RACHEL LEE

RACHEL LEE

THE CRIMSON CODE

MIRA®

ISBN 0-7783-2271-8

THE CRIMSON CODE

Copyright © 2006 by Susan Civil-Brown.

www.MIRABooks.com

Printed in U.S.A.

To Leslie Wainger, who has always
believed in us and who has helped us grow.

Prologue

Jakarta, Indonesia

Arief Sarwano looked at his children sitting in the pew beside him and smiled. Christmas had been kind to his family this year. The electronics firm that employed him had done well, churning out over two hundred thousand units of CyberJoey, the animatronic baby kangaroo that was the year's top-selling Christmas gift in Australia. It had been Arief's project, and he had done much of the design work himself. At that moment, tens of thousands of Australian children were clapping their hands in glee as the plush robot hopped around their Christmas trees and thumped its tail on their floors.

Others might think it absurd that he had poured two years of his life into three pounds of plastic, nylon, silicon and metal that modeled one of the earth's most recognizable animals in a way calculated to attract the attention of five- to nine-year-old children, not to mention the shopping dollars of those children's parents. But as Arief saw it, making children smile was a noble vocation.

And, when a project hit big, a profitable one. The success of CyberJoey had meant, not only a promotion and a raise, but also a healthy bonus. That bonus would ensure that his daughter could realize her dream of going to the United States to attend Notre Dame University next fall. She wanted to study medicine, in America, at the Catholic university. Not *a* Catholic university. *The* Catholic university, the best in America. He chuckled at the memory of the many times she had chided him on that point.

He looked up at the choir and found her in the alto section, slender and beautiful, her long dark hair falling around a face that each day reminded him more and more of her mother. For an instant, he felt the pang again.

The loss of his wife of twenty years, a victim of cancer, had blighted the past two Christmases. Arief had dealt with that loss by pouring himself into his work. In the past months, however, he had come to think that his wife's spirit inhabited every CyberJoey. The toy's eyes had been modeled on hers. And if just one Australian child looked into those eyes and saw love, then Arief's wife was still alive in that child's heart.

The Jalan Cathedral was packed, which was no surprise. The noonday Mass on Christmas was always the most crowded. But it was the one Arief had attended for the past twenty years, the continuation of a family tradition that began at seven in the morning with presents and continued through the late-afternoon dinner. His daughter, rather than his wife, would cook that dinner. But the traditions remained alive, and, with them, a sense of hope that one day Arief would feel whole again.

It was that thought which was shattered by the blinding flash, followed immediately by the crushing force of concussion, as the cathedral turned from a doorway to heaven into the depths of hell in the blink of an eye. Arief's last vision, burned into his retinas, was of his daughter being tossed by an unseen hand through a stained glass window. Then the flames consumed him.

Baden-Baden, Germany

Michael Zeitgenbach could not hear the screams around him. The concussion had shattered his eardrums. In an instant, the still peace of the sunrise Mass had shattered, and in its wake he could feel only the crushing weight of stone on his lower body. His wife, Kirsten, ought to be beside him, somewhere, but the world was black, the air thick with dust and ash.

He ought to be hurting more, he knew. Instead, he could feel only distant pressure from the waist down. As he reached down, trying vainly to push himself free from eight hundred pounds of blood-stained granite, he realized he was going to die. Protruding from his belly was the stem of a chandelier that, seconds earlier, had hung from the ceiling. When he tried to move it, mind-shattering pain exploded through his body. Kirsten, a doctor, would have told him that the metal had pierced his spine.

But Kirsten was not there. She ought to be. They had been sitting together, hand in hand, listening to the traditional Christmas morning readings, when the world had turned upside down in a flash of fire and thunder and darkness. But, reaching around as best he could, he felt no one. No one…except a young girl. Stretching his arm out, he felt the tiny hand.

His niece's hand. He knew it was her, because the wrist still bore the charm bracelet he had given her that morning. One gift, he had said, then the rest after Mass. The rest would never be given, for her hand was limp in his, and he could find no pulse.

Tears prickled at his eyes as he reached to the other side, above him, anywhere, hoping against hope to spend his last moments touching Kirsten. But it was not to be. She might lie only a meter away, or she might be buried beneath the stone that had crushed his legs. Regardless, he could not find her.

And so he took his niece's hand once more in his, the limp fingers the last human contact he would carry with him into eternity.

Boston, Massachusetts

Kevin Daugherty worked with the fury of a man possessed. He had felt the rumble through the floor of the firehouse an instant before the thundering boom had shattered the windows around him. Like the other men of his company, he had resented the Christmas Eve shift. He had wished he could be at Midnight Mass with his wife, Mary, and their two children, his parents, brothers, nieces and nephews. Midnight Mass had always been a Daugherty family tradition.

Well, now he was at the Cathedral of the Holy Cross. Not as a worshipper, but as a fireman. As a son, brother, husband and father, looking for his family. Crouching beneath the wall of water being thrown up by the hose team behind him, he and his partner kicked aside broken glass, and lifted shattered and still burning pews, hoping for any sign of life in the blackened faces.

Kevin's grandfather had told stories about bomb-shattered buildings in France, back in the early weeks after D-day, and a second cousin in New York had helped to pick through the wreckage of the World Trade Center. A four-year veteran, Kevin had seen his share of burned-out buildings. But nothing could have prepared him for what he saw now.

"Daugherty, you have to get out of there." His captain's voice crackled over the radio.

"There may be survivors," Kevin answered. "My family is in here somewhere. I've got to find them."

"We're going to lose the building," the captain said. "You have to get out. Now. That's an order, Daugherty."

Kevin shook his head and kicked aside burning missals, clearing a path to the next row of pews, until he felt a hand on his shoulder, pulling him. He turned and saw his partner, Gerry O'Brien, eyes wide behind the breathing mask.

"We gotta go, Kev," Gerry said, pointing upward. "It's coming down."

Kevin looked up at the roof section above him, watching it swell and recede as if breathing with the heat of the flames. It would not last another two minutes, he knew. Once a building started to breathe, it gave way. It was basic firefighting training: Get out.

But his wife was here somewhere, along with Kevin Junior and little Becky. He couldn't just leave them to the merciless fire, leave them to be nothing but charred forms to be pulled out days later, when the embers had cooled enough for rescue teams to pull apart the wreckage. Mary and Kevin Junior and Becky couldn't be hauled out like so many slabs of barbecue.

"I'm not going," Kevin said. "I have to find them."

"Anyone still in here is dead already," Gerry said. "And we're gonna be dead, too. We're pulling out. Now."

"You go," Kevin said.

Gerry shook his head. "It doesn't work that way, Kev. You stay, I stay. I go, you go. Are you going to kill me, too, along with them?"

And there was the truth of it. Kevin's partner, and the hose team, wouldn't abandon him. If he stayed in the inferno, they would die with him. He had no right to heap their families' grief atop his own. Slowly, slowly, his fingers opened and the fire axe fell from his hands. The bitter tears clouded his vision more than the smoke around him as he shuffled back behind the hose team and began to make his way out.

He could escape the wreckage of the cathedral. He could not escape the wreckage of his heart.

1

Rome, Italy

Renate Bächle had dragged Lawton Caine to Midnight Mass at St. Peter's Basilica. How she had gained the coveted tickets to hear the pope serve one of the two most beautiful Masses of the year, she would not say. She had merely given him a look from those icy blue eyes of hers that these days sometimes even held a twinkle. They had twinkled when he asked.

Lawton Caine, formerly Tom Lawton of the FBI, now a dead man with a new identity working for the U.N.'s ultrasecret Office 119, would ordinarily have skipped Mass entirely. He was a lapsed Catholic who liked being lapsed.

But this Midnight Mass…it was unlike any he had ever attended. There was no sense of urgency, no sense that a schedule must be met, no tired children longing for their beds and keeping parents preoccupied.

No, this had been a Mass devoted to true spirituality. Every moment had been treated as if it were the end in itself. Dignitaries from all over the world had shared in the solemnity and celebration, and Tom had walked out of the Basilica feeling as if he had for the very first time come in contact with the core of his Catholic faith. As if for that brief period he had stepped out of time into eternity.

In short, he'd been wowed.

Renate, too, had been wowed. For those moments, she had allowed herself to feel something she hadn't felt in a long time: vulnerable. She had opened herself to the miracle that the Mass was supposed to be. Of course, that vulnerability couldn't last long. Vulnerability seemed to be something she had virtually erased from her nature.

But after the Mass, she had mentioned to Lawton that she missed home and the *Weihnachtsmärkte,* the traditional Christmas markets set up in every German city and town. She let her thoughts drift back to memories of those festive squares, decorated with holiday lights, where carols, laughter and *Glühwein* flowed in equal measure. To his surprise, she had carried him away with her into the city of Rome, to a small German restaurant that was open all night. There they drank the traditional hot spiced wine, joined in the carols and ate bratwurst that, if it could not take the whole of her back home, could at least take her taste buds there.

Tom, she knew, was missing Miriam Anson and Terry Tyson, friends from his previous life with the American FBI and the closest thing he had to family. She hoped that the restaurant gave him at least some sense of a home.

They left at five in the morning and wandered the darkened streets of Rome, taking in the age of the place, the history that seemed to fill even the air. They spent some time at the Trevi Fountain, shivering in the cool air, receiving a blessing from a passing monsignor who paused to smile at them—probably thinking they were lovers. He made a swift sign of the cross over them, murmuring the Latin words: *In nomine Patris, Filii et Spiritu Sancti.*

Magical.

"Right about now," Renate said, "my parents and the rest of my family are sitting in Mass back home."

She rarely spoke of her family. She, too, was officially dead, as were all of the agents at Office 119. They were a small community of people without country, without family. Save for each other.

Tom reached out and squeezed her hand. She didn't pull away.

All of a sudden, the magic shattered.

They heard a rumble and saw flames rise into the predawn sky. Almost at the same instant, both their pagers went off, hers with a shrill beeping, his with a demanding buzz.

They exchanged worried looks and hailed the first cab they could find. Renate slammed the door on vulnerability. It was time to work.

"The bombs exploded within minutes of each other," the man they all called *Jefe* was saying. In his past life, Tom had known him as John Ortega, a fellow FBI agent. Now his name was unknown and unspoken. He was simply *Jefe*. Chief. "Midnight Mass in Boston. Early-morning Mass in Baden-Baden, and here in Rome. Noon Mass in Jakarta. All were timed for fifteen minutes after the hour. I guess they didn't want to miss the late arrivals."

"Baden-Baden."

Renate whispered the name. Her face went from rosy to ashen in a single instant.

Jefe paused, his attention drawn from the other agents to Renate. "What's wrong?" he asked.

"My...family," she said, breaking the unwritten code of silence about such things, a code enforced by the desire to protect loved ones left behind.

Color returned to Renate's face, but it was not the glow of earlier that morning. Whatever warmth she had felt then was freezing now into a cold, killing resolve.

Tom met her eyes and pressed her shoulder. "Take it easy, Renate. You can't do a damn thing right now."

"Yeah," said the chief. "Besides, the info is still scattered. We don't know anything for sure yet."

Renate's eyes fixed on the chief. "My entire family was at the six o'clock Mass in Baden-Baden."

From outside, the endless wail of sirens could still be faintly heard.

Intel continued to come in to the office, but it remained sparse for hours. The chaos in each stricken city was such that little information was being sent out of the affected areas. Everyone was too busy dealing with the death and destruction.

A huge rear-projection screen displayed a world map, political boundaries in blue, continents outlined in green. As the morning progressed, red dots appeared by more and more cities, as reports came in.

Large television sets built into another wall were tuned to CNN International, Al Jazeera and other European, Asian and American networks. Pictures of destruction began arriving, but little was actually known.

Eventually the news began to identify other targets: a North Sea drilling rig, a pipeline in Turkey, nuclear weapons assembly plants in New

Mexico and Kiev and the computer files of the New York Stock Exchange.

Despite the other targets, the chaotic map soon told a horrifying story. There was no question that the Catholic Church was a primary target of this terrorism. Along with the other targets, a major cathedral had been destroyed in each time zone. The only exception was Baden-Baden, where the target had been a simple family parish in the foothills of the *Schwarzwald.*

"And Baden-Baden doesn't fit," Tom said, looking at the map. "Why two churches in the same time zone? Why not another cathedral? Why not Köln, or Notre Dame in Paris?"

"None of it fits," Jefe said, reading from a computer screen. "The initial reports say no one was injured in the attacks on economic targets. The workers on that North Sea rig say they were given time to evacuate before the rig was blown. And yet they blow up churches with thousands of innocent worshippers. It doesn't make sense."

As he spoke another light winked on, this one in South America. Brazil. Rio.

"Maybe they hit Baden-Baden because there was extra security in Paris and Cologne," Margarite Renault said, her English accented by her French background. A former member of the Sûreté, she was around forty, with classic Gallic features, dark hair and eyes. "The European nations have beefed up their antiterrorist activities. Maybe Baden-Baden was a target of opportunity."

Renate could listen no longer. She knew what had been done—and why. There was no reason to dance around the issue. Justice demanded honesty. "It wasn't a target of opportunity. They murdered my family. They couldn't find me, so they murdered my family."

A half hour later, Margarite found Tom in a side cubicle. She lowered her voice so she could not be overheard. "I am worried about Renate. She is always so controlled, but this…" A shrug. "This she cannot control. It has happened. Now she must—how you say?—deal with it."

Tom nodded slowly. He was more worried about Renate than he wanted to admit. If her entire family had been in the church that had been blown up, he didn't have to guess how she would react. She was tough and disciplined, but the cold, hard look in her eyes left no doubt where her thoughts were running.

His heart would not allow him to leave her alone in her shock and rage. He entered her office and sat in the chair beside her desk. "Renate."

She ignored him, tapping away at her keyboard. "Renate."

Slowly she looked up. He wanted to see emotion in her eyes. Any emotion, even anger. All he saw was the icy coldness of a lifeless glacier. "I'm working."

"You're not working," he dared to say, then plunged on before she could argue. "You're looking for revenge."

Something sparked then in those cold blue eyes. "Don't I deserve it?"

"You don't know anything for sure."

With a swift gesture, she turned her flat-panel monitor toward him. "You see? My family's *kirche*. It's on the list. They are dead."

He felt his heart crack for her. "Maybe…"

"No maybe. Don't tell me maybe. I know." For the briefest instant, a fathomless grief broke through, crumpling her face. Then it was gone, so fast he wasn't sure he had seen it.

"Just remember our mission," he said. "Our mission, Renate. Don't forget who we are. We are *not* them."

"They are animals," she said coldly. "And I am going to kill the ones who hurt my family. I am going to kill them with my own hands."

"Renate."

But she had turned away, pulling her monitor back and resuming her online hunt for information.

Oddly, he found himself thinking of Midnight Mass again, and offering a silent prayer that Renate's family had for some reason not been in that church. But as he turned away and glimpsed the horrific images that were now filling all the TV screens, he decided that God was probably not in a very good mood today. In fact, God was probably not listening at all.

By late afternoon, figures were arriving. None held the mind-numbing counts that had come from the tsunami in the Indian Ocean the previous Christmas, but though the numbers were smaller, the details were just as horrifying. These bombings had not been an act of God. As the acts of men, they were heinous beyond belief, worse even than the Twin Towers in scope. "Black Christmas," as the networks had begun to call it, would undoubtedly go into the annals of history along with 9/11.

Renate sat at her desk, her demeanor a cloak of ice, as if she had frozen every feeling. Tom checked on her frequently, but she never looked up, choosing instead to keep working at the computer, seeking backdoor information.

They were all doing the same. They all had informants, covert contacts in their old agencies, a collective net cast around the world. Weeks ago they had begun to detect signs that a major terrorist operation was in the works, but they had been unable to pin it down. Equally ominous, no one was claiming responsibility. Usually terrorists were all too eager to step forward and thumb their noses at the world.

Silence reigned. From the dust and the fire came only the cries of victims.

So far, heads of state had been quiet, as if awaiting information before speaking. Only the pope had released a brief message, speaking of martyrdom, grief, consolation and forgiveness.

Forgiveness. Tom doubted that there would be much of that for a while.

Riyadh, Saudi Arabia

Betrayal.

Ahmed Ahsami curled his fists in anger as he watched the reports on three television screens. The BBC, CNN and Al Jazeera were unanimous in their focus on the cathedral bombings, with the other work—the real work, carried out by real soldiers—given only a passing mention. He felt the anger burn in his belly like a white-hot flame.

Betrayed.

He never should have trusted them. Fanatics could not advance the cause of Islam. But he had made a deal with the devil, and the devil would have his due.

Three years of careful planning had been turned to dust, and worse, in the past twelve hours. Three years of arguing, cajoling, convincing his Islamic brothers that they would have to walk a new path if ever they wanted true peace and freedom. Three years of reconnaissance, recruiting, training and more training, to create a network of special operations teams truly worthy of the banner of Allah. Three years directed toward a single goal, a day that would mark forever the ascendance of Islam as a major military and political power.

Betrayed.

On a desk beside him sat a DVD, a DVD the world would never see. It was to have been delivered to the offices of Al Jazeera two hours ago. By now the world would have known the name of *Saif Alsharaawi*...the Sword of the East. By now the world would have seen the face of Ahmed Ahsami, the face of moderation and determination, every word in his speech carefully crafted.

True justice, true peace, cannot be bought with the blood of innocents.... Islam, like its cousins Christianity and Judaism, deplores the taking of innocent life.... We have shown that we can strike legitimate military and economic targets anywhere, at any time, and that we can do so with justice in our hearts and Allah on our lips.... We ask only that the West leave the Islamic people to govern ourselves, by our own beliefs and our own standards, to pursue our own dreams with the guidance of Allah....

The speech was to have been an olive branch, offered up with the sincerity of a people who had received too much injustice and renounced delivering more. The days of Al Qaeda and Hezbollah, of suicide bombings intended to cause the greatest possible loss of life, were past. Islam could not stand with its feet in a pool of blood. If he and his brothers were to win this war of ideas, they would have to do so by complying with the true will of Allah…and the laws of war.

These were the arguments he had made again and again, as he had risen to the top ranks of *Saif Alsharaawi.* He had personally approved every target, vetting each for military legitimacy. Oil rigs and pipelines, the nuclear weapons plants, the New York Stock Exchange—the heart of Western materialism—all of those, and the other targets he had intended to strike, were selected after careful evaluation.

The forces of Islam could not match the West in terms of nuclear weapons, guided missiles, aircraft or warships. Ahmed knew that and accepted it. Indeed, he had decided to make that mismatch a cornerstone of his planning. For while he might lack high-tech hardware, he could more than match his opponent in special operations forces: carefully selected, highly trained, highly disciplined and highly motivated. They would be *Saif Alsharaawi,* the Sword of the East, a surgical strike weapon capable of winning military victory without sacrificing political or moral legitimacy.

But he had not had enough strike teams for today's attacks, and so he had made and forged what was to have been an alliance of mutual gain. And his allies had betrayed him.

Worse, they had betrayed Islam. For as efficient as his teams had been, the bombings of the cathedrals had wiped out any possibility of moderation. And the West would strike back not at his allies, but at Islam. The senseless bombing of churches would accomplish nothing except to continue and intensify the Fourth Crusade already being waged against his people.

Ahmed knew what he had to do. And once his anger had passed, he would find a way to do exactly that.

He would turn their betrayal against them.

Moab, Jordan, 1230 B.C.

"It is time."

The young Levite, Elezar, looked at Moses with something akin to fear. The youth was not yet old enough to become a priest, so he was still serving Moses and learning the holy ways, as he had been since his twelfth year. Serving a man who spoke with the Lord through the fire and smoke was often unnerving.

But nothing was as unnerving as this announcement, for it meant that Moses was about to die. Elezar could not imagine a world without Moses. Could not imagine that his own revered great-grandfather Eleazar was fit to take Moses's place. Eleazar was a great priest, true, and could enter the tabernacle that held the terrifying Ark without injury or death but...

Moses was everything to these people, though they often failed to recognize it. They were a stubborn people, difficult to please, often quick to grumble when Moses was not there to steer them. Elezar tried hard not to be that way himself. But now he wanted to cry out to the Lord against the sentence that had been set on Moses.

"Come," said Moses, picking up a staff and waving the young man to do the same. "We must climb Mount Nebo."

Leaving the encampment on the plain behind them, they began to climb into the Pisgah Mountains toward Nebo, the highest peak. Elezar half expected to hear the rumble of the Lord's voice, or see fire atop the peak as his ancestors had seen at Mount Sinai. Which was really not Mount Sinai, but Moses would not tell him where it really was, and none remained among the tribes who could recall, for all who had set out from Egypt with Moses were now dead.

After a long, hot climb, they reached the top of Mount Nebo. Moses spread his arms wide as if to embrace the breathtaking view.

"There, Elezar, you see? There is the land that was promised to the sons of Israel. I will not enter with the tribes, nor will you."

Elezar stiffened. "But I thought..."

Moses turned to him, his eyes kinder than Elezar had ever seen them.

"Let us sit a while and talk, Elezar."

Though it was said he was over a hundred and thirty years old, Moses sat with all the ease of a youth like Elezar on the hard, rocky ground. Elezar sat facing him.

"There are things you must understand, Elezar."

The young man could no longer hold silent. "It is wrong that you cannot enter the Promised Land. It is wrong that you must die for such a small error when so many of our people have made larger ones and lived! Why can you not offer an atonement sacrifice? Why is the Lord being so harsh with you?"

Moses listened to the protests, smiling a little all the while. "My time to leave has come. I am no longer needed here. But I do not want these people to feel abandoned."

Elezar knitted his brow, sensing there was something behind those words.

"Child, do you know your lineage?"

"Yes, I do."

"Do you know the line of your mothers?"

Elezar hesitated. "I know best the line of my fathers."

"You perhaps do not know then that you are descended from my line, as well. My daughters and their daughters married your fathers many times over. You are a Levite, but you are also mine."

The news caused a trembling in Elezar, like a

leaf disturbed by the wind. "It has not been told to me."

"It was as I wished it. Until now. There are things you must understand, mysteries you must learn. These mysteries were once the pride of Egypt. They were set down on a *sappir* gemstone, written by Thoth himself, and discovered by my brother, Pharaoh Akhenaten, when we were but children. We studied the stone throughout our youth. And Akhenaten was the first to fully understand it. Thus he began the worship of the One True God... Aten...our Lord. The stone was once in the Ark. Now..."

Moses opened his leather bag and showed Elezar a polished sapphire pyramid, so small that it fit in the palm of the hand. A blue pyramid that seemed to hold as much depth as the night sky. Elezar gasped, amazed as he thought he saw shapes dancing within the stone. But he could not imagine such a thing, that Moses would steal from God himself.

"Relax, my son," Moses said, reaching out to pat Elezar's shoulder. "As I said, this is not the tablet of the law. This is far older. And far too powerful to leave in untrained hands. The Hebrews are a great people, but too stiff-necked for their own good sometimes. A knowledge such as this, in the hands of a people preparing to make war, would be…horrifying. But I have left them the Urim and the Thummim, which will be enough to aid them."

"What is this power?" Elezar asked. "Is God not the only power that exists?" He felt his world reeling.

"There is only one God, and he is our only God." Moses opened a small pouch and from it poured a fine white powder. "Manna," he said. "The Hebrews think it came down from the heavens. In fact, it is a recipe from this stone, and El Shaddai showered it upon us at night as we camped near the foot of the mountain. Eat some, my son, for it will give you long life."

Gingerly, Elezar reached for the powder, allowing Moses to pour some into his hand. He tasted of it and found it not unpleasant, though not exactly savory. It had the slightest hint of honey to it. The climb had dried his mouth and throat, making swallowing difficult, but he had brought a water skin and was able to wash it down. Moses, too, ate of the powder.

"Now," said Moses, "the people will think I have died. You will descend the mountain and tell them I have gone to my fathers, and then you shall cleanse yourself as the law requires after touching a corpse. By this they shall believe I am dead and that you have buried me.

"Then, by night, you shall return to me. We must go to the place where your real training can begin. The mysteries must pass down, and you will be their messenger."

Elezar's jaw had fallen. "I am to lie?"

"It will not be a lie, for I *am* returning to my fathers. And as far as my people are concerned, I will be dead and gone. As will you. It will be years before you re-enter the world, Elezar, and when you do, you will be a man much changed, for you will know the secret teachings of El Shaddai."

El Shaddai. The Lord of the Mountain.

2

Guatemalan Highlands, Present day

Father Steve Lorenzo had no idea of the carnage spreading around the world on that Christmas. His goal in life had become very simple: to keep himself and his flock alive. For the past fourteen months, he and his Quiche companions had wandered these mountains, hunted by both the Guatemalan police and the rebels. His once smooth chin now sported a bushy beard, and he could hardly remember the sensation of a hot bath.

And yet it was Christmas, and most of his friends were still alive to celebrate it.

He had no vestments. His cassock had long since given way to peasant clothing offered to him by his friends, who could hardly spare even that. He wore sandals one of his flock had made from vine and sections of tire rubber.

And never had he felt closer to God.

When life seemed its worst, as it had often since the police attack on the village of these people, he found a deep well of spirituality that reminded him of the early days of Christianity, when to hold faith in Jesus brought persecution and often demanded flight. Those early Christians had possessed little more than his tiny flock of survivors. In this time he lived as the early martyrs had lived, and it refreshed his faith even as it wore him out.

But his little band was well versed in the skills needed to survive in these mountains. The food might not be as reliable, nor always as familiar, as their rich fields of maize and their herds of sheep, but the forest was bountiful in its own right, and his friends knew how to use everything it provided.

This Christmas morning he celebrated Mass yet again on an altar made of fallen trees, with tortillas made of corn flour he had managed to purchase—along with beans—from a village they had passed a few days ago, with the few quetzals remaining in his pockets. The women had made the tortillas, patting them back and forth to flatten the balls of dough with an expertise that came from lifelong experience. They had been lightly cooked on a rock set amidst the burning coals of a fire. A nearly smokeless fire. Steve was still amazed that they could manage that here in the jungle.

He used the chalice and paten given him on his ordination so long ago by family and friends. The years had burnished them, and now when he touched them he remembered the faces of all his loved ones. Yet he was determined that when the time came, he would sell them without regret to keep these people alive.

It had been a long time since he had even thought of the Kulkulcan Codex, or the reason he had been sent to these people. The Church's concern was so far away now, so remote.

He smiled into the faces of his flock and lifted a tortilla for all to see. *Esto es mi cuerpo.* This is my body.

This was all that mattered.

Fredricksburg, Virginia

Earlier that morning, FBI agent Miriam Anson was in church with her husband, Terry Tyson, a D.C. homicide detective, when her pager began to vibrate insistently. She had been tempted to ignore it entirely until after the service—this was Christmas, after all—when it started buzzing a second time. She turned to Terry, about to whisper an apology, when she saw he had pulled his own pager off his belt and was looking at the number.

Damn! The word exploded in her head, and she touched Terry's arm. He looked at her, and she jerked her head toward the rear doors. He nodded and followed her just as the congregation stood up to sing a hymn. Nearly a thousand voices singing "Pass Me Not" followed them out into the frigid morning air.

Fredericksburg, beneath a bright blue sky and a layer of fresh snow clinging to trees and patches of grass, looked beautiful this morning. Picture-postcard perfect, Miriam thought as she grimly pulled her cell phone from her purse and dialed. Terry turned his back to her and did the same.

If they were both being paged…

"Anson," Miriam said into her phone. "Kevin Willis called me."

Kevin's voice sounded in her ear a second later. "Come in now," he said. "Black Crescent." The current code for terror attack.

All Christmas spirit vanished from Miriam's heart. "I'm on my way." She flipped her phone closed and saw Terry turning to her, his dark face creased with consternation.

"I have to go in," he said.

"Me, too."

Now, hours later, as she sat through one briefing after another on the growing worldwide horror, Miriam wondered at the hearts of men who could perpetrate such atrocities on this holiest of days.

It would be so easy to give in to hate. But hate

would not bring her any closer to justice. It would only push her closer to the very evil she fought.

As the briefing officer presented yet more grim statistics and the anger flashed through her, Miriam reminded herself of the central truth of the Christmas sermon she had heard: God appears in this world in stables, not in mansions or palaces, in the quiet of the human heart and not in a blaze of herald trumpets.

And not in the blinding, crushing explosions of bombs.

No, she couldn't blame God for this one. Humans had done this all on their own. And if Miriam could help track them down, in the dark, silent corners where they hid…that would be the coming of God in this madness.

Rome, Italy

"I have to go to Baden-Baden," Renate said to the chief. Lawton Caine, who was in the office, too, looked at her with something between sympathy and concern.

Jefe looked at her as if she were mad. "Are you out of your mind? You know the rules we play by."

"They murdered my family," she said tautly.

"I know." The chief's voice dropped with sorrow. "But you'll do no good there now."

"I have to go."

"Damn it!" Cursing might be considered extremely impolite by Germans, but for once Jefe didn't seem to care about cultural sensibilities. "Haven't you noticed the pattern? Baden-Baden doesn't fit." He slapped his open hand against the paper map of the world on the back wall of his office, a map that covered nearly the entire space. "If you're right, they're after *you!*"

Lawton stiffened and straightened. "They think she's dead."

She shook her head. "After what happened in Idaho and Montana, they know better. There was absolutely no reason to pick that church in Baden-Baden if they thought I was dead. The grudge is an old one, Law. A very old one. What I did to the Brotherhood…"

The chief compressed his lips tightly. "I'll have to forbid it. You stay here, Renate, where your skills can actually do some good." He sighed. Then he ran his fingers impatiently through his dark hair. "Okay," he said. "Renate, why don't you tell me who would have the funds to support this attack, apart from the Saudi royal family."

Renate regarded him stonily. "The Frankfurt Brotherhood."

"Precisely! So why hit a parish church in Baden-Baden? To get you there. They're hoping you'll go to find out what happened to your family. Bookworm shows up again in her hometown.

Renate, you nearly exposed them a few years ago. I don't think they've forgotten."

Renate lowered her head for a moment. Then she looked straight at the chief, her eyes like chips of glacial ice. "I'll take a job as a dealer at the casino. I'll change my appearance. My father worked there, and there will be talk. Plenty of it."

"You'd be recognized within an hour. Renate, we could even give you contact lenses, hair dye and facial implants, and your old friends would still know you. You're entirely too distinctive."

"I'm not going to let them get away with this," she said. "This is not negotiable, Jefe. I'm going to take the Brotherhood down. And I'm going to take out the son of a bitch who planted the bomb in my family's church. It's only a matter of how."

"Then for God's sake, let's think about the how," Lawton said. "He's right. Going into Baden-Baden would do nothing but sign your own death warrant. Hell, we're not going to find them in Baden-Baden anyway. You know that."

"What's their weakness, Renate?" Jefe asked. "The most you'll find in Baden-Baden is a hit team waiting for you. A hit team you won't even be able to trace back to them. So what is their weakness?"

"Money," she said, instantly. "It's their power base. It's the blood running in the veins of the Brotherhood."

"Well, blood runs back to the heart and the head," Lawton said. "If we follow the money, we find the people who killed your family."

"You can't follow their money," Jefe said. "They're all bankers. They can hide money with the best of them. And you don't even have a thread to pull to get all of it started. Renate, I know how you're feeling, but the right thing to do is to focus on Black Christmas."

"Our entire office is focused on Black Christmas," she said, her voice dripping icy resolve. "The police agencies of the entire world will be working Black Christmas. You can spare me. You know that."

"And we do have a thread to pull," Lawton said. "We have Jonathan Morgan. Edward Morgan's father. Edward was Brotherhood. If he was, his father is."

Lawton had been on the case when Edward Morgan had masterminded the plan to kill U.S. Senator Grant Lawrence—at the time the frontrunner for the Democratic presidential nomination—as well as financing a training camp for Guatemalan revolutionaries in Idaho. Although Lawrence had survived, he was now out of the presidential picture, seemingly content to be the senior senator from Florida. None of it could be proven in a court of law, however. None of it. That loose end still troubled Lawton more than he could say.

"That still doesn't explain how you're going to track their money," Jefe said.

"Banks have a private Internet," Renate said. "That's how they transfer money, and I'll bet the Brotherhood uses that network for its communications. If we can hack into that network, we can find them."

"And how are you going to do that?" Jefe asked.

"I'm going to Frankfurt," Renate said. "I broke in once before. I can do it again."

"You're not going alone," Jefe said. "Lawton, you're with her. You'll need a computer guy, too. Take Assif Mondi from information services."

"We may end up needing more than that," Lawton said. "Niko Petropolis is available. He just got out of rehab. He took a bullet on that operation in Chechnya, remember?"

"I'll have to ask the doctor if he's field ready," Jefe put in.

"So ask," Renate said. Her voice was steely with resolve.

"Oh, I will," Jefe replied. "But first, tell me what you have in mind."

3

Saint-Arnans-la-Bastide, France

General Jules Soult, formerly of the French Army and now retired, sat in his study, enjoying a Cuban cigar as he looked up at the portrait of his renowned ancestor Marshall Jean Soult. The Marshall had built a great reputation in his service to Napoleon, although after Napoleon's first exile he had briefly collaborated with the Bourbon king.

Soult pondered that collaboration as the television behind him continued its incessant assault of news about Black Christmas. Collaboration, he deemed, was often necessary for a man to achieve his ultimate goals. No shame therein.

Jules turned his head a fraction and watched the stream of videotape showing the worldwide destruction. He told himself he was sorry for all the lives lost and crossed himself while murmuring a small prayer as he had learned during his Catholic upbringing.

But the truth was that this plan had been his. Well, with a few added directions from his Order, an order that dated back to the Knights Templar. He still didn't understand why they'd wanted to make that ridiculous detour to the small church in Baden-Baden, but he was a man who followed his instructions—to a point.

He turned back to the portrait of the first famous Soult. They were both military men, and as such they understood that there was a human price for every gain and every loss. Today's activity was a major gain.

While the world reeled and grieved and hunted Islamic terrorists, his men would be doing their stealthy work in the streets.

Jules Soult was a man who studied history intently. George Santayana had said that those who do not study the past are condemned to repeat it. Soult agreed. One must study history in order to learn where the world's great leaders had gone wrong and to improve upon plans that had gone awry in the past, one way or another.

Take Hitler, for example. Napoleon had tried to invade Russia and had been defeated by the winter. Hitler had not learned sufficiently from Napoleon's lesson and had expected too much of his panzers.

Soult was determined not to repeat anyone's mistakes. There was much to be learned in the historical record. Europe had passed the age where an emperor might be accepted, but it had not passed the day when it would accept a strong, unifying leader.

Soult knew he was that leader. His bloodline traced directly back to the Merovingian rulers of Europe, the blood that every ruler since the first century had carried or married into. He might never wear a crown, but he still believed he could reestablish a dynasty.

Much the way Hitler had. Only he would not make the same mistakes. No, he had studied history, and he knew what to avoid.

Hitler had lacked the gift of Islamic terrorism by which to demonize a people. For all of the long-standing hatred of those whom the bastard Church said had murdered the Christ, the Jews had done nothing to harm their European neighbors. And never again would the people of Europe be led to demonize an innocent race.

But radical Islam…that created an opportunity, one that he intended to exploit to the fullest. He had insinuated himself into the planning of Black Christmas—anonymously, of course—and ordered the bombings of the cathedrals. The original Black Christmas plan would not have served his needs. But what had actually happened would work perfectly.

European Muslims would be his scapegoat, the people against whom he could direct violence and thereby distract the people of Europe from his true aims. Moreover, as they joined in the violence against Muslims, they would become inured to hatred and killing. That coldness of heart would serve him well when the time came to recapture the rightful seat of Merovingian power.

Soon the phone would ring, and like Hitler before him, Soult would be given a free hand to conduct espionage against his enemies. He would hire his Ernst Röhm, create his brownshirts to incite the very violence he was sworn to prevent. Confidence in governments would falter, and when it did, he would step into the void.

That much of Hitler's plan had been sheer genius. But he would not repeat that madman's mistakes. No, Soult would do what Hitler could not, nor Napoleon before him. And Black Christmas was the key that had opened the doorway to his future.

He smiled up at the portrait, then took another satisfying puff on his cigar. The ducks were lining up beautifully.

It was a shame so many had died. He would light a candle for them. The Lord would certainly understand, because it was nothing less than the Lord's birthright that he intended to reclaim.

As if on schedule, the telephone rang. He had been told to expect the call, and he knew who she was and what she wanted even before he picked up the telephone. There were advantages to having connections in the highest and most secret circles of power.

"General Soult," he said, speaking in accented English.

"Ah, General," the woman said. "You answer your telephone in English now?"

"I assumed it would be another American reporter asking for an interview," he lied. "Apparently I was wrong. You are German."

"Yes," she said. "My name is Monika Schmidt. I am the director of the European Union—"

"Department of Collective Security," he cut in. "I have seen you on the news many times today. You have had a very bad few days."

"We have all had a very bad few days, General," she said. "Once again, we find that our enemies are more resourceful than we had thought. And that we…"

She didn't need to finish the sentence. The European news media had been finishing it for her for nearly twenty-four hours. How had the vaunted EUDCS, with its contacts in Interpol and the United States, totally missed the planning for Black Christmas? Frau Schmidt did not have an answer for them, though Soult could easily have supplied it. He had, after all, spent much of his career in French military intelligence. And he had used the skills he had learned there to direct the counterespionage operations for the men who had carried out the attacks.

"These things are always more complex than the public realizes," he said, trying to affect a tone that mixed professional sympathy with the wisdom of experience. "It takes many years to develop the kinds of contacts that would have provided warning for such an operation."

"And that is why I call you," she said. "I have spoken with my superiors and explained to them the need for better human intelligence. You served in Chad and directed the French network in Algiers. You have worked in the Arab community before. You know these people."

His contacts had not erred. She was, in fact, offering him a position—the very position toward which he had worked for fifteen years.

"Yes," he said, smiling as he drew on his cigar. "I do. So, Frau Schmidt, how can I be of service to the European Union?"

Riyadh, Saudi Arabia

Monsignor Giuseppe Veltroni carried many problems on his back as he rode in a taxi through the streets of Riyadh to his appointment. To arrive here within two days of the attacks on so many Catholic churches was to put his neck on a chopping block. The people here cheered the destruction, of course. The "man in the street" did not understand the contributions the Church had made toward peace with and for the Muslim world. The average Saudi seemed all too unaware of how much work the Church had done for the Palestinians.

And this little detour was exceptionally dangerous, since he had deserted the protective phalanx the Saudis had provided for him in his capacity as an official representative of the Vatican. But he could not afford listening ears or spying eyes this afternoon. This afternoon he needed to be one-on-one with a man he had nearly come to trust, a man who seemed to have utterly broken that trust.

Beyond that, he was gravely concerned about the fate of Steve Lorenzo. Months had passed since the Guatemalan police had attacked Dos Ojos in an attempt to arrest a rebel involved in the bombing death of the U.S. ambassador. Since then, nothing had been heard from or about the priest he had sent there to find the Codex.

Monsignor Veltroni had virtually adopted Lorenzo, loved him as a son, and felt deep worry about whatever might happen to him. Except… Steve must be dead, or he would have gone to the bishop in Guatemala City, surely?

Veltroni's heart ached and he wished there was something he could take back, some decision he could unmake so that Steve would return whole and unharmed. Yet he could not be sure the priest was dead, for no remains had ever been found. Perhaps he was still searching for the Codex?

If so, and if he was still with the survivors of Dos Ojos, Steve had both the Guatemalan police and army after him.

And perhaps someone else. Rumors had surfaced in Veltroni's extremely sensitive intelligence web that someone called "The Hunter" might be pursuing the Codex, as well. If so...Steve faced more trouble than he could possibly imagine.

With a sigh, Veltroni adjusted his mufti, in this case a *djellaba* with a hood, so that he might blend in better. Beneath he wore his priestly black and his pectoral cross, but he knew better than to think they would save him from harm here.

The cab pulled up before an almost palatial residence. Ahmed Ahsami, a Saudi visionary, was also a member of the Saudi royal family, one of the more minor princes who could live a comfortable lifestyle but not an excessively lavish one. He was also an important official in the oil ministry. Apparently his lifestyle was comfortable enough that one of his employees stepped forward to pay the cab driver before Veltroni could fumble with the unfamiliar currency.

Then, without a word, he was led along surprisingly cool tiled hallways, past beautiful wall mosaics bright with color and into an interior courtyard, where an extravagant fountain bubbled cheerfully and a riot of green plants grew as if this were their native terrain.

The employee—servant?—motioned him to a padded bench. "Sheik Ahsami will send for you shortly."

Shortly turned into ten minutes, but then the servant reappeared and motioned for Veltroni to follow. At once he was led into a spacious room that forsook the grandiosity of the rest of the building for a very businesslike aspect. Ahmed Ahsami, dressed casually in chinos and a blue business shirt, at once rose and came to greet him.

"Monsignor! It is good of you to come. And I can assure you that you were not followed. So we speak freely, yes?"

Veltroni's eyes narrowed. "That is the entire reason I have made this trip, Sheik."

"Please, call me Ahmed. I think we now have more in common than you believe."

Before the discussion could proceed, however, in the best tradition of desert tribes a repast was laid before them on a long table. Hospitality first, then business. Veltroni chafed, but knew he would insult Ahmed if he did not partake with enjoyment and a considerable amount of inane chat.

As he sipped the powerful Turkish coffee, Veltroni studied his host. The initial smile had faded into a look of deep thoughts that did not run in pleasant waters. While he spoke the correct words as dinner was consumed, Veltroni could tell this was not a man in a state of silent celebration. When they had finished and retired to Ahmed's drawing room, Veltroni knew it was upon him to break the ice—or shatter it.

"I needn't tell you how I feel about the Christmas attacks," Veltroni said. "The Vatican is justifiably and righteously angry. This was a very dangerous gambit, my friend…whoever did it."

Ahmed studied him carefully, but Veltroni did not flinch. The accusation hung between them, and the burden lay upon Ahmed to dismiss it. Or to admit to it. Without one or the other, the Stewards could have no further dealing with Ahmed. Promises of peace could not survive acts of malicious brutality.

Finally, Ahmed spoke. "The situation is…complex, Guiseppi. There were acts on Christmas for which I and my men were responsible. There were others in which we were betrayed."

"I know the answer, but I have to ask. You did not authorize the cathedral bombings?"

Ahmed shook his head. "No, my friend. All the attacks were to be on legitimate military, political and economic targets."

"Like the oil platforms?" Veltroni asked.

Ahmed drew a breath. "Yes, like those. And as I'm sure you know, none of the workers there were injured. After all, why else did we choose to act on Christmas, a time when most at the intended targets would be safely at home? My teams had explicit instructions. They carried out their orders with professional discipline. Alas, my *allies*—" he spat out the word with anger "—had other ideas. Now we all lose."

"Yes," Veltroni said. "We all lose. I don't suppose you will tell me about these…allies."

"One betrayal does not justify another," Ahmed said. "Even if they have no honor, I must answer to Allah for what I have done and what I will do."

Veltroni considered that statement. Was there honor in protecting someone who has betrayed you, and who in that betrayal has committed mass murder? Once again, he found himself wishing he knew more of Ahmed's religion. But Islam, like Christianity, suffered from sectarian schisms that rendered simple analysis impossible. Veltroni had no idea of Ahmed's personal Islam or the tenets he held most deeply.

Of course, there was always the possibility that Ahmed was refusing to reveal his allies because he feared retribution if they were exposed. This would hardly be the first time someone had rationalized self-interest in terms of religious belief. Still, Veltroni did not think it likely that Ahmed would bend on this issue. At least not tonight.

"You understand," Veltroni said, "that I may

have trouble with my superiors over this. They will find it hard to sit back and do nothing after so many of our cathedrals have been bombed. And there is only one direction in which they will look."

Ahmed's handsome face creased with both anger and concern. "Of which superiors do you speak? Your superiors at the Vatican? Or your masters in your secret order?"

Veltroni froze. He never would have imagined that Ahmed could have learned anything about the Stewards of the Faith as a secret order. Especially when they appeared to stand in plain sight for all to see.

"I don't know what you're talking about."

Ahmed shook his head. "You don't fool me, my friend. Your Stewards may have a public face and the pope's blessing, but I am not stupid. What we have discussed together tells me that you have a purpose other than the simple ones of the pope."

"The Stewards of the Faith are dedicated to preserving the Catholic Church. There is no secret in that."

"Perhaps not." Ahmed sighed. "Perhaps only your methods raise doubt. Somehow I do not think the Holy Father, as you call him, would approve of some of what you have agreed to."

"The Holy Father lives in a simpler world. Reality must be dealt with."

"Yes," Ahmed answered. "And now you must trust me to handle reality. I will deal with these traitors because they have harmed my cause."

For a few minutes, neither man spoke.

"Trust me," Ahmed said again. "I am as angry as you and your Church."

Finally Veltroni nodded. When he spoke, his tone intimated a threat that his words did not. "We are left to trust in God. God—Allah—will honor our sincere efforts toward peace, however they may go awry."

"Yes," Ahmed said, rising. "Thank you for coming, my friend. You are always welcome in my home. Perhaps you can…buffer…the opinions of your superiors, as they consider these horrors. I have no wish to incite another crusade."

"Nor do we," Veltroni said. "Nor do we."

After Veltroni left, Ahmed Ahsami called for a glass of brandy—one of his few secret vices—and pondered the conversation. Yes, he would deal with the traitors who had blown up the cathedrals. He had already set the wheels in motion to find them and kill them.

But the Catholic Church was now a wild card on the board. The pope had spoken of forgiveness, but Veltroni's words had carried an implicit threat. Perhaps his doubts about the Stewards of the Faith were correct.

But correct or not, at the moment they were not his greatest concern. He could deal with them later if it became necessary. For now he had to find the men behind the true horror of Black Christmas.

And kill them all.

4

Frankfurt Airport, Germany

"You know," Assif Mondi said—in English, for the benefit of the rest of the group, who all spoke English but otherwise diverged greatly in their linguistic skills—"it would have been better if you had wanted to crack into this network a few years ago."

Renate simply stared expressionlessly at him. All the tears she had shed in the privacy of her apartment since Black Christmas had turned into something harder than diamonds. Sometimes her nostrils flared a little, anticipating the scent of blood. The blood of the killers. No one knew it, though, and no one would, because if they learned of it, she would be removed from this case instantly. But deep inside her, the only purpose she had left, the only *desire* that existed, was to destroy any and all who had taken part in the killing of her family.

But Assif was on his hobbyhorse now and not likely to slow down. "A few years ago the banks were on dial-ups. Can you believe it? They used X.25 protocol, which was a good protection, but not unhackable. Now you want me to break into SWIFTNET, a dedicated hardwired network with the most powerful NetScreen encryption devices made. They have firewalls, massive encryption, and worse, they have an untrust fallback."

"Untrust?" Lawton asked.

"If the NetScreen device senses anything unusual in the connection, it will immediately fall over to a backup connection. On a different line."

"Oh, goodie."

Assif looked at him, then nodded. "Exactly."

Renate spoke, feeling a flame-lick of the fury that had filled her since Christmas. Assif, she was sure, had no idea how close to the edge he was walking with her. "Are you saying this is impossible?"

"If I thought it was impossible, I would not have come. I am here. It is not impossible. But don't expect it to be fast."

They were standing on the chilly, windblown concrete platform at the Frankfurt Airport, awaiting a train to take them to the Frankfurt Main Station. From there they would catch a tram to the business suite Office 119 had rented for them.

Right now there were only a few people inside the steel-and-glass tunnel, farther along the tracks, but Renate glanced toward the escalators and saw more arrivals beginning to appear. The sky through the overhead glass remained gray and un-inviting, maybe even promising snow. The chill nipped at her nose.

"Let us talk later," she said to Assif. Then, sur-prising Lawton, she pulled out a pack of ciga-rettes, moved toward the smoking area on the platform and lit one.

Lawton exchanged looks with Assif, who was a handsome Indian with the friendly features of the Punjab. Assif shrugged; then they both fol-lowed her.

"Local color," she said when they joined her. "And the smoking section is here at the end of the platform, where we're most likely to have pri-vacy."

Assif laughed. "Then give me one, please? I haven't smoked since I left New Delhi."

Lawton stepped upwind. Renate noticed the movement, and something almost like amusement flickered in her eyes before dying. Dying again beneath the ice of death.

They let the first, and then a second, train leave for Frankfurt. Assif and Renate were still chatting casually when a compact, powerfully built man joined the growing number of travelers in the smoking area. He watched indifferently as another train arrived and departed. A short time later, he alone remained with them.

He turned and took a couple of strides their way. "Renate," he said, holding out his ticket as if he were asking directions. "Are we all here?"

"Yes, Niko. You know everyone?"

He nodded. "By reputation, at least. You must be Lawton Caine."

Lawton did not extend his hand but simply gave an affirmative glance, as did Assif when Niko greeted him.

When they at last boarded the train to the city, they took seats in separate cars. The essence of the team was now together.

Guatemalan Highlands

Paloma drew Steve Lorenzo away from the rest of the villagers. Most were already asleep, wrapped in colorful wool blankets they carried with them nearly everywhere, blankets that now provided the only protection they had from the elements, except for the tree canopy above. As was so often the case, water dripped steadily from a light rain, and the lanolin in the wool repelled it.

Steve was grateful for his own blanket, a gift from Paloma, the tribe's elderly *bruja*. The word could be translated as witch, but in Steve's estimation it would be fairer to call her a shaman, or, better yet, *curandera,* healer.

Hundreds of generations of knowledge lay behind Paloma's lively dark eyes, knowledge of curative properties that U.S. pharmaceutical companies would give—or take—nearly anything to discover and patent.

"You are a good man, Padre," she said to him as they settled on the damp, dead leaves that carpeted the forest floor.

"I only do what I must, Paloma."

"Only a good man would say that." Her eyes caught a little of the moonlight that filtered through the canopy and seemed to smile at him. "We are approaching a volcano."

He nodded reluctantly. "I've felt the rumblings."

"All the volcanoes have become active since the terrible things that happened in Asia."

Steve had heard the news of the horrifying tsunami in one of his stealthy village visits to buy corn. He had shared it with Paloma, who had accepted it stoically. But what would he have expected? Considering what her people had been facing since the day the village had been attacked in an attempt to arrest Miguel Ortiz, she was hardly likely to care much about hundreds of thousands of dead halfway around the world. These people were in scarcely better straits.

"The gods are angry," Paloma told him now.

He sighed, then smiled when a quiet laugh escaped Paloma.

"I know," she said. "You think your God loves us too much to do such things. But have you forgotten your own stories of the Great Flood? The story of Job?"

Job was a bit of Bible lore that Paloma dearly loved and had taken much to heart. To her, his story seemed to symbolize everything Mayan in some way.

"I haven't forgotten," he admitted.

"So do not deny your god his anger with us. For we have not been a very faithful people."

After living all this time with this particular group of Mayans, Steve could see absolutely nothing in them about which God should be angry, unless it was their unspoken insistence that there was more than one god…something the Bible itself left just a bit ambiguous.

"Paloma, your people have done nothing to earn any god's wrath."

"Perhaps we have not. But there are others… and the innocent always seem to suffer with them. Do you not feel it?"

Steve hesitated. He wasn't sure he wanted to go down this path with her. "Bad things sometimes happen to good people," he said finally, falling back on aphorism. "He makes the rain to fall on the just and unjust alike."

Paloma nodded. "You asked about the Kulkul-can Codex."

Steve froze. All of a sudden time vanished, and he remembered Monsignor Veltroni's charge to him so long ago in Savannah, before he had sent Steve here. "Yes, many months ago. My Church wanted it."

"They fear it."

"Yes."

"And would destroy it."

Steve shook his head. "I don't know, Paloma. They might hide it somewhere, but I'm not sure they would destroy it."

"They *cannot* destroy it."

Steve forced himself to wait patiently. With Paloma he was ever the student, and with Paloma he had learned true patience.

"The Codex," Paloma said presently, "*cannot* be destroyed. It is impossible. It is so old it pre-dates the Maya, the Olmec. It predates the Vira-cocha who brought it to us."

"Viracocha?"

"It is one of his names. You will find he has many and was known throughout this entire part of the world, not just here in the land of the Maya, but among the Inca, also, and perhaps in other ways among our brothers to the north in your country. I do not know. My world is mostly the Mayan world."

Steve nodded, then murmured his understanding, thinking that in the dark of this darkest of nights, she might not see the gesture.

"Viracocha, Quetzalcoatl, Kulkulcan...many names. One man. One very holy man. He brought teachings of love, forbade human sacrifice, although many who followed him did not remember that. He brought the Codex to us, as well, and ultimately it was the Codex that caused the wars that sent my people fleeing into jungles for sanctuary."

"They warred over the Codex?" Steve found that difficult to believe.

"Yes," Paloma said simply. "For the first time in my people's history, we made war not to take captives but to kill. And all for the power of the Codex."

Frankfurt, Germany

The rented suite in a tall office building in the financial district was already outfitted with standard furnishings. In a back room, however, they found the other equipment Office 119 had quietly arranged to have delivered. They spent several hours opening boxes. Since most of them had been shipped from within Germany, their contents were plain to see as bubble wrap and foam popcorn were removed. But a few items, electronics of some kind, had been shipped from outside the country, hidden beneath false bottoms in wooden crates.

It wasn't that the contents were illegal. It was that Office 119 didn't want to leave a trail to this suite.

Assif, Niko and Renate set about connecting all the computer equipment, some of which looked as if it had been intended for military use, while Lawton helped as best he could.

"We have TEMPEST shielding," Assif remarked as he studied some of the equipment.

"Good," Renate said flatly. "I hacked them once before. I am sure they are much more careful now. And if they have any reason to suspect that someone is hacking them now, they will try to track the hacker."

She caught Lawton's confused look and motioned him over to a window that gave him a neck-craning view of some of the surrounding buildings. "You see all the microwave dishes? Many of them are listening, not sending. Without TEMPEST shielding, someone can hear the electronic noise of our computers and decode it to figure out what we're doing."

Lawton nodded. Why did he feel he had just slipped back into the days of the cold war? Maybe he had. The names changed, but the basic plot never varied. "Like the good old bad days of the USSR," he remarked.

Renate leaned back on a desk and folded her arms. "You Americans can be so naive."

He bristled a little. Any naiveté he had once owned had perished on a beach in Los Angeles when a little girl saw her father killed before her eyes and blamed Lawton for it. "And you Europeans think you have the corner on sophistication."

Renate shook her head. "Some do, perhaps. I think we've merely warred ourselves into a terminal case of *Weltschmerz*."

World weariness. Lawton might have laughed at that, had he not been so disturbed by the frightening vibes he kept getting from Renate. She needed watching. "So what are you trying to say?"

"Everyone in Europe wants to say the last pope helped bring down the Soviet Union. Your people want to say it was your President Reagan. Shall I tell you the truth?"

One corner of Lawton's mouth lifted. "I can take it."

"The USSR was brought down by the Frankfurt Brotherhood."

"Oh, come on...."

"It's true. They refused to capitalize the Soviets in any way, which forced them into a state of poverty and bankruptcy. And the reason for that was simple."

"Yes?"

"There was no way for the Brotherhood to

make money on the communist system. They looked at the Soviets and saw huge resources and a huge labor pool they couldn't take advantage of until after the communist government collapsed. Now there are investment opportunities. It may take decades, but the Brotherhood is patient. Very patient. They can wait centuries, if necessary."

Then she went back to work, leaving Lawton to mull that over.

Niko went out to get them a meal, and while they ate, Assif stood next to a whiteboard and began to outline what they would need to do. "First, we have to get into the bank." He wrote swiftly, then snagged another bite of his sandwich.

"Could we pose as an international business seeking access to SWIFTNET?" Niko asked, glancing down at a file folder full of research data. "It says here that banks are offering businesses access to the network."

"No, we can't," Assif said. "First, only a handful of businesses have purchased access to SWIFTNET, and they are all major players in international finance. Second, these business clients are offered only limited access, and they are blocked from the areas of the network I need."

"And most important," Renate added, "our target is a private bank. Like most private banks, it has no public access, no lobby. Clients do not come in off the street. The bank solicits them…personally."

"How can we get on their list?" Lawton asked.

"We can't," Renate answered simply. "The target's clients are very wealthy families, many of them present or former nobility, and huge private trusts. These are not the sort of bona fides that can be manufactured."

"So if I understand correctly, we have no legitimate way to enter that bank," Niko said.

"Correct," Renate answered.

"Utility access tunnels?" Lawton asked. "If we can find their network cables, can we tap in from there?"

"Of course," Assif said. "*If* we could isolate the network cables. But the only way to do that would be to sample all their communications cables at a time when we *know* they are making a SWIFT-NET transmission. And it has to be a transmission whose content we already know, so I can be sure I have the right lines."

"Which brings us back to getting inside the bank," Renate said. "With no legitimate way to do so."

"A black bag job," Lawton said. Renate arched a brow in a silent question, and he continued. "Covert entry."

"Yes, precisely," she said. "A black-bag job."

"Then we need to know their security," Niko said. "Working hours. How many people are in the building at what times of day. Whether there are guards at night, and how many. Electronic security, both external and internal. I'm sure their computers are password protected. If we are going to send a transmission, we will need a password."

"In short," Assif said, staring at the whiteboard as if it might reveal the secrets of the universe, "we need to know their security as well as their security chief does."

Late that night, while Niko and Assif worked steadily in the back room to create what Assif insisted would be an ideal configuration of equipment for the job ahead, Lawton found Renate at the large glass windows in an unlighted executive office.

With her arms wrapped around herself, she was staring out pensively at the Frankfurt night. Beyond the glass, lights sparkled in the cold air. Traffic had almost disappeared, leaving the streetlights starkly alone along the roads. A few offices in the surrounding buildings remained lit, probably for cleaning crews. At any other time, it would have been beautiful.

Right now all Lawton could see was a threat, and he suspected Renate was seeing the same thing.

He moved to her side, joining her perusal of the night beyond the glass.

"You hate these people," he said quietly.

"Wouldn't you?" she asked, her German accent more in evidence than usual. "They tried to kill me. They killed my best friend. Now they have killed my family. What had my family ever done to them?"

"They produced *you*."

She glanced at him, and in the light from without, he thought he detected a flicker of mordant humor in her face. Even that was an improvement over her favored glacial aspect.

"I want to know," she said finally. Her voice seemed thick.

"Know what?"

"Who betrayed me." She faced him briefly. "Someone betrayed me. How else do they know I'm still alive?"

"Perhaps your father…"

"My father knew as much about me being alive as your Miriam in Washington knows."

"Not *my* Miriam," he reminded her.

She shrugged. "She knows. Would she ever reveal that?"

Lawton thought about it. "No."

"My father knew my life was at risk. After all, he had received word of my death long before I was able to tell him I still lived. Think about it, Lawton. He had already grieved for me. Do you think he would do *anything* to make that happen a second time?"

"No."

She nodded once, shortly, then returned her attention to the night.

"What the hell did you do to these swine?"

He thought he saw a faint upward tip of the corner of her mouth, but it was so fleeting it might have been an illusion of the odd lighting.

"Well," she said slowly, "at one time I worked for the *Bundeskriminalamt,* the BKA. Like your FBI."

"Yes, you told me about that when we were in Idaho."

"I was…I think the English phrase is 'a forensic accountant.' Fraud and money laundering."

For a second Lawton was surprised. "In the field, you sure don't act like any accountant I've ever known."

"And you don't act like a lawyer, yet you graduated from law school. We both had to…face difficult and dangerous people. So our training went beyond accounting or law."

"And the Frankfurt Brotherhood?"

"Very quiet, very well concealed. I was not looking for them at first. But then I began to notice strange things. Little fingerprints on affairs reaching far beyond Frankfurt, far beyond Germany. The movement of money can reveal so much."

"It certainly can."

"So I set up a task force. I admit I was the most dedicated. In fact, I admit I became obsessed, especially when it became apparent these people could never be exposed publicly or tried for their crimes. In time I knew more than anyone else. The task force was disbanded as a waste of funds when nothing could be proven."

He nodded, encouraging her.

"So I took my fight underground. Even my superiors did not know what I was doing. I hacked into the Brotherhood's systems and files. And then, quite illegally, I began to give little bits and pieces to the press. I was growing very close to exposing them to the public when they attempted to kill me and instead killed my friend. She was... well, I loved her a lot, Lawton. Not...that way. But maybe even more than that."

"I'm sorry." He could identify with her feelings and had an urge, the first one in a long time, to reach out and embrace someone simply to offer comfort. He had some idea of the hell this woman had gone through.

"That is when Office 119 snatched me away. Literally. Before I could do something stupid, like reappear. When they told me what my job would be here, I refused at first. I wanted to go after them right away. Maybe I should have. Maybe my family would still be alive."

"I'm so sorry, Renate."

She faced him then. Tears were streaming down her cheeks, revealing the grief that was tearing her apart. But her eyes were as hard as steel.

"I will not rest until I have broken them." Her voice was level, harsh. "The world is full of conspiracies, but these...*Schweine.*" She shook her head and a tremor ripped through her. "They are responsible for Black Christmas. I know it. I just need to find out why."

"Power," Steve answered. "Isn't it all about power?"

Renate nodded. Soundless tears still poured down her face. "I know these people. They financed all of this for some arcane reason of their own, and I'm going to find out what it is."

"And then?"

But she didn't answer, as if she knew the Hydra had too many heads. They might foil the Brotherhood's plans, but how could they ever root out all the members themselves?

Another tremor ripped through her, and this time Lawton didn't hesitate. He pulled her close and hugged her. She leaned against him, weeping silently for a long time, and all the while Lawton stared over her head into the night and began to consider the utter hopelessness of their goals.

Wipe out this evil of man against man?

Perhaps when the last two humans disappeared from the planet.

5

President Harrison Rice sat in a wingback chair, looking at his National Security Advisor. Phillip Allen Bentley had not been Rice's first choice for the position. In fact, Rice would not have chosen Bentley at all. When he had announced the nomination, Rice had spoken to the press of Bentley's twenty years of service with the State Department, in a variety of postings. And that, coupled with Rice's close association with the key senators on the Foreign Affairs Committee, had set the tenor for Bentley's confirmation hearings.

The name of Jonathan Morgan had never come up, and certainly not in the White House. But Bentley's presence, so unwelcome, served as a constant reminder.

What Harrison Rice knew—and hoped no one else had discovered—was that his old college roommate and lifelong friend Edward Morgan had masterminded the assassination attempt on Rice's rival in the Democratic primaries: Grant Lawrence. Edward was dead now, a loose end tied up. Edward's father, Jonathan Morgan, had come to Rice shortly after the election and explained Rice's tenuous political position, making it clear that "his people" would expect Rice's obedience. And the death of Edward left no doubt as to the price of disobedience.

Afterward, wild for some escape hatch, he had called for a private meeting between himself and the Director of the FBI, seeking an update on the Lawrence assassination attempt. The meeting had been held away from any possible ears or microphones, at a hunting lodge in West Virginia. Instead of learning that Jonathan Morgan had been lying, he learned that the Bureau had suspected Edward Morgan's involvement but could not find hard evidence. If the FBI couldn't prove it, then Rice had no hope of blowing a noisy whistle on the conspiracy. The "debt" would have to be paid.

Bentley's appointment was the first installment, and although his influence in the administration had thus far been minimal, Rice knew that couldn't last. Black Christmas had changed everything.

"If we handle this well," Bentley continued, "we can form an international consensus. Black Christmas proved to the world what 9/11 should already have made obvious, that Islamic terrorism is an imminent threat to global security. The United States must act, and act decisively."

"Of course we must," Rice said. "But this kind of response…I mean, do we even know for sure who did this? As heavily as we've infiltrated Al Qaeda, wouldn't we have known if they were planning something on this scale? And let's not forget that Pakistan has been an *ally* in the war on terrorism. And they have nuclear weapons of their own."

"Who else but Al Qaeda could have carried out such an attack?" Bentley replied. "We know they've wanted another high-profile strike, and we know they've become a global, pan-Islamic ideological movement. As the 2003 subway bombings in Madrid demonstrated, Al Qaeda's leadership doesn't have to be directly involved in a given attack. They've become a rallying cry for disaffected Muslims around the world. A mention here, a suggestion there, and indigenous Muslim radicals would gladly have performed the Black Christmas strikes on their own."

"But the coordination," Rice said. "You can't tell me these attacks were independent, coincidental actions."

"No," Bentley conceded. "There would have been some coordination in terms of time. But the varying nature of the attacks themselves suggests multiple actors, working independently. And the

complete absence of solid intelligence before the
attacks seems to confirm that. So yes, Mr. President, I think it's safe to conclude that this was an
Al Qaeda coordinated operation. And we know
their senior leadership is clustered in the remote
regions of western Pakistan."

Rice rose to his feet and turned to look out at
the White House lawn. The snow on the ground
was white and even, a pristine backdrop to a conversation that no U.S. president had seriously en-
tertained since the end of the Second World War.
For a moment, he let himself wonder if the mountains of Pakistan were also covered with snow at
this moment, and whether some Al Qaeda leader
was looking out from a cave entrance at a scene
of picturesque beauty. He shook the image from
his head and turned back to Bentley.

"Why not special operations forces? If we
know where these people are, why not go in and
get them?" He picked up Bentley's memo. "I
mean, why *this,* of all things?"

Bentley opened his hands, palms up. "Those
caves are natural fortresses, Mr. President. They
stretch hundreds of feet into the mountains, and
they're interconnected by man-made tunnels.
That's too big a target for commando-style operations. Defense tells me they would need at least
a reinforced brigade to assault that kind of target,
and we would take heavy casualties. Their projec-

tions are based on operations against cave complexes in Iwo Jima and other Pacific islands during World War II. They're saying forty to sixty percent."

Rice recoiled at the prospect of three or four thousand dead Americans. "But this isn't 1945, Phillip. We have better technology now. We have the best military the world has ever known. I can't believe—"

"Mr. President," Bentley said, "cave-clearing operations are straight-up infantry battles. Those fights haven't changed much in centuries. All the high-tech gizmos in the world mean little or nothing in that setting. It would come down to men with rifles and bayonets, groping along in the darkness, having no idea of the terrain ahead of them, against an enemy who knows every inch and is ready to go meet Allah. No, Mr. President, the ground option simply is not militarily viable. It would be a bloodbath, worse than Iraq, and the American people would not stand for it."

Rice nodded slowly. "Okay. And conventional bombs? We have twenty-thousand-pound, armor-piercing bunker busters. We used them in Iraq. Why not there?"

Bentley shook his head. "They are designed for man-made structures, sir. Not for mountains. This is our only viable military option."

"Our only viable military option," Rice echoed.

"You want me to blast a hole in Pakistan—an ally—with nuclear weapons."

"Yes, Mr. President," Bentley said. "With nuclear weapons."

Cairo, Egypt

Guiseppi Veltroni strolled along Midan Talaat Harb, admiring the neoclassic architecture. Despite its haze, Cairo was still a beautiful city. When he had first met Nathan Cohen, years before, Cohen had offered to take him to the Valley of the Kings and the Giza Plateau. But to Veltroni, that was "tourist Egypt," too far removed from the experience of the common Egyptian. Veltroni preferred Cairo or Alexandria, where he could watch the comings and goings of ordinary people, gauge their moods and feel the pulse of their nation.

During the day, Cairo hummed with a rhythm as old as time. Men and women shopped at outdoor markets, bargaining for the best prices on vegetables, meats, clothing and other necessities. It was this sort of human push and pull that had first drawn Veltroni from the tiny village of his birth to the sprawl of Rome, and while he still went home to visit, his heart remained in city life.

His Arabic was barely passable, but he could still learn much from facial expressions and body language. The woman at the lemon stand, for example, seemed untouched by the events of Black Christmas. In her weary face, he saw a woman for whom life was not global in its reach. Not for her the machinations of power or the whispered schemes of men who would do whatever they thought necessary to gain an advantage. Her life was simple, and in that simplicity, he saw a beauty he had long since forsaken.

"You are probably right, my friend."

Veltroni turned to see Cohen standing beside him. As always, the man seemed to appear out of nowhere. Perhaps more irritating, and also as always, Cohen seemed to be able to read his thoughts.

"One day I will learn how you do that," Veltroni said, not extending a hand in greeting.

"It would be better for all of us if you did not," Cohen replied. He pointed to an outdoor café across the street. "Come, let us have fine Turkish coffee and talk. There is much we need to discuss."

"Perhaps," Veltroni said, following Cohen to a table. "If you had news of my brother priest in Guatemala, I would be more inclined to listen to the rest of what you say."

"Ahh yes," Cohen said, sitting. "That would be Father Lorenzo, no?"

Veltroni nodded. "As always, your knowledge of my activities exceeds my knowledge of yours."

"And that, too, is probably for your own good," Cohen said, before switching to Arabic to order for both of them. After the waiter had gone, Cohen turned to Veltroni. "The good Father Lorenzo is alive, my friend, or was when last my sources heard of him. He and the villagers of Dos Ojos have gone into hiding in the mountains, hunted by both the government and the rebels. And also by your enemies."

Veltroni's heart squeezed. While he and Lorenzo had taken the same oath for the preservation of the Faith, an oath that bound them even unto death, he had no desire to test the limits of that commitment, for himself or for his friend and protégé.

"And what can your…sources…do to protect him?" Veltroni asked. "Some quid pro quo would not be amiss."

Cohen shook his head. "Even our reach has its limits, Monsignor. If I could guarantee your friend's safety, I would. But that is not in my power to do."

"And Black Christmas?" Veltroni asked. "Was that in your power to prevent?" It was almost an accusation, a sign that his diplomatic abilities were becoming strained by his concern about recent events—and by Cohen's opacity. Veltroni forced himself to draw a steadying breath. Like it or not, he couldn't afford to offend *any* contact, least of all one about whom he knew so little.

"I wish it had been," Cohen said. "What happened last week served only the basest of human impulses. That horror will only beget more horror. Even now, there are those who are discussing the most awful of consequences."

"Your choice of words is disturbing, Mr. Cohen."

"It should be, Monsignor. There are those who will pause at nothing to pursue their ends, and who will use these attacks as a way to justify more bloodshed."

Veltroni felt chilled despite the warmth of the Cairo afternoon. Time. All of a sudden it seemed there was no time.

"When?" he asked numbly.

Cohen shrugged and sipped his espresso. "The sword must be rattled first. You will hear it rattling."

Veltroni closed his eyes, suddenly wondering how it was that he could be sitting here on a sundrenched street in Cairo, watching ordinary people go about their ordinary lives and discussing the unthinkable.

"Monsignor," said Cohen, leaning toward him, "I will give you something to think about."

Veltroni's eyes snapped open.

"Consider whether you are protecting your Church or your faith. They are not one and the same. As for the Codex you sent your young friend to find…you would be wise to pray that he does not find it. You have no idea what events you and your enemies have set in motion, Monsignor. No idea at all. For myself…" Cohen shrugged. "Armageddon will happen. Now or later."

He rose and threw some money on the table to pay for the coffee. He paused and spoke one more time. "There is a reason, Monsignor, that your Church holds no specific doctrine about whether Yeshua ben Yusef was married. Your Church has shown wisdom in that, and you ought not ignore that wisdom. Be willing to let the truth be the truth."

Then he turned and disappeared into the crowds on the street before Veltroni could say another word.

At that point, if the sky had darkened and lightning had begun to shoot from the clouds, Veltroni would have been no less disturbed. Nor felt any less that he was on the cusp of a division between realities.

His head suddenly rang with Pilate's infamous question: *What is truth?*

And for the first time in his life, Giuseppe Veltroni wondered if he had ever known the answer.

Frankfurt, Germany

Jonathan Morgan rarely came to Frankfurt these days. He was getting too damn old for international flight, even on a private jet. Eight hours in cramped quarters seriously annoyed him. At his age he'd earned the right to spend time fishing and tending his collection of orchids.

Instead, he'd been summoned to a meeting in no uncertain terms. It was all his son's fault, he thought grimly as he stretched stiff joints before attempting to climb down the stairs to the apron. If Edward hadn't screwed up and needed to be eliminated, *he* would have been the one making this hellacious trip.

A car awaited him, he saw. And Frankfurt's winter weather hadn't improved a damn. Cold and gray, threatening snow.

His valet buttoned his overcoat snugly and helped him wrap a muffler around his throat. On his head was perched a stylish gray merino hat.

He descended the stairs easily, now that he had worked out the kinks. For a man in his late sixties, he was in remarkably good shape.

Inside the car sat Wilhelm Tempel, one of the oldest and most esteemed members of the Brotherhood. Wilhelm's family had been one of the founders of the Berg & Tempel private bank, the very core of the Brotherhood. Their association with the bank went back to the thirteenth century. Despite long association and several centuries of marriages between Morgans and Tempels, Jonathan Morgan still fell like something of an upstart beside this man.

"It is good to see you, Jonathan," Wilhelm said warmly enough. "It has been too long."

Jonathan smiled. "That *trip* is too long for men of our age, Wilhelm."

"This could not be discussed any other way. As good as our communications security is, one must never be too trusting of technology."

Jonathan nodded. "I agree."

Wilhelm smiled. "I am told the Hunter is on the trail, Jonathan. He is closing in."

Jonathan felt his heart leap as it had not leaped in years. "How close?"

Wilhelm's smile broadened. "Let's discuss it with the others over the very fine meal my chef is preparing. I even have a bottle of that fine Riesling you enjoy so much."

Jonathan forced himself to be patient, but it was not easy. That the quest might be completed in his lifetime! And if so, he knew exactly what that completion would trigger—and who would rake in the profits.

6

Guatemalan Highlands

This was the dry season? Hah!

The Hunter lay among the thick growth while rain dribbled onto his back. This was supposed to be the best time of year in this godforsaken country, but instead it was miserable. He supposed some weather forecaster would blame it on El Niño or something like that. As if it made a bit of difference on the ground.

He'd been out here for weeks now, following some priest who was supposedly looking for the Kulkulcan Codex. His masters believed the priest would find it faster than the Hunter could. They, of course, were reckoning without adequate knowledge of the Hunter's exquisite interrogation techniques. But then, they wanted the priest, too, as if they suspected him of holding some special information apart from the Codex.

His finely honed sense of people told him the priest was nowhere near finding the damn Codex. Even if that had been Lorenzo's mission, affairs had pushed him onto another tack. The Hunter hadn't experienced the least difficulty learning the story, even after all this time. These *Indios* had little to occupy them other than work, religion and gossip. They loved to talk about almost anything, but they particularly liked to talk about injustices against themselves and their fellows. The story of what had happened at Dos Ojos was beginning to take on all the proportions of an epic myth. Some were even murmuring that the *bruja* at Dos Ojos had made all the survivors invisible.

The Hunter knew better than that. They were invisible, all right, but there was no magic involved. It was simply that they knew the ways of these mountains better than he ever could. No matter what he did, he always seemed to be two or three days behind these people.

And as he plotted each campsite he discovered on his map, it began to seem to him they were moving in circles. Very big circles, but in no particular direction, unless you counted the miles they had put between themselves and Dos Ojos.

He bit into a piece of jerky and watched the rain drip from the narrow brim of his olive-drab porkpie hat. He prided himself on his skills, smarts and utter ruthlessness. But right now he was beginning to wonder if a bunch of ignorant natives were going to outsmart and outrun him forever.

Neither his employers nor his masters would accept that. Either he found the priest and the Codex, or he died trying. There were no alternatives. Cursing silently, he pressed on into the jungle.

Frankfurt, Germany

Jonathan Morgan was pleased with his suite. While the Steigenberger Hotel was comparatively new, especially in a country where businesses proudly proclaimed centuries-old heritages, it offered both luxury and convenience, and had a well-earned five-star rating. Had he been merely a tourist visiting Frankfurt, he might have thought he had tumbled into a traveler's delight.

But he was not on a tourist visit, and as he surveyed the faces of the other men in the room, he found himself unable to relax in the posh comfort of his accommodations. This was business, pure and simple. And it was an ugly business, at that.

"So," the German said, "is your president prepared to use nuclear weapons?"

"He seems resigned to the prospect," Morgan replied. "But this is hardly an easy decision for any man to make. He is a bold man, however. Once he accepts that there are no alternatives, he will move forward with our plans."

"Make sure he does not move too quickly," the Londoner replied. "You must remember that our plan depends on a confluence of events. The Vatican will doubtless object to the use of nuclear weapons, and the Catholic Church still has great sway in many quarters of the world. We need to preempt that objection."

"Our friends are on the cusp of finding the Codex," the Austrian added, nodding. "Its revelation will be major news, despite all that is happening, much as was the St. James Ossuary a few years ago. This, however, will be much greater—proof that Mary Magdalene was the wife of Christ, and that her grandson brought the true gospel of Christ to pre-Columbian America. That will demolish the voice of the Vatican in world events and leave us with an open field in which to operate."

"I am familiar with our plans," Morgan said, trying to contain his displeasure at being lectured. Would Europeans never accept that Americans were not recalcitrant children who needed to be reminded at every step of a process? "But you must understand the nature of American politics. While Harrison Rice is ours to control—to a point—have no doubt that he and he alone is the president of the United States. He and he alone has the power to authorize the use of nuclear weapons. Do not expect him to totally cede that authority, not even to us."

"Hold on," the German said. "You told us that

if this worked, we would—in your son's words— *own* the President of the United States. We took grave risks in underwriting Edward's plan. Were it not for our contacts in your news media, the conspiracy to assassinate Grant Lawrence—and your son's involvement—would have been exposed for the world to see. Now you are telling us that, despite those risks and the ultimate success of the plan, we cannot rely on President Rice to do what he is told, when he is told?"

Morgan paused to light a cigar, both because it allowed him time to frame his response and because he felt it necessary to make them wait for his answer, in order to regain the initiative. He was not accustomed to being interrogated, and the fact that the three of them had obviously prepared privately for this meeting did nothing to make him more amenable.

"Yes," he said, finally, "that's exactly what I'm telling you. He holds the most powerful elected position in the world. It takes little time for the import of that to settle upon a man. He was no one's lapdog, even when he was in the Senate. Now, my friends, he will cooperate with us. But cooperation and slavish obedience are different, and we must accept the former without demanding the latter, lest he decide to use the power of his office in ways that could be even more harmful to our cause."

Rachel Lee

"Unacceptable," the Londoner said. "If you are implying that he might become a threat, then we remove him and replace him with someone more amenable."

"You can't do that," Morgan said, leaning forward, his anger flashing. "I don't have to tell you the geopolitical realities. You now have your European Union, but have no doubt that you are not yet a global superpower. The United States could crush you several times over, with little or no damage to itself. While the U.S. can no longer lead Europe around on a leash like a captive hound, the roles have not been reversed. And there are political sensitivities that Harrison Rice cannot ignore."

"What sensitivities exceed our having bought and paid for his office in blood?" the German asked.

"Anti-Arab violence is on the rise," Morgan said. "We knew it would happen. It was part of our plan. But do not forget the pressure that places on Rice. The American people are demanding a response. He cannot afford to look impotent in the face of what is nothing less than a global declaration of war. And we have told him that only one response is possible. We cannot now ask him to sit on his hands and wait for permission to act."

Morgan rose to his feet, his anger demanding physical movement, lest it manifest in words he might not live to regret. "Your friends must accelerate their search for the Codex. They have been searching for nearly two years. The Codex was to have been revealed months ago, and now you tell me that the president must commit political suicide by waiting indefinitely before responding to Black Christmas? No, my friends, that simply is not possible. At the very least, we must give him a politically acceptable interim response. We must provide a way for him to appear prudent without appearing cowardly."

"Yes, I understand," the Austrian said, his tone softening. "The European people are also demanding a response. Obviously we cannot expect Herr Rice to, as you put it, sit on his hands."

"Yes, of course," the Londoner agreed. "Perhaps we have been too…forceful…in our approach today. I assure you, Jonathan, we are all aware of the political realities. We have spent decades creating those very realities."

"I believe I can offer the necessary alternative," the Austrian said. "We know one of the Black Christmas cells is in Vienna. If we could arrange for their…disposal…in a manner that could be attributed to a joint U.S.-European action, would that assuage the political pressure on Herr Rice?"

"The American people will want results they can see," Morgan said, shaking his head. "After the 9/11 attacks, if you recall, there was a demand for visible action. The fact that covert teams were all over the world, taking down Al Qaeda cells, was not enough. The American people wanted, needed, to see tanks rolling across the desert."

"I am sure it can be arranged for this to be very visible," the Austrian said. "And there will be no U.S. casualties."

"What do you have in mind?" Morgan asked, curious.

"Unless I am very mistaken," the Austrian replied, "our friends will want revenge for their plans having been twisted to our ends. So we will let them have it. Except that we will arrange for Herr Rice take the credit for it."

The plan had merit, Morgan thought. It was elegant, a quality he had always admired, all the more so in recent months. Edward's plan had been too complex, and that had very nearly been its downfall. It was, Morgan thought with satisfaction, good to be working with professionals again.

"That should work," Morgan said, returning to his seat. "Yes, that should work well."

"Very good," the German said. "Which brings us to the final item. How do we find and kill Bookworm?"

Riyadh, Saudi Arabia

Ahmed Ahsami studied the report that his lieutenant had brought that morning. It fit in well with other reports he had gleaned over the past days. Knowing that *Saif Alsharaawi* would find them in the Arab world, the traitors of Black Christmas had instead chosen to hide out in Europe. He should have expected such cowardice.

"Yes, Yawi," he said. "This is quite good. And we're sure of the source?"

"Our colleagues in the Arab Bank are loyal," Yawi said. "I asked them to flag that account number and notify me immediately of any transactions. They have no idea why I asked for the information. But they complied."

"Eight thousand euros," Ahmed said, folding his hands on his belly and looking up at the ceiling. "That is an odd amount. Not enough to buy new identities. Not enough to relocate into anonymity."

"Perhaps they believe they already have," Yawi said.

"I believe they do," Ahmed said. "I think this is for living expenses."

"What a shame," Yawi said, a faint smile on his face.

"What is that, my friend?"

"Their living expenses will be their deaths."

Ahmed couldn't resist the chuckle, though he made a note to pray for forgiveness in tonight's evening prayers. He ought not to take joy in what he was doing, however necessary it might be.

"How soon can we get a team to Vienna?" Ahmed asked.

"We can be ready to leave in two days," Yawi said.

"Fine. See that you are. And leave none alive."

Once Yawi had left, Ahmed considered what he had just done. He had ordered the death of fellow Arabs, fellow followers of Islam. The Koran forbade killing, but most especially the killing of other Muslims. But may Allah forgive him, it had to be done.

Al Jazeera hadn't been alone in reporting on the rising tide of anger against Arabs. It had been too much for even the Western media to ignore. Mosques had been desecrated. Two Arab businesses burned in Los Angeles. Unless the world could see that Arabs would police themselves, there would be no alternative save for more Western intrusion into the Arab world.

And so these traitors must be found and killed. And it must be made clear that they were found and killed by *Saif Alsharaawi*. Then, perhaps, Ahmed could finally release the video he had made before Christmas and begin to paint for the world a picture of a more civilized, if equally determined, Arab leadership.

Ahmed trusted that Allah would understand.

7

Frankfurt, Germany

"Well, there's hope," Niko said, shrugging off his down jacket, careful not to let the melting snow drip onto the sensitive electronic equipment that crowded the office. He looked at Renate. "Your old friends in the Brotherhood are good, but they aren't perfect."

"Meaning?"

"They're smug."

"I assume we finally have some good news?" Renate said, the tension evident in her voice. During the past week she had grown thinner, and everyone in the group had taken to pressing food on her. She had begun to eat again only that morning after Assif had shouted at her.

"If you want to starve yourself to death, okay!" he'd said in exasperation. "But can you at least wait until after the mission? You could endanger someone's life if you're not at the top of your game."

Since then she had eaten two full meals, although it was clear she hadn't enjoyed them.

The past six days had seemed like an exercise in futility. Every plan they had conceived had run into a morass of technical difficulties. Berg & Tempel AG, the target bank, was a tough nut to crack. Any hope of tapping into their communications without making a physical entry into the bank itself had been lost in the spaghetti of optic cables that ran beneath Frankfurt's streets. And Berg & Tempel's ornate, nineteenth-century stone building sat squarely amidst the towering steel-and-glass monoliths of the banking district, where the underground electronic labyrinth was at its most complex.

"I spent the day eating *pommes frites* in the *Jürgen-Ponto-Platz,*" Niko said, taking a seat. "I learned more than I want to know about the murder of Jürgen Ponto, and if I never eat another fried potato, it will be too soon. But it was worth it."

"Yes?" Renate asked. She was in no mood to play the game of twenty questions. "So what did you learn?"

"Berg & Tempel is right across the street, at the corner of Kaiserstraße and Westendstraße," Niko continued, as if unaware of the tart tone in her voice. "I was able to watch their comings and goings all afternoon and into the evening. They're good, but they're also lazy."

"How so?" Lawton asked.

"It's a private bank. No lobby. Customers visit by appointment only."

"Right," Renate said impatiently. "We know this. This is what makes them so difficult to penetrate."

"On the contrary," Niko said. "This is what makes them easy to penetrate. Their security is very lax. They probably don't have a vault, or if they do, it holds no cash to speak of. Most of their work involves shifting investments around and sheltering their clients from taxes. There is little to attract thieves, and thus little reason for the kind of tight security you would find in an ordinary bank. I was able to walk right in, under the guise of delivering a parcel. What's more, once I got past the front desk, I was able to wander the building for fifteen minutes before someone saw that I looked lost and gave me directions."

"So Lawton could make his entry as a *Fahrrad-Kurier*," Renate said. "A bicycle courier."

"Yes," Niko said. "Easily, in fact. And that's not all. I checked out the internal security. Unless they're very good at hiding cameras, there aren't any except at the front door. The computer room uses key cards, as do the senior executives' offices, but beyond that, anyone in the building can go just about anywhere."

"Nighttime security?" Renate asked.

"A guard at the front desk," Niko said. "Unless there were other guards that came in by other entrances, he's the only one. He looks to be a college student making some extra money by working as a night watchman. He locked the doors after the employees left, and twenty minutes later he was drinking coffee with his head buried in a textbook."

"Key cards," Lawton said. "If they have key cards, they probably log entries automatically."

"Right," Assif said, "but those logs would be kept on their computers. Once I know what system they use, I can tell you how to modify the log files."

"This could work," Lawton said, nodding. "I go in just before close of business and disappear into a men's room or closet. Once everyone's gone, and assuming I can get a key card, I'm into the computer room, with comms to Assif, in the utility tunnel below the bank. He tells me what to do to send a SWIFTNET message, so he can tap the correct line, and tells me how to erase my key card entry from the log file. Then I hide out until morning, wait until things are busy, and leave as if I had just dropped off the parcel. It's simple, and clean."

"Yes," Assif said. "That can work."

"If we can get a key card," Renate said. "And if we can get Assif to the right utility junction box."

"And don't forget the bicycle," Niko said.

Lawton looked at him. "I don't understand."

"The couriers lock their bicycles at a rack outside the bank," Niko said. "Someone will notice if it's there when they leave and still there in the morning. So one of us will have to pick up the bicycle without looking as if we're stealing it, then return it the next morning."

Renate walked to the whiteboard and began to write. "Lawton in the bank. Assif in the utility tunnel. Niko, you will handle the bicycle, and be on watch when Assif enters and exits the tunnel. I'll be here, monitoring our communications and the police scanner."

Lawton nodded. "So we need to find the utility junction box and get a key card. Then, I think, we're good to go."

Renate looked at Niko. "I need you to go back to the *Jürgen-Ponto-Platz* and watch the bank employees as they come to work. We need to identify those who work in the computer room."

"And how am I supposed to identify which employees work in the computer room?" Niko asked.

"I'll go with you," Assif said, breaking into a smile. "I can spot a fellow geek from a kilometer away."

"Good," Renate said. "Then we start surveillance on the computer room employees. One of them is sure to be single and male. And I will get the key card from him."

Her tone left no doubt that she would do anything, anything at all, to achieve the downfall of those who had killed her family. Whatever conscience she might once have owned had been blown away by a bomb in a simple church.

Vienna, Austria

Yawi Hassan had spent the day in a café on the Gellerplatz, watching the apartment house two blocks down Quellenstraße. Three hours earlier, laughing children had streamed from the Catholic school across the street. Yawi was struck by the irony: terrorists who had murdered thousands of Catholics on Christmas Day were hiding out in an apartment house two blocks from a Catholic school.

Now a last group of students, young teenage boys, Yawi guessed, freshly showered after an athletic practice, approached him. With his limited German, Yawi realized they were asking him to settle a dispute over which Austrian football club would be strongest that year. Although he knew nothing of Austrian football, Yawi chose from among the team names the boys pressed upon him.

"Rapid ist sehr gut," Yawi said.

"Ja!" answered the boy who had offered that club. *"Rapid wird immer dominieren! Die san leiwand!"*

As the boy broke into a wide grin, the other boys objected. Much to Yawi's relief, for he had not understood the boy's reply, they took the disagreement with them as they walked to the tram station. He smiled and shook his head as they left. In whatever language, in whatever culture, boys would be boys.

Now alone again, Yawi reviewed the plan in his head. All the pieces were in place. The last of their seven targets had returned to the apartment only a few minutes before, after a quick stop at a corner market. Even now, Yawi knew that his men were moving into their final preassault positions.

The target was a third-floor apartment, and Yawi and his men had gone over the interior layout several times. Each of his men had a specific assignment from the moment they burst into the open front room. They had rehearsed the assault in an identical apartment building across town until everyone on the team could perform his mission in total darkness and absolute silence. There would be no arrests tonight. Their orders were clear.

Kill them all.

"Ready," a quiet voice whispered in Yawi's earphone.

Yawi strolled down the street, taking a final look around. His secondary objectives were to minimize civilian casualties and to extract his men without their being identified. He saw no *Polizei* in evidence, and at this late dinner hour, there was little traffic on the street.

"Two minutes," he whispered.

Ninety seconds later, he entered the building and began to ascend the back stairs. He didn't need to check to ensure that the back exit was neither locked nor blocked. The Austrians were very careful about such matters. And even if they hadn't been, his men had already verified that fact. As he climbed the stairs, he screwed a silencer on his Tek-9 automatic pistol and cycled the bolt to chamber a round.

Yawi reached the third-floor landing and pulled his ski mask down over his face, then placed his left hand on the shoulder of the last man in his team. That man in turn placed his left hand on the shoulder of the next, until the fifth commando, first in the line, placed his left hand on the door leading from the stairwell into the interior corridor. Now, simply by squeezing the shoulder of the man in front of him, Yawi gave the silent signal to go. In less than a second, the message had been relayed to the lead man, and he pushed open the door.

The corridor was clear, and they moved silently, each holding up fingers to count the doors they passed. *One...two...three...four.* Yawi checked each man's count, for in the stress of an assault, he knew not to overlook even the smallest, most basic detail. Certain that they were at the right door, he patted the shoulder of the man in front of him.

That action was repeated up the line, and the lead man extracted a tiny video camera with a fish-eye tubular lens. As the tube slid beneath the door frame, Yawi studied the distorted image on the handheld monitor. He counted six people in the room, two on a sofa along the left wall, two in the kitchen area to the back and two at a small dinner table. A shadow moving in the distance marked the seventh target, walking along the back hallway.

As the lead commando withdrew the camera tube, Yawi relayed the information to his men with hand signals. Each nodded. Now the second man squeezed two small gobs of putty into the gap between the door and its frame, one at the catch for the doorknob, the other at the dead bolt. As that man pressed detonators into the plastic explosive, Yawi and the others readied flash grenades. The second man held up a thumb.

All was ready.

The men flattened themselves against the wall, and Yawi nodded. The second man squeezed a tiny plunger, and two muffled pops sounded almost simultaneously. Yawi felt a momentary rush of satisfaction. His man had done his job precisely as he had been trained, using the minimum amount of explosive necessary to blow the door. The satisfaction was quickly lost in the moment, however, for now he and his men burst into motion.

The lead man kicked the door open, and four flash grenades were tossed in immediately. Two seconds later, the grenades exploded with a rushing *whoosh,* as Yawi and his men shielded their eyes against the blinding, blue-white glare.

"Go!" he snapped.

The command was unnecessary, for his men were already in motion. The first two men burst in, pistols leveled, marking their targets, the quiet pops as they fired lost in the cries of panic within. Yawi followed and saw that two of the targets were already slumping to the floor, red holes punched in their chests.

Yawi pressed on toward the back of the apartment, his arms extended, left hand beneath his right, supporting the weight of the weapon, moving it side to side, tracking with every turn of his head. A light beneath the bathroom door flicked off, and Yawi fired through the door at the same instant that it seemed to spout holes from within.

He felt the three rapid punches in his chest, knocking him back against the wall, but kept firing, the flimsy door now almost disintegrating before his eyes. He realized he was sitting on the floor, his back against the wall, with an unbelievable tightness in his chest, making it all but impossible to breathe.

Through a gaping hole in the door, he watched his target rise and come toward him, gun in one hand, the other vainly trying to staunch the angry geysers of blood spurting from the side of his neck. Yawi was dimly aware of one of his comrades coming around the corner to check on him, of the target turning and raising his pistol, of three more shots, of the target finally crumpling to the floor, half-atop him.

Mission accomplished, Uncle, Yawi thought. *We killed them all.*

And then the darkness swelled around him.

Frankfurt, Germany

It all sounded so simple, but Lawton knew it wasn't. Nothing could be that simple. He drew Renate from the back room into one of the executive offices. "We need to talk."

"About what?"

"This sounds too simple."

"Anything sounds simple when it is laid out this way."

Damn, she was so distant again, as if everything that made her Renate had flown away to another star system.

"Renate, listen to me."

"I *am* listening, Law."

"Then think about it. If this bank really contains the kind of information you think it does, why isn't it better guarded? The entire Frankfurt Brotherhood could take a fall if their computer records were breached."

She turned to face him directly. "What are you saying?"

"I'm saying the only reason they'd do this is if their records are so heavily encrypted that we'll probably be wasting our time anyway."

She shook her head. "First we go for their communications. We hack into their computer system and view their private Internet messages. If we find what we need there, we can talk about what to do next to nail them. But trust me, if we follow the money we'll find them."

"But how will we break their encryption? Even the NSA can't hack SWIFTNET. When they want the information, they get a subpoena."

She gave him a tight smile. "You must have faith in me. And in Assif. We have done this before."

"Why do I feel like there's something you're not telling me?" he asked.

"Because there are some things that it's better not to know," she replied, her icy eyes fixed on him. "Trust me, Lawton. I know what I'm doing here. And we *will* get what we need."

She left to rejoin the others, and he followed reluctantly, thinking that he didn't mind putting his neck in a noose if he could be certain it would serve a purpose. He wasn't sure of that with this job yet.

Niko was regaling Assif with the story of the murder of Jürgen Ponto.

"He was the head of the Dresdner Bank, back in the 1970s. It was a terrible time in Germany, in Europe. Lots of terrorist groups active. Suzanne Albrecht was Ponto's godchild, the daughter of a man he'd known since childhood. But he didn't know she'd joined the Red Army Faction. She showed up at his door carrying a bouquet of roses, acting like the loving godchild. Then she and her two companions tried to kidnap him. He fought back. They shot him five times."

"Wow," said Assif, shaking his head. "His godchild?"

Niko nodded. "It makes you think, doesn't it? You can know someone from the day they were born and still not know them at all."

"He was the enemy," Renate said quietly.

"The anger of disaffected youth," Niko said. "So easy to twist young minds."

Assif's face froze as he looked at the television news. "Yes. And it's happening again."

8

Saint-Arnans-la-Bastide, France

General Jules Soult sat in the comfortable leather armchair in his library. He puffed on a cigar and studied the papers that had arrived by pouch from Frau Schmidt only a short while ago. The courier was cooling his heels outside, awaiting Soult's response.

It would be positive, of course. He had every intention of taking over intelligence operations for the European Union Department of Collective Security. He also intended to make very sure that these documents he was to sign would hamper him in no important way.

He was quite pleased to discover that there was nothing to object to in the papers before him. He was assigned full intelligence responsibility and ordered to report directly to Frau Schmidt herself.

Apparently the good German woman had no desire for any dirt to get past the two of them. That pleased him.

His operational budget would be generous, and while his operatives were forbidden to use deadly force except in self-defense, Soult wasn't worried about that detail. His people would ensure that he retained plausible deniability.

Satisfied, he signed and initialed the first set of documents, keeping a copy for himself, and slipped the executed version back into the pouch. He touched a button on his desk, and moments later his butler appeared. An English butler, of course. There was something about the way the English buttled that remained without compare.

"For the courier. Then I should like my brandy."

The man bowed, accepting the pouch. "At once, Monsieur le Général."

Soult sent the butler on his way, then reached into his top right desk drawer and pulled out a remote control. With the touch of a few buttons, the library wall to one side opened and revealed a large-screen television. As always, it was already tuned to a news network. Today he chose to listen to one out of Germany. It always paid to have a wide variety of sources.

What he saw pleased him immensely. Students in Berlin were burning pictures of Osama bin Laden. The Islamic Center in Vienna had suffered from graffiti and broken windows. The violence was still only in the stage of small outbreaks. But it would provide perfect cover for what was to come.

He was still smiling when his butler returned with his Napoleon brandy on a silver salver. The man placed the snifter carefully on Soult's desk and began to bow out.

"Wait, Devon."

The butler paused and straightened to attention. "Monsieur?"

"Have you seen the news about the public attacking mosques? And protesting?"

"Yes, sir."

Soult turned to look the man in the eye. "What do you think of it?"

"I can understand the anger, monsieur, but the actions accomplish nothing of purpose."

Soult nodded slowly, and dipped the mouth end of his cigar in the brandy for a moment. "What would be *your* idea of a proper response?"

Devon's eyes widened only a fraction, and only momentarily, before he resumed his customarily formal demeanor. "I'm quite sure I don't know, sir. I am merely a butler."

Soult chuckled. "And a diplomatic one at that. Don't you feel the least urge to strike back, to seek vengeance, no, *justice,* for these atrocities?"

Devon hesitated. "What I feel, sir, is not necessarily a wise response. Yes, I feel loathing for persons who could commit such crimes. But does that give me the right to take the law into my own hands?"

With that, before he could be questioned any further, Devon and his salver disappeared from the library.

Soult studied the curl of smoke rising from his cigar, then glanced at the news again. Devon would bear watching, he decided. Then, a moment later, he changed his mind. Devon had spoken as a rational, mature man who had been raised in a culture of law. And everything that he himself was about to do would be under the color of law. And if it were so, then Devon should have no reason to object, not that Soult had any intention of letting his butler in on his secrets. Still, he knew better than to presume that a butler—even one as impeccably trained as Devon—would be oblivious to what happened around him.

Reaching for the phone, he placed a call. When his comrade answered, Soult spoke in flawless Spanish. "I have the position, but I must attend to administrative details before I can issue a contract. However, you may begin your recruiting efforts immediately."

He hung up and sat back in his chair. Everything was going as it should. Another smile creased his face. Every revolution required an army, and soon he would have his. What's more, the very government he intended to seize would be paying for that army. The effortless irony of his plans gave him a heady feeling of power, almost a rush. Better than Napoleon brandy and Cuban cigars.

But even as he was feeling smugly content, the news broke away from its coverage of random acts of malice to something far more deadly.

"Today in Vienna," the reporter said, "special agents of the EU and the United States carried out a joint strike on a terrorist cell believed to have been involved in Black Christmas...."

Soult sat forward quickly, brandy forgotten, and turned up the volume. Pictures of bodies being carried out flashed across the screen, along with exterior shots of a nondescript concrete apartment house of a type that had become common after the war, a type Soult felt was a blight on the beauty of Europe.

Bodies. Nine terrorists killed in a fierce gun battle. And then the face of the American president, Harrison Rice. "This is only the beginning," the president said. "We will hunt down these terrorists to the last man. In cooperation with our European allies, we will not allow these atrocities to go unavenged. Thank you."

Soult sat back slowly. For the first time that day, he sensed something at work that was beyond his knowledge. Beyond his control.

Every bit of triumph he had been feeling vanished like a puff of smoke from the end of his cigar.

Riyadh, Saudi Arabia

Ahmed Ahsami watched the television, absolutely livid. *His* men had gone in there to take out those terrorists, but the situation had been snatched away. Among the nine "terrorists" whose pictures were now being broadcast to the world was Yawi. His sister's son.

He slammed his hand down on his desk over and over, grief and anger warring on a scale that was beyond speech, beyond description. At that moment he could have blasted the entire world into oblivion.

Someone was using him. Someone he thought was an ally. Nothing else could possibly explain this. The information had come to him about the location of the terrorists, but it had apparently gone to someone else, as well. How else could Austrian and American commandos have arrived just minutes after the survivors on his team had withdrawn? That could not have happened by coincidence.

His nephew and Isa had been killed, offered up like sacrificial lambs, and were now being labeled as part of the terrorist cell. And the American president was standing smugly before a bank of microphones, his Alabama drawl and artificially confident smile reminiscent of nothing so much as a plantation owner swearing that rebelling slaves would be hunted down.

Why? Why had someone done this? To prevent him from showing his message to the world, that Arabs could police Arabs? That there could be peace? That the rest of the world needn't intervene in the affairs of Muslims?

He slammed his hand on the desk again, heedless of the pain. He had been used. Again. And now blood would spill. Thoughts of fealty to Allah faded as his rage grew. Blood would spill. The blood of his betrayers.

Reaching for his phone, he called the Vatican. Either Veltroni was involved or he would know who was. Either way, he would feel Ahmed's wrath.

Washington, D.C.

Harrison Rice sat in the Oval Office, his back to the room, watching the early-winter night settle over the snow-covered gardens. From time to time someone would enter the room and tell him that his approval rating was shooting through the roof since his press conference announcing the successful raid in Vienna.

Strangely, he felt little joy in hearing that his approval rating was somewhere in the eightieth percentile, having leaped up from the basement into which it had fallen following Black Christmas.

What he felt, what he truly felt, was relief that he could avoid the use of nuclear weapons. At least for a little while. But thinking that over, he was surprised at how swiftly Bentley had wanted him to announce the raid in Vienna and claim the credit. Too fast, thought Rice. No time to even absorb events or get the full details. Just get out there and say, "Look what we've done."

Rice knew his strings were being pulled, and he found it distasteful and ugly. He wished there was some way he could fight back. He had no intention of leading the world into annihilation for the sake of agendas that were hidden from him.

He felt as if he were caught in a spiderweb, and struggling only mired him deeper. Somehow he had to find a way out of this trap. But until he knew just what the trap was, and what purpose it served, he had no way to know the right direction in which to move.

He was a very unhappy man.

Polls be damned.

"You should be grateful, Mr. President."

From behind him came the all-too-familiar voice of his National Security Advisor. Had the man come to gloat?

"Grateful?"

"Yes, sir. This buys us time. Time to think about what to do in Pakistan. Time to explore other options, if there are any. It takes the political heat off of you, Mr. President, and gives you the opportunity to make a cool and rational decision. One you'll be comfortable with."

Rice pivoted his chair and faced Bentley. "Yes? How can that be? Nine men could not have pulled off all of the Black Christmas attacks. We both know that. If you were trying to placate the American people, you can take it from me—this won't do it. They will figure out that these nine men didn't work alone, and they'll do it faster than you can spread butter on a biscuit."

"I'm not concerned about the American people."

"Obviously not."

Bentley, who was actually a short and stocky man, nevertheless seemed to tower over Rice. "I have to look beyond our borders, Mr. President, to the future of the entire planet."

"And using nuclear weapons is for the benefit of the people whose lives will be erased in an instant?" Rice asked, sarcasm dripping from every word.

"Mr. President," Bentley said, "it's time for you to learn to take the broader view. There is more at stake than the future of *this* country. And we can't prepare for that future if we feel shackled by domestic politics. This raid loosens the shackles, sir."

Perhaps, Rice thought. Perhaps it loosened one

set of shackles. But he knew that Bentley represented another, and those were growing ever tighter.

Vatican City

Giuseppe Veltroni's stomach burned after the phone call from Ahmed Ahsami, and it was still burning when he entered the private apartment of Pablo Cardinal Estevan, the society's titular head.

The cardinal had cast aside his official uniform in favor of slacks and a smoking jacket. Before him on the coffee table in the deceptively unofficial sitting room sat a small glass of amber liquid. The cardinal neither greeted Veltroni courteously nor offered him a drink—something that deepened Veltroni's concern and caused his stomach to roil even harder.

"This Ahsami," the cardinal said without preamble, "may be in the process of becoming a serious hindrance to our goals."

Veltroni, who had long since resigned himself to the fact that the Stewards of the Faith held aims of which he was unaware, nevertheless could not let that statement go without response. "Ahsami is merely the man with an idea. *Saif Alsharaawi*, The Sword of the East, will continue without him. It has to, for it is the only way that Islam can make peace with the West."

Cardinal Estevan reached for his drink and sipped deliberately. The ormolu clock on the mantelpiece now seemed loud. Veltroni found himself listening to the seconds of his life ticking away. Wasted time, sitting here indulging this cardinal who was dragging out this interview simply to enjoy Veltroni's discomfort. May the Lord forgive him, but he had never liked Cardinal Estevan.

"We must preserve the faith at all costs," Estevan said finally. "That is our entire purpose in founding this society."

Really? thought Veltroni, who was at that very moment wondering if the cardinal spoke the entire truth.

"You must tell this Ahsami," said Estevan after another deliberate sip, "that we had no inkling of this raid in Vienna. Tell him we regret that someone else became involved. That he would be wise to look at his other allies."

Something icy seemed to wrap itself around the monsignor's heart. "Other allies?"

One corner of Estevan's mouth lifted. "You surely did not think that we alone held an interest in *Saif Alsharaawi.*"

"If not, then why wasn't I told?" Anger was beginning to build in Veltroni. "If I am to be effective, I must be informed."

"You receive all the information you need. Whether this Ahsami chooses to recognize it or not, there are other actors on this stage." Estevan put up a hand to silence Veltroni's objection. "Who those actors are, and what their roles were in Black Christmas and Vienna, are not our immediate concern. But they *are* Ahsami's concern, and he would be well advised to deal with them."

Estevan shook his head and for the first time said something that Veltroni could truly agree with. "We want peace, Monsignor. Peace for the world. We have no desire to create Armageddon. But others do. And they must be rooted out. We had hoped Ahmed Ahsami might be the man to ally with. His influence in the Islamic world was growing, and it may yet grow again. And he has even less reason to desire war than we do. Isn't that what you said to me?"

"Yes. Yes, I did."

"And you still believe it?"

"I do."

"Then speak to him again. Tell him to look back to the thirteenth century. There he will find his enemies, the ones who betrayed him."

"I need more than that!"

Again Estevan lifted a hand. "It is all I can give you. Now, how is your priest doing in Guatemala?"

"I haven't heard from him yet."

"Then he is dead. We must send someone else. The Codex must not fall into the wrong hands. It is more important than you can conceive, Monsignor, and not just for the story it might tell."

"I have wondered," Veltroni said carefully. "Since the Church has no official doctrine on whether our Lord might have married and sired children."

"Of course not," Estevan said with a shrug. "We don't know, and even if the Christ were married, it would not affect our faith. No, Monsignor, this Codex is far more dangerous. If it falls into the wrong hands, there *will* be war. A war more terrible than the world has ever seen."

Estevan leaned forward, staring intently at Veltroni. He emphasized his next words by tapping the tabletop with the tip of his index finger. His episcopal ring flashed fire. "It is for God to decide when the end of humanity will happen, not for man. But there are some who would make the decision themselves."

Veltroni was shortly out on the street again, even more troubled than before. He had been told to send Steve Lorenzo to Guatemala in order to prevent the discovery of the Magdalenian secret. And he had done so. But Estevan was right. The exposure of that secret, if it were true, would cause only small ripples. So the Codex represented something far more. Something he could not imagine.

Being in the dark was not something he liked.

But it was in the dark he was going to have to function. As for his friend, Steve Lorenzo... Veltroni whispered a silent prayer. Dear God, let Nathan Cohen have spoken the truth when he said Lorenzo still lived.

There were some things Veltroni's conscience could not have borne, Lorenzo's death among them. No amount of ritual penance and forgiveness from his confessor would erase such a stain. Thinking back over his conversation with Cardinal Estevan, the monsignor wondered if he had become involved in things not even God could forgive.

Croton, Italy, 460 B.C.

His days and evenings swarmed with students; time to simply reflect had become a rare and precious commodity for Pythagoras. He was getting on in years, and, perhaps because of a life spent traveling all over the known world to learn from the wisest of men, he tired easily these days.

He no longer cared to become involved in politics, although wherever he traveled he seemed to become mired in them…even here in Croton, where he had finally fled to escape the ugliness in his home of Samos.

But tonight his thoughts were far from Samos, or his students, or even the current invasion of Croton, which he thought would prove to be minor compared to other invasions he had endured during his life.

No, tonight he had no thought for his students, nor for the past, nor for the war. Tonight, hidden away in the small cave he had turned into a hermitage, he was looking at a sealed metal box that had been delivered from an old friend in Egypt. The friend had promised to send the contents to him if ever he thought he could not keep it safe.

Now it sat before him, the concealing box, seeming to dance a bit as the flame of the small oil lamp in the niche nearby flickered in a draft.

Pythagoras's eagerness knew no bounds, but still he held back, enjoying the anticipation.

He knew what lay within: the tablet of Hermes Trismegistus, or Hermes Thrice Great, as the Greeks called him. Thoth to the Egyptians. Messenger of the gods. To some, a god himself.

Pythagoras cared not whether Hermes-Thoth was really a god. What he knew from his experiences in Egypt, Babylon and among the Chaldeans, from his travels in many parts of the world, was that the tablet contained the old knowledge. The knowledge nearly lost during the great flood that was recorded in the chronicles of Sumer and the Hebrews.

It was a knowledge many spoke of quietly but few had ever truly gained access to. It was a knowledge that allowed the refineries of Sardis, in Lydia, to separate silver and other metals from gold. But, according to his Egyptian friend, that was the most base of uses for the knowledge in the tablet.

It was only a small beginning. The tablet was said to contain the secrets of sacred geometry. The secrets that allowed transmutation of gold into *mufkyzt*, the ancient Egyptian secret of life. The Fire-Stone. Its powers were said to be beyond imagining.

But that was not so much what interested Pythagoras. Yes, the sacred geometry. Yes, the transmutation of gold, but not because he wanted the gold. No, he wanted what the power of the transmuted gold could give him: the power to pierce the veil of this world and see beyond to the eternal.

His entire life had been a search for knowledge and purity, not for personal gain, but for the sake of knowledge and purity themselves. To know everything was to become truly pure. To become… pure knowledge.

This tablet could give him that, if he were worthy enough to understand it. He had been preparing for this day ever since he had heard of the stone of Hermes.

The hermetical knowledge lay before him now, and he feared he would open the box and discover that all his study and preparation were inadequate. That he might need more years than remained in his life to understand.

Abruptly aware that he was sitting on the cold cave floor wasting whatever time he still owned, he reached out with a knife and broke the lead seals on the box. His hand trembled as he lifted the lid and peered within.

He could see only a thick wrapping of leather and fur. Gently he reached in and closed his hands around the contents. To his amazement, he could feel what lay within the wrappings, and it was no tablet. At least nothing that he thought of as a tablet.

Disappointment speared him momentarily, but then he lifted the bundle from the box and began to unwrap it. Leather and fur fell aside, revealing a cloth threaded with gold, probably from Sardis, where artisans worked wonders with gold, managing even to turn it into thread.

That wrapping, too, fell away, revealing a thickness of papyrus that looked like a ball. It gave beneath his fingers, however, and in his mind's eye he began to see the shape of what lay within.

Pulling the papyrus away with trembling, eager hands, he at last freed the gift completely.

His breath caught in his chest as he stared at an emerald pyramid no larger in any dimension than his palm. He lifted it carefully, feeling its weight, admiring its quality and shape.

But then his heart plummeted, for he could

see nothing written on it. Nothing at all. Perhaps it was the light?

He reached out and picked up the oil lamp, bringing it close. No shadows appeared on the perfectly smooth surface. Nothing in any way indicated that anything had ever been written there.

But then, as he began to put the oil lamp back, he happened to pass it behind the emerald.

At once his breath caught again, for within the stone he could see symbols, symbols that seemed to be moving in some kind of dance, as if they were somewhere else, beyond the weight of gravity, and the pyramid was only a door through which to view them.

Then, in an instant, he knew. This was not some mere tablet but a sacred mystery itself. A sacred mystery left by the hands of the gods.

9

Renate watched the young man from across the bar. True to his word, Assif had been able to spot his fellow geek. After four days of subsequent surveillance and a brief conversation on a tram, Assif had confirmed that Jürgen Hausmann was indeed a computer operator at Berg & Tempel, and, just as important, that he was single. Neither of those facts surprised Renate in the slightest, now that she had the opportunity to observe Hausmann.

Although he was boyishly handsome, he was cursed with a gangly body that seemed to move as if each limb were making the decision independently. That awkwardness extended to his speech, each word seeking permission before emerging.

One part of Renate felt pity for the young man, who was obviously earnest and sincere in his fascination with his chosen career. But the larger part of her simply saw him as a resource and his awkwardness as an opportunity to exploit that resource.

She gracefully lit a cigarette, after making sure she had caught his eye, and smiled at him. It came as no surprise when he smiled back, nor when—after she had fashioned a look of exasperation as she studied the screen in front of her—he made his way across the Internet café to her table.

"Haben sie Schwierigkeiten?" he asked, in the singsong Frankfurt dialect. *Having problems?*

"Ja, die habe ich," Renate replied, smiling as she adopted the same melodic pace. *"Ich kann nicht finden was ich suche." Yes, I am. I can't find what I'm looking for.*

"Perhaps I can help?"

Renate smiled, nodding to an empty chair. "Please. I promised a friend that I would find this for him, and it's just hopeless."

"What do you seek?" he asked, sitting on the edge of the chair as if fearing that at any moment she would shoo him away like an annoying insect.

"My friend will visit America," Renate said. "I need to find him a map of Boston, so he can find his relatives there, but all I can find are hotel sites. Sometimes the Web is just impossible."

"It can be," Hausmann said, reaching for the

keyboard. "Let's see if we can find something more useful."

A half hour later, she had a complete map of the Beacon Hill neighborhood in Boston, along with complete directions and a map from Logan International Airport to the address of her nonexistent friend's nonexistent relatives. She even had a list of local restaurants, theatres and other attractions.

More importantly, she had a date with Jürgen Hausmann. And two hours later, she found herself trying to hear herself think as they sat in a crowded dinner club, surrounded by what appeared to be a convention of the undead. Hausmann seemed to sense her discomfort and offered a sheepish smile.

"I was very into the Goth scene when I was younger," he explained. "I must have eaten in this club six nights a week while I was at university. I suppose this isn't a good choice for a first date, though."

"No," Renate said. "It's fine. You chose a place where you would feel comfortable."

"*Ja,*" he said, smiling. "But the food is wonderful, I promise. They have the best *Maultaschensuppe* in all of Frankfurt."

Renate had always been fond of the traditional German ravioli soup and accepted his recommendation, adding an entrée of roast pork with sauerkraut and oven-roasted potatoes.

Just as their soup was served, she saw Niko enter the club and take a seat behind Hausmann. With his smoldering Greek features, Niko had no difficulty attracting the admiring glances of the young women in the club. That he had donned black eyeliner and lipstick only added to his rakish charm in a place like this. Within minutes, Niko was cycling to and from the dance floor, each time careful to let his chair jostle Hausmann's just slightly.

Renate ate slowly, watching Hausmann's eyes each time Niko returned. By the time they had finished the soup—a rich pork broth with leeks, hosting the ravioli stuffed with pork sausage—Hausmann no longer seemed to notice the slight bump as Niko sat down.

As the waiter brought the entrées, Niko rose again, deftly slipping a hand into the open fanny pack that rested on the floor beside Hausmann, extracting his key card. This time, however, Niko headed not for the dance floor but for the door, where he passed the card to Assif before returning.

Twenty minutes later Assif signaled from the door, and once again Niko rose from his chair. After retrieving the key card, he returned to the dance floor, this time with a girl who could not yet have been twenty, and engaged in what Renate's parents would have described as a *Ludentanzen*...a whore's dance. The couple returned to Niko's table, the girl plopping into Niko's lap. As she sat, Niko's well-timed kick sent the fanny pack tumbling.

"*Ach! Es tut mir Leid,*" he said, pushing the girl from his lap and reaching for the sprawl of personal items that had fallen from the pack. "*Ich werde Sie helfen.*"

"*Nein, macht nichts,*" Hausmann replied, shaking his head as he bent to grab his pack.

But the objection was too late. Niko had already gathered a handful of credit cards and a Palm Pilot, adding them to the key card he already held. With an apologetic smile, Niko handed the items to Hausmann, who returned them to his fanny pack.

A few sputtering phrases later, Hausmann returned his gaze to Renate. "I suppose I should have chosen a quieter place to eat."

"No," she said, reaching across to brush his hand. "This is fine. As you said, the food is wonderful."

"Yes, thank you," Hausmann replied.

After Niko had left, with a young girl on his arm who would doubtless go home disappointed, Renate and Hausmann sipped coffee.

"This is good," he said, as their cups emptied. "I haven't…been on a date in…a long time."

"Neither have I," Renate said. "And yes, it is nice to meet new people. One never knows what one will find."

"I hope you are not too disappointed," he said.

"No, Jürgen," she said, smiling. "I'm not disappointed at all."

Guatemalan Highlands

Miguel Ortiz slipped out of the jungle and arrived at Father Steve Lorenzo's side without giving the priest any sign or sound of his approach. Miguel was the reason the villagers of Dos Ojos had been running for well over a year now. The youth had belonged to a group of rebels who had killed the U.S. ambassador in Guatemala City almost two years ago.

The police had attacked Miguel's entire town in their effort to find him, and the locals had fought back. Since then, Miguel had joined the townspeople in flight, and the rebels had joined the search for Miguel.

Everyone wanted a piece of him, it seemed.

Yet, in repenting his part in the guerrilla operation, Miguel had become a valuable asset to his family and friends. He knew ways to protect them and cover their trail. He had taught others how to keep the women, children and old men safe.

And he had made his confession to Father Steve, who had long since followed the rule that when God forgave sins, He tossed them into the deepest part of the lake and put up a No Fishing sign. The past was past, and Miguel had atoned.

The forgiveness of the villagers had been readily given, as well, even though they had lost everything but their lives. But Steve often thought that these people were unusually forgiving, perhaps because they were so downtrodden to begin with. Perhaps because they could easily understand what might drive a young man to do what Miguel had done.

Or perhaps they were just closer to love.

Miguel crouched down beside Steve, keeping his voice to a whisper that could barely be heard above the wind in the trees and the night sounds of the teeming forest around them. "We are being followed."

Steve stiffened, his assignment shooting immediately to the forefront of his mind. "You're sure."

"*Sí.*" Miguel cocked his head to one side. "About two thousand meters back, Padre."

"How many?"

"One man. He is well trained."

"Are you sure he is after *us?*"

Miguel nodded. Starlight caught and reflected from his dark eyes. "He has been following us for days. We must move at once. And we must not make fires again, for they leave a track we cannot hope to cover."

"He is not that far away. How can we hope to elude him now?"

"I will do something. But you must wake Paloma and get the others moving immediately. Paloma will know the best way to go." With a jerk of his head he indicated the volcanic peak that barely showed through the trees, and then only because moonlight fell on it. "There are caves. She knows them. Follow her lead. But go at once, Padre. He cannot kill us all, but I am sure there is someone he wants who is among us."

And none should die anyway, Steve thought as he watched Miguel disappear once again into the shadows. Then, as quietly as he could, he crept over to where Paloma slept.

Within ten minutes the entire band was on the move, heading straight for the volcano's cone, toward the mountain that belched steam and shook the earth. The mountain that might, at any moment, move beyond rumbles and steam to rain fire and ash and death upon them all.

But, to quote a military friend's favorite aphorism, that decision was above his pay grade. Steve had accepted the fact that he was just a priest. He was the shepherd of this flock but not their owner. He could guide them, at least spiritually, but decisions of life and death, of the changing of the seasons, of whether a hurricane would sweep through these mountains and bury them all beneath a sliding mound of mud...those were not the decisions of a priest. They were the decisions of God, and God alone.

Steve thought back to one of the first homilies he could remember from his seminary training, classic in its structure, its clarity and its poetry. *Let God be God,* the instructing priest had said. *Let the Church be the Church. Let me be a priest.* The instructor had offered this homily as a model for one that a priest might give to introduce himself to a new parish. But Steve had come to realize that it might serve equally well as a daily prayer.

He had come to Guatemala on a high mission, to protect the Church from knowledge that might prove embarrassing, or even damaging. But in these past months, wandering the jungle with these companions, he had begun to fall back on that homily and the prayer it encapsulated. It had become a buttress to support the weight of both daily decisions and the larger decision that hung always over him: what he would do if and when he found the Codex.

Yes, the mountain ahead rumbled, but whether it moved from rumbling to rage was a decision for God. To worry about that was to place himself in the role of God, and he had come to accept that he must let God be God.

Yes, sooner or later the decision of what to do about the Codex would move from future to present, and with that decision the fate of his church and his faith might seem to lie in his hands. But the Church was bigger than one historical fact, and its protection lay in hands bigger than his. So let the Church be the Church.

And yes, one day he might face death with these people, whom he had come to think of as his family as well as his flock. When that day came, he knew he could do little but repeat the final stanza of his personal prayer. Let me be a priest.

As the rain began to fall again, he realized that his prayer encapsulated all the best that he could hope for. A life of simplicity, of service, of love. The many distractions that had once plagued his consciousness fell away like the raindrops that landed on his face. He was where God had put him, doing what the Church had asked of him, endeavoring to serve his flock.

And that, he knew, was enough.

10

Life offered an infinite number of ways to make oneself miserable. Sometimes Renate Bächle believed she had tried them all, at one time or another.

Memory, however, was one of the most effective. Her past was a book she had been obliged to close after the Frankfurt Brotherhood had tried to kill her and she had joined Office 119. It was also a book best kept closed, because opening it was like Pandora opening the box and releasing all the woes of the world.

Most of the time she kept the book firmly shut. That Renate was another person, in another time. As far from the person she was now as it was possible to be.

But as the chilly gray light of dawn began to seep through the sky and into the office, memory demanded its due. The loss of her family had torn away her last private anchor. She might carry out this assignment as if she were content with it, but a fire burned in the pit of her stomach to remind her that this would not be enough. Not ever. She would not rest until she had destroyed the Brotherhood and all its evil influence.

Guilt was eating her alive. It was because of her that her family was dead. Because of her that her best friend had died. She had dared to go after the Hydra and had yet to clip the heads off any of the snakes. But she would, she vowed. They would pay.

That cold place in which she had forced herself to live since cutting herself off from her past and joining this organization was beginning to melt. The glacier within her had cracked; she could feel the heat of anger burning it away.

With a sort of detachment, she forced herself to look at what was happening inside her heart and mind. It was not good. Too much was at stake here for her to lose her cool head.

But that glacier was made of the frozen waters of loss and grief, and it did indeed want its due. It wanted to be acknowledged, experienced, felt. It wanted to take her back to more innocent days when she had believed the world was a good place and wonderful things were possible. It wanted to return to the days before she had learned that powerful men manipulated the world in secret and considered the rest of humanity to be expendable pawns.

She heard a faint rustle from the doorway behind her and knew that Law had come to check on her. He was always checking on her, worrying about her, watching over her in some way, since Black Christmas. She had been his mentor during his early days with the office, and now he had become her personal broody hen.

Part of her didn't mind. Another part of her resented the intrusion he represented into the places she guarded behind icy defenses higher than the Alps. All of her knew it was a dangerous thing, this emotional attachment. They had to work together, and must remain professional for the sake of their work and their lives. There was no room in what they did for personal involvement, not even with him as a broody hen.

But for this little time, she let it go. Later she would speak of how detachment was necessary to their survival. But right now she needed to know that someone in the world gave a damn about her and the grief that was dangerously near to tearing her apart.

The rustling came closer, and finally she turned her head to watch his approach. He was wearing sweats, the official pajamas of the group, for at night the entire building temperature was turned down. On his feet he wore thick socks, and in his hands he carried two big mugs of coffee.

"Care for some?" he asked, offering her one of the mugs.

"Thank you." She accepted it gratefully and wrapped her icy fingers around its warmth.

"Can't sleep?" he asked as he settled into a chair nearby. She looked at the brightening sky; he looked at her.

"It's going to be another gray, cold day," she said, nodding toward the window.

"Me, neither," he said, answering his own question.

She looked at him again, taking in his disheveled hair, the pillow crease on his cheek and his general all-American good looks. Whatever his ancestry, it had blended well, giving him none of the identifying features that could label his background.

"I won't say I'm wired about this operation," he continued, as if they were already in the middle of a conversation. "I've been more wired about other things I've needed to do."

She responded with a small nod, figuring he needed to talk about some detail of the plan.

"We've got the blueprints of the building. We've got the best information we can get in general. As black bag jobs go, this isn't the worst. Not the best, but not the worst, either. It'll be tense, though."

She nodded yet again. He sipped his coffee and stared off into space, as if thinking. Then he shocked her.

"I'm not sure I trust you."

Her breath stopped, and her heart slammed. All of a sudden emotion wasn't something to think about; it became the substance of her being. Her anger flared. "How dare you?"

He held up his hand, shaking his head. "Hold on, Renate. Just let me finish."

She had to set her mug down; then her fists clenched until her nails bit into her palms. Only by a huge effort of will did she remain silent.

"I'm not saying you might betray us or that you're a spy for the Brotherhood, or anything like that," he said. "But you have a huge emotional investment in this operation. I know you're not happy with this assignment, and that you'd rather be hunting killers than trying to get proof of the Brotherhood's involvement in Black Christmas. I think you resent the way you've been reined in. And I can't say I blame you."

She looked at him from hot eyes, still angry. "I always do my job," she told him icily. "Always."

"I know. That's your reputation. Everyone I've met at Office 119 says the same thing—*Renate is the job*. It's as if they see you as the perfect Office 119 agent, with no emotions, no distractions, no past and no personhood."

"And what do you see?" Renate asked, unsure whether she wanted to hear the answer.

"I see a human being who can be hurt," he said. "And has been. Badly."

"Tell me," she said, leaning forward to fix him with a stare that, she hoped, would freeze his soul. "How would you feel if you learned they'd killed Miriam Anson?"

"I'd be furious," he said. "I'd want revenge. She was more than my mentor at the Bureau. She and Terry were the closest I've had to a family since my dad died. And I hope that you would be professional enough—and enough of a friend—to have this same talk with me. Before I went off and did something that might not only get me killed, but might well compromise Office 119 and put all our lives at risk."

"Is that what you're afraid of?" she asked. "That I might put you in danger?"

"No," he said. "And certainly not by intent. I'm just reminding you that you're not alone on an is-land. We may all be dead, Renate, but we're dead together. When I agreed to join this group, I ac-cepted a responsibility. And I don't mean just the job. I mean a responsibility to you and Jefe and Niko and Assif and Margarite and everyone else in this organization. Because if I make a mistake, it won't be just my neck on the line."

He leaned in, meeting her gaze. "Like it or not,

Renate, you did the same thing. You're responsible *to* us and *for* us, just as we're responsible to you and for you. You don't have the luxury of rage…or revenge."

Renate knew he was right. And the fact that he was right only made it worse. "You sound like my father."

"I'm sorry," he said.

"No, Lawton. You're not sorry. Nor should you be."

He smiled. "Okay, you're right. I'm not sorry."

Her thoughts seemed to swirl like the tendrils of cream at the top of her coffee mug. Finally she spoke. "The Brotherhood used my family like pawns on a chessboard. They killed my parents to draw me out. I have to make their deaths mean something. I have to make my friend's death mean something. It's the only honor I can give them. Otherwise, I'm sacrificing them as pawns. And then I'm no better than the bastards who killed them."

She scrubbed a tear from her cheek, angrily. The glacier was crumbling. She could not afford that. But it was happening, whether she liked it or not.

"My dad was a great card player," she said. "I knew how to play pot-limit Omaha poker almost before I knew how to read. And I'm good, Lawton. My friends at university had jobs to pay for cars and clothes and pizza. I didn't. I went to the casino on weekends and took money from rich tourists who thought knowing the rules meant knowing the game. And that paid for my car and clothes and pizza."

"Remind me never to play poker with you," he said, a smile creasing his features.

"Yes. You shouldn't. But my dad was better. He'd played, and dealt, so many hands in his life. It was as if the cards spoke to him, whispered their secrets to him. He didn't have to calculate how many outs he had or whether the pot odds justified a play. He'd done it so often that it was automatic, like breathing. And he played the game of life the same way."

"What do you mean?" Lawton asked.

"He was the wisest man I ever met," she replied. "He always saw through the consequences of every decision. He knew when to take risks, when to play it safe and when to walk away. And he tried to teach me to live the same way.

"When I was in my first year at university," she continued, "I thought I'd met the perfect man. He was smart and gorgeous, and I thought the sun and the moon spun around him. He was in his last year, about to graduate and move to Berlin. I wanted to leave school and go with him, anything just to be with him."

"I'm guessing your dad didn't like that," Lawton said with a wry chuckle.

"You would guess correctly," Renate replied.

"But he didn't get angry. That wasn't his way. Instead, he talked about poker. He told me to suppose I'd had a bad run of cards and suddenly I picked up a pair of weak off-suit aces. Would I want to get all my money in the pot before the flop on just a pair of aces with no support? I said of course not. It looks like a good hand, but in Omaha poker it's a hand that can turn to trash very quickly, because the cards don't work together."

She drew a breath, sipping her coffee. Lawton sat quietly, waiting for her to continue. After another long breath, she spoke.

"So he looked at me and said, '*Liebchen,* if you leave university to go with this young man, you're moving all of your money in on those weak aces. He seems like a good man, but your cards don't all work together. If things don't go well with him, where will you be then?'"

"Broke," Lawton said.

"Exactly," she replied, nodding. "If he'd put it any other way, I would have gotten angry and fought with him. But he had taught me poker too well. I knew he was right, and that summer I found out that Herr Perfect had been cheating on me all along. If I'd gone to Berlin with him, I would have been devastated. But my father had shown me how to make the right decision."

"He was a great dad," Lawton said, smiling.

"He was. And he adored my mother, and she

him." Her voice hardened. "And now they're dead. People like that should not just die and go away. They should not be pawns on a chessboard. Their lives, and their deaths, should mean something. I can't let them have died in vain."

He nodded slowly, his eyes fixed on hers. For the first time in as long as she could remember, it was she who looked away. Outside, the city was waking up, the sounds of trams and automobiles making their way through the window glass, the quiet moans of a city's morning stretch. A year from now, the city, the planet, the universe, would still wake and breathe in their own way, regardless of what she did. Suddenly she felt very small.

"Renate?" he asked.

His voice seemed to pull her back into the room, to force her to remember who and where she was.

"Yes?"

"Your dad, your mom…" He paused, as if looking for words. "Every time you do the right thing, the wise thing, take the well-considered risk, or play safe, or walk away…they're still alive. Because you're living the values they cherished. You're being the woman they hoped and dreamed you could be. And I'll guarantee you that, to them, there is no higher honor you could give them."

The tears forced their way out again, but this time she lacked the strength to hold them back.

Lawton made no move, simply watching as she felt her head fall into her hands and the sobs begin to rock through her chest. The city woke, the earth spun on its axis and circled the sun, the universe expanded, and all of it unaware of her as she sat and wept.

And that, her father would have said, was the beauty of the game of life. The cards didn't care into whose hand they were dealt, and she wasn't responsible for which cards fell into her hand. But she *was* responsible for how she played them. And in this moment, the best play she could find was to cry for the memory of two people who, if only for a moment in the span of the universe, had given her life and love and wisdom beyond measure.

She could honor them, in this moment, with her tears. And once she had done that, she knew, there was a job to do. An important job. A job worth doing well. And if she did her job well, the Brotherhood would pay, not only for the lives of her parents but for all the lives it had so callously swept aside.

That would be her parents' legacy.

They would not have died in vain.

Guatemalan Highlands

On the side of a volcano, the soil was rich, full of nutrients brought forth by centuries of eruptions. That combined with the rain to produce dense undergrowth, and Miguel sometimes needed his machete. He kept its use to a minimum, however, for fear of alerting the man who was hunting the people of Dos Ojos.

As often as he could, he chose to climb over or under obstacles, or simply move very slowly through them, allowing his trail to close up behind him.

The villagers could not do that. There were too many of them, too many children. Their machetes had been carving paths through the forest for a long time now. Along with the fire pits, this was guiding the Hunter behind them.

But now, as the people climbed higher on the side of the mountain, the forest changed. The undergrowth lessened, making it possible for them to move without carving their way.

It occurred to Miguel that if the Hunter realized this, he would make his move soon. Miguel was determined not to let that happen. He doubted he could take the pursuer mano a mano. The Hunter was clearly well trained, and a much bigger man than he himself was. Nor did he have a gun. While his sturdy AK assault rifle would hold up forever, even with minimal care, he had long since run out of ammunition.

Paralleling the trail the villagers had taken, Miguel was certain he could backtrack until he came up behind the Hunter. Then he would find a way of stopping the man, or sending him in another direction.

Guilt goaded him as much as love for the people of Dos Ojos, as much as his love for his sister and her family. Guilt because he knew his village would not now be running except for him. In quiet moments he wondered why he could not have seen what was going to happen to them if it became known that he had participated in the assassination of the American ambassador. He wondered that he could have been so heedless and naive.

Padre Lorenzo said, *Hindsight is always twenty-twenty.* Once he'd explained the saying to Miguel, the young man had nodded agreement and accepted that this was so. But he continued to feel guilty anyway. Neither the forgiveness of God, nor the freely given forgiveness of the villagers and his sister, could quite wash away his sense of guilt.

He owed them. And now he was going to find a way to protect them, whatever the cost.

Finally he had traveled far enough back that he felt it was time to cross over to the path carved by the villagers as they had moved through yesterday. Then he would follow the one who hunted them until he could take action.

He was sweating, despite the relatively cool temperatures at this altitude, by the time he once again emerged on the newly hewn path. Yes, he was behind the place where he had last seen the man.

It was good. Stealthily and alertly, he moved forward, trying to emulate the jaguar of sacred myths older than his people. He would become the jaguar, silent, patient, deadly.

Between one step and the next, it happened. Something hard hit the back of his head, causing him to see bursts of light before he sank into utter darkness and fell to the ground.

11

Frankfurt, Germany

Niko and Assif had donned workers' uniforms with
the name *Deutsche Telekom* emblazoned on them.
Even now, Renate knew, they were entering the utility tunnels that wound beneath Frankfurt's streets.

Law was studying the blueprints for the Berg
& Tempel building, so Renate sat by herself, listening to Niko and Assif's brief snippets of conversation on the radio. This was probably the
easiest part of the operation in terms of safety:
they were going to locate the junction box where
the lines from the bank connected with the rest of
the system. On paper it sounded so easy as to be
not worth the effort, but they all knew that in the
real world of darkened tunnels, where even real
utility workers sometimes tore at their maps in exasperation, nothing could be taken for granted.

And that maze posed a far greater danger than the remote possibility that Niko and Assif might be detained for a few minutes by some overeager *Polizei*. Each carried a handheld GPS tracker, as well as a tunnel map. But neither the maps nor their link to the Global Positioning System satellites was a firm guarantee against getting lost in an underground warren where landmarks were nonexistent and time seemed to stand still.

At least, Renate reasoned, the Brotherhood itself was no threat at this stage of the operation. Its world was also a rabbit's warren, but the bankers would never sully their wingtips in a utility tunnel. Instead, they tunneled through the ones and zeroes of the international banking networks, silently shifting huge sums of money to tip the scale here or balance it there.

When she had first caught their scent, as a forensic accountant with the BKA, it had been the whiff of transactions that seemed to have no rhyme or reason: money from here to there, then to somewhere else, and then back to its source. Soon she had become persuaded that the bank was involved in some kind of shell game, shuffling money around so that it could not easily be traced. Money laundering, perhaps. But what money were they laundering? Where did it come from?

As she had pursued those answers, she had

begun to uncover an unpalatable truth. The conspiracy had little or nothing to do with money laundering. They were buying influence, and peddling it. And, she had noted uneasily, one of their major profit centers lay in the world's arms manufacturers.

Indeed, the same collections of shell companies—all of them ultimately run by a handful of bankers—seemed to hold significant or even controlling interests in many of the world's largest arms dealers. That in itself did not shock her; weapons research and production was both very expensive and highly speculative. Of course businesses would need to diversify their holdings and thus protect themselves against a single calamitous canceled contract.

No, her growing sense of unease had come from the tight nexus between the bankers, the arms dealers and the political elites of Europe and the United States. The further she dug, the more she saw the connections repeated across national and even ideological borders. Power, guns and money had become an unholy worldwide triumvirate. And whether a given transaction was legal seemed to be entirely irrelevant to the men who made the connections.

It was as if these men saw the law—and morality itself—as little more than an impediment to be ignored, swept aside or purchased outright. In their minds, it mattered nothing whether an arms deal, or a war, was legal. The question was simply whether it was likely to be profitable. If so, then the pieces were quietly moved around the board—the politicians corrupted or co-opted, the news colored, the public distracted—and the plans put in motion.

She hadn't been able to prove it back when she'd worked for the BKA, and her strategy of leaking information to the press had come to an abrupt end as the power of money did its work and they tried to kill her. Now she lived in a shadow world, yet somehow they had discovered that she was still alive.

"Be careful," she heard herself whispering to Assif and Niko. "These people…"

"We know," Assif said. "We know."

Of course they knew. They wouldn't be doing this otherwise. While she still could not prove all of what she knew about the Frankfurt Brotherhood, she had been relieved to discover that her superiors at Office 119 not only believed her but had information and suspicions of their own. It was one such investigation—into the murder of a U.S. ambassador in Guatemala and the attempted murder of a leading contender for the U.S. presidency—that had taken her to the United States and given her the opportunity to recruit Tom Lawton, now Lawton Caine, into Office 119.

She smothered a sigh and cursed the circumstances that forced her to sit here, listening to the radio, while Niko and Assif were out and actively pursuing her enemies. She wouldn't have an active role in this operation again until they were hooked into the bank's SWIFTNET lines and could begin to decrypt their messages. Until that time, she was more spectator than participant. But once they began to decrypt the data...then would come her time to strike.

For the sake of her sanity, she hoped that was soon.

Then, crackling over the radio, came Assif's voice. "We have found it."

She snatched the radio. "You're sure."

"As much as we can be."

Lawton reached for the fleece-lined windbreaker that was draped over the chair behind him.

"He's leaving now," Renate said into the radio.

It was time.

Riyadh, Saudi Arabia

"Look back to the thirteenth century for your enemies."

Ahmed Ahsami read the cryptic note one of his aides had scribbled and attributed to "Yusefi." Veltroni, of course. But what did he mean?

Ahmed almost crumpled the slip of paper with the anger he had been feeling since Black Christmas, but he stayed himself just before he clenched his fist.

Veltroni was trying to tell him something. Perhaps even Veltroni didn't understand the message he had passed. Ahmed had known from the beginning that Veltroni, while higher than many in his secret society, was far from the top. Perhaps someone above him had told him this. Had ordered him to send this message.

If so, Ahmed knew no more than before except that the Stewards of the Faith were at least pretending they had played no part in the unexpected turn of events that had become Ahmed's nightmare.

Closing his eyes, he mentally reviewed every contact he had ever had with Veltroni, seeking any hint of deception. But no, Ahmed believed that Veltroni and his group really wanted what they said: a more peaceful world, one that all faiths could inhabit without conflict.

But that didn't necessarily mean they hadn't alerted U.S. and European authorities to the presence of the terrorist cell in Vienna.

He put his forehead in his hand and looked at the slip of paper in front of him, covered with the graceful Arabic script of his aide.

Perhaps the Stewards of the Faith hadn't realized the statement Ahmed had wanted to make after the cell was taken out. Perhaps they were concerned only to see those who had attacked their church brought to justice. He could understand that.

But no more than that.

The thirteenth century? The era of the Crusades? What did that mean? How could his enemies today arise from those times?

He had studied the history of the Middle East and knew something about that period, but not nearly enough. Rising, he went to the bookcases that covered most of one wall and searched through them. He had some English books about the history of the Crusades, and while he had preferred those written by Muslim sources because of the bias of the English, he nevertheless pulled one of them out now.

Go back to the thirteenth century? He would do exactly that. He certainly wasn't finding his answers in the present.

La Rochelle, France, October 12–13, 1307

Silently, in the dead of night, the ships belonging to the Knights Templar slipped their moorings and headed toward the open ocean. Soon they would be joined by the rest of the fleet, even now sailing silently from Paris.

The wooden ships creaked mightily and sat low in the water, burdened as they were with the immense weight of fleeing men and holds full of gold.

Chevalier Maurice d'Valmy stood at the stern of one of the ships, watching the dark hulks of the others following them. No lights guided them, for fear they might alert those ashore to the Templars' flight. Captains and crews were relying on their intimate knowledge of these waters, with only starlight to show the way.

D'Valmy gripped the wooden rail so tightly that he wouldn't have been surprised if his hands left permanent prints in the wood.

Betrayed! The word chimed in his head with every heartbeat. To this very moment, even as he and his fellows were in the midst of flight, he struggled to believe it was truly happening.

Over the past week, messengers had spread silently throughout France and neighboring countries with the scarcely believable news that the French king, Philip le Bel, had conspired with the pope, and that upon the morrow, soldiers would be arresting every Templar they could find as heretics.

This, after all their service to the pope, after all they had done to support and finance the monarchies of Europe.

But that was the problem, wasn't it? he thought bitterly. Philip was heavily in debt to the Templars, and rather than attempt to repay them, he wanted to steal their entire fortune for his own coffers. According to the Grand Master, Jacques de Molay, they were all fated to be tried by the Inquisition.

So he had ordered the majority of the Templars to take to sea with the fleet and the great treasure that Philip so desperately wanted. The heroic de Molay and a handful of other Templars would remain behind to face the Inquisition and defend the order...and probably die.

Flight ran against every inclination in d'Valmy's heart and soul. Given a choice, he would have remained behind and faced those devils and their devious schemes. He would have called the Templar Army to the sword and fought back. He would have done anything but this.

But the Grand Master wouldn't hear of it. "This is better, Chevalier," he'd said when d'Valmy had confronted him two days ago. "It is time for us to vanish. The pope no longer cares for us and fears our power. If we cannot serve the pope, then we must serve only our God."

Maurice d'Valmy had long ago sworn to do that very thing. To serve the Cross, to serve the son of David, to protect the secrets that had come down to them from a past so distant it was hardly mentioned in any history he had ever come across.

But of course it had not been mentioned. The Church had strangled the knowledge, fearing it as godless. Even so, the Church had willingly profited from it, and from the Templars' good relations with the Muslims in Jerusalem...at least until Saladin had driven the Templars out.

Maurice touched the leather bag hanging from his sword belt, checking that the *real* treasure, the treasure greater than gold, was still with him.

"You must hide," the Grand Master had said. "You must melt into the shadows, into far countries.

"We shall continue our banking businesses, and one family has agreed to run it for us. You will know them when they come to you and speak of the Red Shield."

D'Valmy had nodded acquiescence. Red Shield, red cross, rosy cross...they were all names for the same thing. The same Rose.

"As for the rest," de Molay had continued, "they shall become a new order. The Order of the Rose. In Scotland you will find as much safety as you and the others can. England will shelter you, but there is a royal marriage with France that may eventually become a problem, so take the greatest treasure to Scotland. The money will be spread out over the years throughout Europe. Many banks will begin to appear. But it is not the money and gold I worry about. They were only a way to conceal the greater power."

He had leaned forward and gripped d'Valmy's forearm. "You must guard the fire-stone with your life, Chevalier. It must never fall out of our hands. The gold—" he waved a hand "—when the time comes, pass most of it to the family of the Red Shield, but also pass some of it to the Teutonic Templars. They will stay strong despite the evil to come. They will defend their territory, and I have given them permission to do so. But the rest of you…flee."

Remembering the conversation now, as La Rochelle fell away behind them, d'Valmy understood why he had been chosen. Only a few understood the power of the stone in his pouch. Only a few knew how to use it, and d'Valmy was one of them. To him had been entrusted the secret and the power.

A power, he realized now, he must never use in a way that might draw attention. He must see that his brothers escaped and reached safe shores, see that the gold fell into hands that would use it to advance the well-being of the others and righteously exercise the power that money gave.

But the fire-stone must never fall into other hands. It was too dangerous, too powerful. Its misuse was the very thing the Knights tried so hard to prevent, even at the cost of sacrificing some of their numbers to the Inquisition and vanishing into the mists of myth.

Maurice d'Valmy squared his shoulders and turned to face forward into the night. Much as it went against his nature, he would do as he had been ordered.

12

"Es ist sehr kalt," Lawton said as he entered the bank, the parcel tucked beneath his left arm. *It's very cold.* He glanced at the clipboard in his right hand. *"Ich habe ein Paket für Herr Stolzmann."*

"Ja," the receptionist said, her mouth smiling, but her eyes betraying impatience. She was obviously ready for the workday to end. *"Im ersten Stock."*

"Ja, danke," he replied.

Although she had directed him to the first floor, in Germany that was the one immediately above ground level. He headed for the elevators at the back of the entry hall. Once inside, he pressed the button marked 1 and dutifully exited after ascending one level.

But rather than turning left toward the office of Mr. Stolzmann, to whom the package was addressed, he walked to the stairwell. He paused for a moment at the landing, listening, then descended to the basement, where the bank's computer room lay. Three doors past the computer room, he knew, was a janitorial supply closet. He opened that door and slipped to the back, wedging himself between tubs of floor wax and stacks of toilet paper. Then he keyed the microphone on his walkie-talkie.

"I'm in."

"He's in."

Renate's voice crackled in Niko's ear. At that moment, having left Assif at the junction box, Niko was shucking his uniform coverall at the tunnel's entrance. After pulling a nondescript wool coat from the toolbox he had carried with him, he slipped it on and emerged from the tunnel, his posture ever so slightly hunched, looking for all the world like a homeless man who, having slept the day away safely removed from the disapproving eyes of the *Polizei,* was now headed out in search of a meal.

He could as well have donned a cloak of invisibility, for in the manner of people around the world, those he passed on the street studiously avoided eye contact, which was precisely what Niko wanted and needed as he made his way down the sidewalks of Frankfurt's banking district. Only as he approached the bicycle Lawton had left in front of the bank did his posture straighten, and in that slight shift he became a respectable junior employee, finished with his daily labor, retrieving his bicycle so that he could return home to a young wife and child.

As he bent to unlock the chain that held the bicycle in place, he pressed the microphone button on the walkie-talkie in his shirt pocket.

"I have it."

Lawton listened to the stirrings in the corridor outside. He had no need to glance at the illuminated dial of his wristwatch, for the sounds told him the time as reliably as any quartz crystal. The employees of Berg & Tempel were nothing if not punctual.

Perhaps ten minutes had passed since Niko's brief transmission. He could only trust that the receptionist, seeing the bicycle gone when she left work, would assume that Lawton had made his delivery and departed without her having noticed. If she did not—if she noticed that a courier had entered without leaving—things could get dicey. He would simply have to rely on human nature, on the receptionist making the most logical assumption based on the evidence. After all, she had no reason to suspect anyone would try to break into her workplace. He told himself not to worry as the sounds of departing employees swelled, then slowed, and finally stilled.

* * *

Renate's thoughts echoed Lawton's. This was perhaps the most dangerous phase of the operation. Niko was stashing the bicycle in a shopping area half a kilometer away. Assif was in the utility tunnel. Lawton was hiding in the supply closet. And she was here, monitoring their radio and the police scanner.

That left no one to observe and report on the reaction of the receptionist as she left the building and saw the empty space where the bicycle had been. No one to assess whether a shrug indicated acceptance that she must have overlooked the courier's departure. No one to warn Lawton if she suddenly reentered the bank with a look of alarm on her face.

They had discussed this, and whether it might be better for Lawton to enter a few minutes earlier, giving Niko time to hide the bicycle and return to watch as the bank employees left. But that, too, had carried an implicit risk: that the receptionist, while still inside the bank, might grow suspicious at the passage of time and alert someone that a courier was in the building.

After weighing the risks on both sides, their deliberations had turned to a single, inescapable fact. This was a one-time-only attempt. If Lawton were caught inside the bank and asked to leave, the receptionist would surely remember him if he tried to return on another day. Thus, there was nothing to be gained by having Niko on hand to alert him to trouble. Either the operation worked or it didn't.

And that meant Renate could do nothing but wait for Niko to stroll past the bank and confirm that the security guard had arrived and settled into his studies. The sweep of the second hand was agonizingly slow, and she repeatedly caught herself holding her breath, as if by so doing she might be silent on Lawton's behalf. She resisted the urge to light a cigarette, although her hand repeatedly crept toward the pack in her purse as if with a will of its own. The long muscles of her legs began to burn, and she realized she was clenching them, her body preparing for both fight and flight, though her mind knew neither was possible.

"I am back," Niko's voice finally said. "All is ready. Let's go."

Lawton heard the transmission and was already slipping from his hiding place as Renate repeated the call. He pressed an ear to the door for a long moment and heard only the quiet hum of a sleeping building.

"Coming out now," he said.

The corridor, now only dimly illuminated, looked different than it had only a half hour before. Every sound seemed magnified by the absence of ambient noise. Reason told him that the sounds of his breath could not be heard through the ceiling and floor above, where the security guard would be focused on his homework. Yet still he forced himself to breathe slowly, through his nose, as he silently approached the computer room door.

He swept the key card through the slot, and even the muffled *clunk* of the bolt sliding back made him start. He pulled the door open a fraction and held it, listening for any sound within or without that might indicate danger.

There was none. He knew there would be none. He was not breaking into the offices of the CIA, after all. This was simply a bank, closed down for the night, with a lone security guard, whose sole job was to press the fire alarm if the smell of smoke should distract him from his reading. The guard wasn't even armed. With no vault full of cash and valuables to protect, the employees of Berg & Tempel had little to fear.

Shaking his head, Lawton opened the door and entered the computer room, letting the door close silently behind him. He tore open the parcel he'd been "delivering" and pulled out the printout of instructions that Assif had prepared, then placed it beside the keyboard of the nearest console and settled into the worn desk chair. Atop the monitor, he recognized photographs of the Hausmann family.

"Okay," he said into the walkie-talkie. "Let Assif know I'm ready to start."

But the only answer was the hiss of static.

Guatemalan Highlands

They had to take a break. Father Steve was no longer the young mountain goat he had been, and he figured admitting to his weariness would not only get him a brief rest but would get Paloma one, as well. She might be elderly and in some ways frail, but that woman had a will of steel. He could see the fatigue on her face, but she kept trudging along.

The forest had thinned, making it possible for them to advance without leaving an obvious trail. At Steve's suggestion, they had broken up into three different groups, so their tracker would have to make a decision as to which trail to follow. At least the majority could escape the Hunter.

"I have to rest," he said finally. At once the small group halted. Had he been asked, Steve would have said they all looked relieved that someone had finally suggested it.

"Not yet," Paloma said firmly. "Nearby is a cave where we will be safer."

"No argument from me." If Paloma could do it, then so could he. It troubled him a bit that he wearied this way, considering that before he had come here he had run several miles a day. But something in their way of life now had depleted him… and made him aware that his knees were aging. Or maybe it was just all the constant walking on uneven ground.

He shrugged those thoughts aside and trekked forward with the rest of his group. The increasing altitude was at least making the air drier, for which he was grateful. Hiking like this was so much more comfortable in low humidity.

Shoving a hand into his pocket, he found his rosary and began to pray again where he had left off earlier. Their little band could use every bit of divine help that might come their way.

Paloma walked beside him, steadying herself with a stout stick. She seemed to have gone far away in her thoughts, but then, so had he. He was suspended somewhere between heaven and earth, having a silent dialogue with God while he murmured the familiar prayers.

So, he said to God, *I don't suppose it does any good to point out that these people have suffered enough. I don't suppose that really matters.*

God didn't answer. Of course not. That might or might not come later. But God had broad shoulders, and Steve felt like complaining a bit.

I realize that these people aren't suffering by your will. Miguel made a choice that caused evil to befall them. Their flight is the only way they can protect themselves, since they fought back against the police. You know, I can understand why they fought back. The police did not come to make an arrest. They invaded a village.

God listened.

But still, there has to be some end to this. Some safety for them somewhere. As it is, I can barely help school their children, we have so little time to hold still. What future do these people have without Your intercession?

Steve quieted himself then, focusing on the familiar prayers, leaving his heart open for some kind of answer. He had long since learned that if you spent too much time talking to God, you couldn't hear when He answered.

But at the moment there was no answer of any kind. Silence and a deep-rooted ache were all that filled Steve's heart. He wanted so badly to save these people from this misery, yet he could not see the way.

Paloma's voice dragged him out of his preoccupation. "Padre," she said quietly. "The cave is just ahead."

He could not see it, but scarcely a minute later the members of his band began to disappear into some bushes in single file. Then he, too, passed between the bushes, and the mouth of the cave was plain to see.

"A lava tube," he said. As he spoke, the ground beneath his feet trembled as another quake shook the mountain. A lava tube. They were going to seek sanctuary in a lava tube on the side of an active volcano. He didn't know whether to laugh or groan.

"This is dangerous," he said to Paloma. "Do you know what this is?"

She nodded, and her eyes crinkled around the corners. "I know. Your Lord will protect us."

"Uh...our Lord also said we should not test God."

Paloma shrugged. "He has been testing *us*, has he not? We will be safe. If we are not...then it is meant to be. But for now, we must hide from the hunter who seeks us. There is no better place. A rabbit would get lost in these caves."

He argued no further. Everything was in the hands of God, as it had always been.

"It is good," Paloma said, linking her arm through his. "And once we are settled, I will tell you a secret. For I have not long left in this world, and I must pass it on before my days end."

She paused to look at him. "It is the secret you came here for, Padre. The secret of the Codex."

Frankfurt, Germany

"We've lost him."

Renate sat bolt upright, her heart jamming into

higher gear as Assif's voice came over the radio. "Lost who?"

"Law. All we're getting is static. We can't reach him."

Oh God! For an instant something squeezed in her chest, and she could scarcely breathe. She forced it to give way to icy calm.

"Why would that happen?"

"Perhaps there's interference from the computers," Niko said.

"No," Assif said before Renate could say a word. "I can't believe I didn't think of it before. It's TEMPEST shielding…." His voice trailed off; then he said something sharp in his native dialect. From the tone, Renate guessed it was some kind of curse. "The room," Assif said.

"The room?" Renate was confused.

"Of course the room!" Assif said. "It's shielded. And it's also blocking his walkie-talkie transmission. I can't believe…"

"Assif!" Renate spoke his name sharply. She couldn't have said why. And she didn't want to admit how worried she was.

"I'm an idiot," Assif said grimly.

"No, no," Renate said as soothingly as she could. She couldn't afford to have any team member lose his head. "None of us anticipated this. We should have, but we didn't. Okay. That's done. So now to the problem at hand. Do you think Law can pull it off anyway?"

Assif was silent for a moment. "I gave him printed instructions. I went over them with him. If he paid attention and remembers everything, he can do it."

"Then perhaps," Renate said icily, "you'd better start looking for that SWIFTNET transmission."

13

Not very often did Jules Soult open the hand-crafted book that contained his lineage. A monk had begun illuminating it in the fourth century. Other monks had added to it with the passing years, some creating works of art, others with less talent simply inscribing names, dates, marriages.

The papers used were exquisite, the finest to be had at any point in time. The volume had originally begun as a papyrus scroll, but at some point one of the monks had transformed it into a book that contained enough empty pages so that even after all these centuries, Soult did not have to worry about beginning a new volume for his children.

The tome was heavy, decorated fancifully in gold leaf, with no title to indicate the treasure it contained. The oldest pages showed signs of aging but so far had not cracked or crumbled. Soult's father had arranged for a controlled storage environment for the book, in a well-hidden safe, so that further deterioration would be delayed even longer. And no one, but no one, ever touched these pages without wearing fresh cotton gloves.

It had been many years since Soult had brought out this volume. Sometimes he thought of trying to find someone who could turn it into a family tree that would be easier to read than this listing of marriages, births and deaths. But each time he considered it, he abandoned the notion, for he was not yet ready for anyone to know his true bloodline. There was no one he could trust to do the work and keep silent.

But later, when he had assumed his rightful position in the world, then he would have this made into a huge family tree for all the world to see.

Others shared his ancestry, and many of them belonged to the same Order of the Rose that he did. But only Jules Soult could claim an unbroken *female* line of descent from the earliest Merovingian kings. Therefore his blood was the purest.

Soult opened to the first pages, inscribed so long ago that even the precious ink had faded a bit. He daren't keep the book out long, but he couldn't stop himself from touching the page where the line began.

What had come before that no one could say

with absolute certainty, although the Order of the Rose firmly believed that the Merovingians, also known as the Fisher Kings, had married into the bloodline of Mary Magdalene and Jesus, of the royal house of David.

One only had to look at the fleur-de-lis, as old as the monarchy in Europe, to guess the truth, for that symbol was an idealized form of the iris, a flower symbolic of the House of David. The French royal coat of arms had also contained the Lion of Judah.

Soult believed the myths. But more importantly, he had proof of his direct descent from the original European kings. A lineage so precious that even Napoleon had married into it, taking an Austrian princess as bride in order to legitimize himself.

Hah. And the Austrian royals had thought they were the purest line extant.

Slowly, Soult closed the book and for a moment sat with his hand resting on the cover, his eyes closed as he savored a dream close to fruition. Then, carefully, he restored the volume to its wrappings and placed it back in the safe.

Not much longer now, he promised himself. As soon as Frau Schmidt gave him permission to hire Hector de Vasquez y San Claro, the next, and most important, piece would be in place.

Hector was an old friend and also a member of the Order. Together, they would accomplish the impossible.

But there was one more thing, one thing that would give him the incredible personal power he would need. The Crimson Codex, also called the Kulkulcan Codex. And the Hunter was even now closing in on it.

With his eyes closed, Soult imagined holding the treasure in his hands and learning the secrets of its power. His family legend held that it was this the Magi had brought to the young Jesus, called "gold" but in reality the lodestone of Hermes Trismegistus, the writings that would allow gold to be transformed into something even more powerful, something even more valuable, something known only as she-mana.

The story that had so carefully been passed down from generation to generation held that the Magi had come from the East not simply because the stars told them that a Judean king had been born but because the stars told them that *the* Judean king had been born, the son of the House of David, the one who would transform the world.

And so, in the gift called *gold,* had come the stone with the ability to transform gold into something protective and healing and ultimately powerful, a power that nothing could defeat.

The story said that before his death, Jesus had given the tablet to Mary and told her to take it abroad and hide it. Mary Magdalene had eventually come to the south of France, with their daughter, Sara. It was directly from Sara that Soult was descended, or so the story went. But there had been two children born of Sara, one a daughter, the other a son who had sailed with the tablet to begin a new ministry elsewhere.

For most of his adult life, Soult had been searching for even a hint that someone knew where the tablet had been taken. Then, little more than a year ago, he had learned that the Church was searching in Central America.

And now the Hunter was on the trail.

Soult smiled and lit another cigar. All the pieces were coming together beautifully. He could have asked for no better omen for his plans.

Guatemalan Highlands

They celebrated Mass again, using the remnants of the tortillas they had carried with them from their last camp. The rest had been eaten with fruits they had gathered along their way. What they would eat tomorrow lay in God's hands. They had flour but could not make a fire. Collecting fruit again would mean stepping outside this cave into danger.

Yet none of his flock appeared especially concerned. Their absolute faith that things would work out often amazed Steve. Their acceptance of the way things were was a lesson he would do well to take to heart.

He moved among them, dispensing the Eucharist, and all received it reverently. As he passed, he blessed the very young children who were not yet old enough to partake of the sacrament.

Then he ended the Mass. Gradually the villagers settled down in groups of family and friends, preparing to spend the night on the hard cave floor.

Paloma came for him then, drawing him away from the others into a small antechamber he hadn't noticed before.

"We must speak very quietly," she warned him. "Sounds echo in these caves."

He nodded.

"My time is ending," she said then, making his heart sink.

"Yes, you said that earlier. Are you sick?" he asked anxiously. "Why haven't you said something?"

She shook her head. "I am not ill. But just as your God speaks to you, the jaguar speaks to me. I have little time left. Let me use it wisely. Just listen, Padre."

Steve closed his eyes. This was what he had been sent to discover, yet if he carried the Codex out of here, as the Stewards wished, he would be abandoning these people. He could not do that.

He opened his eyes and looked squarely at Paloma. "Don't tell me."

She smiled faintly.

"I'm serious, Paloma. Don't tell me. If you tell me I'll…have to disobey my orders, and I took a vow of obedience."

Her smile deepened. "Is your vow of obedience more important than your true calling?"

His heart was thumping in his chest. He looked downward, as if his hands held the answer, but all he could see in the flickering light of their one candle stub was the dance of shadows.

"Listen," she said. The same commanding *Oye* she used when she wanted the attention of the villagers. This was Paloma the shaman speaking now, not Paloma the friend.

"I have known that I would need to pass this on. To pass on the care of these people. Since we fled from our village, you have repeatedly proved that you are the one. You have cared for my people as I would have cared for them. You have nourished their hearts and souls as well as their bodies. Never once have you complained about the burden. You are truly a priest. You are our leader, the one my people can rely on."

"But…"

"Silence, Padre," she said flatly. "I have had ample time over the years to search out the one who will follow me. You are the only one I have ever found. And under these circumstances, my people cannot be left to fend for themselves."

He wanted to argue with her further, but he could see the steely resolve on her face.

"When the time comes, you will know who to share the secret with," she continued. "But first, let me tell you why it is so dangerous."

Almost in spite of himself, he leaned forward so he would not miss a word.

Frankfurt, Germany

Of course...the room is shielded, Lawton thought. It made perfect sense. Computers, like any electronic equipment, released faint radio signals as their components operated. Sophisticated listening devices could detect and decode those signals, and track the data being processed as efficiently as if the listener were standing over someone's shoulder.

The solution—adopted by the military, most major corporations, law enforcement agencies and all financial institutions—was the same TEMPEST shielding they were using for their own computers. It was simply a fine copper mesh laid into the walls, a Faraday cage that blocked incoming and outgoing radio signals. The bank used it to prevent outsiders from listening to its computers. But now it was also preventing Lawton from communicating with the rest of his team.

Like the others, he was so accustomed to operating with TEMPEST shielding that he no longer thought about it. That, he realized, was why none of them had considered that he would not be able to communicate from this room. After all, he reasoned, we don't think of gravity…until we drop something.

Rationalizing the oversight served to calm his nerves. They had, after all, anticipated that there might be some kind of communications failure. That was why Assif had printed out the instructions that now lay open on the desk, and why he and Lawton had rehearsed this part of the operation. They had prepared for this as well as they could. Now that preparation would be tested.

Lawton drew a long, slow breath and read the first paragraph of instructions, hearing in his mind Assif's voice in every word. *Step one: See if the computer operators left their consoles active overnight.* If not, Lawton would have to power one up, and Assif had given him detailed directions for how to do that.

He pressed the space bar on the keyboard, and the monitor sprang to life. Just as Assif had hoped, the operators simply put their consoles into sleep mode when they left for the day. It saved time when they arrived in the morning. And it made Lawton's task that much easier.

He paged past the now unnecessary instructions for powering up the console and compared the display on the monitor to the diagram Assif had drawn. While it was not exact, it was close enough. Forcing himself to relax, he clicked the mouse and began to type.

In the tunnel beneath the bank, Assif studied the dim screen of his laptop. A four-inch-wide flat cable emerged from the side of the computer like a tongue, then split into dozens of tiny wires, each of which was connected to the junction box by means of tiny alligator clips. If any signal passed through that box, the laptop display would show which line was active. The plan had been to track the signals at the exact moment that Lawton said he was sending a message. Now he would have to hope that he could detect which signals were Lawton's transmissions and thus which cables carried the bank's SWIFTNET transactions.

A flicker across the monitor was followed almost immediately by an echoing flicker. A SWIFTNET e-mail sent to a nonexistent address, followed by the automated error response message? If it happened three times in rapid succession, Assif would know.

Once again, Lawton typed in the message and the fictitious e-mail address. Once again, he clicked the send button. Once again, he quickly got the error notification. Then, again, for the third time.

* * *

"I've got it," Assif said, as the third set of impulses flickered across the screen. "Damn good job, Lawton."

"He can't hear you," Renate replied, the relief in her voice evident, even over the walkie-talkie. "But I'll be sure to tell him when he gets out of the computer room. So we're done?"

"Almost," Assif said. "Now he has to erase the logs of his entry and the logs of the bogus e-mails."

"And that part is simple, yes?" Niko asked.

"It is, if they're using the standard operating system software," Assif said. "If not...well...that was when I was going to talk him through it."

The same thought passed through Lawton's mind as he studied the final pages Assif had given him. If the bank's computers had used the software Assif's research had indicated they would, this next part would have been easy. But, in the manner of geeks the world over, Jürgen Hausmann had modified the software for the specific needs of Berg & Tempel.

And those modifications affected exactly the processes Lawton now needed to access. He was sure that a handful of commands, had he known them, would have erased all evidence of his hav-

ing been there. Assif would have known how to
do it. Lawton did not.

At that moment he heard the faint melodic
whistle in the corridor outside. Someone was
coming.

14

Guatemalan Highlands

Miguel Ortiz awoke facedown on the forest floor. The rich smell of loam and rotting leaves filled his nostrils, but he hardly noticed. His head throbbed as if someone were hammering on it, and he struggled to remember what had happened to him. What he had been doing. And why it was dark.

Slowly, cautiously, he sat up. The night was thick, unbroken by the glimmer of either moon or stars. He wished for night-vision goggles so that he could at least see his surroundings.

It hurt. Gingerly, he reached up and touched the back of his head. Some crustiness indicated he had bled from his scalp, and the lump and tenderness there filled in the rest of the picture.

All of a sudden he remembered. The Hunter. The man must have circled back behind Miguel.

The young man felt shame at his failure, but the shame didn't last long.

The Hunter now had hours on him, hours that Miguel would not be able to recover in the pitch darkness of the night.

He was struck then by another thought. Why hadn't the Hunter killed him? Why had the man merely rendered him unconscious? What was going on here?

Frightened for Paloma and his fellow townspeople, Miguel pushed himself to his feet. The world reeled, and he almost fell again. But he could not afford weakness. Not now. If ever he'd had an opportunity to redeem himself, this was it. If he caught the Hunter in time, he would save a life, perhaps several lives.

He could see nothing at all, but he was accustomed to nights as dark as this, nights when, if heavy clouds moved in, there was no light at all except what man could make to hold back the shadows. *Darker than dark,* his American trainer had once described it.

But the night brought its advantages, too. The night hunters and their prey were moving in these woods, making sounds, however quiet, that could cover any he himself made. From time to time something screamed, signaling that some hunter had found his meal.

The ground beneath him began to shake. He

was already unsteady on his feet, so all that kept him from falling was a tree he found when he threw out his arms.

"*¡Madre de Dios!*"

The exclamation was drawn from him not by the shaking of the ground beneath his feet, nor by his near fall. Instead it burst forth as he looked up in terror at the mountain above him. The volcano peak now broadcast an orange glow bright enough to drive back the night. And his people were climbing toward that very horror.

Almost before he knew it, his feet were running along the path they'd cut only days before. He had to reach them as swiftly as possible.

Because, hiding in the caves, they might not realize the peak had come to glaring life.

Deep within the cave, Steve felt the ground shudder violently beneath him. Around him, he could sense the others coming awake. He himself could not sleep. What he had heard tonight had become a heavy weight on his soul. What Paloma had said flew in the face of many of his lifelong beliefs—*if* he believed her. If he didn't, then he was engaged in an act of disobedience so grave that he would have said it was not within his nature.

But the rumblings of the mountain shook him from his thoughts and back into the here and now. He wondered if he should move everyone out of the caves right away. This was the hardest and longest tremor they had yet experienced, and from what little Steve knew of volcanoes, it boded no good.

He was worried, too, about the two other parties who had split off from them. He had wanted to travel with one of them, but Paloma had insisted he stay with her. The others, she had said, would know how to care for themselves. They had set a rendezvous point where they would meet in four days' time.

But still he worried about them. Would they fully understand how dangerous this mountain was becoming?

Then he scolded himself. These people had lived with this volcano all their lives. They knew what it could do, if not from personal experience, then from stories handed down to them. Indeed, they probably knew even better than he the dangers of this place.

He pressed his hands to the cave floor and felt a warmth there that worried him. At this point, he didn't know whether they were safer in here or out there. It would depend on the kind of eruption, he supposed, and whether this lava tube had ever been sealed off by previous eruptions.

The truth was, he had no idea what their best course of action would be.

"Paloma?" He called out her name, since the others were all awake now, and fussing babies were being put to their mothers' breasts. "Paloma?"

"She went out," said one of the men. "To look at the mountain."

"Gracias."

With care, he pulled out a prized flint and lit the candle stub that remained to him. Using it to light his way, he edged around people until he could see the cave opening.

He saw Paloma's slender figure in the mouth of the cave. Her silhouette would have been welcome but for one thing: it wasn't dark, but orange.

His heart slammed, and he quickened his pace. Before he could reach her, however, a crack resounded, cutting across the mountain's rumbling, and Paloma fell to the ground as if she were a puppet suddenly cut loose.

The Hunter!

Steve started forward, realizing he had to try to save her. But even before he had completed his first step, two men ran out before him and quickly dragged her back into the cave, barely missing being shot themselves.

"Está muerte," one of the men said. *"¡Ay Dios, ella está meurte!"*

Dead. Paloma was dead. Steve hurried to her, reaching for the pouch of sacred oils he kept strapped to his chest. He must do the anointing and do it swiftly.

His hands trembled as he brought out the vials and began to murmur prayers that were all too familiar. As he spoke them, he realized that while he should have been reflecting on the sanctification of the dead in Christ, all that filled his mind was the realization that he and these people were trapped between an erupting volcano and a merciless hunter.

God help them all.

Frankfurt, Germany

Lawton looked around the computer room. It was notably lacking in hiding places. The hum of a buffing machine told him that the janitorial crew was working in the hallway. Looking around, he realized that the computer room was spotlessly clean. Perhaps they'd cleaned it the night before and wouldn't need to do it again tonight. Or perhaps they cleaned it every night. Given how carefully the bank guarded its computers, he doubted the janitorial crew would be allowed to work in it unattended, regardless.

In the meantime, he needed to find out how to erase his presence. That was the critical task, and he tried to steady his nerves as he studied Assif's instructions.

Since Hausmann had modified the operating system to Berg & Tempel's specific needs, Lawton realized he needed to put himself in Hausmann's shoes. The man was a computer operator who spent his days in the bowels of a bank, ensuring the data flowed smoothly. The photos on the console indicated a sense of territorial possession.

This was not Berg & Tempel's computer. This was *his* computer. So whatever Hausmann had done, whatever changes he had made, whatever passwords he had added, he would not have locked himself out. Whatever Lawton needed to do, it could be done from this console.

With that in mind, he began the steps that Assif had laid out. No, there were no visible files that looked like logs. But the files would be there. And if they were there, then Hausmann would have made sure he could access them.

Lawton began to explore the various screen menus. Within minutes he found a menu item named "Show Hidden Files." Selecting it, he saw that the visible files were only the tip of Berg & Tempel's iceberg of data. Assif would have understood, and might even have explained in terms that Lawton could grasp, why computers needed so much hidden data in order to function. Perhaps later Lawton would ask him. For the time being, however, he focused on the massive list of files, most of which had names he could not even begin to fathom.

Dates, he thought. *Log files would be organized by date and time.* There were hundreds of files with largely numerical names, but most of them had too many or too few digits to be dates. Reminding himself that the Germans, like most Europeans, recorded dates in day-month-year format, he scanned through the files for likely candidates. He found three that seemed to fit and opened the first. It appeared to be a transaction log, and after scanning it to ensure that it did not record e-mails, he closed it and turned to the second.

It was filled with time-stamped entries, each of which seemed to have two coded names and a number. Perhaps e-mail addresses and the size of the e-mail? He scrolled to the bottom, and sure enough, there were six entries time-stamped only a few minutes before. The three bogus e-mails he had sent as a test and the three automated replies he had received. He selected the six lines and hit the delete key. The computer responded with that most annoying of messages, asking if he was sure he wanted to do what he had just done. He clicked the Yes button, and the six lines of data—the only record of his having used the SWIFTNET system—vanished.

The third file also had time-stamped entries covering several days. These were far fewer and, for the most part, far more regular. While there were a few exceptions, there were regular entries at the opening and closing of business each day, and again during the noon hours. These were, he realized, the logs of key card usage. Once again, he scrolled to the bottom of the list and found an entry from an hour ago.

Had he really been here for an hour already?

The computer insisted that he had, and he deleted the entry, after once again affirming that yes, he really intended to delete it. The single coded line—and the last trace of his presence—vanished.

And then the computer room door opened.

Guatemalan Highlands

"Come, Padre," Rita Quijachia said quietly, pulling at Steve's arm. "There is another way out of this cave."

"But…Paloma…" he began.

"Paloma is with God now," Rita answered. "And the mountain will care for her burial. Miguel is still out there, and he will distract the Hunter somehow. We must leave now, Padre. We haven't much time."

He knew she was right, and still he found it difficult to leave the woman there. He had dedicated his life to God, had spent most of his adulthood in the presence of those who purported to be spiritual. And yet, it was in the eyes of this woman that Steve had seen the truest face of the Almighty.

Still, Rita was right. The eyes that had been mirrors of love and holiness were no longer alive. All that remained was a body, along with her presence in the memories of every man, woman and child from Dos Ojos. And the legacy she had left to Steve.

Rising, he followed Rita back into the rumbling mountain, holding her hand as she led him through pitch blackness. Ahead, he could hear the footfalls of the others, faint slaps of handmade sandals on stone. He could see nothing, and he knew they could see no more than he, yet they moved with a calm certainty that infused itself into his own heart. God was leading them, Steve realized. Whether by memories of long-ago legends or by some divine presence, he knew that he was being guided to safety. He could not have led them, but he knew in his heart that he must trust them.

His free hand trailed along the tunnel wall, to balance himself against the deafening shudders that passed through the rock. In the absolute darkness, with the ground so alive, he realized he was losing his sense of orientation. Only by an act of intense concentration could he discern up from down, and more than once Rita's strong arms caught him as he lurched against her.

It was after one such lurch, as he reached for the wall again, that he felt it. A niche in the rock, hardly wider than his hand.

In the heart of the living earth, Paloma had said, *the hand of God has touched the rock. Five steps past and two steps to the left. There you will find the Codex.*

If it had been in this mountain, would she not have told him? And yet he knew—in a way beyond knowing—that this niche was the marker to which she had referred. It was to this place, at this moment, that he had been led by duty, by faith, by Paloma, by Miguel and Rita and the rest of the village.

He counted the steps, forcing himself to keep his balance. As he took the fifth step, another ear-splitting crack echoed through the rock, and he felt the wall to his left crumble away. Without thinking, he turned.

"No, Padre!" Rita yelled into his ear, although he could barely hear her voice. "We go this way!"

"I must," he answered. "Paloma."

Her voice rose again, but the challenge died in her throat. "Yes, Padre. I will come with you."

"I'm sorry," he said. "This I must do alone. Go with the others. Find Miguel. Keep them safe. I will catch up with you."

"Padre!"

"I command it!" he yelled. "Trust in God, and hurry!"

He felt her touch leave his and realized he was now alone. He turned to the crumbled wall and stepped into the newly revealed chamber. One step. Two. And now he felt around him, forcing himself to trail his fingers over each fissure of the rock, ignoring the sting as his palms were rubbed raw by the rough pumice.

A gap, so tiny that he was sure his arm would get stuck within it. He reached in, farther, farther, until his shoulder was wedged in the narrow crack.

And then his hand closed over something impossibly smooth, impossibly perfect. In the instant that his torn fingertips touched it, he knew what it was.

The Codex was within his grasp.

He drew it out slowly and tucked it into his bag. Then, retracing his steps, he turned in the direction Rita had gone. His heart raced as he made his way through the twisting, quivering caverns. With no one now to guide him, he gave himself over to the most primitive instincts, trusting his first decisions at each fork in the tunnel, his eyes closed, his thoughts swirling, yet strangely still.

Right. Then left. Left again, and then once more. Then right. It was as if the rock itself spoke to him, step by step. He had no impression of where he might be in the mountain, yet he knew this angry, smoldering, quivering beast meant him no harm.

Suddenly the stench of sulfur burned at his nose, wafting on a breeze that blew into his face. And then the darkness around him changed. Not black, but gray, like dirty snow whipping past. He was outside the volcano, and the dirty snow was volcanic ash, carried on the eddies caused by the mountain's heat.

"Padre!"

Somehow Rita's voice cut through the swelling roar, and he ran toward it, heedless of the loose rocks that seemed to give way with nearly every step. Forms emerged in the gray darkness, arms reaching out to him, and in a few more steps he found himself in their embrace.

"I feared you had lost your way," Rita said.

"I had," he answered simply, as he followed her and the villagers down the slope, toward what little safety the tree line offered. "I *had* lost my way. But it was found for me."

"Now we must find Miguel," Rita said.

"No," he replied, as they reached the lee of a fallen tree. It was meager shelter, but it was better than no shelter whatever. "We must stay here. Miguel will find us, Rita."

"He's my brother," she said. "I can't leave him out there."

Steve took her hands in his. "God will guide his footsteps, Rita. Just as He guided mine."

"God is angry!"

"If God were angry with us," Steve said, "He would have taken me in the mountain. No, Rita. We have done all that skill can do. Now we must trust to faith."

15

Frankfurt, Germany

"*Oh mein Gott!*" Lawton said, jumping in his seat as the security guard opened the door. Then he caught a breath, offered a sheepish smile and added, "*Sie erschrecktet mich!*" *You startled me!*

"*Es tut mir Leid,*" the guard answered, obviously as startled as Lawton. *I'm sorry. Excuse me.* "*Entschuldigen sie.*"

"No problem," Lawton said with a sad smile. "These upgrades. They're more work than they're worth."

"Yes," the guard answered. "I was told they were still working out the bugs."

"We sure are," Lawton answered.

It had been an educated guess. If the bank had a computer system and a skilled operator like Hausmann, there were certain to be an endless series of upgrades to the system. It was the way of computers and the people who used them. If the software could do *this*, then of course, with only a little extra work, it could do *that*, too, yes? Such work kept people like Hausmann employed and had given Lawton the excuse he'd needed.

"But," he added, "I think I'm done for the night."

"I can let you out," the guard said.

Lawton smiled. "That'd be great. Would you do me a favor, however? Don't mention that I stayed late tonight?"

"Um, sure," the guard said, looking dubious.

"They've been complaining about overtime," Lawton explained. "If I file for the hours, they'll be upset. But if they know I worked late and didn't file for the hours, they'll think I'll do that any time they want."

"Yes," the guard said, chuckling. "Give them a drop and they want the pitcher."

"Exactly," Lawton agreed. "Let me just gather up my stuff."

He rolled Assif's notes into one hand and hunted through the menus until he found the Sleep mode, then selected it and watched the screen go black.

"Someday," he said, holding up the notes, "someone will be able to explain why computers just generate more paperwork."

"Don't hold your breath," the guard said with a laugh. "Come. I'll walk you out."

* * *

Ten minutes later, as he rounded a corner, Lawton spoke into his walkie-talkie. "It's done and I'm out. Assif, did you get the signals?"

"Yes," Assif replied. "We're all good."

"You're out of the bank?" Renate asked.

"Yes," Lawton answered. "The security guard walked in, and I gave him a spin about having to work late and just having finished. Fortunately, it seems, he doesn't know the bank staff. So he walked me out."

"Let's hope he doesn't decide to mention that to his relief," Niko said, his voice heavy with concern. "This was supposed to be invisible, remember?"

"I had no choice," Lawton said, the cold night air stinging his lungs. He quickly explained why and how he had asked the guard not to mention it. "He seemed like a decent kid. I doubt he'll even remember it by the time he clocks out."

"Let's hope not," Renate said. "Okay, Assif, set the bridge to relay the bank's signals here, and everyone get back here. We've taken enough chances for one night."

Lawton had no argument. Perhaps, he thought, in an hour or two, his pulse would return to normal.

Brussels, Belgium

Walking out of Frau Schmidt's office, Jules Soult felt as if he were walking on air, but he didn't let his elation show. A somber mood was called for under the current international situation, and somber he appeared.

"We must," Madame la Directrice had said, "find as many of these terrorists as swiftly as we can. Use whatever means necessary, Monsieur Soult, as long as I can explain it legally somehow. The American president is thinking of using nuclear weapons."

For an instant Soult froze. That was a wrinkle he hadn't imagined. "Has he gone mad?"

"We must wonder." Frau Schmidt, who otherwise might have been a beautiful woman, was frowning so deeply that she looked at least twenty years older than her calendar age. "I fail to see how that will help anything, but you know the Americans. Patience is not one of their virtues."

Soult pondered the threat. It made his skin crawl, frankly. "Do you have any idea who they intend to go after?"

"Parts of Pakistan where terrorists are believed to be harbored. There are other targets as well, but so far my intelligence hasn't been able to determine them."

Soult nodded. "I will find out."

Frau Schmidt looked at him from eyes circled purple with fatigue. "We must stop this, Monsieur Soult. Which means you must move swiftly to locate those at fault."

Soult nodded. Twenty minutes later he departed with what amounted to carte blanche. Very well. So he would have to add an additional task to his plans. There would be no joy in leading all of Europe, as was his birthright, if the world were dying in a nuclear holocaust.

Not that he wouldn't have used tactical nukes himself if he had believed it to be in his best interests. That much he could understand about President Rice. The problem lay in the fact that Pakistan, too, owned nuclear weapons and would surely retaliate, thus escalating matters. And this time, unlike 9/11, the entire world had already suffered, so there was going to be precious little sympathy for the Americans if they took such horrific action.

Still, he was feeling very good, humming under his breath as he made his way from the building to the street and hailed a taxi. Now to his hotel, where he would meet with Hector de Vasquez.

He and Hector went back a long way, both of them having served in the military, and thus with NATO, for long careers. They had found much common ground on which to agree in their visions for Europe's future, a future that put Europe at no one's heel. Hector's eldest son was Soult's godchild, a tight bond in both their worlds. They had become, in effect, extended family. And they both belonged to the Order of the Rose.

But thus it was when hearts and minds met in common cause.

He found Hector awaiting him in the hotel lounge, a quiet, dark room at this time of day, occupied by only one other person, who sat at the bar. Hector had found a distant corner and ordered them each a Napoleon brandy. Of course.

Hector and he also shared their bloodline in the distant mists of time. Both had Merovingian claims, but Soult's was the purer, and Hector was content to be second. Second, after all, promised many perquisites.

"How did it go?" Hector asked immediately. He spoke in Spanish, as would Soult, for Belgians spoke French. Neither wanted to risk being understood if they were overheard.

Soult glanced once again at the man at the bar and decided he must have had a fight with his wife, for he seemed determined to drown some kind of sorrow.

"I have carte blanche, Hector." He watched the smile stretch Hector's handsome face. "Carte blanche," he repeated savoring the words. "All Schmidt wants is—what is that American phrase?— plausible deniability."

"Congratulations, my friend." Hector lifted his snifter in a toast, and Soult followed suit. "To the future."

"To the future," Soult agreed.

Hector finished his brandy in one gulp and signaled the bartender for another. Until the barman came and went, the two remained silent.

"So," Soult said, "it will be as we discussed. We must find at least some of the terrorists. But the second part is more important. There are other enemies who must also be seen to. And we cannot ride in as the saviors of Europe if Europeans do not first feel threatened. Spare nothing."

And that was no easy thing, Soult thought, as he watched Hector nod again. Europeans tended to be rather more blasé about these things, having already experienced years of terrorism from groups like the Red Brigades and the Beider-Meinhof Gang. A decade or so ago, there had been riots in the streets of Germany against immigrating Turks who were filling jobs. Even now, most of Europe was angry at Spain for its liberal immigration policies which allowed a flood of North African immigrants. And once those North Africans arrived in one EU country, they could travel freely to any other.

Spain, Soult sometimes thought, was the only country in the world that failed to suffer from xenophobia. He still hadn't decided whether that was a good thing. Of course France, less willingly, now had large populations from its former colonies and a significant Muslim population.

All of which was going to aid his plans.

"But there is one more thing," Soult said. The seriousness in his tone caused Hector to lean forward. "Schmidt told me that the Americans are thinking of using nuclear weapons as a response against the terrorists hiding in the mountains in Pakistan. She also thinks they must have others in their sights."

"Mother of God," Hector said. His color paled. "That must not happen."

"I agree. I have some friends with connections inside the White House. I will contact them and find out what is happening there. Simply be aware that we do not have the luxury of time, my friend."

"As you suggested, I had already begun recruiting," Vasquez said. "I can have teams in position within the week."

Soult nodded, satisfied. "Finally, there are the financial details. You will of course need a contract with the EU."

Hector smiled and lifted a large envelope from the seat beside him. "I have taken the liberty of preparing it for you. It is basically our standard contract, and there are four copies."

Soult nodded. "As soon as I have signed these, I will arrange for your first payment. For operating expenses. Then the standard form will apply—you submit your bill each month. To me. I will take care of it. Frau Schmidt really doesn't care to know much about this."

"As we hoped." Hector smiled. "I'll begin the street demonstrations immediately."

"Just hurry. And if we occasionally make a mistake, but there is no proof of that...I will not necessarily be upset. One must break eggs to make an omelet, *non?*"

Hector nodded. "I shall break eggs as it becomes necessary. Our long-term plan is paramount." He shook his head. "They played into our hands, Jules. Right into our hands."

Guatemalan Highlands

Ash fell in waves from the sky over the next two days. With blankets covering their mouths and noses, Steve's party made their way around the rumbling cone to the far side. Since they had emerged from the mountain at quite a distance from where they had entered, they seemed to have lost the Hunter, at least temporarily. And each new wave of ash buried their footsteps, as did each tremor that ran through the mountain slope. The ash sifted downward, filling in their deepening footprints.

It was three days of sheer hell before they reached the relative protection of the lower forest, where the growth was thick enough to act almost like an umbrella. Ash sifted through, of course, but not nearly as much.

Then it began to rain. The stuff, so incredibly

light before, became a miserable, heavy mud that irritated the skin. The smell of sulfur had become their constant companion. Few of them felt like eating, except for the babies, whose hunger paid heed to nothing else.

At least, once they were in the jungle again, fruit became plentiful, and gradually they began to harvest it and eat while they kept moving.

But they could not keep moving forever. Weariness had reached the point that many were stumbling over their own feet. Soon they would have to halt, volcano or no volcano, hunter or no hunter.

Finally, just as they were all about to give out, they stumbled upon a grotto from which water, clean water, poured. It was a sheltered place, partly a cave, partly protected by a thick growth of trees that blocked the sky and let only a hint of sun seep through.

There they collapsed, and Steve said prayers of thanksgiving, absolutely certain that God had at last sent them some relief.

Everyone refilled their water skins. In the pool below the falls, many bathed, ridding themselves of layers of ash and dirt. Even the infants received a dip in the icy waters to rinse away the grit that was so hard on their delicate skin.

The water seemed to refresh many of them, and a number of the men set out to find food.

Steve added another prayer of gratitude for the bounty of these forests.

He bathed, too, careful not to offend anyone by removing his clothing. Well, his clothing needed washing anyway. Then he crept up inside the grotto until he sat almost behind the waterfall.

Here the world was even dimmer, and the curtain of falling water cut off all sound from the outside. For a little while he could be alone, and he discovered that he desperately needed the solitude. He hadn't really enjoyed a moment to himself since they had fled the village.

The weight of the bag hanging from his belt pulled at his mind as much as it pulled at his waist. Finally he decided he had to know what the Codex looked like, especially since, according to Paloma, it had cost many people their lives over its long history. He loosened the drawstring and pulled it out.

Even in the dim light, the sight of it was enough to make him gasp. It was a perfectly cut ruby, a perfectly cut pyramid.

He stared at it in amazement, then ran his fingers over its flawlessly smooth surface. He could just hold it in the palm of one hand, and he lifted it, admiring the workmanship that so long ago had created such perfection and beauty from a single gemstone.

Had Paloma's people fought over it because it

was so beautiful, and thus priceless? But no, she had said it was powerful. The kind of power people were willing to kill for.

Steve's stomach rolled nervously as he tried to remember what Paloma had told him that night they had sheltered in the lava tube. Power, she had said. Great power for anyone who could master the secrets of the Kulkulcan Codex.

But how could this be a Codex? Nothing was written on it.

He lifted it a little higher, trying to catch more light. Suddenly, as if something inside the ruby had caught a hint of light and magnified it, there was a flash that illumined it from within. For an instant he thought he saw symbols of some kind, but he also had the feeling that during that instant he was looking through a doorway into a place far beyond the ruby he held.

Then, just as quickly, the light vanished.

Steve's hands trembled, and he quickly tucked the ruby back into his pouch. Whatever it was, it appeared it was not simply lifeless stone. That lent credence to all that Paloma had told him, and in that instant he knew he must hide this ruby from everyone. *Everyone,* including the Stewards, for even men of deep faith could be corrupted.

He put his head in his hands, trying to decide what he should do next. Save the people of Dos Ojos, if that was humanly possible. Hide the ruby somewhere, so it would never be found. As if he could think of such a place.

Then, unbidden, he thought of the symbol that adorned the U.S. one-dollar bill: the pyramid with the all-seeing eye.

He'd always dismissed that as a symbol of boys at play in their secret societies. Men were forever doing things to make themselves feel special, as if they belonged to some group that knew secrets that could not be shared. The Masons claimed a lineage that went back to ancient Egypt. He had never before believed it.

But now… He thought of the pyramid in his pouch. Maybe the Masons really didn't hold any esoteric knowledge. But maybe they held the memory of it. And maybe that came from some-where else.

All he knew for sure was that Paloma had been killed, so somebody either wanted this gem or wanted to prevent it from falling into other hands.

That alone made it both dangerous and valu-able. And if it was what Paloma had hinted…

He had become the guardian of a terrible, ter-rible secret. One that might well upend reality. One that might, as Paloma had warned, set off the ultimate war.

Despite his worries and sorrow, sleep crept up on him anyway, and he dreamed of Moses on the mount, receiving the tablets of the law, dreamed of the Ark of the Covenant and its contents, dreamed of things that had never happened. Things that might have happened.

His mind jumbled them all together, as if trying to work a puzzle. In his sleep he mumbled uneasily, trying to find answers to questions he couldn't quite form.

It was a nightmare, and he stood squarely in the middle of it.

16

Tel Al-Amarna, Egypt

Nathan Cohen sat bolt upright in bed. Through his eastern window he could see red streamers as the sun prepared to climb over the Sinai.

But it was not the light that had awakened him, although it was near the hour when he said his prayers to the Great Light. No. Even in his sleep he had felt a temblor in the threads of reality. Somewhere, someone had found one of the two missing Codices.

An icy vice gripped his heart, and he tried to assure himself that even if someone had indeed found it, he would not know how to use it. Years of study and the passing of arcane secrets through the generations were necessary to begin to unfold the stones.

But someone had briefly touched upon the

power. He had felt it, and he was sure it was not one of his brother or sister priests.

Rising swiftly, he pulled a cloth around his waist, a cloth such as his predecessors had worn for millennia. Then he crossed to a safe that was hidden beneath the floor, a true anachronism in this simple hut made of mud. In this town he was known as the rabbi who studied the Kabbalah. They came to him, Christian, Muslim and Jew alike, for advice, and he dispensed it carefully, not wishing the full nature of the power at his disposal to be revealed.

His family had lived in this area since the days of Akhenaten, when a rich and glorious city had risen from these sands around the new worship of the One God. Generation after generation, they had been sages of one kind or another, descended in direct line from Akhenaten's vizier.

But that was knowledge he kept to himself. Over the centuries the family had worn many names, but in these parts they were known and trusted, whatever religion they seemed to be at any time.

He opened the safe, then drew out a golden chest and opened it. Inside, the fine white powder of shemana shone brightly, seeming to contain a light of its own. Carefully, he removed a pinch and sprinkled it over himself.

An instant later he stood on a featureless plain in a place that had no sun yet was bright enough to see clearly. Above, the blue sky was as feature-less as the plain and seemed deeper than an ocean.

Before him, on the smooth sand of the plain, atop a pillar of gold, sat the sappir stone, the sap-phire pyramid of light. Hidden here, in another di-mension, it was safe from thieves.

He laid his hands upon it and closed his eyes, calling to his brothers and sisters.

One by one they materialized, until the twelve stood together around the sappir.

"Someone has found one of the missing Codi-ces," Cohen said. "What is worse is that he stirred its power somehow, or I might never have known of it."

The others frowned deeply. They had only two missions in life, and one of them involved keep-ing the pyramids out of the hands of others until the time came to bring them together.

"The time is approaching," said Ulel, a priest-ess who wore her years gracefully. "Perhaps it is time to gather the stones."

"But," said Maram, another of the elder priests, "while it may be approaching, it is not yet here. Bringing the Codices together prematurely could cause effects we do not yet want."

There were murmurs of assent from the others. Ulel shrugged. "So be it," she said.

"But," Maram said, "we must find out who has

the stone and what they plan to do with it. Can you do that?" He looked directly at Nathan.

"I have a suspicion. One of the Stewards of the Faith confided they had sent a priest to seek out the Kulkulcan Codex."

"Which is?" asked one of the others.

"The Crimson Codex," Cohen explained, using a euphemism designed to conceal the real nature of the stone. "The ruby pyramid."

"You think he may have found it?

Cohen nodded slowly.

"Will he bring it back to his superiors?"

"Probably." Cohen sighed. "My brothers and sisters, our goals are not so very different from these Stewards, although they do not plan as grandly as we. They do not know what they seek, and their reasons for seeking it are petty. It is likely that this priest will consider the pyramid to be something he must return to his superiors, for that was his assigned task. But it may be that Paloma told him enough to convince him to pro-tect it."

Heads bowed momentarily, in silent obser-vance of Paloma's passing. She had been one of them for a very long time.

"It may be," Cohen said, "that she passed the knowledge to him. That she may have chosen him as her successor."

Again silence answered him.

"Find him," Maram ordered. "Find him, and make sure he will protect the pyramid."

"Or take it from him," Ulel added. "His life is irrelevant."

Frankfurt, Germany

"Any traffic yet?" Lawton asked, glancing in the bathroom mirror as he scraped a razor over his face.

"Nothing that seems important," Niko replied. "Assif and Renate are working on the decryption now, but judging by the sender and receiver addresses, I'm guessing all we have so far are routine bank transactions."

Niko was using the adjacent sink to do what he called "a field bath," washing from the waist up. In the absence of a shower—and the office suite had none—it was the best they could do. An angry red welt creased Niko's back from right shoulder to left hip.

"That looks like it still hurts," Lawton said.

"It does," Niko replied, "when I have time to think about it. I usually don't let myself."

"Chechnya, wasn't it?" Lawton asked.

Niko nodded. "I did something dumb, and I paid for it."

"What happened?"

"We'd penetrated an Al Qaeda cell operating there. They were holding a big meeting, so we sent in an ops team. I was the team leader. I thought we had good intel. Everything looked set."

"And then?" Lawton asked.

Niko's face took on a faraway look. "Either someone had misinterpreted the intel, or they moved the meeting ahead by six hours. This wasn't the kind of place where my team could just ride up in a couple of Land Rover vehicles. We were slipping in by ones and twos. The idea was that everyone was supposed to be on scene two hours before the meeting started. I only had half my team ready."

"And you went in anyway," Lawton said. It was not an accusation, merely a statement of fact.

"I did," Niko said. "I didn't think I could count on them sitting around talking for six hours while the rest of my men showed up. Besides, it was possible that our source had tipped them off and they'd moved up the meeting to set a trap. If that was the case, it was better to hit them while they were unprepared, even if we had fewer men."

"Sounds logical," Lawton said. "It was a command decision, Niko. You had to make one, and you did."

"Tell that to Otumbo and Kaleek," Niko said. "We didn't have sniper cover yet. Kaleek was spotted moving across a square, and they opened up on us from the second-floor windows. If I'd had my snipers in place..."

"We have a saying in America," Lawton said.

"Coulda, woulda, shoulda. Could have, would have, should have. You can play that game over every decision you make, Niko. You made the best decision you could with the information you had available."

"Yeah," Niko said. He tapped his forehead. "I know that up here. But part of me still wonders.... Kaleek went down in the first volley. Otumbo and I went into the square to get him while my fourth man covered us. We got him almost back to the corner when a new shooter opened up from the roof. One of the bullets took off the top of Otumbo's head before it hit me. The fourth man dragged me to cover and held off the shooters while I called the snipers in. He and I piled into the back of their Land Rover, and we got the hell out of there."

"And two months later, here you are," Lawton said.

"Exactly."

"The situation might well have turned out exactly the same way, even if you'd had your entire team in place," Lawton said.

"I know," Niko said. "Doesn't change the fact that I want to get back at the bastards who killed my men. You know, Otumbo had three younger brothers and two sisters in Rwanda. He was a sergeant in the Rwandan army before he joined 119. The insurgents had a price on his head, and on the heads of his family. So he 'died,' like the rest of us. He thought that would protect his family. After he was killed in Chechnya and Al Qaeda found out who he was, word got back to Rwanda. The insurgents wiped out his brothers and sisters while I was in the hospital. Now here we are, sneaking into a bank, looking for the people who killed Renate's family, when the rest of the Black Christmas plotters—the same people who killed Otumbo, the same people who butchered his six-year-old sister—are still out there."

Lawton turned to face him. "You think this operation is a waste of resources?"

Niko shrugged. "I do. I think we're on a vendetta. Renate wants revenge."

"As do you," Lawton said, impassively.

"You're right," Niko said, his features taut and hard. "I do. But she wants the people who killed her parents and her cousin. I want the people who killed thousands of innocent people on Christmas, the people who go right on killing thousands every month in places no one cares about."

"I can see that," Lawton said, nodding. "But it's just possible that Renate's right. That we're after the people who financed Black Christmas. So who are the real killers, Niko? The angry, disaffected kids who pull the triggers, or the people who strip them of hope, build the training bases, buy the aliases and the fake IDs, and put the guns in their hands? Do you blame the arrow or the archer?"

"Americans," Niko said, smiling. He put a hand on Lawton's shoulder. "You really do believe that you can make it better, don't you?"

"Don't you?" Lawton asked.

"No. We're still cops, Lawton. Cops don't stop crime. Not most of the time. We've had cops, or people like cops, for as long as we've had civilization, and still there is crime. We're just cops, trying to bring criminals to justice."

Niko shook his head slowly and took a breath. When he spoke again, his voice was muted. "No, my friend, we're not saving the world, you and I. Your country wants to bring democracy to the world. But we Greeks invented democracy, and it took us almost two thousand years to spread it over all of Greece. We're not missionaries. We're cops, trying to round up the current crop of bad guys. Maybe, if we do our jobs well, we can stay ahead of the tide, so the water doesn't flood the city. But the ocean will always be there."

"Maybe you're right," Lawton conceded. "But we have a job to do. And Renate deserves the same justice you want for Otumbo."

"Yes," Niko said. "But after that…I want *them.*"

Assif Mondi was chafing at the bit, too, although he never would have said so aloud. He had too much respect for Renate. He was not, however, as certain as she that finding the people responsible for the deaths of her parents would lead them to any great revelation about those responsible for the entirety of Black Christmas.

Yes, he understood the reasoning that the Frankfurt Brotherhood might well have funded the operation and that they might have left their footprint by trying to draw Renate out. But on the other hand…well, tapping into the Brotherhood's communications was not likely to yield a confession. People like this were far too smart to send self-congratulatory e-mails, even in highly encrypted form.

"You know," he said to Renate when they took a brief break for coffee and a snack, "these guys may have had nothing whatever to do with the attack on Baden-Baden."

She looked at him from hollow, too-tired eyes. She had been pushing so hard he was beginning to wonder if she might not make a critical mistake in their attempts to find the correct decoding sequence.

"How can you possibly think that?" she asked.

"Well," he said carefully, "I'm not sure the attacks on the churches and the attacks on the nonreligious sites were perpetrated by the same group."

Tired as she was, she nodded slowly, listening. Thinking. He could almost see the wheels spinning.

"They're different," he said, pressing on, now

that he had her full attention. "It's almost as if two different groups with different agendas were involved. As if…" And here he really hesitated. "…as if one group were using the other for cover."

Something sparked in her eyes. Her head lifted sharply. "I've been thinking that, too. But the only trail we really have to follow is the money. Only the money would link the two. Only the money will tell us who the players are."

Assif drew a deep breath. He was all too aware that months could be wasted while they tried to build a financial trail. People like the Brotherhood were adept at laundering money through enough points of disbursement to make tracking it nearly impossible. Sometimes he wondered how they even knew what they were doing themselves.

"Renate," he said finally, gently.

Her icy eyes lifted to his, as she detected his change in tone.

"Our time is limited," he said. "Very limited. You know what the Americans are hinting at."

"I know. But I was ordered to do this, rather than seek answers in Baden-Baden."

"There are no answers in Baden-Baden. You know that. Whoever committed that atrocity and all the others…they were long gone by the time the police moved in. Already in another country or on a different continent."

"What are you saying, Assif?"

He hesitated. "You know these people and their tricks as well as anyone. You hacked into their system once before. How likely is it we will overhear them plotting their next attacks?"

"Infinitely more likely than it was before we hacked into their computers," Renate answered coldly.

He nodded and scooted his chair just a little closer to hers. "Think about it, Renate. I know how hurt and angry you are. But in terms of the world, is it better to run down the Frankfurt Brotherhood or to find the perpetrators of Black Christmas?"

A weary smile lifted the corners of her mouth. "They are one and the same, Assif."

A sigh escaped him, his entire mood seeming to change on that breath. "You want to know something?"

"Of course."

He looked at her again. "If I were the American president, I would use those weapons and much more after this."

Renate stiffened. "How can you say that?"

He dared to meet her gaze. "I'm getting so tired of these people who don't care how many innocents they kill. Who don't believe they're bound by any morality, any laws. I lost friends on Black Christmas. I'm not sure that any justice in this world will be enough for these savages. So maybe the American president is right. Maybe the only answer is to exterminate them all."

17

Madrid, Spain

Barak Al-Ibrahim heard the alarm and rolled over sleepily. It was 2:00 a.m., and he was not yet ready to face another day. Last night, at dinner, his son had announced his engagement. The bride-to-be was a fellow Muslim, the daughter of a long-time family friend. The celebration had lasted long into the evening, far beyond Barak's usual bedtime. With only four hours' sleep, he knew he was in for a very long day.

Still, he had responsibilities, not only to his family but also to his community. He was a baker, and his shop had served his neighbors for five years, since he'd immigrated to Spain from his native Algeria. It was said that most people eat to live, while Spaniards live to eat. If that were true, Barak helped to feed them. And he took pride in that.

The alarm was insistent, and he forced himself
to sit up and open his eyes. Looking out the window, he saw dots of orange light, as if fading stars
had settled over the city. But these were not stars,
he realized. They were fires, and now, as he
reached over to silence the buzz of the alarm, he
heard the distant wail of sirens.

"What's happening?" his wife murmured sleepily, as if sensing his unease.

"Nothing, my love," he replied. "Just fires
somewhere in the city. Probably the cold. People
use those electric heaters, and they ignite the dra-
peries. Go back to sleep."

"Anwar will marry," she whispered, reaching
over to squeeze his hand.

"Yes," he said. "Anwar will marry. And I am
certain that you will make sure it's the most beautiful wedding in all of Spain. And since I will
have to pay for it, I must go to work."

"Listen to you," his wife said, a quiet lilt of
humor in her voice. "You already sound like an
old man."

He chuckled. "This morning, I feel like one."

"I could make you feel…young again," she said.

"I am sure you could," he replied. "But not this
morning. This morning, I must work."

"Go, then," she said, playfully pushing him out
of the bed with her foot. "Go and bake your bread."

"Do not think of it as baking bread," he said,

lightly grasping her toes through the blanket. "Think of it as baking Anwar's wedding cake."

"Oh yes," she said, her smile radiant even in the dim light. "With that thought, I will have happy dreams."

Thirty minutes later, Barak had shaved, dressed and quietly slipped out into the brisk nighttime air. The scent of smoke hung heavy, biting his nostrils, and he told himself that he would need to seal the shop carefully, lest his breads and pastries smell of it. The short walk to his shop woke him, as it always did.

Usually at this hour he had the streets almost to himself, and he took the time to converse with Allah and meditate upon the Koran. There had been much to speak with Allah about lately. The horrible acts that his fellow Muslims had perpetrated at Christmas were, as Barak had expected, rebounding on the Islamic community. Many of his non-Muslim customers no longer came to his shop, and those that did—even people he had known since the shop had opened—seemed to eye him with suspicion. While he could understand their feelings, it still hurt that they lumped him in with the kinds of animals who could kill innocents.

He understood the anger of the Arab nations. For far too long the West had treated them as little more than giant petrol stations. So long as the pumps remained open and the prices low, the West cared nothing for the Arabs' lives or liberties, their hopes or hurts. One did not need a degree in political science to understand why the Arabs felt used, and why they wanted to shake off the bonds of economic imperialism.

But to destroy churches and murder innocent women and children was no answer. Allah would bring justice in His own way, in His own time. A righteous and divine justice, such that no man could resist or deny. Until that time, Barak knew, it was the duty of Islamic peoples throughout the world to practice *jihad* in the true meaning of the word, as the holy and lifelong struggle to discipline one's heart and mind to the will of Allah. For only in that struggle could anyone find true peace.

Such thoughts were the staple of his morning walks, reminding himself of his place in the great struggle to bring the world into alignment with the perfect will of Allah, to bring peace and justice to all mankind. That struggle began in his own heart, with the quieting of anger, with forgiveness of those who looked upon him with suspicion, and with the celebration of joys such as those his son had revealed last night. If Barak could discipline himself to such thoughts, then—in that tiny way— he made the ultimate triumph of Allah ever nearer.

Against the smell of smoke and the drone of sirens, Barak raised these thoughts like a shield, and within them he walked as if on an island of peace.

Once at the shop, he closed the door, then wetted a towel and tucked it into the gap beneath. His customers would have fresh bread this day, and the sweet scent of pastries to greet their noses when they came into his shop. And he would create that sweetness even as fires burned in the city.

He shrugged off his coat and started the ovens, then turned his mind to the simple, soothing task of preparing dough. He had loved this process from the time he had sat with his mother in their tiny kitchen in Algeria. Flour and water, yeast and eggs, butter, sugar and salt. Measure and mix, knead and allow to rise, roll and bake. In a task that others might find sheer drudgery, Barak found joy and fulfillment.

Until the firebomb crashed through his shop window.

Frankfurt, Germany

Lawton awoke from a catnap to find that Niko had turned on the television set. When he heard Lawton stir, he turned and said, "Come, my friend. You need to see this. Europe has exploded in rage."

Hastily rubbing his burning eyes, Lawton sat up, then moved closer to the screen. In their own way, the pictures were nearly as bad as Black Christmas. Mosques burning. Muslims being beaten by crowds. Vicious slogans spray-painted on walls.

"My God," he said.

"I knew it had been happening here and there," Niko said. "But most people are law-abiding. This…" He shook his head. "This kind of thing has not been seen in a long, long time."

Renate's voice intruded from the doorway. "Not since Hitler." Her voice was hard, icy. *"Kristallnacht."*

Lawton looked again at the screen. "What are you saying?"

"On November eighth, 1938, the Germans erupted in violence against the Jews. Over one hundred fifty synagogues were attacked that night, and over seven thousand Jewish businesses were burned or looted. It came to be known as *Kristallnacht:* the night of broken glass."

Lawton stared at the screen with a growing sense of anger. "I don't understand. The Jews weren't terrorists."

"Of course not," Renate said. "But that's not my point. *Kristallnacht* wasn't a collection of spontaneous, random acts of violence. It was seeded, organized, encouraged by Nazi thugs. And this is, too. It's too big and too widespread not to be."

"So what are you saying?"

"I'm saying someone is working behind the scenes to incite violence against Muslims, for political gain, just like Hitler did with the Jews. Someone is walking in his shoes, following his plan." She paused. "I just wish I knew who. Perhaps Assif and I can crack the encryption. We are now reading e-mail headers from Berg & Tempel."

Lawton turned in his seat. "Anything interesting?"

She nodded slowly. "In a way. The Brotherhood is moving more of its investments into weapons manufacturing. They are expecting war."

"At this point you don't need a crystal ball to guess that."

She shook her head. "In the past six hours, there was a flurry of message traffic with the U.S. Messages routed through the Federal Reserve."

"Oh my God," Lawton said.

Renate nodded. "It may be time to talk to your rose."

Lawton studied her eyes. To contact Special Agent Miriam Ansen would be a violation of Office 119 protocol. Miriam had been his mentor when he worked for the Bureau, in a life that was now past. That she might be a useful source in this investigation was irrelevant; every Office 119 agent came from a law enforcement background, and each of them had old friends who might be useful sources. But the strict and necessary secrecy rules prohibited agents from contacting anyone they had known prior to coming to Office 119. To violate that would be to risk the exposure—and the destruction—of all.

Lawton looked at Niko and Assif. "Would you excuse us for a moment, please?"

"There is no need," Renate replied. "We are a team. There is nothing we cannot say in front of them."

"Perhaps," Lawton said.

Renate turned to them. "I have asked Lawton to contact a woman he knew at the FBI. They worked together on the Lawrence case."

"You know we are not allowed…" Niko began.

"She already knows he's alive," Renate said, impatience clear in her voice. "We coordinated with her in the final assault on Wes Dixon's Guatemalan mercenaries. She has kept his secret this far. I see no reason not to trust her."

"We should talk to Jefe about this," Assif said. "We have rules for a reason, Renate."

"Yes," Lawton said. "And Miriam has rules, too. She can't simply walk into the Federal Reserve and demand to see their e-mail traffic. And unlike us, she can't tap their phones without a warrant. A warrant she can't get just because we've picked up increased traffic between Frankfurt and Washington over the past six hours."

"What if we could read the e-mails?" Renate asked.

"If we can read them, and if they say what you think they will, then yes," Lawton said. "But if I'm going to contact Miriam, I need hard evidence. Not speculation."

"Then we must decode those e-mails," Renate said.

"That won't be easy," Assif said. "The banks use excellent encryption. It has taken me a week just to crack the headers."

"Then you've made progress," Renate said. "Keep working on it. Before all of Europe is in flames."

Brussels, Belgium

Monika Schmidt was not a happy woman, and Jules Soult was sitting in the hot seat in her office. He had known beforehand that scenes such as these were going to take place, and he had resigned himself to them. They were, after all, part of the game he was playing, part of the price he would need to pay.

"These riots have to be stopped," she was saying as she paced behind her desk, arms folded tightly. "Apart from the ugly face it shows the world, the important thing is that the people of the EU can't possibly feel safe while these mobs are filling the streets. And all—" she turned to face him "—I repeat, *all* of the people of the EU member nations should feel safe."

Soult, who wanted no such thing just yet, merely nodded and agreed.

Frau Schmidt threw up a hand in exasperation and distress. "First the terror attacks, and now our *own* people carrying out terror attacks? Against their neighbors? Against their former friends and associates?"

"I'm sure it's not quite that bad."

"No?" She glared at him. "I don't care if these people are street toughs taking advantage of the situation. I don't care about their politics. They are *thugs,* and they are attacking people with whom they were coexisting only days ago. Tolerance, something we Europeans have prided ourselves on since the last war, has become an empty word."

Soult murmured agreement.

"I will not have it," she said firmly. "And it is your job to stop it."

"I know. But I have barely begun to organize my operations." A lie, but necessary.

"You should have had enough people in place to have at least sensed this was going to happen!"

"The few people I have so far put in place are searching for terrorists, Frau Schmidt. How were we to know that we would be dealing with popular uprisings?"

"I am not so sure these uprisings are popular."

Soult's heart skipped a beat. Had she heard something? "What do you mean?"

"I mean that I do not believe the majority of Europeans support them. In fact, I believe the majority are fearful of them. Civil unrest is always frightening."

Civil unrest and a frightened European population were Soult's goals. The longer the unrest continued, the more frightened the average citizen would become—and the more likely to want someone in power who was strong enough to make them feel safe.

With all modesty, Soult was sure he was the man to do that. "I will attempt to speed the creation of my organization," he assured her. "But even so, I must choose people of whom I am certain. I cannot risk hiring the wrong people."

"No, of course not." Frau Schmidt sighed and seemed to let go of some of her tension. "These are ugly times, General Soult. The European Union is new, and not entirely trusted. If we cannot show strength and the ability to secure ourselves from within, then..." She left the thought incomplete, but her meaning was entirely clear.

"I understand." Indeed he did. He was counting on it, in fact.

"I'm sure you do." She shook her head again. "This makes us appear weak, General."

He nodded. Of course it did. That was the entire rationale behind it. "Let me speak to my people and see what I can do."

"Thank you. Keep me informed."

"But of course."

He took his leave, his heart lifting with each step he took.

Things could not have been going better.

Not for his purposes, at least.

18

Washington, D.C.

Harrison Rice finished up his economic briefing with a sigh of relief as he watched his advisors file out of the Oval Office. A glance at his watch told him he had fifteen minutes before several congressmen arrived to discuss an education bill that especially interested him. It had, in fact, been one of the issues on which he had run for office: the improvement of public schools and universities.

But before he could settle into an issue with which he was comfortable, Phillip Bentley walked in as if he owned the place. Which, thought Rice angrily, he probably did.

Even after all these months, Rice was still trying to figure out how he had reached these straits.

But that was moot now, he thought, as he watched Bentley enter. He was stuck. Whatever his own moral scruples, he wasn't sure he had the cojones to stand up to Bentley—or, more importantly, those who stood behind him.

Rice could feel himself becoming increasingly paranoid, and these days he sometimes wondered if he'd been deliberately planted as Edward Morgan's roommate, just to give these people their foot in the door.

But that was ridiculous, he told himself sternly as he watched Bentley turn on one of the televisions that were artfully concealed in a wall. How could anyone then have known that Rice would someday be in a position to run for president?

No one could have known, he assured himself. Although...although he sometimes wondered if invisible hands hadn't been helping his political career all along. The fear did nothing to improve his mood.

"What is it?" he asked Bentley irritably. "I have a meeting."

"Not for a few minutes," Bentley said as he picked up the remote and flipped through channels.

"What's going on?"

"You need to see the news out of Europe. Most of our domestic news networks won't cover it before tonight. Ah, there we go."

The picture bloomed in living color and horrific detail. Mobs marched in the streets, carrying

banners in several languages, many in English.
The English ones screamed for death to Muslims.

"Good God!" Rice said.

"It's happening all over the continent," Bentley said. He turned up the volume, and a German narrator, sounding less than calm, gave a staccato description of events. Though Rice couldn't understand the rapid-fire German, the voice added urgency to the pictures of rioting mobs, of shop windows being shattered and Molotov cocktails being thrown. The camera drew back and showed Berlin, with spotty fires raging.

Then the view changed to Madrid and stretcher bearers carrying a badly burned man from what appeared to have been a bakery. Even as the injured man was being carried out to an ambulance, crowds shook their fists and shouted angrily.

Bentley switched off the TV.

"Everywhere?" Rice asked.

"Everywhere but Britain, so far. And with what happened in London last year, I'm sure they'll be next."

"But…" Rice didn't want to believe what he had just seen.

"It's spreading, and it's spreading fast, Mr. President. Our analysts believe that it will spread to us, as well."

Rice's mind spun into high gear. "We'll need to call out the Guard. Alert the police."

"Martial law," said Bentley.

Rice's head jerked. "Not unless it's absolutely necessary."

"It will become necessary. It's best to be prepared."

Rice felt a surge of anger. "Did you bring your crystal ball, Bentley? How can you be sure that our people will react this way and to this degree? So far—"

"So far," Bentley interrupted, "very little has been accomplished. We've taken out one terrorist cell, a mere nod to the enormity of what happened on Christmas. Do you think Americans are feeling very safe right now? We haven't taken out even one cell in *this* country. Soon the American people are going to realize that. Soon the American people are going to vent their rage just as the Europeans are doing."

Rice knew what was coming. The Vienna action had been merely a reprieve. But before Bentley could speak the words again, before Bentley could again remind him of the armed military officer who sat patiently outside with the "football" chained to his wrist, Rice spoke.

"Get out of here, Bentley."

Bentley bridled. "You don't give me orders."

"Yes, actually, I do. And if you want to be National Security Advisor this time tomorrow, you'll get out of here and let me think."

"May I remind you—"

"You don't need to remind me of anything. I know what you're holding over my head. But until I'm impeached and convicted, or arrested, I'm still the president, and I can still fire you. So get the hell out of my office."

Bentley's face was red and angry, but he left with the cultivated grace of the East Coast upper crust. Good breeding.

Fuck breeding, Rice thought, as he sank onto one of the sofas. Fuck it all. He had to start thinking and think fast, or the world was apt to come to a brink it hadn't seen since the Cuban Missile Crisis.

And Harrison Rice didn't want that to be his legacy.

Riyadh, Saudi Arabia

Ahmed Ahsami watched the news with a growing sense of horror. All his dreams for *Saif Alsharaawi* were crumbling about his feet. Ever since Black Christmas—a day that was supposed to have demonstrated Arab strength and self-control—everything he had tried had turned to dust. The Black Christmas attacks had been subverted and turned into a worldwide massacre. His attempt to put down some of the plotters in Vienna had been cast as the West putting down the bad Arabs. The goodwill he had hoped to build now

lay in ruins as mosques and shops burned across
Europe.

Perhaps the most radical of his brethren were
right. Perhaps there was no basis for peace with
the West and the only option was a war of annihilation where only one was left standing. It
would certainly end the problem, one way or
another.

But Ahmed had no illusions as to the outcome
of such a conflict. While Muslims were huge in
number, and while they predominated in vast areas
of the world, they could not win a world war
against the West. Arab armies had tried to conquer
Europe before, and they had failed. Even if they
could succeed today, the massive engine of Western economic power—the United States—lay
safely between two oceans. While Arabs could
cross those oceans to deliver pinpricks—and despite their horrifying human cost, in terms of un-
seating American power, even the 9/11 attacks had
been pinpricks—there was no way any Arab army
could cross those oceans in sufficient force to sub-
due the Americans. A war of annihilation could
mean only the annihilation of the Islamic lands.

And yet, while he was loath to admit it, Ahmed
knew that he was responsible for the current crisis. Over the past few hours, that responsibility
had settled over him like a sandstorm, rasping at
every nerve ending. He had spent these past weeks

raging against his betrayers, when he should have been raging against himself. His reach had exceeded his grasp.

The Christmas attacks had been far too wide-ranging in scope. He had known that, and he should have trimmed the plan, so that his own operatives could carry it out. Yawi had argued for that, but Ahmed had refused. Instead, he had chosen to rely on outsiders, even knowing that his view of Arab ascendancy was very different from the views of those upon whom he was relying.

He had been blinded by his own ambition, blinded by his vision of a world waking up on Christmas morning to discover that "those Arabs" were far more powerful, far more capable and far more disciplined than the Western media had portrayed them. In Ahmed's mind, Westerners would wake to discover that the Islamic world was its equal, and they would then be willing to negotiate as equals.

That had always been a fantasy, he realized now. Even if the attacks had been carried out precisely to Ahmed's plans, the West could—and probably would—have counterattacked in ways he and *Saif Alsharaawi* could not have matched.

The simple, shameful truth was that the Islamic world was not equal to the West. Even the most powerful of the Arab nations lacked the means to produce modern aircraft, warships or tanks. Their armies, however powerful they might seem, relied on weapons produced by Western nations, Russia or China. In a war of attrition, with the American and European navies and air forces blocking new shipments, the armies of Allah simply could not replace their losses. Sooner or later, they would be ground down.

Even oil, that lone resource of the Arab nations, was a two-edged sword. When the OPEC nations had attempted to use its power, with the embargoes of the 1970s, the West had responded with devastating economic sanctions. While the rest of the world was dependent on Arab oil, the Arab world relied on the West for nearly everything else. The sanctions had hurt the OPEC nations far more than the embargoes had hurt the West.

As those bitter realities settled through the fog of illusions fed by clerics and princes, Ahmed saw through to the core truths. Though he served Allah, as the operations director for *Saif Alsharaawi,* he knew he could not rely on divine intervention to solve the problems faced by his Arab brethren. Allah worked through his children, and the children of Allah were his hands in this world. As Ahmed saw it, the Islamic world had only two options.

The first was to seek some level of military

parity. In simple terms, that meant acquiring nuclear weapons. If *Saif Alsharaawi* were in possession of a nuclear deterrent, then it could assume a true leadership position in the Islamic world. Then it could negotiate with the West, not as a supplicant, but as an equal. Of course, any attempt to acquire such a deterrent would most likely bring down Western wrath even more firmly. No, force was not the way.

The second was to employ that most useful of Arab gifts, guile. It was as his father had told him so many times as a child: *Ahmed, the greatest weapon you will ever possess is between your ears. Discipline your mind with faith and knowledge, and none can be your better.*

As military operations, *Saif's* performances in Black Christmas and the attack on Vienna had been masterpieces of planning and execution. As political operations, both had failed miserably. He had allowed his enemies to outthink him and thus to turn his military successes into political failures. But no more. Now it would be Ahmed who gained the mental advantage.

Veltroni had said that the secret lay in the past, in the actions of the *Hassassim* and the Knights Templar. And whatever his spiritual inadequacies, the intelligence of a Jesuit was not to be dismissed lightly.

So what had become of the Knights Templar?

Languedoc, France

Jules Soult had chosen the inn carefully. It had a view of Rennes-le-Château and two of the Templar forts on nearby hilltops. But it was not for the view that he had chosen it. It was for its relative isolation. Unlike Rennes-le-Château, which had been overrun by tourists ever since that book about the Priory of Sion had been published, this inn remained out of the way, catering to the select clientele who already knew of it.

Soult not only knew of it, but his family tradition held that on this very spot Marie Madeleine— or Mary Magdalene, as she was more commonly known—had looked out over the vineyards on the surrounding slopes. Sitting in the bow window of the inn, at a small table, Soult fancied the view hadn't changed much since the Magdalene had dwelt here.

Later had come the Templars, full of the secrets they had learned in Jerusalem, recognizing Marie Madeleine as the wife of Christ. They had built those forts with an eye to defending sacred ground. Instead, they had been forced out by Philip, calmly marching down the mountain path to their execution.

Soult puffed his cigar and gave a nod of admiration for those men. Out of their end had sprung his Order of the Rose. The Priory of Sion—also supposedly sprung from the same past, though before the Templars—was a less legitimate branch of Merovingians, accorded a status they didn't deserve and publicly denied when questioned.

But Soult knew his own line as well or better, and would never deny it.

The Rose. Her secret name through the centuries as the Church had steadily persecuted any and all who disagreed with Rome. Oh, they had sainted her, naming her the Apostle to the Apostles, but then Gregory VI had decided that the Magdalene had become too important for a woman in the male dominated church and preached a sermon naming her the prostitute in the New Testament whom Jesus had saved.

It was all balderdash, of course, and many were today realizing that the Magdalene had been falsely accused. But Soult had long since realized that history was written by the victors.

Soon, however, he would write his own victorious history. Smiling, he puffed on his cigar and waited for Hector to arrive.

Twenty minutes later, Hector did indeed appear, full of apologies for having taken a wrong turning in the lanes that ran through the mountains. Soult waved the apology aside. "A minor matter," he said graciously.

"So," Hector said, speaking in Spanish, "it goes well, no?"

"Yes. Very well." Smiling, Soult held up his cigar and watched the smoke curling from its tip. "Frau Schmidt wants me to use every power at my disposal to quiet the unrest. I of course agreed."

"Of course." There was a glint in Hector's dark eyes. "But instead?"

"But instead we must now encourage Muslims to retaliate for what has been done to them."

"An excellent idea."

"Yes, I think so." Soult, feeling genuinely beneficent in light of the success of his plans so far, smiled warmly at Hector. "You can do this, yes?"

"I have always said so. My men are in place. Give me a day or two to make sure all is in order."

Soult leaned toward Hector, lowering his voice. "We are close now, Hector. Very close."

Hector nodded, and Soult leaned back, satisfied. "The people will cry out for safety and peace." He extended a hand, cupping it, then abruptly tightening it into a fist. "We will give them peace, Hector."

"Yes. And you shall be a hero to all."

Soult raised a brow. "And the Europa Prima party?" he asked, referring to his own political party, which until now had gained relatively few members, as it was a party dedicated to the European Union. While most Europeans embraced many of the benefits of the Union, they were still leery of giving it too much political power. The mere existence of an international political party engendered more suspicion than trust.

But that was about to change. Of that Soult had no doubt.

"The party is ready to take center stage and name you its leader," Hector confirmed. "Right at the moment of your greatest acclaim."

Soult nodded again, content, feeling pleasant anticipation in his stomach. "You know, Hector, it is so odd."

"What is?"

"How people claim to cherish freedom but are so willing to throw it away in exchange for safety."

Hector's eyes narrowed. "You will not move too fast on that?"

Soult blinked, then laughed and stubbed out his cigar in the ceramic ashtray. "Of course not, Hector. That would be foolish. I was just reflecting on the oddity of human nature. Those who have power, such as ourselves, are the only ones who truly have freedom. Everyone else has the illusion of it, an illusion they will toss away in exchange for the promise of safety."

Hector nodded, satisfied. "Forgive me," he said. "But we are working so hard toward this end, and I sometimes forget that you are a greatly patient man."

Patient? Soult thought. Yes, he was patient. Not many could have spent so many years in pursuit of a single goal. He smiled to let Hector know that no offense had been taken. After all, Hector had served him well for many years.

Soult called for another brandy, then gave himself up to looking out the window and enjoying the perfect day.

19

The letter in the mailbox outside the door appeared innocuous enough. Miriam looked at it, wondering who would have bothered to write to her from New York. These days, the phone and e-mail had all but replaced the letter as a way of communication.

She studied it for a moment, not recognizing the handwriting, and almost tossed it as one of those "hand addressed" sales things. But she paused before she let it drop into the trash can. First-class stamp, not a postal meter. Return address "White Rose," without a street number.

Suddenly her heart was hammering. This had to be from Tom Lawton. He had promised to let her know he was still alive from time to time by sending a rose. Beyond that, all contact had ended, leaving a small hole in her life and a larger hole in her heart.

Tom had a new life and a new name now, and she didn't really know what to expect inside the envelope. Was he in New York? Did he want to meet?

Her fingers trembled with excitement as she slit open the envelope and drew out the single sheet of paper. Inside was a typed message.

A friend needs to meet you. Thursday, 8:00 p.m. Chez Peter. He will carry something from me. T.

Her hands still trembling, she burned the letter and put the remains down the garbage disposal. This wasn't innocent, she thought. Something serious was going on or Tom Lawton wouldn't have broken his silence.

For a few seconds she wondered if she should tell Terry. Then she decided against it. If she was getting into something dangerous, she didn't want to drag him in with her.

She looked at the envelope she still held and realized she needed to burn that, as well. No e-mail, no phone call, no cell phone. Nothing the NSA might listen in on or pry into. Nothing that would leave a permanent trace of the note that had been delivered by what was still the most private trans-

mission system in the world: the good old-fash-
ioned U.S. Mail.

She started to laugh as she lit the corner of the
envelope, letting it fall into the sink and burn as
the letter had.

And she thought she had been paranoid before?

She was still laughing when Terry arrived
home. He wanted to know what was so funny, but
she only shook her head. "I'll tell you sometime,
love. I promise."

Sometime was not good enough for Terry. He
said nothing but, "Hurry home," the next morning when she announced she was going to a late
meeting in Georgetown and wouldn't be home
directly after work.

He watched her go out to her car and begin the
long commute to D.C., and thought that they really needed to move closer to the city. Neither of
them needed this kind of commute every day.
Sure, they liked their apartment and their church,
and the feeling that they were really "away" when
they were off duty. But this was a bit too far away.

He decided to wander around some of the bedroom communities nearer to Washington, since it
was his day off. If he started looking and found
some ideal little house for them, Miriam would
probably jump at the chance to move.

Whistling, he set about getting dressed. Of

course, after his day of real estate exploration, he had every intention of following his wife when she left work that night.

Not because he didn't trust her. Because he did. But this meeting was out of normal parameters and had roused his every instinct to high alert. Miriam often kept late hours, but the FBI rarely sprang for dinners. And if not the FBI, then who? He knew his Miriam, and it wouldn't surprise him if she were in the process of getting into something way over her head.

Miriam never noticed Terry behind her. Not that she expected a tail. The letter had been a burst of sheer genius, and she was sure no one had read it but her.

She was grateful to find a parking place near the bistro, although Thursday wasn't one of its busiest nights. That was the reason she and Tom had often come here for dinner after work. Until she and Terry had fallen in love, that was. Terry had changed everything, and Miriam still celebrated that change every day of her life.

Inside, she was shown to a small table near the back. She explained that she was expecting someone, then ordered an appetizer and a soft drink.

Her drink had just arrived when a small man in a business suit came up to her with a smile and handed her a white rose.

She smiled and motioned him to sit. The waiter

materialized before they could exchange a word, and in a slightly accented voice the man ordered a beverage. Only when it appeared, along with Miriam's appetizer, did he begin to speak.

"Tom and I work together," he said.

"I thought so." Miriam, who had absolutely no appetite, lifted a small pâté-covered cracker and bit into it. She knew from experience that the pâté was exquisite, but right now she couldn't taste a thing.

"I call him Law," the man said, sipping a glass of wine. "That's his new name."

Miriam dabbed her lips with a napkin. "Apropos."

The man smiled. "You may call me Diego."

"Miriam."

He nodded. "Law speaks highly of you."

Miriam was in no mood for social pleasantries. "I suppose there is a purpose for this meeting?"

"Ah, yes. But first we must ensure this fussy waiter will not disturb us for a while."

The waiter was back again, almost as if summoned by Diego's mention. They both ordered their entrées, then Diego leaned over and whispered something to the young man.

After he had left, Diego gave her a rueful smile. "I told him we needed time alone. That I was trying to decide whether to ask for your hand in marriage."

"I hope he's a romantic."

"Aren't we all, when we are young?"

Miriam found herself smiling. "I suppose we are."

"But to business," Diego said.

"Please."

"Law asked me to tell you that a series of encrypted e-mails has been sent from a private bank in Frankfurt to the U.S. Federal Reserve here in Washington."

Miriam nodded slowly. "Interesting."

"These e-mails were sent over the international banking network, not the Internet."

Miriam raised a brow. She knew little about the ins and outs of bank transaction processing, but she knew enough. "Meaning NSA would never see them."

"Not without a warrant. The concern is that someone in the Fed is passing them to someone in your government. Someone high enough in the food chain to have considerable influence with the Rice administration."

"Have you read these messages?" Miriam said.

He paused for a moment, and nodded. "Only in part. Our decryption is not complete. Their security is very good, and it will take time to decode them. And that is time we do not have."

"Why?" Miriam asked, feeling her stomach lurch.

"You have heard about the violence in Europe?"

"Of course," she said.

"It will happen here in America, as well. The messages seem to suggest that the recipient should wait for that violence before taking decisive action."

"I don't understand," Miriam said. "What kind of decisive action?"

He looked at her, sadness in his eyes. "Your government plans to employ tactical nuclear weapons against suspected terrorist targets in Pakistan."

"Oh my God." Miriam's stomach sank so far that she shoved the appetizer away, unable to even look at it.

"Exactly," said the man.

"But why?" Miriam tried to collect her thoughts. "I mean, I'd heard rumors, but I thought it was just Beltway gossip. Or, at worst, posturing. You're saying they're true?"

Diego nodded. "America has signed a comprehensive nuclear test ban treaty," he explained. "You haven't tested any devices in years now. There are some in your Pentagon who worry that your weapons manufacturers no longer know how to build a working bomb. For them, this is a way to prove that the new devices work."

"So they'll kill people just to prove their expensive bombs are worth buying in bulk," Miriam said with obvious disgust.

He nodded. "Others want to stabilize the region

at any cost, so they can build factories and take advantage of cheap labor, which they cannot do in a climate of unrest."

Miriam nodded slowly, though she still felt sickened. "What should I do?"

"Law was hoping you might be able to discover the final recipient of these messages."

"I'll try." But the thought of trying to track messages from the Fed to the White House was daunting, to say the least.

"I have brought copies for you," he said.

"And if I do find out who these messages are going to...what then?"

Diego shrugged. "It is possible he may be removed one way or another. We must do everything in our power to prevent a nuclear strike. Because it will not stop with Pakistan. You and I both know that."

She never did eat, though Diego somehow finished his meal. He paid the check, then slipped an envelope into her hand before they rose from the table. She tucked it into her briefcase.

"How will I let you know if I learn anything?"

"My card is in the envelope. I am assigned to the United Nations. Speak to no one but me."

Diego parted from her on the street.

Terry was sure she never realized that he was parked six cars away on the far side of the street, all too aware that she had met a man for dinner and come out carrying a white rose.

There were no words to describe how much relief he felt when she suddenly tossed it in the gutter with every appearance of distaste.

Her guardian angel followed her all the way home.

Riyadh, Saudi Arabia

Ahmed Ahsami had nearly finished wading through the book about the Knights Templar. He had, despite his anger and unhappiness, found it rather interesting to read how the Templars and the Muslims had once worked together in Jerusalem and Palestine. That was something he had not heard before, and he might have considered it a lie except that the English writer seemed to think the information spoke poorly of the Templars.

According to the writer, that association had eventually helped bring about the fall of the Templars. The men who had undertaken to give everything to their God and protect pilgrims coming to the Holy Land had somehow gone astray, becoming wealthy beyond belief, making friends among the Muslims—even, it was said, reading the Koran. They had briefly placed a "king" in Jerusalem, a man who was said to have descended from the line of Davidic kings.

Ahmed snorted at that. The sons of Ishmael had lived in that land longer than the sons of Isaac. The Arab claim was far older.

The Templars, he learned, had come to nearly control Europe through their wealth. They had virtually created international banking, and any king, prince or duke who wished to wage war was beholden to them for loans. Eventually, every royal house in Europe was indebted to them, many so deeply that they were little more than Templar puppets.

Then he read of their downfall, when the king of France and the pope had conspired to wipe out the order and take their treasure. But the Templar fleet had vanished, and with it the untold wealth that had for so long financed Europe.

Ahmed sat back in his chair, rubbing his chin and thinking. The wealth had disappeared. Or had it?

He thought of the huge sums of money that had come his way to fund his plan, and he began to see how he might be a cog in a larger plan, a much older plan. One that didn't care about God or Allah at all. One that had betrayed its very foundations.

If the Templar wealth had not disappeared, then where would it have gone? Who had inherited the true role of the Templar Order, that of banker to the princes of Europe? The nexus of international banking had been Frankfurt for over two centuries, until, by the time of the First World War every major participant was borrowing money from the same group of men. The war devastated Europe, but the bankers grew ever wealthier.

Armed with this information, Ahmed called his contact in the Saudi national bank. It was time to find out where the money for Black Christmas had originated and what projects those men were investing in next.

He was through with running a step behind.

20

Guatemalan Highlands

The volcano rumbled twenty-four hours a day. By night it cast an orange glow on the mountains and slopes surrounding it, and sometimes, in the perpetual cloud that seemed to hover over it, bursts of orange light could also be seen. So far no lava had poured down its slopes, no lava bombs spat out to ignite the forests below. So far the mountain remained a seething cauldron that raged only with showers of ash.

But Miguel knew better than to count on the mountain remaining restrained. Worse, he had to make his way through the sea of ash on its slopes before it rained, for then he would be caught in a mire that would wash him away.

And he knew the mountain could make its own rain. Whatever the educated people might say,

Miguel knew the lore, the treasured knowledge of his Mayan people. He knew the mountain was a living, breathing beast, and he knew there was no way to placate it once it woke. It would have its way, and a puny man scrambling over its slopes could not withstand its force.

It could pour fire from the sky or cause rain. That was its great power. And either one would be equally destructive. Or it could send silent killers down its slopes, the ghosts of jaguars that would grab men by the throat and choke them to death.

He kept a bandana tied over his nose and mouth, hoping to escape the power of the ghostly jaguars. More, he prayed every step of the way that the mighty mountain would take no notice of him. And on every other breath he sent a plea to the Christian god to protect him.

By the night glow he followed the Hunter. He had no idea why the man had killed Paloma, nor did he care. For that alone the stalker must die, and Miguel called on the power of the jaguar to aid him.

Miguel knew, as the Hunter he pursued had evidently surmised, that there was another way out of those caves. During the time the mountain had shaken like a cat trying to shrug off some pest, he had lain watching the man, watching him search the opening to the cavern, watching him emerge again as if he thought it was all over.

The man had stood for a long time, braced

against the quaking earth, and for a while Miguel thought that his quarry was going to descend toward him, to meet the end that Miguel so longed to give him.

But then it was as if the man had another thought, and he began to struggle around the side of the mountain, through deepening ash, grabbing trees for support. Only when he had vanished did Miguel climb to the cave to learn what he could about his family.

It was there that Miguel had found Paloma. A great cry had risen in his chest, but he had swallowed it. While rock shook free from the walls and ceiling of the cave and threatened to crush him, he had stood over the frail body of the *curandera* and prayed that her return to the heavens would make her happier than this life had.

Then he bent and took the small pouch she wore around her neck. It was a medicine pouch, she had said, and the contents were to be sprinkled over her when she died.

She had told them all, and no one had questioned her. No one would ever have dared question Paloma. She was too well loved. Too well respected.

Opening the pouch, he had found a fine white powder that glowed faintly. For a moment he could only stare in amazement, but then another rock fell, this one too close, recalling him to the present.

Carefully he had pinched the shining powder

from the pouch and sprinkled it over the old woman. Another pinch to complete the job. It had glowed where it fell, seeming to cover her with light.

He had thought about pouring the rest of the powder over her, but something stayed his hand. Instead, he had tightened the drawstring on the leather bag and tucked it into his pocket. She would want the padre to have it. Somehow he knew this as if she had told him.

Then he had turned and hurried swiftly out of the dangerous cave. Behind him, Paloma's body shimmered in the darkness.

For days he had continued to follow the Hunter, had watched him find the other cave entrance, and finally, just this night, had seen him pick up the trail of the refugees in the valley below the rumbling mountain.

Now the hunt would move more swiftly, for the Hunter had scented his prey. On impulse, Miguel pinched a bit of the shiny powder from Paloma's bag and ate it. Dimly he remembered that she had given him some once when he was a very small and very ill child. It had strengthened him almost immediately. He prayed it would do the same now.

Because if he didn't get to the Hunter first, the man would probably kill the rest of the refugees.

And Miguel was not going to allow that to happen. No matter what.

Rome, Italy

Renate's senses went on high alert as the train pulled into the Termini Station. Its graceful, modern appearance, rather like a ladies' fan spread out over the arrival area, belied a danger she had come to know only too well in the past three years. Pickpockets and baggage thieves, often aided directly or unwittingly by begging children, phony taxi cab drivers and other assorted miscreants, prowled the station grounds in search of unsuspecting tourists.

Lawton had arrived in Rome earlier, having taken an overnight train from Frankfurt. Renate had stayed with Niko and Assif until morning, surviving on coffee and adrenaline, hoping that Assif's legendary cryptography skills would yield more information from the intercepted e-mails. Finally, convinced that she would have to wait for further decryption and having been summoned back to Rome by Jefe himself, she had boarded the train. She had slept for much of the fifteen-hour journey, but she did not feel rested. She had begun to wonder if she would ever feel rested again.

Perhaps it was her eyes darting about at the ragged edge of exhaustion, or perhaps it was her usual heightened state of alert when walking through Termini Station, that tipped her to the presence of the man walking a few meters to her left and one step behind her. At first she dismissed him as a routine pickpocket, but something about the way his eyes continually swept between her and the down escalator toward which she was walking sent a cold chill down her back. If he was indeed a pickpocket, she knew she was the only target he had in mind. And pickpockets looked for targets of opportunity, not specific people.

She glanced around, quickly estimating the most likely sites for an attack. It would be the escalator, where even at this hour people were standing in close quarters, with their attention distracted by panels displaying directions and posters advertising the city's attractions. That would be where *she* would attack, up close and personal. A knife or ice pick, probably. Done correctly— and she doubted the Brotherhood would hire an amateur—she would be collapsed at the foot of the escalator, with him on his way to a train, before anyone noticed. Her death would be written off as random street crime, a tragic story of a Dutch national killed by a mugger, with perhaps a brief story in *la Repubblica,* or perhaps not even that.

Just as she expected, he began to close in as they neared the escalator, pacing himself so that he would be a step behind her. She knew this was no place for a fight. He would be above and behind her, with leverage, giving her no freedom of maneuver. Clicking her tongue as if she had forgotten something, she turned and headed back toward the main entrance to the station. Jefe would have to pay for a taxi. At least the broad, semicircular cabstand in front of the station would give her a greater opportunity to defend herself.

She heard him turn to follow and went through a mental inventory of her weapons as she quickened her pace. As a rule, she didn't carry a handgun in Europe, especially not when traveling. Europeans had adapted to the threat of terrorism far earlier and far more than their American counterparts. Gun laws were strict—and strictly enforced. Even as a BKA agent, she had not been authorized to carry a gun except for specific assignments, and Office 119—which did not officially exist—could not authorize her, regardless.

That left her keys, potentially lethal if she could get in close, but to do so would also expose her to whatever weapon her attacker had. Apart from that, she was armed only with her wits and her training, and she had no doubt that he was her equal in both regards.

As she stepped through the front door of the station and approached the row of taxis, she slipped one hand into her purse and grasped her keys, the key ring in her palm, the keys protruding between her fingers, just beneath the knuckles. It was not much, but it was all she had. That, and the knowledge that he was there, perhaps not suspecting that she was aware of him.

She walked up to a taxi, speaking rapid-fire Italian, her eyes flicking between the driver's face and the muddled reflection in his less than spotless passenger window. She saw only a shadow approaching, blocking the bright lights of the station entrance, but it was enough.

Turning her hips to the left, she pushed off on her right foot, her right hand rising at her side, shoulders squaring, left hand in a defensive position, lunging onto her left leg, her right arm extending fully with the entire force of her body behind it. For the first time, she got a clear view of the man's face as she felt the keys gouge deeply into the soft flesh of his throat.

His eyes widened in shock for an instant, before his face contorted in pain. His hands rose to his throat, and she caught the dull gray glimmer of something falling to the ground. The *Polizia* would later establish that it was a stiletto, the blade blackened ceramic, a combat knife used by special forces operatives worldwide, available in any of a number of military equipment catalogs.

But Renate could not take note of such things. Instead, her focus was on finishing what she had begun, and she drove her left fist into his solar plexus, hearing the rush of breath as he doubled over. Her third strike, again with her key-studded right fist, slashed into the side of his head, just beneath the ear, penetrating skin and muscle before shredding his carotid artery.

Behind her, the cab driver gasped as a fountain of blood erupted from the side of the man's neck, spraying across the sidewalk. Renate stood over her attacker as he collapsed to the ground, her vision crystalline clear, the coppery scent of blood strong in her flaring nostrils, her muscles tingling in anticipation of actions that would never happen.

The taxi driver would later tell the police that seconds seemed to stretch into hours before the blond woman realized what she had done and slumped against his taxi, hands trembling, trying to catch her breath, her eyes still wide in terror.

But he would be wrong. It was not terror that her eyes radiated with almost searing intensity. It was rage.

Renate, Lawton and Margarite sat in Jefe's office, Renate still simmering with an anger that hung in the air like a cloud. If ever human eyes had looked feral, hers did. This was not the woman he had met in Idaho, Lawton thought, the woman whose face had borne the shocked and horrified look of someone who has just taken a human life. There was no shock or horror in her now. She wanted more of the Brotherhood's blood.

Jefe looked up from the police report that a source had obtained. He appeared tired, his Latin features sagging as if the weight of the world lay upon his shoulders.

"The *Polizia* are saying it was self-defense," he said. "They will report it as an attempted robbery of a tourist. But it wasn't, was it?"

"No," Renate said. "He was no street mugger. He was an assassin."

"There's no question now," Lawton said. "They know she's alive."

"I agree," Jefe said, nodding. "The question then is, how much do they know about the rest of us? Has Office 119 been compromised?"

"He might have spotted her in Frankfurt," Lawton said, with more confidence than he felt. "The Brotherhood knows her and knows what she looks like."

"Maybe," Jefe said. "Regardless, we must assume the worst. The Brotherhood is an organization with a worldwide reach and a worldwide agenda. They can communicate using one of the most secure networks there is. I always thought it was a bit foolish to assume that no one would ever suspect our existence."

"Maybe not," Renate said, her voice cold and firm. "The Brotherhood has been after me for years. They knew I was alive, or they wouldn't have killed my parents. They don't have to know about Office 119 to know about me."

"But how did they track you?" Jefe asked. "How did they know you would be on that train, arriving at that time? You were supposed to have traveled with Law, the night before. Staying overnight was a spur-of-the-moment decision. *I* didn't even know about it until Law got here."

Lawton drew a breath. "Somehow, they picked her up in Frankfurt. There's no other way it could have happened. Think about it. If they were onto us, there's no way I could have gotten into Berg & Tempel. If they were onto the whole team, they'd have taken us all out in Frankfurt."

"But consider this," Renate said. "Even if they were just watching me, they probably spotted the rest of the team. That means Niko and Assif…"

"Relax," Jefe said, holding up a hand. "That was my first thought. As soon as we heard what happened, I sent a message to Niko and Assif. And I have a three-man security team on the way there now."

"That's a lot of resources," Renate said. "And all because of me."

"Well," Jefe said, "for the time being, I can spare them. With these new EU Department of Collective Security operators all over the place, I had to order our European teams to stand down."

"What's the deal with that?" Lawton asked. "I heard about the riots, but now they raided a mosque in Nice?"

Jefe nodded. "The word is that General Jules Soult, the new deputy director for intelligence, has a private security firm under contract."

"Mercenaries," Margarite said.

"Yes, exactly," Jefe agreed. "It's all legal, but I still don't like it. Anyway, Soult said he had good intel that an Al Qaeda cell was operating out of that mosque, so he sent a team in."

"Yeah," Lawton said, shaking his head. "Four dead, seven wounded, including six kids. That's going to go a long way toward stopping terrorism. Did we have any intel on the target?"

Margarite shook her head. "Not a thing. We had static about another mosque in Nice, but we couldn't confirm it. Nothing on that one, though."

"Is our French intelligence *that* bad?" Renate asked.

Margarite looked at her, anger simmering in her eyes. "No, it is not. That mosque was clean. As the raid showed."

"Prickly," Renate said, a flicker of a smile crossing her features for the first time since her arrival.

Margarite ignored her. "I have known of Jules Soult for years. He is a political opportunist from a family of political opportunists."

"Is he one of *those* Soults?" Lawton asked, dimly remembering his Napoleonic history.

"The very same," Jefe said. "Great-great-bunch-of-greats-grandfather was a Marshall of France."

"And not a very good or honorable one," Margarite said, the tone of her voice leaving no room for debate. "General Soult—the current one—commanded the Foreign Legion in Chad for several years. There were rumors."

"What rumors?" Renate asked.

"That he was a man who would spare no blood in the defense of France," Margarite replied. "Not his soldiers' blood. And certainly not his enemies' blood. When it was rumored that a terrorist cell was training in a mountain village outside Goz-Bieda, he went in and took it out. Not just the camp. The entire village. According to the rumors, when his superiors asked why, he said 'They knew, or should have known.'"

"That's…ruthless," Lawton said.

"Yes," she replied. "But by the time he left Chad, terrorist activity had all but ceased. So any excesses were swept away. That he would raid a mosque, on minimal intelligence, is not out of character."

"Regardless," Jefe said, "with Soult's operatives fanning out all over Europe, we don't have a lot of room to operate. So I can spare a security team in Frankfurt. Now, with that out of the way, tell me about these messages to Washington."

Lawton spoke. "I contacted Miriam Anson. You remember her from the Bureau. The contact was indirect, via our man at U.N. headquarters. She's going to try to find out who the messages were meant for."

Jefe nodded. He looked at Renate. "I think it's now inarguable that the Brotherhood is up to something. It's not clear, however, whether they're taking advantage of events or instigating them."

"Instigating?" Lawton asked. "You mean the riots?"

"We're getting indications they're not spontaneous."

Both Lawton and Renate responded with silence as they absorbed the news.

Lawton finally spoke. "How sure are we?"

"Fairly sure. The problem is tracking down the agitators. The signs of organization are there, buried in the chaos, but that's all we know for sure. Somebody hopes to accomplish something with this civil unrest." Jefe tipped back his chair and closed his eyes for a moment.

Renate said, "The Brotherhood loves nothing more than a good war."

Jefe opened his eyes and nodded. "But street violence is different. Civil unrest makes investors nervous. That doesn't help the Brotherhood. They may be funding someone, but I would guess that someone isn't marching precisely to the Brotherhood's tune."

"Perhaps," Renate said. "At the very least, the message traffic seems to show the Brotherhood pushing for American intervention in Pakistan. Nuclear intervention."

"Let's hope your friend can track down the recipient," Jefe said to Lawton. "I know I don't need to remind you that we represent the United Nations. Our first and primary purpose is to ensure the safety of all peoples. A nuclear exchange in south Asia will kill a lot of people, but it won't make anyone safer."

"You'll get no argument here," Lawton said.

"In the meantime," Jefe said, "I've told Assif to put all his resources into decoding today's traffic."

"Today's?" Renate asked.

Jefe looked at her. "They know you're alive. They sent someone to kill you. It didn't work."

"Which means," Lawton said, "they'll be talking about it. That should tell us who was involved."

"Then we kill them," Renate said, her gaze flat and unbending.

"No," Jefe said. "We can't kill our only leads, Renate. We have to find out what they're up to and who they're working with."

"Fine," she said. "We do it your way. For now."

* * *

A short while later, Lawton followed Renate into her office. She sat at her desk and logged on to her computer, ignoring him as if he weren't there. He was used to it and ignored it.

"I know how you feel," he said.

"Oh you do, do you?"

"I most certainly do." He felt a spark of irritation. "Look, Renate, you're not the only person who's had loved ones killed and feels responsible. There are plenty of us out here with that on our consciences." To this day, he could not think of the girl in Los Angeles who had watched her father die, and had blamed him for it, without wanting to rip someone to shreds.

Her jaw set tighter, and she tapped on her computer keys as if he had vanished.

"Listen," he said finally. "If you let your anger get in the way, more people are going to die. And this time, it *will* be your fault."

Her gaze finally lifted to him, and for an instant the icy cold in her blue eyes gave way to a hunted, haunted expression that triggered an ache in his chest. That was another feeling he couldn't afford, and he almost wished he hadn't confronted her.

But he also knew what this woman was capable of, and he didn't want her haring off on her own.

Finally she spoke, once again shielded behind

her glacial facade. "Are you going to help me capture the people who killed my family?"

"Of course," he said. "And most especially the people behind the plot. But we have to keep our eyes on the ball, Renate. This isn't just about your parents. It's about eleven thousand people who died on Black Christmas, not to mention the thousands who will die if Rice decides to use nuclear weapons. They all deserve justice."

"Fine," she said. "Then let's get to work."

Cambridge University, 1669

Isaac Newton sat in the office of his mentor, Isaac Barrow. Barrow held the recently created Lucasian Chair in mathematics and had taken Newton under his wing, though many could not understand why. He had even attempted to gain his pupil attention in the world of mathematics by sending copies of one of Newton's papers to some of the more prominent mathematicians of the day.

To many, he knew, Newton seemed a rather undistinguished scholar, but largely because he did his best work when on his own. The period of the plague outbreak—when he had been forced back to his home to avoid infection—had proven to be some of the most fertile years of his life.

Barrow had seen a thirst in the young man, however, a deep and abiding thirst for knowledge, and an unwillingness to be bound by conventional thinking. It was this that had attracted him, since he'd been rather unconventional most of his own life, as well.

But now he had momentous news for the younger man. "I have decided to give up this chair, Newton."

The younger man lifted his eyebrows. "Whyever should you do that, sir?"

"Because I am weary of it. In my youth, I pledged to study divinity. I think 'tis time I kept my pledge."

"But, sir…"

Barrow shook his head. "Do not argue with me, Master Newton. I have made my determination, and I have taken the necessary steps. I have also chosen my successor."

"I hope you did not choose Phyfe."

Barrow laughed. "You know me better than that, I should have thought. No, I have named you. When I depart at end of term, you shall replace me."

"But—"

Barrow waved an irritated hand. "Enough. I have chosen well. But there is something I must share with you, and I must give you some instruction with before I depart."

Newton nodded, unconsciously sitting forward in his chair.

"As a young man, I was considered somewhat troublesome…particularly after a speech I gave on the anniversary of Guy Fawkes Day. It was considered expedient to send me on travels throughout Europe, to report back to Cambridge on the universities over there. You may have heard of that?"

"That you traveled, yes."

"Well, I certainly traveled, and in the event I traveled rather more than anyone expected, including myself. My ship, at one point, was attacked and set afire by pirates. Great adventures, Newton. The kind worthy of a book, I daresay. But not necessarily enjoyable while they were happening."

"Pirates, eh?"

"Pirates. I escaped with nothing but the clothes on my back and a little something I picked up when I was in Smyrna." Barrow chuckled. "Which is to say I escaped with the only thing that mattered. I intend to pass it on to you. I think you will make far better use of it than I ever could. What do you know of alchemy?"

"A little. I have looked into hermeticism, as I have into many things."

"Well, I believe you will want to look into it a bit further now. And I believe you will also begin to unlock some of the mathematical puzzles with which you have struggled."

Newton edged forward a bit more. Excitement

was written all over his face. "Why do you say that?"

"Because I am about to pass to you an ancient mystery. It is, I believe, a part of the ancient mysteries the Scottish Rite mentions. But I also feel that this may be but one part of a larger puzzle."

"What are you talking about?"

"This." Rising, Barrow went to a wall panel. He did something quick with his fingers, and the panel opened to reveal a space behind it. "No one knows this is here but I—and now you," Barrow said. "The man who built it for me died in the plague. Sad story. But it is now our secret, and ours alone."

Newton rose and went to stand beside him. In the cavity was a small chest of beaten, aged copper. Barrow lifted it out and sagged a little, as if it were heavier than its size indicated. He carried it to the reading table and set it down. A moment later, he released a spring and the top popped open. Inside was a leather-wrapped object.

"'Tis said to be one of the tablets of Thoth," Barrow said.

Newton gasped, his entire face lighting with amazement as Barrow pulled aside the wrappings and revealed an emerald pyramid.

Carefully Barrow lifted it in his palm and held it toward the window. "Within this stone is a window," Barrow said. "I believe you will be able to understand what you see better than I, which is why I pass it to you. It is said this once belonged to Pythagoras, who got it out of Egypt."

Newton leaned closer, peering into the depths of the stone. He was the picture of amazement.

"It is yours now," Barrow said gently, and placed it in the younger man's hand. "Yours to study and learn from. But keep it secret, Isaac. Very secret. It could be worth your life if anyone learns you have it."

21

Prague, Czech Republic, Present day

Kasmir Al-Khalil had been too nervous to eat that morning, yet now he found himself ravenously hungry. Soon, he thought. Soon he would exit the subway train and make his way up the escalator to the car awaiting him at the Invalidovna station. By the time he and his driver arrived back at their safe house, where his sister would have a meal waiting, hundreds would be dying.

As well they should. Kasmir had been aching for another chance to act again ever since Christmas, when he had destroyed a church full of infidels in Baden-Baden. In the weeks since, hundreds of Muslims had died in wave after wave of reprisals. It was time to strike again, to exact justice for those who felt they could kill with impunity.

The planning for this operation had been simplicity itself. Indeed, the hand of Allah was clearly visible in the events of the past two weeks, ever since intermediaries had introduced Kasmir to the chemist from Chechnya, who had once been a major in the Red Army. Ricin, a lethal toxin derived from castor beans, could be had, if the price was right. As it turned out, that price had been well within the operating budget for Kasmir's group. Within a week, Kasmir had one hundred milliliters of atomized ricin, a poison so toxic that a droplet the size of the head of a pin was sufficient to kill an adult.

Now that deadly bottle rested in an open backpack beneath Kasmir's seat. Kasmir had chosen his seat with care. It was directly beneath the speaker that broadcast announcements. That, coupled with the sounds of the train itself, would mask the hiss as the ricin was released into the air. To start the process, Kasmir needed only to pull the string that ran from his backpack to the ring on his middle finger. Then he would exit the train and be safely away before the poison concentration in the air reached toxic levels. If their calculations were correct, that would happen as the train reached the busy Florenc station, where the yellow and red subway lines met, beneath the main bus station in Prague. Kasmir had chosen that site to yield maximum exposure.

The static-filled speaker burst to life, announcing the Invalidovna stop. Kasmir pulled the string as he rose from his seat, then walked to the exit door and waited. This was the time of greatest danger, he realized. If someone noticed that he was leaving his backpack behind, they might call him back for it. And there would be no way for him to retrieve it without receiving a fatal dose of the toxin. His heart pounded as he counted the seconds until the door opened.

Ten seconds and Kasmir almost leaped from the train. He walked briskly, forcing himself not to run, so as not to attract attention, and made his way out of the station into the morning sunlight. Only then did he realize he had been holding his breath.

"How did it go?" his partner asked as he climbed into the car.

"Fine," Kasmir answered.

"Praise be to Allah."

"Yes," Kasmir said. "Praise be to Allah."

For Magda Gross, it had been a very ordinary Tuesday morning. The emergency room at the Kotol Hospital had not been exceptionally busy, and apart from a cardiac case and treating the abrasions of a cyclist who had been struck and fallen in morning traffic, she had spent much of the day reviewing treatment charts for the few patients left from the overnight shift and thinking about how she would tell Stefan Dubcek that she could not marry him.

Now, as she sat in the hospital cafeteria with her lunch, she considered again whether she should accept his proposal. Stefan was a good man, after all. They were both doctors, so he would understand her demanding work schedule and her dedication. He was kind, if sometimes a bit brusque, and even an adequate dancer. He played the violin, she the cello, and while neither of them had had much time for their music of late, it was still a shared interest and a common topic of conversation. All in all, any woman in her position ought to consider him a perfect catch and leap at the opportunity of marriage.

And yet, she noted with a pang of self-doubt, somehow the spark just wasn't there. Perhaps it was that he was a neurologist, with all the psychological oddities that so often accompanied that specialty. When they discussed music or medicine, he could be charming. But then there were the long periods when he seemed utterly lost in his own thoughts and she felt utterly alone. Even the sex, after their first novelty-heightened encounters, had become routine. He was an adequate lover. He would make an adequate husband. But did she really want "adequate"?

She had gone back and forth over these same thoughts for two days, and in the end she kept coming back to the same place: that marriage should be something more than merely good enough. Again and again, she heard the voice of her late father echoing through her mind: *Choose the man who makes your heart sing and your life will always be filled with music.* Stefan was a good man, but he did not make her heart sing.

Her heart tearing at that thought, she almost did not notice the insistent buzzing at her belt. She reached down and switched off her pager, knowing already what it meant. Rising to her feet, she left her lunch uneaten and made her way back to the E.R.

"Forty-six-year-old female presenting with acute respiratory distress," the head nurse said, guiding Magda toward the treatment room. "Nonsmoker, no personal or family history of respiratory disorders. Pulse is eighty-five, blood pressure is ninety-five over fifty, temperature thirty-seven-point-two, lips are cyanotic."

"Thank you," Magda said, quickly scanning the chart as she stepped into the room. "Ivana Navatny? I'm Doctor Gross. When did you start to feel sick?"

"About an hour ago," the patient said through the clear plastic oxygen mask. "It was as if I could not catch my breath."

"Was anyone else at work ill?" Magda asked as she looked at the monitor. The woman's face was pale and her lips faintly blue. Magda lifted the woman's hand and saw that the flesh beneath her fingernails was also bluish. The oxygen monitor read ninety-two percent. "Ivana? Was anyone else at work ill?"

But the woman did not answer. Indeed, she seemed unable to focus her eyes, and beads of sweat had broken out on her forehead. The digital temperature monitor now read thirty-eight-point-seven degrees, well above normal, and the oxygen reading had slipped to eighty-nine percent.

"Increase oxygen," Magda said, her voice crisp and cool as she tried to make sense of the symptoms. Patient cyanotic. Respiratory distress. Fever. Now the woman's hands began to quake.

"Doctor Gross," another nurse called from the door of the treatment room.

"Not now," Magda said.

"Please," the nurse said. "Another patient just arrived with the same symptoms."

"Watch her oxygenation," Magda said to the head nurse, indicating Ivana as she herself made for the door. "If it gets worse, we'll need to intubate her. Schedule a chest X-ray. It looks like influenza, but the rapid onset has me concerned."

Four hours later, with twelve more patients admitted and at least fifty others at other hospitals, Magda grew far more concerned. That evening, when the Prague police discovered the backpack and the empty aerosol bottle within it, the source

of the mysterious illness began to become clear.
Three days later, after the bottle had been shipped
to a laboratory in Paris and examined, the "Prague
Flu" would be confirmed as ricin poisoning.

But that news would come too late for Ivana
Navatny and one hundred twelve others, including Magda herself, who had inhaled the toxic particles wafting from her patients' clothes.

Two days after Ivana Navatny arrived at the
E.R., Stefan Dubcek held Magda's hand as she
struggled for her final breaths, her lungs hemor-
rhaging and kidneys failing.

And, in those final moments, Magda heard
the music.

22

Strasbourg, France

"*Mesdames et Messieurs,*" Soult said, his voice clear and strong, "we find ourselves at a unique moment in the history of mankind. We—who for centuries wasted our youth and our resources making war on one another—now stand united under a single constitution. We need no longer cower under an American umbrella. We need no longer live in the shadow of the American economy. We are many languages, many cultures. And yet we are one people."

He paused to let that thought resonate in the minds of his audience. He knew it was a message that would sit well with the members of the European Parliament, before whom he had been called to explain why events like Prague could still happen when the Department of Collective

Security had redoubled its efforts. A lesser man would have bristled under the implied criticism, but Soult had expected it. In fact, he had planned for it. These hearings gave him the opportunity to address not only the Parliament but also the hundreds of thousands of Europeans who were watching on television. It was for this reason—and not, as some had suggested, a noble offer to fall upon his sword—that he had persuaded Frau Schmidt to put his name forward to be questioned.

"But the events of these past weeks," he continued, "have left us all deeply scarred. Representatives, there is evil in this world. An evil that destroys cathedrals and murders the faithful. An evil that seeks to sabotage our factories, our banks and our livelihoods. An evil that disperses deadly poisons in our subways and seeks to make us afraid to leave our homes. We have repented for the sins of our ancestors. We have retreated from our empires. We have negotiated. We have bargained. We have opened our doors. And how does this evil respond? With more terrorism."

Now the members hissed, loudly and continuously. While he could not see through the TV cameras into the faces of those who were watching in their homes, he knew that he would have seen echoed there what he saw before him: righteous anger. That was one half of the equation. Now came the time to add the rest.

He lowered his tone, his voice now sober and direct. "As you know, I am honored to serve the European Union in the Department of Collective Security. In that role, I have become intimately familiar with both our strengths and our vulnerabilities. Honesty compels me to report that our vulnerabilities exceed our strengths. Our borders are all but unguarded. We lack the resources to investigate immigrants. Most of all, we lack the will to do what must be done in order to identify and protect ourselves from terrorists in our midst. In our noble dedication to liberty, we deny ourselves the very tools we most need to combat this menace. When we board a train, a tram or a subway, we hope that no one has planted a bomb. We can only hope, because we lack the vigilance to *know.*"

The members were hushed, shifting uncomfortably in their seats, nodding. Fear. That was the other half of the equation. Fear and anger, seeded and watered, tended and directed. Those were, and had always been, the keys to control the will of the masses.

The time had come to play upon the weakness of this particular audience. Under the EU Constitution, the role of the Parliament was severely constrained. Only the President of the European Commission—the executive branch of the EU government—could propose new legislation. And while the Parliament elected the President, it was hardly a free and open election. The European Council—comprising the heads of state of the member nations—nominated a single candidate, who the Parliament could only approve or disapprove.

Constrained to vote upon only those laws proposed by the President, and only for or against the Presidential candidate proposed by the Council, the Parliament had but one real power. It could, at any time, issue a vote of no confidence and thereby remove the President and his Commission from office. It was this provision that made Soult's ultimate plan possible, and he intended to make full use of it.

Soult smiled, his posture friendly and open. "Members of Parliament, I have two dogs. You no doubt saw them in the media coverage of my appointment. I had no idea that a simple walk around my lawn would acquire such attention or gain them such fame, but such is the way things work in our day and age."

The members laughed, as he had expected. He had been walking his dogs when two television reporters approached him to ask about his new job. In waving to the reporters, he had dropped one of the leashes, and the smaller of his dogs, René, a springer spaniel always eager to make new friends, had dashed forward to greet the female reporter. In a comic scene, captured in full on film and broadcast on every news report in Europe, Soult had coaxed the wayward pup with a dog treat. The moment had instantly humanized him to the people of Europe, and indeed, that had been precisely his intent when he had dropped the leash.

"Fortunately," he continued, still smiling, "it was the smaller of my dogs that slipped away. The other, the Great Dane, would no doubt have knocked the poor woman off her feet in his attempt to befriend her."

Again they laughed, and he let the laughter die before he continued, his voice now firm. "But perhaps it was not mere fortune. For while I hold René's leash with a light hand, I wrap Jacques' leash around my wrist. It is not that I love Jacques any less, or consider him inferior in any way. I simply recognize that, owing to his size, he is the greater danger."

He let that thought settle for a moment. "Members, I regret to say that I am not permitted to apply the same common sense in my profession. Yes, there are European terrorists. There are those who would attack this very institution, those who espouse nationalism and decry European unity. And yet, let us not deny what we know, what the attacks in Madrid, and London, and Black Christmas, and now Prague, have made indisputably clear. Not all dangers are equal. Some are tiny springer spaniels, while others are Great Danes."

He lifted a hand, quieting the few murmurs of dissent. "None of us can sanction or excuse the recent wave of violence against peaceful European Muslims. But neither can we safely ignore that vox populi, however shameful and inappropriate its expression may be. Our people recognize the greater danger of Islamic terrorism. And have no doubts among you, the people act because we will not.

"In the name of equality, we ignore the greater danger. In the name of fairness, we are required to examine all threats as if they were equal, even when we know they are not. Black Christmas and the Prague attack happened because the Department of Collective Security was neither permitted nor given the legal tools to focus on the gravest threat."

The murmurs of dissent had spread, as he had expected, and now he sat and waited for them to settle. He suspected the members' voices rose as much as a nod to principle as to any real opposition to what he had said. That they quieted so quickly only confirmed his opinion.

"Let me be clear," he said. "I speak not of a pogrom. Europe has known far too many of those, and we must never forget the blood that was shed in the name of religious intolerance. When I walk my dogs, I do not hold Jacques by the throat. That would be shameful. That would be as evil as the evil we face. But I recognize that I must watch him more closely, be more aware when he is tempted away from our common path. For if I were to wait until he began to charge, it would be too late. Just as it was too late on Christmas Day. Just as it was too late in Prague.

"Most of our Muslim neighbors are fine citizens. Indeed, in the wake of what has happened in these past weeks—with so many of their mosques desecrated, so many of their businesses destroyed, and so many of their number beaten and killed— I have no doubt that they, too, would like to be free of the stain of their radical brethren. They, too, would like us to root out the evil among them, so that they can live their lives as safe and peaceful members of a calm and prosperous Europe.

"I cannot give them that hope," Soult said, his voice now in full force, "without the legal authority to focus my efforts on the greater danger. You cannot grant me that authority unless the Commission proposes legal reforms that recognize that greater danger. Members of Parliament, I ask you to press the Commission for such a proposal. Beseech them, in the name of good and decent European Muslims, in the name of all Europeans. Give me the tools to do the job you have put before me. For if I cannot, then the cycle of senseless violence will continue, and more lives will be needlessly lost. I applaud these hearings, and it would be my honor to answer your questions."

* * *

Later that evening, as dinner settled with a fine cigar and a glass of brandy, he watched the coverage of the hearings in the comfort of his hotel room. He did not think himself a man given to self-satisfaction, but even he smiled at his performance.

He turned to Hector Vasquez, who sat beside him. "It went well, I believe."

"Yes," Vasquez said. "You were very persuasive. I myself would have believed you, had I not known better. Perhaps you were an actor in another life."

Soult chuckled, then drew slowly on his cigar and let the smoke rise from his lips. "The Prague incident was brilliant, by the way. Flawless."

"Thank you," Vasquez said. "In the wake of the street uprisings, every extremist group in Europe was eager to exact revenge. I had only to place one of my men among the Prague cell for a few days to provide them with the ricin, then step away and let their anger do our work for us."

"We are still monitoring them?" Soult asked.

"Of course," Vasquez said. "We have had them under surveillance since you told me about them. We can pick them up whenever it will be most useful."

"Let them be for a while," Soult said, now stroking his chin. "We will need them for the final act. We have given the people their *Kristallnacht.* Now we must give them their Reichstag

Fire. Then they will be truly ready for change, for strong leadership, for protection from their fears, for revenge against their tormentors."

"And then," Vasquez said, raising his glass, "we will have them."

Soult raised his glass and completed the toast. "We will have them all."

Washington, D.C.

Miriam Anson was pinned to her desk. Not literally, of course, but she felt the same as she would have if her feet had been nailed to the floor.

Since she had received the partially decoded e-mails from the U.N., she had been living in a world of divided loyalties and secrecy. She couldn't afford to let the Bureau know what she was about for fear word would get back to the wrong people. For fear that they would tell her to bag it.

So she worked on the messages as her other tasks permitted, feeling on the one hand that she might be betraying her own agency and government, and feeling on the other that she might have a larger loyalty to the world.

Conflicted barely described it.

If messages from Germany to the Federal Reserve were also traveling to someone in the White House, then they were traveling in pouches she could not trace. E-mails would have been nice, but a lot of agencies relied on couriers for things that needed full secrecy. This town was awash in couriers. How could she possibly know which ones to watch?

Nor would watching them tell her a damn thing.

So, taking advantage of the quieter hours and feeling pressed by the increased nuclear saber-rattling from the Rice Administration since the Prague attack, she'd been staying later and later at her desk.

That night she finally let Terry in on the secret. Marriages couldn't withstand secrets, not secrets that were having such an effect on one of the spouses. She had to tell him why she was working so late so often. She had to tell him why she was so worried and distracted.

At first he was overjoyed to hear that Lawton was still alive. He even accepted Lawton's employment with a secret U.N. organization. But when she started talking about the encrypted messages…that was when he got tough.

"Let me see them," he said.

"But…"

"Miriam." His voice took on a warning edge she had never heard from him before. It was enough. She couldn't handle this alone any longer.

She went to her home office and took the papers out of her safe, then gave them to Terry. While he scanned them, she filled him in on what she knew. Which was little enough, actually.

"Basically," Terry said finally, having scanned all the e-mails, "Tom thinks there's a plant in the White House who's pushing for the use of nukes."

"That's the basic outline."

Terry nodded, his dark face creased with thought. "It does seem fishy. You said these messages originated from a private bank in Frankfurt and went directly to the Fed in Washington?"

"Yes."

He nodded again and lifted his gaze. "Have you ever heard my favorite conspiracy theory?"

"What's that?"

"That big money rules the world. Like a huge shadow government, bound by no law except to fulfill the…shareholders' own wishes. That wars are good for them because they generate profit. That peace is sometimes good because it generates investment. But basically, Miriam, they rule the roost, and decide when we have war and when we have peace."

Miriam was looking at him with astonishment. "What makes you think that?"

"Life. I'm a cop. A detective. I've been paying attention to the news for a long time. The news and editorial opinion. I can see the shadows behind the puppets. Always have."

He smiled crookedly. "Call me crazy if you want."

"I might have a couple of years ago. I can't now, Terry."

He rose, tossing the e-mails on the table, and began to pace their apartment. "I was thinking about moving closer to D.C. This commute is killing us both."

Miriam gaped. "What?"

"Just muttering. While you've been working all the time, I've been house hunting."

"Any luck?"

"Not yet." He turned and faced her. "And it's going to have to wait until we sort this out. Tom's right, Miriam. Someone is pushing Rice."

"How can you be sure of that?"

He held up the messages. "Maybe you should read these again. Or maybe you should just watch Rice's face when he makes a speech. Remember how he used to be? All folksy Southern charm? You couldn't help but like the guy, even if you didn't like his opinions. But now…" Terry shook his head. "Now he looks as if he's been gutted."

"Black Christmas gutted us all."

"That's not what I mean. There's something in his eyes. I don't think he believes what he's saying anymore."

"About using nuclear weapons?"

"About much of anything. I'm used to reading

people's faces, honey. It's as if he's mouthing someone else's lines. So the question is, who in the government might have a link with that Frankfurt bank? Or with the people who are using the bank for a front?"

"Someone with banking connections." Miriam nodded. "Well, that covers about a quarter of the White House and cabinet."

Terry chuckled. "Ain't that the truth."

"But it would have to be someone in a position to talk to Rice privately. To really press him."

"To twist his arm with some kind of information. Rice doesn't strike me as the type to sell out for money."

"Me neither." Miriam thought for a few minutes, then rose from the couch and headed for her computer. "I need to do some background checks on Rice's senior appointees."

"I'll bring the coffee." Terry Tyson had no intention of being left out of this one.

Two hours later, they both spoke the same words at the same instant: *Morgan-Redstone.* Miriam looked up at Terry, and he nodded.

"It's got to be him."

Everyone in America, and many around the world, knew about the attempted assassination of Grant Lawrence. He had locked up the Democratic nomination with a near sweep of the Southern primaries and had just finished giving his victory speech in Tampa, Florida, when he was shot twice in the chest. Miraculously, Lawrence survived the shooting, but it had been a near-run thing, and he had been in and out of a coma for weeks afterward. As a result, the Democratic nomination had passed to Alabama Senator Harrison Rice.

But only a handful of people knew what had really happened in those fateful months. The official explanation was that Lawrence had been shot by a deranged loner, a former army private from Atlanta. And indeed, that man had pulled the trigger. But that had been only the tip of a larger conspiracy, including an Idaho rancher named Wes Dixon, who ran a training camp for Guatemalan insurgents. The attempted assassination—and the training camp—had been paid for by Edward Morgan, a senior vice president at his father's bank… Morgan-Redstone.

Miriam had led the FBI SWAT team that had taken down Dixon and his Guatemalan mercenaries. But Dixon had been killed in the firefight, and Edward Morgan had vanished in New York. With Morgan's disappearance, all ties between the assassination and Morgan-Redstone had evaporated. With no way to press the investigation forward, Miriam had given in to the inevitable and allowed the FBI to portray the Grant Lawrence shooting as an isolated act.

Perhaps not even Harrison Rice knew that he owed his presidency to a brutal, criminal act financed by Edward Morgan. There was certainly nothing in his behavior to suggest any involvement. While Morgan had been Rice's college roommate, Miriam had found no evidence linking Rice to the Lawrence shooting.

But neither Miriam nor Terry could see any reason for the nomination of Phillip Allen Bentley to the position of National Security Advisor. Bentley had no background in intelligence and had never belonged to any of the dozens of foreign policy think tanks that comprised the national security apparatus. Apart from a dry dissertation on the history of international credit banking in feudal Europe, there was no evidence that Bentley had any interest in or aptitude for a national security appointment.

And yet, there he was, nominated by Rice and swiftly confirmed by a nearly unanimous Senate.

Miriam was less interested in what Bentley's résumé lacked than what it said. For the fifteen years prior to his appointment, Phillip Allen Bentley had been a senior executive at Morgan-Redstone…and a personal protégé of Jonathan Morgan himself.

Jonathan Morgan was a star on the international banking scene. He had three times served on the board of directors of the World Bank and had headed a debt relief agency for Eastern European nations emerging from the Soviet Bloc. A thirty-year member of the Council on Foreign Relations, Jonathan Morgan himself would have been a logical choice for National Security Advisor.

And Jonathan Morgan was Edward Morgan's father.

"It was a proxy nomination," Terry said. "Rice couldn't nominate Morgan—there would have been too many questions about his son's disappearance. So Bentley got the job instead."

"And he probably still answers to his old boss," Miriam said. "Morgan has close ties with the European banking community in Frankfurt. His son paid for the assassination attempt on Grant Lawrence. His protégé becomes National Security Advisor. And we have encrypted messages from a Frankfurt bank to someone who is close to the President. It all fits."

"Yes," Terry said. "It does. The question is, what are you going to do about it?"

23

Riyadh, Saudi Arabia

Ahmed Ahsami reviewed the pages of transaction reports and banking network message traffic with the sharp, cold eye of a desert adder. His source in the Saudi bank had been eager to help after Ahmed had explained how the man's former contact, Yawi Hassan, had been killed. His source had used his access to the banking network, coupled with computer skills that stretched far outside the law, to unearth a mountain of data about international banking traffic from Frankfurt to individual Muslims and Islamic organizations. The man's eagerness had been both a blessing and a curse. A blessing in that the man had done his research quickly. A curse in that the man had been so thorough that now Ahmed was forced to wade through hundreds of pages looking for the single thread he needed.

The call to *maghrib,* or sunset prayer, was a welcome distraction. Ahmed spread his prayer mat on the balcony outside his office and knelt facing Mecca.

In the name of the merciful and compassionate God. Praise belongs to God, the Lord of the worlds, the merciful, the compassionate, the ruler of the day of judgment! Thee we serve and Thee we ask for aid. Guide us in the right path, the path of those Thou art gracious to; not of those Thou art wroth with; nor of those who err.

This opening chapter of the Koran, the *Fatiha,* began each of the three cycles that composed the sunset prayer. With each cycle, Ahmed stood, then knelt, turned his head to the right, then to the left, and finally prostrated himself to manifest his submission and devotion to Allah. Although no one was near enough to hear him, he concluded the sunset prayers with the traditional benediction: *May the peace, mercy, and blessings of God be upon you.*

Hoping that a merciful Allah would guide his eyes, Ahmed decided to forgo dinner and return to the sheaf of papers on his desk. It was then that he found the series of transactions from a private bank in Frankfurt, via an intermediary in France, to the terrorist cell his men had attacked in Vienna.

Berg & Tempel AG.

Ahmed could not help but to chuckle at the way the bank's founders had hidden their secret in the open. *Berg* was the German word for "mountain" and *Tempel* the word for "temple." Mountain & Temple. Temple Mount. Veltroni had been right after all.

Ahmed had found the heirs of the Knights Templar.

His search grew far easier now, as he focused on the transactions and messages to and from Berg & Tempel. It was all there. The disbursements for Black Christmas. The transaction in Vienna that Yawi had found, which had led Ahmed to send him to his death. And, three weeks ago, the disbursement to Prague. Each funneled through an intermediary in France, a different intermediary each time. Doubtless those were single-use accounts, set up for and closed immediately after each transaction. He knew there was no way to track down the intermediary. The men behind this would be far too clever for that.

But perhaps he could track down the final recipients. He had done so in Vienna, after all, although he now realized that information had been bait. Ahmed had snapped at that bait, and Yawi had died for it. But now Ahmed was inside their information loop, and what he had was not bait but critical intelligence, evidence of their involvement in murder on a global scale.

Ahmed briefly considered taking the evidence to the authorities, but only briefly. He had no good reason to be in possession of it, and no wish to explain his own role in the events of the past months. Nor did he wish to burn his source at the Saudi bank, a dedicated young Muslim whose only crime had been to peel back the layers of secrecy that shielded money and those who moved it.

No, this was something he would handle himself. As he continued to scan the documents, he spotted a second set of disbursements ending in Prague, dated four days ago. A second payment for the ricin attack? Perhaps, but not likely. The first payment had been substantial, more than Ahmed had spent on any single target on Black Christmas. Ricin, it seemed, was an expensive weapon.

But if not a second payment for the subway attack, then what? Obviously the same terrorist cell had been paid for another attack. He checked again the dates for the first payment to Prague and the subway attack. Twelve days apart. The pattern was consistent with Ahmed's own practice of shifting funds as late as possible, lest a bank auditor get suspicious and investigate the transaction before the operation could be launched.

Ten days. At most. And probably less.

That was how long Ahmed had to find the cell

and organize an operation against them. He picked up the telephone and called his deputy.

"We must go to Prague," he said without preamble. "Make the necessary arrangements. We leave tomorrow."

Vatican City

Monsignor Veltroni looked across the tea table at Pablo Cardinal Estevan. Both sipped Earl Grey, and ate biscuits and cakes in the English style, a custom the cardinal had adopted a generation ago. It was one of the many ways Estevan used to put his guests off guard. Veltroni had long since learned to withstand the charm and the food.

"So, what are you hearing from your young priest in Guatemala?"

"Nothing," Veltroni said, wondering why they were once again covering this ground. "I still believe he must have died during the raid on the village where he was assigned."

"But surely that would have been reported to the bishop."

"I doubt it, Your Eminence. Why would the Guatemalan police want to tell a bishop they had killed one of his priests? No, such a thing would be conveniently overlooked."

"Perhaps. Perhaps." The cardinal nodded dubiously. "But you will tell me if you hear anything?"

"Of course." Then Veltroni could no longer hold in the question that had been plaguing him since the outset. "Eminence, why are we concerned whether some Mayan codex indicates that the Savior might have married and had children? I understand it would shock people, but it would expose no flaw in our faith."

Estevan frowned as he nibbled on a small biscuit. "No, you're right. It would expose no flaw in our faith. Merely a flaw in our story. It makes us appear liars."

"Not if the information was presented in a positive light. The Holy Father could announce that we had learned something new and wonderful about our Lord."

Estevan sniffed. "That codex must come into the hands of the Church. Only the Church can rightfully judge its contents and decide what, if anything, needs to be made known to the world."

"Yes, Eminence."

Estevan smiled, but there was little warmth in the expression. "Remember your vows to the Stewards, Monsignor. We will protect the faith with our lives, if necessary."

"I remember."

Indeed, he remembered very well. But protecting the faith with his life was a far cry from lying about it. Veltroni hoped he concealed his feelings for the rest of the visit, and when he at last escaped he felt as if he were emerging from a dungeon, rather than the well-appointed apartment of a senior member of the Curia.

The stroll back to his own much less impressive apartment would take about ten minutes unless he encountered someone he knew…which on any given day proved nearly inescapable. On this late, rainy afternoon, however, he met no one and reached his apartment without delay.

Once inside, he indulged himself by stripping off not only his coat, but his cassock, as well. He donned his favorite pair of pajamas, though it was still too early, and made himself a cup of rich hot cocoa, even giving in to the temptation to top it with whipped cream.

The blustery weather seemed to justify the indulgence, along with the fact that he had no further appointments or duties that day. It was a rare occurrence indeed when a monsignor in the Vatican could simply put his feet up at five in the afternoon and declare the day over.

The decadence of the hot chocolate satisfied some deep craving. He chose a novel rather than television, which might actually intrude on his perfect moments of escape with reminders of reality, and the rattle of the cold wind against the elderly windows made him feel snug.

But the novel couldn't hold his attention. His thoughts persisted in drifting back to his conversation with Estevan and his inescapable sense that there was more to the Codex than the Cardinal was telling him.

After all, he thought, his gaze drifting from the printed page to the gray world beyond his window, an ancient Mayan codex probably only hinted at things that could be interpreted as referring to Christ. It couldn't *prove* anything. Not even all of the legends that Cortez had encountered—and the crosses to go with them—had been taken as proof. Why should a codex, containing the roots of a myth, be considered powerful enough to weigh against the gospels?

Gospels that, he knew, were utterly silent on whether Jesus had married. Gospels that had clearly been edited. And all of which revealed at least some political purpose.

The Word of God, as he knew from his studies, had passed through the minds and hands of many men before reaching its final form. The truth was still undeniably within the pages of the Bible, but one had to make allowances for the times in which they were written, the men whose hands held the pen, and the audiences for whom they were intended. The Codex, if it were ever found, would probably be accorded even less status than the Nag Hammadi gospels, which the Church actually suggested that the faithful read for purposes of comparison.

So…again his mind balked. Rain rattled at the windows now, a wintry rain with little gentleness. His apartment was growing chilly, and he wasted a moment or two trying to decide whether to light the fire or just wrap up in a blanket. At the moment, either one seemed like too much effort.

Sighing, he set his book aside. Estevan was up to something, and a poor monsignor would probably never know what it was. All he knew for certain was that he regretted sending Steve Lorenzo into that hornets' nest, and his prayers morning and night begged for the life of his young friend.

A rap at his door startled him. He wasn't expecting anyone, and friends always called first, because they were all so busy most of the time.

Putting aside his beverage, he went to answer the knock. Outside his door, in the yellow of the overhead hallway lights, stood a young man wrapped in a heavy coat.

"Monsignore," he said in accented Italian, "I have been asked to give you this letter."

"Thank you." Veltroni's hand automatically went to his pocket for a tip, but he was in his robe and pajamas, and the young man disappeared before he could ask him to wait a moment.

Curious.

The monsignor closed his door and returned to his sofa, where he had enough light to see. Outside, the wind and rain blustered almost angrily.

His name was typed on the envelope. The return address was that of the Vatican press office. Interesting.

He tore open the flap and pulled out a thin sheet of paper.

Under the letterhead of the press office he read:

Monsignore, we received this message in error. It appears to be personal. Forgive our intrusion.
Salvio Viglio, O.F.M.

Another sheet lay beneath it, smudged and dirty, but clearly addressed to him.

Monsignor Giuseppe Veltroni, the Vatican.
Joe, I am alive and well, but you will not see me again. I am committed to my work here. That which was hidden is hidden once again and must remain so. Steve.

Veltroni read the missive three more times, then decided that he needed a fire after all. It had been well laid by the person who cared for his apartment, and in a few minutes the blaze in the fireplace was bright. Without another thought, he threw both sheets of paper and the envelope into the flames.

Then he offered a prayer of thanksgiving, both for Steve Lorenzo's safety and for the young priest's decisions. Veltroni was but a monsignor, bound by vows of obedience and too exposed here in Rome to keep secrets. But Lorenzo was half a world away, far removed from overseers. The good father had apparently reviewed the Codex and decided, for reasons of his own, that its exposure might bring harm to his flock.

Lacking any basis to second-guess Lorenzo's decision, Veltroni could both accept and celebrate it. That night, for the first time in months, he slept the sleep of the righteous.

Rome, Italy

The Poisoning in Prague, as the media had dubbed it, had Office 119 teams in Eastern Europe scrambling, but so far their efforts had been hampered by the more direct and visible work of the Czech and EU authorities. Crackdowns on mosques and madrassas had been swift and unrelenting, yet thus far they had made no headway in identifying the attackers.

That in itself had begun to trouble Renate.

It was unrealistic to expect as lucky a break as the FBI had received after the 9/11 attacks. On the evening of those attacks, Boston airport authorities had found two suitcases that were to have been on one of the hijacked aircraft, but which had missed the flight due to a late connection. In those suitcases, FBI agents found complete plans for the attacks on New York and Washington, including pilot training materials, the names of the terrorists and the journal of the lead hijacker, Mohammed Atta. The evidence had literally fallen into the FBI's lap, courtesy of an airline baggage-handling screwup.

Neither the FBI nor Interpol nor the national and local authorities—nor Office 119—had been as fortunate after Black Christmas. Two months had passed, and, despite hundreds of agencies fielding tens of thousands of agents worldwide, there had been no arrests. There had been only a single raid in Vienna…a raid that, for all the media hype, had developed no new evidence, nor even confirmation that those killed had been involved in Black Christmas.

It was maddening, and yet, for Renate, it was something more than that. It was suspicious. She knew it was impossible to commit a perfect crime, and certainly not on a scale such as Black Christmas. That operation had doubtless involved hundreds of planners and operatives, and yet, if any of them had boasted to a wife or friend, it had not reached any investigator's ears. The physical evidence—the remnants of the bombs themselves—pointed in too many directions to point anywhere at all. On the one hand, there had been near-surgical operations aimed at industrial and economic targets. On the other hand, there had been indiscriminate killings in the church bombings. Thousands of potential witnesses had been interviewed, but none of the stories correlated on enough relevant facts to convey any significant information.

Yes. Something was very wrong.

The ringing of the telephone distracted her.

"Yes?" she asked.

"I have good news," Assif said from Frankfurt. "I have decoded a transaction from almost three weeks ago. A substantial transaction. To Prague."

Renate quickly ran through dates in her head. "The ricin attack. We've got them."

"Hold on," Assif said. "There's more. There was another transaction to the same account two days ago."

"A final payment?" Renate asked.

"Maybe, but given the amount of the first transaction, I doubt it." Assif paused for a moment. "I think they're planning something new."

"Send me copies of everything," Renate said.

"Already sent," Assif replied.

"Good. I'll take it to Jefe as soon as I print it. Good work, Assif. This time we have the jump on them."

24

Guatemalan Highlands

You had to be a mountain goat to live here, Steve thought. The mountains were rugged, the result of volcanism, almost all steep cones, except where they ran together. The soil was fertile, the gift of the eruptions, creating thick growth everywhere. The rain had let up, though. The dry season finally seemed to be in full swing.

But even those in flight had to rest, especially the children, though despite the ruggedness of their path, Steve could have traveled another few hours. His body was better conditioned than it had ever been.

But not the children. They wearied faster, and their parents could carry them only so far. One of their party, acting as a scout, had found a sheltered place beside a brook that appeared to be steadily drying up. For tonight there would be enough water, however. A gift from the rains and the mountains.

Men and women, older children in tow, scattered outward around the camp to find edible fruits and plants, and perhaps, if the men were fortunate, some meat for tonight.

Steve and two women were left behind to watch the youngest of the children. The women tended the infants, while Steve provided the daily lessons as best he could, a few minutes each of reading, writing, basic arithmetic and catechism. It was not, he knew, an adequate curriculum, for he was well aware of his limitations as a teacher. But it was better than nothing at all.

Later in the evening, after the day's gatherings had been prepared and shared, the adults settled into the tasks that had consumed Homo sapiens for tens of thousands of years before the advent of agriculture and civilization. They preserved the uneaten food as best they could, wound strippings of vine and animal sinew into twine, fashioned bone and wood and stone into tools to supplement what little they had picked up along their journey, set watch, laid out pallets and slept.

Steve found it difficult to fall asleep that night, however. Three years ago, he would have attributed that to the uneven ground that seemed to provide bumps and hollows in all the wrong places, but he had long since become accustomed to such privations. No, it was his mind and not his body that lay uneasy in the darkness. A vague but certain foreboding seemed to hover in the air like the silk of a spider's web.

Miguel had never rejoined them. Steve kept his sorrow quietly in his heart, for there was nothing else he could do. He watched Miguel's sister, Rita, grow daily quieter, but she never brought the subject up, and he felt in some way that as long as no one ever commented that Miguel was missing, she could cling to her belief that he must still be alive.

But his absence most likely meant one thing: the stalker had killed Miguel. In which case the stalker was still following them. For days Steve had cherished the hope that the Hunter hadn't been able to follow them after they exited the caves on the far side of the mountain, but he didn't really believe it. Anyone good enough to move silently and unseen through these mountains would be able to figure out what they'd done and pick up their tracks again.

Now, trying to sleep, with the feeling of uneasiness seeming to grow with every drip of dew from the leaves above…

He was failing, he thought. He was failing these people. He was failing his church. He had refused to complete his mission.

Odd, he thought, how things seemed to change out here in the jungle. He believed in God, of course, and in Jesus, but…out here, all the rules changed. In fact, almost all the rules became superfluous. They depended on God and each other for every little thing. There was no time for anything else. No time for finer points of theology and doctrine.

Everything had boiled down to the very basic. "Love God above all else, and love your neighbor as yourself." The most important commandment of all.

The thought brought him comfort somehow, and he began to drift off at last. And as he drifted away, he felt himself rise above his sleeping body, then above the canopy of the forest that sheltered them, and then he flew among the stars.

Such a beautiful dream. Peace flowed through him.

You have been chosen.

An empty plain materialized around him, and twelve people, men and women, clad in shimmering robes. He looked down at himself and saw that he, too, wore such a robe.

"Paloma chose you as her successor."

He looked up into a wise, ageless face. "Who are you?"

"You will learn all in due time. For now, it is enough that you call me Nathan."

"All right." He felt no impulse to object, despite his anxiety. Even in the dream, he realized this was more than a dream.

"You have been chosen," Nathan repeated. "Paloma chose you when she entrusted you with the Ruby Codex."

"Chosen for what?"

Nathan smiled. "To be a Guardian of Light, servant of the one true God."

Steve considered that. He had already dedicated his life to God, so that aspect didn't disturb him. But he sensed that being chosen probably involved more trouble than he was already in.

"Why me?" he asked.

"Because Paloma chose you," Nathan answered. "The Guardians are few, because few have the wisdom to know what we know, what you saw when you looked into the Codex."

"What did I see?" Steve asked, remembering the swirling symbols that almost screamed of a deeper meaning, but one he could not ascertain.

"What do you think you saw?"

"Secrets," Steve said without hesitation. "The secrets of the universe itself. But what did they mean?"

"In time," Nathan said. "But first…"

Nathan waved a hand, and suddenly Steve was standing a few feet away from his own sleeping body. As he watched in horror, a man he didn't know crept stealthily out of the woods. In moments he had silently cut the leather thong that tied the bag containing the ruby to Steve's belt.

"I must stop him," Steve said, trying to wake himself. "I must…"

Then he was back on the plain with the twelve. A woman stepped forward and touched his arm.

"This must happen," the woman said, her bright blue eyes boring into him. "This was meant to be."

"I promised!"

"We know of your promise," Nathan said. "But one cannot promise more than that of which one is capable. This was meant to be, so that you can protect your people. With the Codex gone, you can settle your people, and they can build their lives anew. For now they are safe, and safe they will remain."

"All of this was meant to be," the woman said, squeezing his arm. "All of it from the very first day. But now you have a mission."

"Yes." Nathan nodded. "When your people are settled, you must return to the Vatican. Tell your friend Veltroni that the Codex has been stolen. Do not tell him of what you saw, for he is not ready to know. Tell him only what you have been told to say: that the Codex has been stolen. He will join you on the next stage of your quest."

"Why not simply stop the thief now?" Steve pleaded. "Why don't you let me awaken?"

"There are powers that must be laid low," Nathan said. "This is as it must be. This is the only way we can force them out of the darkness. Look now, and see…."

The dream shifted to visions of war. Steve tossed and turned, but he could not pull himself out of the mire of horror. He knelt over charred, maimed bodies, anointing them and praying. He listened to their cries for God, for death, for relief. Women and children lay among the maimed and burned. Lifting his head, he looked around and saw that bodies stretched as far as he could see, all of them screaming in pain and terror.

"This," Nathan said, "we cannot allow. This is what you must prevent. It is why Paloma chose you. It is why the Light has chosen you. Be ready, Priest Lorenzo. Your time has come."

Steve shook himself awake and saw that the sun was rising. The trees above him seemed to glisten in the early light. He could not shake off the dread that had grown as he dreamed, and for long minutes he lay flat on his back, telling himself it had been only a dream. None of it was real. It could not be real. Finally he forced himself to roll onto his side, and horror shook him to his core.

The Codex was gone.

Washington, D.C.

"Miriam?"

Miriam looked up from her computer screen, in

part upset to be distracted from her search of Phillip Bentley's preconfirmation background check, and in part grateful for the break. So far, she knew Bentley was linked to Jonathan Morgan, and she knew he was receiving private messages from a bank in Frankfurt. But that wasn't enough to barge into the office of the National Security Advisor and accuse him of blackmailing the President.

"What is it?" Miriam asked.

"You have a visitor," the secretary said. "A woman named Katherine Dixon. Were you expecting her?"

"No," Miriam said. Katherine Dixon? In an instant, she combed her memory and connected the name. Wes Dixon's widow. "But that's not a problem. Tell her I'll see her in five minutes. And, Jessica, I want to meet her in a clean room."

"Certainly," the secretary said.

Miriam closed the document she was viewing and quickly opened her file on the Dixon case. Yes, she had remembered correctly. Katherine Dixon was not only Wes Dixon's wife, she was also Edward Morgan's sister and Jonathan Morgan's daughter. Scanning the file quickly, Miriam refreshed her memory on the case, then rose and walked out to the lobby.

Katherine Morgan was a striking woman, with strong, patrician features, sandy blond hair shot through with streaks of gray, and tired eyes. She rose as Miriam approached, obviously recognizing her from the many television news reports following the Dixon affair. Her smile was artful, graceful and patently out of step with her true emotions.

"Special Agent Anson?" she asked.

"Yes," Miriam said. "And you're Katherine Dixon. Please come this way."

The J. Edgar Hoover Building had several interrogation rooms, but only a few of these were classified as "clean." The clean rooms were windowless, equipped with the latest countersurveillance technology, with none of the customary video- and audio-recording equipment or two-way mirrors. Clean rooms were reserved for interviews of the most sensitive nature. Miriam couldn't imagine anything more sensitive than what she was about to discuss with Katherine Dixon.

"Thank you for seeing me," Katherine said as she took her seat. "I remembered your name from the news. You are the woman who killed my husband."

"Yes," Miriam agreed, feeling an unpleasant jolt. "I didn't kill him personally, but I was the scene commander. So, yes, you could say I killed him."

Miriam didn't tell her that Wes Dixon had had a rifle trained on her when he had been shot. Or that he would almost certainly have killed her, had Tom Lawton not shot him first. There was no point in antagonizing a grieving widow, and Katherine Dixon didn't seem the type of woman who would come in just to harangue Miriam.

"I know," Katherine said. "I also know he was as good as dead long before you ever saw him in Montana. He'd been dead for a long time."

"How do you mean?" Miriam asked.

"The man I met, the man I married, was a wonderful man," Katherine said. "He was intelligent, diligent, well-read. He loved his country, and he loved the army. And he loved me. Probably in that order."

Miriam didn't respond. It was clear that Katherine intended to tell a story, and Miriam was content to listen. Later, she could ask questions to fill in the gaps. But as she had learned all the way back in her academy training: when a subject is willing to talk, don't do anything to get in the way.

"I guess it started as soon as we got married," Katherine continued, "but I didn't notice it until after the Gulf War. Wes began to keep secrets from me. I'd been told that was fairly common for men who had seen combat. And Wes's brigade did see action south of Basra, so I thought that's all it was. Later, I told myself it was because he'd been promoted and assigned as the division intelligence officer. He couldn't talk about his work, so I figured he'd gotten into the habit of not talking at all.

"Whenever we went back to visit my family, Wes and Edward and my father would go off fishing or trapshooting, or excuse themselves after dinner to go to my father's study and talk. I knew Wes couldn't talk about military secrets, and besides, Edward and my father weren't foreign spies, they were just bankers. Even so, when I'd ask Wes what he had talked about with them, he'd just shrug and say it was 'guy stuff.'"

Katherine paused for a moment. To Miriam, it seemed obvious that the older woman had thought through and planned what she was going to say. She would not have been shocked to find out that this pause had also been planned.

"Finally," Katherine said, "I confronted him about it. I told him I didn't want state secrets, but I didn't want to be married to a ghost, either. We'd tried to have kids, but that had never worked out. I was living on army bases, and I didn't find much to talk about with most of the other wives. They resented my family's money. So many of them were barely scraping by, and Wes and I could afford to live comfortably, even when he was a junior officer. I had no reason to work. So I sat home all day waiting for a man who, when he did get home, barely said three words to me. As you can guess, we had quite a row about it."

Miriam nodded. Everything Katherine had said so far had been preamble; that much was obvious. Setting herself up as the innocent, unknowing wife.

"Still," Katherine said, "it got better after that. But a year later, he left the army. I asked why, and he just said he was tired of it. But he had loved the army, loved the discipline, loved the structure, loved the sense of mission and purpose. Then, when he said we were moving to Idaho, I knew something was wrong. Neither of us had ever lived out west. It made no sense. I didn't ask where the ranch hands came from. I thought they were probably illegal aliens, passing through, like migrant workers. But Wes's face slowly got tighter. Harder. The man I'd met was hardly there anymore."

Miriam leaned forward, making eye contact, tired of the charade. "So you're saying you didn't know that the ranch you and your husband owned was just a front for a terrorist training camp?"

"No, I didn't," Katherine said, almost convincingly. "Sometimes I heard gunshots, but I thought it was just hunters, or Wes trapshooting with his friends. I had no idea Wes was training guerillas."

"I find that hard to believe," Miriam said, impatience clear in her voice.

"Believe what you want," Katherine said. "My husband is dead. And my brother is dead, too. You didn't kill my husband, Special Agent Anson. Edward did, by dragging him into all of this. And when it all came apart, my father killed Edward."

"First," Miriam said, "the FBI has no evidence that your brother is dead. For all I know, he's living the high life in Monte Carlo. And second, what is 'all of this'?"

"I guess you wouldn't have any reason to read the *New York Times* obituaries," Katherine said. "Edward's body was found last week by a lobster fisherman in Maine."

Miriam sat back, catching the momentary flicker of a smile in Katherine's eyes. Yes, Katherine had planned this entire conversation, right up to the point of saving that revelation until it would have the greatest impact.

"How did—" Miriam began, but Katherine cut her off.

"He was murdered, Special Agent Anson. Gunshot wound to the back of the head. Tied into a weighted canvas sack and dumped into the ocean. He might never have been found, except the sack had torn and snagged on a lobster trap."

"How did they identify the body?"

"My brother was wearing a Rolex wristwatch," Katherine said. "Rolex watches have serial numbers stamped on them, inside the waterproof case. The detectives in Maine sent the serial number to the Rolex offices in Switzerland, and it came back registered to my brother. After that, they checked dental records."

It was plausible, Miriam knew. The same method had been used to identify bodies in the past, most notably in the infamous Albert Walker murder case in England. She could certainly verify the information easily enough.

"What makes you think it was your father who killed your brother?" Miriam asked.

"The last time my brother was seen was the day you tracked down Wes," Katherine said. "He was supposed to go fishing with my father that morning, but my father said he never arrived at the boat. I had no reason to question it at the time. I knew Wes was in trouble, and I knew it was Edward's fault. I was furious with him. Like you, I thought Edward just decided to disappear. But when his body is found, after having been dumped at sea, after he disappeared the day when he was supposed to be fishing with my father…"

"Yes," Miriam said. "I can see where you would draw that conclusion."

"If my father killed my brother," Katherine said, fire flashing in her eyes, "then he knew what my brother was doing. That means he also knew my husband was involved. I knew my father was a cold, ruthless man, but I never suspected… I want you to get him, Special Agent Anson. I want you to get him for all of it. And I'm willing to help. I'll tell you everything I know. Everything I've learned since Wes was killed. I'll take a polygraph. Wes was a good man, and my father turned him into an evil one. I won't forgive that. I want you to get him."

Miriam nodded. If everything up to that moment had been scripted, that last speech had come from somewhere else. The rage was evident in Katherine Dixon's eyes, the eyes of a woman who wanted vengeance. That part, at least, was true. The case surrounding Edward Morgan had always been a bottomless pit. Now, it seemed, that might change. And Katherine Dixon's timing could not have been better.

"Okay," Miriam said. "First, though, tell me what you know about Phillip Allen Bentley."

"You mean Daddy's lapdog?" Katherine said. "What do you want to know?"

"Everything," Miriam said. "Everything."

25

Jan Kott was a former barber who had turned to local politics after the former state of Czechoslovakia split into two nations, the Czech Republic and Slovakia, in 1993. In the years since the "velvet divorce," Jan had become a respected member of the state parliament, both campaigning on and working for an internationalist platform by which his country would meld seamlessly into the European Union.

He was also an Office 119 intelligence asset.

Renate had recruited him four years earlier, during her investigation of an anti-EU bomb plot. Although Jan had not been involved in the plot, he had been a married man romantically involved with a young woman who was among the conspirators. Jan had been in love, and the woman had been using him to get information on security arrangements.

When Renate had approached him, his horror at learning that his young flame meant to ignite more than his passions far outweighed any reluctance he might have had to be a willing spy. Renate had saved both his marriage and his political career, as well as helping him to safeguard his country.

So when he met Renate and Lawton at the train station outside of Prague, it was not with the customary reluctance and resentment that spies usually felt upon meeting their handlers. Instead, he greeted Renate with a warm smile and a long embrace. Movement on the local in-city service hadn't yet been resumed and might not be for some time. They all squeezed together into a small white Mini Cooper and headed into the city.

"Have you learned much?" Renate asked Jan as they drove through winding lanes hardly wider than the medieval carts for which they had originally been designed.

"Yes, the Minister of Banking and Finance was very forthcoming," Jan said. "The problem was not getting the information but keeping him from sharing it with our own police. There is considerable political pressure for a quick and *local* solution to this atrocity."

"I'm sure there is," Renate said. "But this is part of a larger puzzle. I don't just want the people who set off the ricin in the subway. I want their entire network, and that includes many people who are outside the reach of the Czech police."

Jan held up a hand. "I understand. And I gave the Minister of Banking my assurances that this matter would be handled both swiftly and effectively. I said no more than that, nor did I need to. There are advantages to chairing the committee on internal security."

Renate nodded. "I know. That's why I recruited you."

Jan chuckled. "Really? I thought you recruited me for my charm and good looks."

"Those helped," Renate said. "They got you into the trouble that made you vulnerable for recruitment."

For an instant Jan's face began to darken, because Renate's eyes were glacial. But then she offered the briefest flicker of a smile, and Jan broke into a hearty laugh.

"Guilty as charged," he said. Then, with a chivalrous bow of his head, he added, "And eternally grateful for your rescue."

Lawton could see why the man had been so successful in politics. If he could extract a smile from Renate under these circumstances, he could sell ice makers in Siberia.

"So who is the banker we are after?" Lawton asked.

"His name is Mikael Rotel," Jan said, making eye contact with Lawton in the rearview mirror. "There's a dossier beside you in the backseat. Not that there is much to it. He comes from an old banking family. Sixth generation. His family's bank remained open through the Nazi occupation and the Soviet rule. On the surface, they appeared apolitical. In fact, they were simply shrewd businessmen, willing to make such appeasements as were needed in order to keep the bank functioning."

"That fits," Lawton said.

"Here is your hotel," Jan said, pulling to the curb beside a stately building that dominated the block. "The bank is two blocks down, on the left."

"Thank you," Renate said, already reaching for the door handle, but Jan put a hand on her arm.

"If your mission should require you to do anything that might be…embarrassing…you will give me advance warning, please?"

"Yes," she said. "If we can. You are a good man, Jan. I have no desire to compromise you. But I cannot give you promises. Our sources indicate that there is another operation under way, so we may have to act very quickly. There may not be time for…courtesies."

"Of course," Jan said. "Do what you must. Stop these bastards."

"We will try," Renate said, climbing from the car.

"If you need anything at all…" Jan said, letting the sentence trail away. "In my position, I have access to…certain assets."

"Just do what you can to keep your police and the EU Collective Security forces out of our way," Renate said. "That will be enough. We can do the rest, and it will be better for you if we do it ourselves."

At the same moment, twelve blocks away, Ahmed Ahsami and his team were unpacking in a tired apartment that had most certainly seen better days. The outside of the building still bore clear scars from World War II, and the inside bore the scars of careless tenants since. Still, it was within his diminished operating budget.

His cousin in the Saudi Bank had pinpointed the origin of the money here in Prague. A banker named Mikael Rotel, a man descended from the Court Jews of old.

Ahmed had found that story *very* interesting, for while Rotel was no longer Jewish—in fact, his family had found it expedient to become Christian during the nineteenth century—Ahmed could not help feeling some sympathy for what the Court Jews had endured in times past. In fact, it gave him what he believed was a key to why Rotel would become involved in the ricin attack in Prague, as well as the attack on the Catholic churches.

Court Jews had been the moneymen for many of Europe's monarchs after the Templars had been executed and driven away. But while these men had funded the excesses of those who had ruled by "Divine Right," everything from fancy jewels to armies, they had been reviled and abused by those who depended on them.

So even if Rotel's family had found it wise to become Christian early in the nineteenth century and thus had avoided Hitler's purge of European Jews more than a century later, Ahmed suspected Rotel had grown up hearing of his family's mistreatment by the royalty and gentry they had financed.

Ahmed knew all about long memories. His people suffered from the same problem. Add to that the problems of the modern day, and some very angry people emerged. Scarcely surprising that Rotel, a Semite, might choose to join other Semites—Arabs—in a war against Christianity.

But he also knew that Rotel was merely a courier for a bigger cabal. Rotel had not personally funded *Saif Alsharaawi's* attack on Christmas. The money had come from Frankfurt, and no doubt the same people had funded the other Christmas attacks.

But Rotel was his point of entry into the European banking cabal. The Saudi Bank dealt on the fringes of that group, wealthy enough to be a power in its own right, but not entirely welcome in the oldest banking circles in the world. Banking circles, he had lately discovered, that seemed to like to fund *both* sides in a confrontation, thus ensuring they had backed the victor no matter the result.

Ahmed shook his head. Anger he could understand. Rotel he might well be able to understand. But a group of people who worshipped money as their god and had no other moral measuring stick… He thanked Allah that he had a strong faith and the Koran to guide him.

His appointment with Rotel was late in the day. After hours. His cousin had said that Rotel often worked late, so there was nothing unusual in an appointment at such a late hour. Ahmed felt less sanguine. The late hour could have been chosen because Rotel did not wish to be seen with an Arab.

He could have chosen a Western business suit, but for some reason Ahmed decided he preferred to present himself as who he was: a Saudi, a member of the royal family, however minor, and a highly ranked oil minister. He would see if Rotel objected to being seen with such a one as himself by appearing flagrantly Saudi.

He donned the *thobe,* the long white garment that covered him from neck to ankle, and the *ghutra* and *igal,* the embroidered red-and-white scarf and its black rope crown, which secured the scarf. Then he chose his most expensive black *bisht,* the over-robe he wrapped about himself. It was widely bordered with fine gold embroidery, suitable to his station. Because of the cold weather, however, he opted for Western shoes.

A glance in the mirror told him that he appeared as exactly who he was. It seemed important to him this night not to be covert, not to deny his heritage by wearing a Western suit. It seemed important to let Rotel know he was not dealing with just another malcontent but a man who held power in his own right.

Satisfied, he headed for the door of his room. He deliberately left his bodyguards behind. Tonight he sought information, and he felt he would achieve his purpose better without a threat of violence in the background.

Lawton and Renate sat in a Mini across the street from Rotel's bank, sipping strong coffee and trying to keep warm as night descended over the city. They had been warned about Rotel's late hours and might well have avoided this wait, but they had decided they didn't want to risk missing him. They didn't want to have to wait another day. Another day might result in another terror attack.

"I hate stakeouts," Lawton remarked, simply to fill the silence.

"Me, too. They're one of the worst parts of the job."

"Yeah, second to getting shot at."

She started to chuckle, a sound that warmed him more than it probably should have, but the chuckle was cut short by the arrival of a black limousine. From it emerged a man in full Saudi dress. The bank's doorman escorted him inside.

"Interesting," Lawton murmured.

"*Ja.*" Renate was silent for a moment. "Law?"

"Yes?"

"Can you think of any reason why a Saudi would want to visit a European bank?"

"Well, yes, actually. I understand that when things in the Middle East get tense, a lot of wealthy Arabs move their money to European banks."

"And?"

He turned to look at her. "Are you suggesting we hijack a wealthy Saudi?"

"I'm suggesting we go in right now and have a talk with them."

"Do you have an appointment?" The question was half joking.

"No, but I have a badge. Interpol."

He shifted uneasily. "Umm…"

"I know. But it's better than trying to kidnap the two of them on the street to find out what is going on."

He couldn't argue with that, but using false police credentials, such as an Interpol badge, was strictly against Office 119 rules. It was more likely to make the agent memorable. Still, there was little choice.

"Rules were made to be broken," he said finally. "Let's go."

Washington, D.C.

Night thickly blanketed the icy world outside, and Harrison Rice had the feeling it was crawling in through the glass of the Oval Office windows and reaching out with damning tendrils. Tonight he was facing not only Bentley, but Bentley's allies, as well.

"We have to take strong action," General Carlisle was saying. "After the incident in Prague, we *have* to show that we're not going to stand for this. We need to strike a blow that will get the world's attention! *Before* they use ricin or sarin in the New York subway system. Or here at our heart, in the D.C. Metro."

"I want a measured response," Rice said, but he could hear the uncertainty in his own voice. "And I want the perpetrators, not innocents."

"Do you think *they* care about that?" the secretary of defense, Harvey Schiller, asked. "They've been attacking innocent people from the beginning. Suicide bombers in restaurants and buses in the Middle East. Businessmen and secretaries and firemen on September 11. Commuters in London. Catholic churches all over the world, including that Catholic church in Pakistan a few years ago, where they killed worshippers at mass. Now the trains in Prague. Do you think *they* care who they kill? It's about terror, Mr. President. And they think they can keep tweaking us without a response. They think we *won't* respond with all our force. They're counting on it, in fact."

"I couldn't have said it better," Bentley added. "They keep pulling the tiger's tail with impunity. All we do is roar. It's time to let them know that we can bite."

"And we know for a fact," the general chimed in, "that there are terrorists hiding out in the mountains between Afghanistan and Pakistan. At this point it doesn't make a bit of difference whether they were directly involved. The important thing is to let them know what we're going to do to them wherever we find them if they don't stop this."

"But nuclear weapons? They'll leave the place uninhabitable for centuries to come. The radioactive dust will kill many people outside the area."

Bentley nodded. "Yes, Mr. President, it will. But these are bunker-busting nukes. What are we going to leave uninhabitable? Caves and a few nomadic villages around them? It's hardly a loss for the world, sir. And I can guarantee you that there will never be another terrorist attack if you do this."

Rice smiled mirthlessly. "You want to put that guarantee in writing?"

"I will. Gladly. The point is, these damn terrorists feel safe. We hunt them like criminals, and they keep slipping away. I say it's time to fight them as if they'd declared war on the Western world. Because they have, Mr. President. They have."

Rice turned away and looked toward the windows. The night was pressing in, and he began to feel it in his bones. "These are low-yield, tactical weapons?" he asked.

"Yes, sir," the general answered. "They'll burrow into the ground and detonate in the caves and bunkers where these bastards run their operations. We'll minimize the collateral damage but still make the point that the tiger has teeth. Nuclear teeth."

Rice closed his eyes for a few moments, trying to find a way around this. He couldn't. He thought of his own daughter riding the New York subways to classes at Columbia. What if someone used ricin there? What about all the other people in this country who relied on public transportation? Was he to offer them up as sacrificial lambs in this unholy war?

Something deep within him stiffened. He turned and faced the waiting men. "Do it," he said. His voice was firm. "But I reserve the right to recall the planes if at any point I feel it will serve our interests."

The general stood up, grabbing his hat. "We

won't arm the weapons until you send the codes. And we'll keep you apprised at every moment where the task force is."

The darkness had filled him, and all the reassurances from his advisors couldn't make him feel any better. He had just made a choice no president since Truman had made. He had never guessed just how lonely he was going to feel in this office.

26

Prague, Czech Republic

Getting past the doorman and building security proved far easier than Lawton would have expected. Apparently people in Europe were more impressed by a badge than in the U.S. Or at least that seemed to be the case here in Prague, where years of Soviet oppression had perhaps made them less likely to question authority.

They passed through the door without a moment's hindrance, and the security guard at the front desk eagerly directed them to Rotel's office and promised not to warn Rotel they were coming.

Oddly, Lawton believed him. The man had paled at the sight of the badge and clearly preferred not to engage Interpol's attention.

If he hadn't seen the same reaction from the doorman, Lawton might have wondered what the man was hiding. Instead he thought it was a damn shame that so many people had been taught to cower before any sign of authority.

In the elevator, he remarked to Renate, "I prefer my criminals demanding warrants."

She looked at him blankly. He decided the explanation would be too involved and let it go.

"We start pleasantly," she reminded him.

"As long as they do." Sometimes he grew a bit irked at the way Renate seemed to consider him in need of instruction. He'd been a field agent longer than she had.

The elevator doors opened jerkily. Apparently not everything had been repaired since the birth of the Czech Republic. Eighth floor, to the right, and there was the office. Lawton tried the door and found it unlocked. Inside was a receptionist's office, but she had apparently left for the day. Everything on her desk spoke of compulsive tidiness.

From beyond the inner door they could hear male voices. "Knock and announce?" he asked Renate quietly. After all, she was the one with the phony credentials.

"No." Reaching out, she placed one hand on the doorknob and raised her Interpol credentials as if they were a shield. A second later, they were in the room.

Of all the things Lawton had expected to see,

the scene he found was not among them. Rotel was sitting behind his desk with his hands up. The Saudi was sitting on the other side of the desk, pointing a 9mm pistol at the banker.

"Interpol!" Renate said firmly. "Drop the gun!"

At least that was what Lawton assumed she said, since she had spoken in German. Automatically he stuck his hand under his jacket to feel for a gun that was no longer there. The gesture served its purpose, however. The Saudi lowered the pistol and placed it on the floor beside him.

Rotel started shouting in Czech, but Renate silenced him with a few sharp words. The man seemed to shrink in his chair.

For a few seconds no one moved, no one spoke. Lawton thought almost wryly that where once he had been concerned about setting off some kind of international incident by interfering with the banking affairs of a wealthy Saudi, he was now concerned that they had walked in on a crime in progress and couldn't do anything about it.

Surprisingly, it was the Saudi who spoke—in English.

"I am," he said, "Ahmed Ahsami. I am a Saudi, and an oil minister for my country."

"And the gun?" Renate asked, staring him down.

"I have reason to believe," Ahsami said, "that this man provided the funds for the recent ricin attack. He has blackened the name of all Arabs."

"A lot of Arabs have blackened their own names, too," she answered coldly.

He gave a dignified bow of his head. "That is true, but it is an Arab problem. Arabs must take care of their own problems, including terrorism. It is not for the rest of the world to become involved."

Lawton could scarcely believe what he was hearing. "So you came here like the Lone Ranger to take him out?"

"Lone Ranger?"

"Never mind. What were you going to do with that gun? Execute him?"

"I need information. There is another operation under way, and I intend to stop it." Ahmed paused. "I have devoted my life to finding a way to settle our problems without bloodshed. But some people—powerful people—seem to have another goal. They are willing to kill innocents, even if it is forbidden by the Koran."

"It is forbidden by the Bible, too," Renate said bitterly. "That doesn't seem to make any difference."

"As Mohammed, blessed be he, noted, we are all people of the Book. We are bound by the same rules. But there are those who feel the rules do not apply to them."

"And you want to stop them?"

Ahmed nodded. "Indeed. The situation is spiraling out of control. Just today, the American president began talking publicly about nuclear strikes in Islamic lands. Blood for blood, and more blood for that. It is madness!"

Rotel had been slowly lowering his hands, and now Lawton turned on him. "Move your chair back, away from the desk. *Now.* Or I'll ask Mr. Ahsami to pick up his pistol."

"Tying him up would be good," Ahsami remarked.

Lawton pulled a pair of flex cuffs from his back pocket and cuffed the banker's arms behind the chair. Then he looked at Ahsami. "I have a pair for you, too."

"Not necessary. I will tell you a story…a true story. It will help you understand."

Renate nodded at the pistol, and Lawton closed in carefully, using his foot to move it well out of reach of the Saudi before he picked it up. Then he sat in a chair in the corner, the weapon pointed in the direction of the two men near the desk. Renate's shoulders relaxed a bit, and she, too, sat— out of the line of fire.

"I'm listening," Lawton said.

Ahsami closed his eyes briefly. When he opened them, they were intense. "For five hundred years after the wars of Christian aggression— what you call the Crusades—your people left the Arab lands alone. We ruled ourselves, resolved our disputes and conducted ourselves according to Islamic law. Then, in the mid-nineteenth century, everything changed."

"Oil," Renate said.

"Precisely," Ahmed said. "The British found oil in my country, and in Iraq, just as the Industrial Revolution was creating a demand for that commodity. And, in the manner of a people who believed themselves entitled to whatever they wanted from non-European peoples, your people set to work dividing up our lands among themselves, as if we who had lived in those lands for centuries out of mind had no say in the matter."

"You're talking about Israel," Lawton said.

"That is only the excuse, my friend," Ahsami said. "For while the Palestinians justly feel that they were driven from their homes, one might also note that no Arab nation took them in as brothers and helped them start new lives."

Lawton nodded. "The thought has crossed my mind."

"No, this goes beyond the state of Israel. This is a two-hundred-year legacy of imperialism, an imperialism that continues to this day."

"The Arab nations were granted independence after World War II," Lawton said. "If not immediately after, then certainly within a decade or two. Your people aren't living under colonial rule anymore."

"You think not?" Ahmed asked. "Who do you

think owns our oil reserves? Our 'independence,' as you put it, was paid for with long-term leases on our oil fields. Our national borders were drawn by Europeans, without regard to our traditional identities. Our ruling families were chosen by Europeans, given free rein to be as corrupt and oppressive as they wished, so long as the wells continued to pump. Even when we nationalized our oil production in the 1960s, the drilling and processing equipment was still owned and run by Western businesses. After the regime of Saddam Hussein was overthrown, the British authorities in Basra hired local Iraqi contractors to operate the port facilities. The U.S. canceled that contract and instead installed one of its own corporations. Yes, my friend, we still live under colonial rule."

Renate spoke. "Is this how you really see it?"

"This is not how I see it," Ahmed said. "This is how it is. Millions of people are massacred in Africa, and the Western nations do not intervene. But let there be a problem in a place where oil can be found, and suddenly they have a responsibility to act."

"So Western nations act in self-interest," Lawton said. "That justifies terrorism?"

"Hardly," Ahmed said. "But consider this. The Jews fought to drive the British out of Palestine. They used terrorism to do it. And they succeeded. Do you think the Palestinians did not learn the lesson? Do you think other freedom fighters in Islamic lands did not learn the lesson? Terrorism is the warfare of the weak against the strong, my friend."

Lawton nodded, absorbing what he was hearing, but making no judgments as yet. He wanted to hear everything before reasoning it through.

"Instead of seeking peaceful solutions, we have used violence." Ahsami shook his head. "Instead of aiding our Palestinian brothers, we chose instead to invade Israel to try to take their land back by force. Instead of attacking legitimate military targets, we slaughtered the innocent."

"So," Renate said, "is there a point to this story, beyond history that we could read for ourselves?"

Ahsami hesitated, clearly thinking. "I am trying to find the words to properly explain the purpose of *Saif Alsharaawi.*"

"Wait. Who is that?" Lawton leaned forward, certain he had never heard the name before.

"The English translation would be 'Sword of the East,'" Ahmed said. "We are determined to gain true independence for all Islamic peoples. The independence of an equal among equals, not of weak peasants begging their feudal lords for crusts of bread. We cannot achieve our goal so long as some among us behave like animals, leading the Western nations to feel the need to occupy us in order to protect themselves. Before *Saif* can negotiate with the West as an equal, we must first demonstrate to the world that we can police ourselves, that we can clean our own house."

"And that brings you to Prague?" Renate asked. "Pardon me, but this is hardly your house."

"When a man's children destroy another man's property, can he deny responsibility because it did not happen in his own home? The ricin attack was carried out by Muslims. Whether they acted in Muslim lands is beside the point." Now Ahmed turned to face Rotel. "And this man paid them. That means he knows who they are." He returned his attention to Renate and Lawton.

"So," he concluded, "I have explained why I am here. Now, may I ask why you have come? And please don't insult my intelligence by claiming to be from Interpol. Interpol acts through the local authorities, and neither of you is Czech. So...who are you?"

Washington, D.C.

Special Agent in Charge Kevin Willis looked across the desk at Miriam. "Do you know what a political shit storm this will create if you're wrong?" he asked.

"Of course," Miriam said. "I'm not stupid, Kevin."

"We're talking about the National Security Advisor," he continued. "A coconspirator in the shooting of Grant Lawrence? The Rice Administration a puppet of this shadowy cartel of international bankers?"

"Come on, Kevin," she said. "You went with me to Idaho. You were there in Montana when we took down Wes Dixon. You know the story we put out about the Lawrence shooting—yet another crazy lone gunman—was a crock. You can't tell me you're all that surprised."

"How reliable is Katherine Dixon?" he asked.

"As reliable as she needs to be," Miriam said.

Kevin's sigh approached exasperation. "How am I supposed to read that?"

"She has an agenda. It involves nailing her father because she believes he killed her brother and was directly or indirectly responsible for her husband becoming tangled up in the whole mess. She wants revenge."

"That'll sound good on a witness stand."

"It doesn't mean she's lying. She's got names, dates, amounts of money and inside information. What's more, she's getting papers from her husband's files for me."

Kevin's brows lifted at that. "Paper I can use."

"We'll have it in a couple of hours. But we don't have time to waste, Kevin. You know that. Once Rice launches that attack…"

"Nobody knows for certain that he's going to

do it," Kevin said. "So far it's all been saber rattling."

Miriam half smiled. "Katherine told me. She
overheard her father discussing it on the phone
with someone. She's not sure, but she thinks it was
Bentley."

Horror spread across Kevin's face. "Jesus H.
Christ!" He popped out of his chair as if ejected
and started rapidly pacing the confines of his office. "You can't expect me to interfere with a decision made by POTUS and his advisors!"

"Not even if one of those advisors is a mole?"

"Miriam, why the hell would they want this?
What good would it possibly do a *bank?*"

"Banks have and make investments. Banks
make money on war, because they own shares in
the defense industry. And they make money when
an unstable region of the world is…pacified…by
financing investment there. For international
banking, this is a win-win situation. For international banking, only inaction is a loss."

She leaned forward, tapping her index finger
on his desk. "Do you want me to show you? Do
you need to see the actual proof that the people
who funded the Allies in the Second World War
also funded Hitler? Would you like to see how the
same banking family funded both Napoleon and
the British? How far back do you want to go, Kevin? They have no side but their own. And if they

need to own or blackmail a U.S. president in order to get their war... Are you adding this up?"

She could tell by his face that he was, but all he said as he continued to pace was, "This is insane. It's conspiracy horse manure."

"Oh, it's a conspiracy, all right. As near as I can tell, it's been going on for centuries. But the fact that it's a conspiracy doesn't make it insane."

"It *sounds* insane."

"But you know I'm right about the history. What makes you think it ever stopped?"

He ceased pacing and faced her. "If I'm going to go into the West Wing and arrest the National Security Advisor, then I need *proof,* Miriam. Not a bunch of theories and bits of history. You'd better hope this Katherine Dixon comes through."

"No, we'd *all* better hope she does—before those bombs are unleashed."

27

Guatemalan Highlands

The day had turned misty, a thick fog had crept under the dense trees and through the heavy undergrowth. The band, still struggling toward their appointed meeting place with the other two groups, decided finally that they could go no farther lest they have a mishap in the fog.

The mountain had at least stopped rumbling, Steve thought with gratitude as he settled on the ground, his back resting against a thick tree trunk. No more ash. Although even the small amounts that had sifted through the thick leaves above and fallen with the dew and occasional light rain had made parts of their trek unnecessarily miserable. The stuff, unlike the ash from a fire, seemed to turn to concrete when wet. Some of the people were coughing, and he was certain they must have inhaled some ash despite their efforts to cover their faces.

The women started a fire as soon as they could, and soon the pleasant smell of wood smoke filled their campsite, and not long after that the aroma of roasting vegetables and fruit.

As soon as he could, he thought, he was going to have to find a way to buy these people more corn. A way to ensure they could survive until they had rebuilt their lives in some isolated spot.

And why was he suddenly so certain that the time had come for that? Because of a dream? He must be losing his mind. Yet…it felt right. They couldn't run forever.

"Hola, Padre."

Startled, he twisted his head and saw Miguel walking toward him, a Miguel who looked much older than he had a week ago. A Miguel who clearly had barely eaten since he had separated from them.

"Miguel! Praise God, I thought you were dead."

"I almost was." Miguel squatted beside him. "When I doubled back on the stalker, he saw me and hit me on the head. I do not know how long I was unconscious. When I awoke, I started tracking him. I lost him two days ago."

"It's all right. I think he got what he wanted. I believe he's gone."

Miguel nodded, but his face was hard. "I saw Paloma."

Steve reached out tentatively to clasp the young man's shoulder. "I'm sorry. We had to run and didn't have time to bury her. But I don't think she suffered."

Miguel shrugged. "We all suffer, Padre. That is life. But it is good you did not bury her." From around his neck, he lifted a leather pouch that hung by a thick leather cord. "Somehow I know Paloma wanted you to have this. She chose you, didn't she, Padre?"

Steve nodded reluctantly.

"Then take this pouch. I used what I needed when I buried her. The rest is for you."

"What is it?"

Miguel shook his head. "I don't know. But I think it gave her power. The power is yours now."

"But…"

Miguel silenced him with a gesture. "Maybe when I understand why an old *curandera* like Paloma is shot by a hunter in the woods, I can explain that power to you. Right now, I don't understand anything, and I must go find my sister. She must think I am dead."

"I think she alone of us kept faith that you were alive."

Miguel smiled faintly. "I must talk to her. If I turn myself in to the police, the villagers can settle somewhere safely. Perhaps it is time I paid the price of my actions."

"Miguel…"

But the youth was already disappearing into the fog to seek his sister around the fire. Steve looked down at the pouch in his hand and resisted the urge to hurl it away into the fog.

Who was he to replace Paloma? As far as he could see, he had never done anything except fail these people. But he kept gripping the pouch anyway. It was his last link to Paloma, and he couldn't let it go.

He opened the pouch and saw the familiar white powder that she had shown him before. Licking a fingertip, he touched it to the powder, then brought it to his lips. At once the bone-deadening weariness seeped away, leaving him, if not refreshed, at least relaxed. It was what happened a moment later that shocked him.

Once again, he stood in a vast, black emptiness. Once again, eleven figures slowly materialized. Once again, the woman spoke.

"You would call it manna," she said. "But it has many names in many cultures. And though few know that it even exists, and fewer still its potential, it has been both the blessing and the bane of humanity for millennia. Its baser form is the treasure of kings. But this…this is the treasure of the Light himself. It is his gift to us, to nourish and strengthen us, to bring us closer to his infinite perfection. But like every great gift, it carries with it great responsibility. Very few have the grace or wisdom that such a gift demands. Very few have the courage to resist its temptations."

"Paloma has chosen you," the man called Nathan said. "Each of us was chosen by a predecessor. Not all of us were the first choice, however. Beware of temptation, my friend. Guard yourself against it in every moment. For only those who live in the Light can serve the Light. Seek neither power nor glory nor vengeance, nor even justice. Seek only the Light, Steve Lorenzo. Only that can save us. Or we will all perish in the fire to come."

"What fire?" Steve asked. "Who are you? Am I…is this a hallucination?"

"It surely must seem so to you," the woman said. "For it is not the reality that you have been taught. But we are as real as the young man who now stands behind you. Ask him. He will tell you."

Steve turned, and saw Miguel and his sister. But only Miguel seemed to be aware of the others. *"Madre de Dios,"* he whispered softly.

"¿Que es?" his sister asked. *"¿Miguel?"*

"¿No veces?" he asked. *Do you not see?*

"No. No veo," she replied. *"¿Que es ese?"*

"Apparently it is not for you to see, Rita," Steve said. "I cannot say why Miguel can see them, or why you cannot. Your brother and I must talk now, Rita. We will join you shortly."

Rita retreated into the fog, leaving only Miguel and Steve in the infinite blackness. Miguel's face was filled with terror and wonder, in equal measure.

"Do not worry," Steve said. "They are friends."

"Angeles," Miguel asked.

"No," Nathan replied. "We are not angels, Miguel. We are mere servants, as Father Lorenzo is a servant, and you, as well."

"I am not worthy to serve," Miguel said. "I have too much blood on my hands."

"No more than I had," Nathan said. "Less than some of us. No one comes to the Light from the light, Miguel. We all come from the darkness. It can be no other way."

"What must I do?" Miguel asked.

A moment later, the figures vanished, and Steve and Miguel were once again alone in the jungle.

"I must go to Rome," Steve said. "I do not know where the road leads, but only that it begins there."

"Then I will go with you, Father," Miguel said. "Wherever you go, I go also. That is my pledge and my promise."

Steve felt tears forming in his eyes. "Thank you, Miguel. I will not betray your trust. Come. Let us get the others settled. We must find them a place where they can stay and resume their lives."

"I know of a valley," Miguel said. "It is to the west, perhaps three days' journey. When I was with the rebels, we trained there for a brief time. But then the jaguars killed two of…it was…we could not stay. Perhaps that place was reserved for the people of my village. Perhaps the jaguar god was saving it for us."

"Then there we will go," Steve said. "And may the jaguar protect them always."

Prague, Czech Republic

"Who are we?" Renate asked. "I'll give you the very simplest answer. Black Christmas killed my parents."

Ahmed nodded. "Black Christmas killed a lot of parents, I'm sad to say."

"That's true," Renate replied. "But in my case, it wasn't mere chance. The people behind Black Christmas—the money people like Mr. Rotel here—wanted *my* parents dead. Specifically."

"How can you know that?" Ahmed asked, studying her. "Why would they—"

"They died in Baden-Baden," she said. "In a simple parish church. All the other church bombings were major cathedrals. This wasn't a 'statement.' It was a murder, intended to draw me out into the open, so they could kill me, too. As for why they want me…that I can't tell you. But I think that, at least for the moment, we are on the same side, Mr. Ahsami."

"And that is not good news for you, Mr. Rotel," Lawton said, leveling the pistol at a spot between the man's eyes. "Not good news at all. But you are a banker, not a martyr. You want to live another day. So you're going to tell us what we want to know, right?"

"If I can," Rotel said, his eyes flitting around the room, avoiding the hole in the barrel of the gun. "I don't know anything about Black Christmas."

"Ah," Renate said, taking a piece of paper from her purse. "I didn't expect that you would. But you're in luck, because we didn't come to ask you about that. This is just a routine banking inquiry. We simply want to know who owns this account. I've highlighted it for you."

"I would have to use my computer," he said. "I don't have such things memorized. How could I?"

Renate smiled. It was not a pleasant smile.

"My friend here," she said, "the one with the gun pointed at your head, has some experience with your bank's computer system. He'll be more than happy to take care of that, as soon as you give us your password."

"Marita-zero-five-one-three," Rotel said quickly.

Renate chuckled. "Wife's name?"

"Patron saint," he said. "I am a Christian man. I would not have given money to terrorists if—"

"Save it," Lawton said, as Renate typed in the characters. "I'm sure the Czech police will have more than enough patience to listen to your excuses. But I don't." He glanced at the screen, then at Renate. "Press F-four. Now the account number, then Enter."

Renate followed his instructions, and soon a name and address popped up on the screen. Kasmir Al-Khalil.

"That address is in the Arab Quarter," Ahmed said. "I know because we are staying nearby."

"We?" Lawton asked.

"I brought a team with me," Ahmed said. "For when I received this information."

"Then let's go," Renate said. "The clock is ticking."

Lawton opened Rotel's center desk drawer and began searching through it.

"What do you want now?" Rotel asked.

"A razor blade would be good," Lawton said. "A sharp letter opener might suffice."

"I have a letter opener," Rotel said. "Top right drawer."

Lawton opened it and found the four-inch blade with a mother-of-pearl handle. He laid it on the desk. "Very classy. Probably not sharp enough, but you can try."

"Try what?" Rotel asked.

"Those are nylon flex cuffs," Lawton said. "If you can cut through them, you won't have to stay here all night waiting for someone to ask embarrassing questions in the morning. On the other hand, you might want to be careful. Wouldn't want to slash your wrists trying to get free."

"But…" Rotel began.

"Have a nice night," Lawton said, following Renate and Ahmed out of the room.

"Why did you give him a way to get free?" Ahmed asked.

"Where I come from," Lawton said, "we have a saying. You can shear a sheep many times, but you can only skin it once. We may need Mr. Rotel again at some point."

"And where *do* you come from?" Ahmed asked. "Your friend has explained why she is here. You haven't."

"No," he said. "I haven't. She's the boss. I'm the help. That's enough for you to know."

"If we are to work together—" Ahmed began, but Renate cut him off.

"Work together? I said we were on the same side…for the time being. That doesn't make us partners. I don't know that *you* didn't plan Black Christmas."

"You need me," Ahmed said. "My team can operate in places where yours cannot. My men are not out of place in the Arab quarter. Yours would be. We are a very tightly knit people here in Europe, all the more so with what has happened lately. You would not get within a block of that address without someone alerting Mr. Al-Khalil. He would be gone before you arrived. That is why we created *Saif Alsharaawi.* Only we can police ourselves."

"We go with your team," Renate said.

"Renate—" Lawton began.

"He's right," she said. "His team can do this better than we can. But I don't trust him enough to let them do it alone. We're going with them. Our team will monitor police communications and stand in reserve."

Lawton simply nodded, and Renate felt a surge of relief that he had caught her meaning. She and Lawton had come alone, intending to call in an operations team when they had the information. But she didn't want Ahsami to know that.

"When do we go?" Lawton asked.

"My men can be ready in three hours," Ahsami said.

"Fine," Renate said. "We go tonight. I will go with Mr. Ahsami. Lawton, you go back and brief the others."

"But…" Lawton said.

"She knows us better than you do," Ahmed said, smiling. "Even if we were *Jihadists,* there is no glory in killing a woman. To do so would bring shame on an entire family. She knows she will be safe."

"Call my cell when you've finalized your plans,"

Lawton said. "I want to be there with the takedown team."

"I will call you with the plans," Renate said. "But you need to stay with our people, on ready alert."

"I don't like it," Lawton said.

"You don't have to," she replied. "It's as you told Mr. Ahsami. I'm the boss. You're the help."

28

Prague, Czech Republic

Lawton didn't like the arrangement at all. He had no team to lead, and no way to monitor the Czech police. In truth, he was simply sitting in a hotel room, waiting for the telephone to ring. Renate was on her own, working with a team of armed Arabs who might well be the very terrorists they were looking for.

He understood her reasoning. It was even more dangerous for Ahmed Ahsami to believe that he and Renate were here in Prague without any backup. So long as he was here with a nonexistent operations unit, ready to back her up, Ahsami had to respect the possibility that Lawton could intervene if need be. And given the Arab attitude toward women, Renate would indeed be safer with them than Lawton would. At least he hoped so. On very rare occasions, sexism had its advantages. But that didn't mean he had to like it.

The first thing he'd done upon returning to the hotel room was to call Rome and ask for a check on Ahmed Ahsami. Jefe had called him back within a half hour, transmitting a brief biography and a photo. Yes, the man Lawton and Renate had met at the bank was indeed Ahmed Ahsami. Yes, he was a minor Saudi prince and a senior official in the Saudi oil ministry. But one fact bothered him. Ahsami's nephew, Yawi Hassan, had been killed a few weeks ago in Vienna, part of the terrorist cell that the combined U.S.-EU operation had taken down. Somehow Ahsami was connected to Black Christmas. And Lawton intended to find out how.

He'd ordered dinner from room service—roasted veal and vegetables in a peppery Bordelaise sauce—but he was too nervous to eat it. The intense bite of the sauce had set his stomach alight with the very first mouthful. So the food sat on the tray, growing cold, as he paced the hotel room, waiting for his cell phone to ring.

When it did, he nearly knocked it off the table in his rush to grab it. "Renate?"

"I'm fine," she said, obviously picking up on his anxiety. "They've reconnoitered the target, and we're ready to go. Is everything set there?"

"Yes," he said. "Ahmed Ahsami is who he says he is. But there's a catch."

"What's that?" she asked.

"His nephew was in the Black Christmas cell that was taken down in Vienna last month. And if his nephew was involved in Black Christmas…"

He didn't have to finish the sentence.

"We can discuss that later," she said. "We're moving out now."

"Be careful, Renate."

She paused for a moment. When she spoke, her voice was different. Muted. Sincere in a way he had rarely heard. "Thank you."

Renate was dressed in a *burka*. This had been, she realized, another reason why Ahmed had brought her along. Veiled, save for her eyes, her blond hair and Western clothing concealed under the flowing black robes, she would attract no attention as she moved with Ahmed's men.

As a show of trust, Ahmed had given her an Uzi machine pistol with a collapsing stock. It, too, vanished beneath her robes. His four men were similarly armed, and Renate could tell they were well trained. There was a coldness in their eyes and an efficiency in their movements that could only be born of experience. They reminded her of Niko and the other Office 119 operations men she had met. Men who were accustomed to violence, up close and personal. Men who had mastered their fear more than once and knew they would master it again. Killers.

But she, too, was a killer. She didn't like it, and she doubted she would ever face it with the cold, ruthless, mechanical efficiency that these men showed. Still, she had killed a man in Idaho and another in Rome. She had done it face-to-face. She had seen the surprise in their eyes, the shock and pain, and the emptiness as life left them. The first time had sickened her. But in Rome, she had felt only anger.

Was that how it was? Was that all that divided so-called civilized people from terrorists, murderers and savages? Simply having done it…the act of taking a human life? Had she become no different than the people she hunted?

This was no time for self-analysis, she knew. And yet, something within her screamed out for justification, for a reason to feel she fought with the angels and not alongside the devil himself. Since Black Christmas, she had been on a mission of vengeance. She had tried to tell herself that she was simply doing her job, working to bring the perpetrators to justice. But she knew better. She had known better all along.

Now she was going into battle alongside men who were very likely part of the same organization she was supposed to be fighting against. Ahsami's nephew had been in the Vienna cell. Had that cell been the one that bombed a church in Baden-

Baden? She had stepped into a shadowy maze, where no one was what they seemed. In truth, the only person left that she truly trusted was Lawton Caine. And what had he said, just before they hung up?

Be careful.

She would be careful. Not for herself. For him.

"We're here," Ahsami said quietly. "It's the next apartment building."

"Yes," she said. "I see."

"Stay back, with me."

"Ahmed…"

"I have no doubt of your capabilities," he said. "Your eyes frighten me, and I do not frighten easily. You would kill in an instant, just like my men. But they have worked together for months. Each knows how the others will react, whatever should happen. You don't know them, nor they you. Let them do what they must, Renate. Let not your cold eyes grow colder."

"Let's get on with it," she said. "I will stay back with you, but I'm going to be in the room. And I want them alive. We need to question them. Dead bodies can't talk."

"I understand," he said. He lifted a hand to his face, as if he were brushing away a fly. In fact, he was lifting a wrist microphone to his mouth. "Go."

The men were in motion almost before the word was finished. They moved swiftly, silently, a single organism slipping through the darkened hallway, up the stairs, then coalescing around a door. Silent hand signals and brief nods were their only communication as stun grenades were readied. One of the men kicked the flimsy door open, and the grenades flew in. The organism moved in behind them, no longer silent, words barked out rapid-fire in Arabic.

Less than a minute later, it was over.

"Clear," Ahmed said. "No one is there."

"Then we search the place," Renate said, stepping forward. "And nobody takes anything out unless I see it first. Agreed?"

"Agreed," he said.

The apartment was small and cramped. Renate went first to the kitchen, holding a hand over the stove burners, then to the oven door, then to the electric coffeepot on the counter. All cold. She opened the refrigerator and saw only a single wedge of goat cheese, carefully wrapped in plastic, and an unopened bottle of milk.

"No one had dinner here tonight," she said. "No sign of breakfast or lunch. He probably left yesterday."

"Yes," one of Ahmed's men said. He seemed to be the leader of the team and had obviously undergone the same training she had. "He has left for some time now."

"He's already left for the next operation," Renate said. "We need to know where he went. I want every scrap of paper. Every photograph."

Ahmed repeated her instructions in Arabic, and the men set to work. Kasmir Al-Khalil was a careful man. A framed diploma on his wall indicated an engineering degree. The apartment was meticulously clean.

Renate tried to build a portrait of the man who lived here, the man who had loosed ricin on the Prague subway. He would be precise in every detail. He would keep careful notes. The question was, would he keep those notes after an operation was concluded? There was a blank space on the desk where a laptop had obviously been, cords to the printer and modem clipped precisely in spring clamps on the back of the desk. Had all of his notes gone with the computer?

Probably not, Renate reasoned. A small filing cabinet beside the desk was packed with papers, carefully indexed. Bills that he had paid, with printouts of the electronic transactions that had paid them. Tax records, to the last receipt. No, this was not a man who would trust his life to a computer file that might be wiped out by a single power surge. The evidence was here, in this apartment, somewhere.

Ahmed's men were rifling through the bedroom and bathroom, and she could see they were doing a thorough job of it. Here in the front room, apart from the desk and filing cabinet, there were only a faded sofa and a stained dinette table with a single chair. She made quick work of the sofa, finding nothing. She went through his files, page by page, knowing all the while that he would not have been so foolish as to keep records of his operations in so obvious a place.

She returned to the kitchen. The records would be here. She opened the cupboard doors and found only a few mismatched dishes. They had probably come with the apartment, along with the sofa and table. The pots beneath the counter were clean and neatly stacked, largest to smallest, all the handles pointing to the left. Precision.

The knives and silverware in the drawers were set out with equal precision, stacked neatly, with no wasted space. Everything gave Renate a greater sense of the man who lived here. His operational notes would be stored in the same way. Stacked neatly, with no wasted space. They would not be exposed to cooking grease or food spills. That ruled out the stove, ventilation hood and the space beneath the counters.

Somewhere clean. Somewhere that he could get to them easily. Somewhere that no one else would think to look. Somewhere safe. Inviolate. Almost hermetically sealed.

She opened the freezer. Four neat stacks of frozen dinners. Nothing else. Nothing else, and yet… on one of the sixteen frozen dinners, just one, a corner of the box was raised. It was out of place. And she knew it was what she was looking for.

She pulled the boxes from the freezer and set them on the counter. The flaps at the ends of the boxes were still glued closed, or had been glued again. Most likely it was the latter. She tore one open.

A sheaf of papers, carefully wrapped in plastic. Condensation on the outside of the plastic obscured the papers for a moment, but when she tore the plastic away, her heart slammed in her chest.

Plans for the church in Baden-Baden.

Kasmir Al-Khalil had murdered her parents.

Washington, D.C.

Kevin Willis and Miriam, plus three other investigators, rapidly sorted through all the papers Katherine Dixon had delivered. She had brought an astonishing number of boxes. In fact, Miriam concluded, she must have been gathering them for a long time, at least since her brother's death.

With every passing minute it became evident that a team of investigators and lawyers, given a few months, would be able to nail Jonathan Morgan to the wall on any number of illegalities.

But they didn't have months. They might only have days. Or, worse, hours. Kevin himself was looking increasingly disturbed, and every ten minutes or so he would look up from the papers he was going through to remind everyone that they didn't need an airtight case; all they needed was enough to get into the West Wing and go after Bentley.

"We can build the case later, people. Right now I need a smoking gun on Bentley, and only Bentley."

They all knew it. The reminders were merely Kevin's way of tamping down his growing anxiety.

"Hey, Kevin," somebody called from the doorway. "You need to see this. POTUS is making a live speech."

Kevin's gaze met Miriam's instantly. She saw the dart of fear in his and felt it herself as her heart slammed.

Kevin stood up. "Keep looking, people. And hurry. Miriam, come with me."

Two doors down, in a break room, Harrison Rice's face filled a thirty-six-inch television screen. Miriam felt a jolt of shock as she looked at him; he must have aged a decade in the weeks since Black Christmas.

"...with great difficulty and much prayer," he was saying. "After the terrible events of Black Christmas, we and the other civilized nations of this planet believed we could treat these perpetrators as criminals, hunting them down wherever they hid. I'm sure you all recall the successful raid in Vienna a short time ago. We all hoped that would be merely the beginning of our roundup of the worst terrorist force this world has ever seen."

He lifted his head, looking directly into the camera. His face was deeply lined with sorrow— and something else. Fear? Miriam wondered. *Good God, he looked horrified.*

"Then," he said heavily, the smallest crack in his voice, "we saw the terrible, terrible ricin attack in Prague. My heart, and I'm sure the hearts of all Americans, goes out to the victims and their families. As you know, we have sent all the medical aid we can. We have made every humanitarian effort we can after all these strikes.

"But, my fellow Americans, I have reached the conclusion that that is not enough. We are no longer safe anywhere in this world, not in our churches, not in our subways, not in our offices, or even the sanctity of our homes. I can no longer call this terrorism. I call this war.

"As a result, I am officially asking Congress to declare war on all terrorists worldwide. I am not talking about seek-and-arrest missions anymore. I am talking about *real* war. We will use every technology, every weapon, at our disposal, bar none, to erase these vermin from the planet. What happened on Black Christmas is not going to happen again. What happened in Prague is not going to happen in this country. Not on my watch. We will declare war, and then we will unleash our military to take any and all actions it deems necessary to protect our shores.

"Thank you and God bless America."

A shudder went through Miriam. "Oh my God."

Kevin looked at her. "He's stalling."

"Stalling?"

"Asking Congress to declare war. He's buying a little time."

She shook her head. "It's not going to be much, Kevin. Congress will meet tonight, if necessary, to pass the resolution."

"I know." His fists clenched. "There's one thing we haven't discussed, Miriam."

"What's that?"

"There's no precedent for getting a warrant to get into the West Wing or White House. I don't think we can do it. And I don't think Bentley's going to come out of there until this is over."

She drew a long shaky breath. "We've got to do something! You heard what he said. Any weapons. Any means."

"I know. I know. Once he has the resolution past Congress, there's going to be no stopping it. Those nukes will be unleashed."

Just then a reporter came on screen. "We're trying to find a member of Congress to comment on the president's speech, Larry," he was saying.

"But they all seem to want to reserve their comments for later. It's my understanding that they're going to suspend all other business to vote on this declaration of war immediately."

Miriam tuned him out. "I've got it," she said suddenly.

"What?"

"Senator Grant Lawrence. He still owes me a favor, and I'm going to call it in right now."

Without another word, she turned on her heel and strode to her office.

29

Saint-Arnans-la-Bastide, France

Jules Soult watched the American president's speech with a feeling of deep satisfaction. The threat was now on the table. He had no doubt that, when combined with the terrorist attacks, the actions America was about to take would be seen as destabilizing, as a major threat. Especially since he and his men would make the connection obvious.

Now the people who were still quibbling about the European Constitution because they feared loss of primacy, or because they were xenophobic, would stop quibbling. Instead, the demand would grow for a stronger union, one that could stand militarily against the U.S. and all other dangers, including the Muslim Jihadists. And France, with its nuclear capability, would be seen as the country that should take the lead.

In fact, now that the president had made his threat, Soult's own people would start the outcry. And as France grew closer to preeminence, Soult would become more and more the hero, because his men were about to put down the street violence.

But not just yet. He went to open the safe once again, and from it he took the leather-wrapped ruby pyramid. Few understood its powers, but Soult did. And he was about to go to Strasbourg to make himself a hero.

When he was done, none would doubt the divine right of Jules Soult to run the European Union.

Prague, Czech Republic

Renate and Ahmed Ahsami returned to the hotel and joined Lawton in his room.

"Ahmed is going to help us decipher these papers that were found," Renate told Lawton. She tossed him the plastic-wrapped packet she had found, then tugged the *burka* over her head, revealing her jeans, jacket and bulletproof vest. "His men are fanning out in the area around Khalil's apartment to see if they can learn anything about his activities."

"Good, good," Lawton said. Right now he was feeling like an utter fraud as Ahsami's eyes swept the room, apparently noting the absence of the kind of equipment one would expect to find in a command post. "The local authorities are backing off for now."

Renate nodded in answer to his lie. "Good. The last thing we need is them moving in right now."

Something in Ahsami relaxed, and he moved around the room, switching on all the lights. The day outside was turning grayer by the minute, and the room was darkening. He looked different in his black Western clothes, Lawton noted. More catlike. More dangerous. When he tossed his jacket over the foot of the bed, his black turtleneck outlined the body armor beneath.

"What I want to know," Ahsami said, "is how these people are always one step ahead."

"Except in Vienna," Lawton remarked.

Ahmed looked at him, dark eyes burning. "*Someone* was ahead of us. When I sent my team in to take out the cell there, they were attacked, too. My nephew died, my friends died, and they were called terrorists, too."

Lawton's eyes widened at this revelation, and he looked at Renate. Her look left no doubt. She believed Ahmed. And Lawton did, too.

Ahmed continued. "Everyone thinks they were part of that cell, but that was not so. Who is ahead on all of this? Who is planning this? I swear to you, it is not Jihadists, for I would have caught wind of their plans."

Renate reached out and touched his arm briefly,

lightly. "I know who it is, but I can't prove it. We need to go through these papers."

He nodded sharply, as if barely restraining himself. Then he took the packet and went to sit at the small desk, where he ripped open the plastic and began to scan the tightly written lines of Arabic.

"Lawton?" Renate said.

He looked at her.

"Break silence. Call Miriam. I'm getting really worried."

"Me too," Lawton agreed. "I'm starting to see tentacles everywhere."

"Yes," Ahsami said, looking up. "Tentacles. That is the name for them. And they are indeed everywhere, my friends."

Lawton nodded, pulling out his cell phone. "I'll have to ditch this phone after I call. And the call could still be traced."

Renate shrugged. "I don't think we're going to be in Prague for very long anyway. Somehow I suspect Khalil has moved on to another job."

Her face sagged a little then, and her blue eyes, no longer glacially icy, met his straight-on. "This man killed my family, Law."

"You're sure of that?"

She nodded. "Beyond any doubt."

"Then we're going to find him and nail him to the wall. I promise."

"Don't make promises you might not be able to keep."

"Good advice," Ahsami said bitterly. "In this world, it seems promises are made to be broken."

"Not mine," Lawton said. He and the Saudi exchanged looks, and for an instant, just an instant, there was perfect understanding between them.

Renate nodded to Lawton, and they stepped into the hallway, leaving Ahmed with the papers.

"Did you hear?" she asked. "He sent a team to Vienna. They were the ones who took out that cell. His nephew got killed in the attack, and the police swooped in and just counted his nephew along with the terrorists."

Lawton nodded. "He's telling the truth about that part. But the way he moves, and what I see in his eyes…he's dangerous, Renate."

"Yes, I know," she said. "I saw his men in action. If he doesn't have special operations training, then he's hired people who do. They move fast, and they hit hard. We ought to contact Niko. If we can get photos to him, he might be able to identify some of them. That's a pretty tightly knit community."

"Yes, most of them train together, in the U.S. or in Britain. Niko might recognize them, especially if they're Saudis."

She nodded. "And they probably are. I don't think he's hiring from the radical Islam community."

"He might be a good asset," Lawton said. "If we can control him."

"Yes," Renate said. "If we can control him. Well, let's go back in and see if he's found anything."

Ahmed was hard at work, intently focused on the precise lines of Arabic, taking notes on a pad of paper. From time to time he shook his head and scratched out a word or two, then wrote again. So intent was his focus that he did not appear to have noticed their departure or their return.

"Anything yet?" Renate asked.

Ahmed held up a finger, asking for a moment, as he studied a page and then wrote more. After a minute, he looked up. "What is happening in Strasbourg this week?"

Renate looked at Lawton.

"The EU Parliament is in session," he said.

"Yes, it is," she said.

"That would be a choice target," Ahmed said. "Very high profile. And it would make a pointed retaliation for how the European security forces have treated Arabs here lately. It's exactly the kind of target Al-Khalil would be willing to attack."

"We need to get to Strasbourg," Renate said. "And we need a team there waiting."

"My team can be ready on an hour's notice," Ahmed said. "And I want them there."

"How do I know we're not just letting you walk

in the front door?" Lawton said. "Not to put too fine a point on it, but why should we trust you? This won't be in an Arab quarter. We can do it."

"Because I know where Al-Khalil is staying," Ahmed said, holding up a sheet covered in Arabic characters. "And you don't read Arabic."

"He has a point," Renate said. "On the other hand, we have translators."

"And how long would it take them to pore through these documents?" Ahmed said. "Are you sure you have the time? Because I'm not."

"We go in together this time," Lawton said. "Your team and ours. Together."

Ahmed shook his head. "Our men have not worked together."

"I somehow doubt that is true," Renate said, her eyes turning cold and hard. "I watched your operation tonight. I would bet money that your men trained at the same bases ours did."

Ahmed gave a noncommittal shrug.

"We could do this all night and into tomorrow," Lawton said. "Bottom line remains the same. We go together or we take you down."

After a long moment, Ahmed nodded. "I need it to be known that *Saif Alsharaawi* did this. It is important. More than you can know."

"That is fine," Renate said. "It's better, in fact."

"Yes," Ahmed said. "You can remain invisible."

"We always do," Lawton said. "We don't exist."

Washington, D.C.

Phillip Allen Bentley did not want to take the call that was about to be put through. Though nominally the National Security Advisor, tasked with giving the president insight and advice on military and intelligence matters, in the past three weeks he had become the de facto chief of staff. What was about to happen was far too important to be left in the hands of the hack political appointees who populated the other key positions in Rice's administration. Too many important people had too much at stake for Rice to be permitted to make mistakes.

To avoid that, Bentley had been working long hours over the past weeks, often into the wee hours of the morning, making sure that everyone in the decision loop was on message and had no doubt as to Rice's commitment.

Predictably, men of conscience seemed to balk at the prospect of unleashing the unthinkable. No one had used nuclear weapons in war since the bombings of Hiroshima and Nagasaki. And while the strikes Bentley had planned would not release citywide devastation in the manner that those had, there was still hesitation at the prospect of opening that Pandora's box. The Pakistanis had nuclear weapons, after all, and no one thought they would accept this attack passively. It was only natural that the aircrews and their commanders would be loath to carry out their duties.

Those men's only source of confidence would be their confidence in the unwavering resolve of their commanders, including their commander in chief. Dissent could not be permitted from any quarter. Already the navy admiral commanding the Sixth Fleet had been removed, officially to be "promoted" back Stateside to head the Naval Military Personnel Command, but in fact because he had transmitted a message to the president, expressing his doubts about the upcoming mission. Bentley had intercepted that message and, by removing the admiral, sent a message of his own to everyone involved: *The president's mind is made up, and dissent will be expunged.*

All the extra effort might have been unnecessary if Harrison Rice could have been trusted to do the right thing on his own. But Rice himself still harbored doubts, and Bentley knew he had to provide the certainty and firm hand that a spineless president could not. Bentley had to shield the president from any information or opinions that might embolden his doubts. With so many people seeking access to the president, that was more than a full-time job.

And now this. Grant Lawrence, of all people. Why him? Why now?

Bentley did not believe in coincidence. In his world, the illusion of coincidence was exactly that: an illusion, manufactured to cover the carefully orchestrated actions of those who did not wish to be seen. The difference was that Bentley was accustomed to seeing behind the curtain, to knowing who the secret players were, who was in the process of creating the coincidences that a gullible public would swallow like fresh bait.

Grant Lawrence was not supposed to be one of those players. But for the vicissitudes of fate, Lawrence would be cold in the ground, forever removed from the political scene. He had always been too much of an independent thinker for Bentley's tastes, and for those of Bentley's superiors in the Brotherhood. Early in Lawrence's senate career, he had been sounded out to determine if he would be willing to do as he was told for the right price. When that had failed, they had sought to find some leverage that might be used against him, but there was none to be found. Grant Lawrence had been implacably honest in his political life, with a fiercely loyal coterie of personal friends from whom he sought advice and guidance. Despite the Brotherhood's best efforts, Grant Lawrence's inner circle had remained as impregnable as a medieval fortress.

Had Lawrence been content to remain the junior senator from Florida, working on his pet legislative projects while leaving the real business of running the world to those who knew what ought to be done, the Brotherhood might well have let him be. In America, as elsewhere in the world, the halls of government were sprinkled with a small handful of committed idealists, men who could not be compromised, men who would be faithful to the principles and promises by which they had risen to their positions. The Brotherhood was content to let such men be, to let them labor away in comparative obscurity, to be fondly remembered by their constituents for a smattering of trivial accomplishments that never threatened the true agendas of power. Indeed, such men provided the illusion of representative government and noble principle by which the ignorant masses were kept docile and obedient.

But Lawrence had not been content to keep his place on the periphery. He had sought higher office, the highest in the land—indeed, the most powerful position in the entire world. His charisma and vision might well have seduced the American people into electing him. And the prospect of a U.S. president who was beyond the Brotherhood's reach was simply not acceptable. The office of the President of the United States was far too important to be left to the whims of the American electorate.

For that reason, Lawrence had been targeted for death. Had one of the bullets that struck him been an inch farther to the right, or had the doctors not responded with such skill, or had Lawrence not shown such damnable strength of will, he would indeed be dead. Instead, he was alive, and he had returned to his senate duties and was at that moment on the other end of the telephone line that blinked on Bentley's desk.

With a heavy sigh, Bentley picked up the phone.

"Grant Lawrence, this is Phillip Bentley," he said with feigned warmth. "It's so reassuring to hear you're back to work. President Rice was so worried for you, and so elated when you pulled through."

"Thank you, Mr. Bentley," Lawrence replied with equal charm. "The president's warm wishes meant so much to all of us. My wife and daughters were especially grateful for his letter, and for the Medal of Freedom."

Decorating Lawrence with the nation's highest civilian award had been a calculated act, Bentley's suggestion, and heartily endorsed by Rice. With the country traumatized by the attempted assassination, Rice had needed a way to endear himself to the people, lest he begin his presidency as a political lame duck. Within a week after honoring Grant Lawrence—at a ceremony conducted at Lawrence's hospital bed, when there was still doubt whether he would fully regain his faculties, and then rebroadcast by a consistent, calculated media machine that celebrated Rice's "grace" and "humility"—his approval ratings were in the mid-sixties, giving Rice the clout he needed to pursue his policies.

To pursue the Brotherhood's policies.

"What can I do for you, Senator?" Bentley asked.

Bentley could almost see the phony smile on Lawrence's face as the senator spoke. "Well, as you know, I was barely conscious when the president presented me with the medal. In fact, I hardly remember it, apart from what I was shown later in the news broadcasts. I never had the chance to thank him personally for that honor. So I'd like to set up a meeting with him, just a few minutes of his time, to tell him how much that meant to me and my family."

Bentley pursed his lips for a moment. "I'm sure the president would appreciate that, Senator. But as I'm sure you know, this is a difficult time for him. For all of us. These terrorists have declared open war on the entire free world. The president is busy with other heads of state, trying to coordinate a focused and effective response. We can't afford to end up going it virtually alone again."

"I understand, Mr. Bentley," Lawrence said. "And I promise not to take much of his time. I just…well, at a time when my wife's heart was all but shattered and my daughters seemed beyond hope, President Rice stepped in and gave them a message of hope and pride. I can't let such a kind act go unrewarded, Mr. Bentley. Belle, my youngest daughter, thinks that medal saved my life. She sits in my office sometimes, just looking at it, saying 'thank you.' This is…well…it's important to me, and I can't let it go. I need to thank him. Personally."

Lawrence's voice had cracked as he finished his plea, and for a moment Bentley almost found himself falling for the famous Lawrence charm. Lawrence had a long reputation for sincere gratitude, even among his political enemies. More than one adversary had given him an opening, knowingly or not, in response to his personal charisma.

But Bentley knew Lawrence was no saint. He could not have achieved what he had without a cool, calculating political mind, and he'd earned a reputation as one of the most subtle, savvy and skillful operators on Capitol Hill. It was for that reason, and no other, that Bentley knew he had to accede to Lawrence's request. There was an iron will beneath the velvety words, and Bentley was not naive enough to think a refusal would be allowed to pass. Somehow, somewhere, Lawrence would have a backup plan, and he would not hesitate to spring it if the need arose.

Bentley would simply have to control the meeting. With Grant Lawrence, that would be no easy task. But there was no other way.

"The president has a full morning tomorrow, but he may have some time tomorrow afternoon," Bentley said. "I have a ten-minute window in his calendar, between his meeting with the ambassador from India and his economic briefing."

"That would be perfect," Lawrence said. "Perhaps knowing how much he means to Karen and the kids would help his dinner to settle easier in these difficult times."

"Yes, perhaps it would," Bentley said. "I'll pencil you into the schedule at three-twenty, Senator. But if something comes up…"

"I understand, Mr. Bentley," Lawrence said. "I'll be there. I'll have an FBI agent with me. Unfortunately, the director doesn't want any of us to travel without a keeper. As you said, dangerous times."

"Of course," Bentley said.

"I'll see you tomorrow," Lawrence said.

"I look forward to it."

Bentley hung up the phone and looked up at the ceiling. So the Director of the FBI had acted on Bentley's instructions to assign "protection" agents to the key members of Congress. It was Bentley's way of keeping an eye on the major players on the Hill. If Lawrence had any ulterior motives, the agent would let the director know.

And the director would let Bentley know.

Bentley smiled. Yes, the meeting would be fine.

30

La Petite France, Strasbourg, France

Kasmir Al-Khalil reviewed his schematics one last time, then double-checked the circuit board in front of him. What he was working on was far too important to fail due to hasty carelessness. This operation would send an unmistakable message to the Europeans who wanted to use Arabs as their modern-day Jews. These Jews would fight back, and fight back hard.

Kasmir took a breath and looked out the window. He was staying in the area of Strasbourg known as *La Petite France*. It was an area where tourists were commonplace and a strange face did not attract attention. It was a picture-postcard neighborhood, pale buildings with exterior beams crisscrossing their facades. Attic dormers, sometimes two levels of them, spoke of no space wasted.

Across the street, tourists were already massing at the Au Pont Saint Martin restaurant, tempted by the promise of legendary cuisine in one of the most beautiful settings in all of France. Most of them would spend the day wandering along the well-kept streets, spending their euros in the shops, perhaps looking out over the river that wound through the neighborhood like a glistening ribbon.

A few might make their way across town, to the European parliament complex, a gleaming celebration of steel and glass, with graceful curves and a sweeping view of the river. Many would stop to look at the statue in front of the main entrance, a man and woman locked in an embrace, their thighs forming a heart-shaped union that Kasmir had found pornographic and repulsive. No true Muslim could enjoy such a statue nor any union that it symbolized.

Still, that afternoon, Kasmir would make his way to that same building and past that same statue, not to admire either the architecture or what Europeans thought passed for art, but to wreak the vengeance of Islam upon a cruel and faithless culture.

This bomb was more complex than the one he had used in Baden-Baden, because it had to do more than merely destroy a church full of worshippers. This bomb had to destroy an idea, a dark and terrible vision that would try once again to crush Islam. This bomb had to inflict a horror so total that the infidels would never again dare to threaten Islam or those who worshipped the one true God.

This time his contact had enabled him to purchase two kilos of the plastic explosive Semtex, along with one kilo of cesium-137, a radioactive waste product from nuclear reactors. One-half kilo of Semtex was in a simple pipe bomb. Its purpose was simply to wound and maim those who were standing nearby, and attract would-be rescuers into the blast area for the second bomb. The remaining Semtex was packed into a ball, surrounded by the cesium. When that bomb exploded, ten minutes after the first, it would rip a hole in the building. But the cesium would be the real killer.

Dispersed into the air, its particles would be inhaled by those who had survived the blasts themselves. It would be distributed throughout the soft tissues, causing nausea, pain, disorientation and a host of other disorders. But the real damage would come later, as the radioactive particles emitted beta radiation, warping cell nuclei, turning healthy cells into cancerous ones, eating away flesh from the inside, destroying organs, leaving the victims to endure slow, agonizing deaths.

Those deaths would be symbolic of the slow death that their infidel leaders had inflicted upon them by rejecting Allah. In this act, Kasmir would raise Allah's name to new heights, striking hard at the empty, materialistic hearts of Allah's enemies, leaving them leaderless, demoralized, decaying from within, just as their society was decaying from within.

And for this, Kasmir had to make sure every detail was perfect. The timing device was sealed inside a lead case, along with a brass plaque on which Kasmir had engraved a message: Justice from Allah! The case would survive the blast and be found by the investigators. There would be no doubt as to who had done this, and why.

Kasmir had built the timer himself, along with a mercury antitamper device, also sealed inside the lead casing. Once he had armed it, the bomb could not be removed without detonating it. From the lead casing, steel conduit curled through the cesium and into the center of the Semtex. Inside that conduit ran the wires connecting the battery to the detonator. The wires could not be cut without moving the bomb, and the steel conduit itself would create more fragments in the immediate blast area.

Both would be placed in the Tour, the towering atrium entryway of the Louis Weiss Building in the EU parliament complex. This was the primary entrance and would be the site of tonight's formal reception, hosted by the President of the European Commission and his other commissioners. Dozens, if not hundreds, of members of parliament would be present, to see and be seen, to quietly press their ideas in snatches of conversation. The ugly business of government would already have begun amidst the pomp and circumstance, but Allah and Kasmir's work would change all that.

It was, Kasmir thought, the most effective and efficient use of his resources. When this day had ended, the world would know that Islam could strike anywhere, at any time, even in the most closely guarded circumstances. The armies of Islam were no longer ragtag desert Bedouins who could be massacred with machine guns. They were skilled commandos, men to be reckoned with and respected.

On this day, the West would quake with fear at the power of Allah. This was how it should be.

Avenue La Liberté, Strasbourg, France

The hotel that Office 119 had chosen lay in the heart of Strasbourg's university area. It was—in the opinion of Margarite Renault, who knew the city better than any of them, the best place in the city for a group to disappear. No matter the city, students tended to be focused on their studies, their romances, their jobs and themselves, not necessarily in that order. Being accustomed to new classmates and new places, they tended not to notice the arrival of a dozen new people in their neighborhood.

Lawton and Renate had a detailed model of the *Institutions Européennes* alongside a small-scale map of the city. Margarite Renault had come from Rome to provide local knowledge and translations where essential. She had three contacts in the city, one of them a member of the parliament itself. Their knowledge was not complete, but it was as complete as they could make it.

They were now briefing the strike teams, who stood in two wary groups, Ahmed's four men on one side of the table, and Niko's three-man Office 119 squad on the other.

"Al-Khalil works alone," Renate said, holding up a file that had expanded considerably overnight. Agents in Rome had put together a detailed dossier on Al-Khalil: age thirty-nine, born in Chechnya, immigrated at age twelve, educated in Köln, London and Stanford. "His cell in Prague appears to have been very small, and his associates have no roles in his operations except to procure materials and provide intelligence."

"We haven't rounded up the others yet," Lawton added, "but I agree with Renate. Al-Khalil is most likely alone. That makes him a harder target to find. But Margarite has some ideas."

Margarite rose and pointed to the map. "Based on the information Ahmed translated, he is staying somewhere between *La Petite France* and the Rue du Dome. This is the tourist area of Strasbourg, and it attracts visitors from all over the world. If a man alone wants to hide, that would be the best place to do it. No one will notice a new face. No one will question him, so long as he has euros to spend."

"And he does," Renate said. "We know that from the bank transfers. We need to plan an inter-cept point between the *Place de la Cathedrale* and the European parliament complex. We know that this is where he's going to strike. Ahmed, if you could fill us in?"

Ahmed had been awake most of the night, translating the documents they had found in Al-Khalil's apartment. His eyes were worn, but still clear and sharp. He nodded and walked over to the model of the EU parliament buildings.

"There is a reception tonight, a ceremony that will officially open the new session of parliament. The President of the European Commission, along with his other commissioners, will greet the members of parliament. The reception will be held here, in the Tower."

"La Tour," Margarite said. "Please."

"As you wish," Ahmed said. "This is the most open space in the entire parliament complex. It's the perfect site for the kind of bomb Al-Khalil is going to use."

"And that's a dirty bomb," Lawton said. "Al-Khalil's notes talked about a radioactive material known as cesium-137. If that's mixed in with the bomb, and the bomb goes off while the room is full, it will kill everyone. If not at first, then later, from radiation poisoning."

"It would be a monstrous act," Ahmed said, nodding. "One that would bring the wrath of Allah and the nations of the West down upon our people. We *must* find that bomb."

"I also want Al-Khalil," Renate said, her face grim and determined. "And I want him alive. He's a pawn in this chess game. I want the king. After that…"

Her voice trailed off. She didn't need to finish the sentence. She and Lawton had argued this point back and forth for much of the night. The simple fact was, she *did* want Al-Khalil dead, and dead by her own hand. But Lawton was right. They needed the information that only Al-Khalil could provide: his contacts, his superiors, how he had been recruited, who selected his targets.

For her part, Renate didn't believe Al-Khalil would even know those things. He didn't seem like the type of man who would commit atrocities in the service of European bankers and power brokers. He would believe his motives were pure, that he was acting on the orders of Al Qaeda or some similar group.

Still, they had to question him. He was their only tangible thread in this shadowy web. So she would not kill him. Not yet.

"A question," said Geoff O'Connor, former

SAS and now an Office 119 operations officer. "Why so many of us? We're looking for one man working alone. We know where he's going to strike, and we know when. Why not just tell the EU security people what we know, pass them a photo of Al-Khalil, and let them take him down when he tries to plant the bomb?"

"Two reasons," Lawton said, jumping in before Ahmed could answer. "First, Ahmed's team needs to be the public face on this one. I don't have to tell you how things have been for European Muslims in the past few months. And the vast majority of European Muslims had nothing to do with Black Christmas, or the subway attack in Prague, or any of the rest of it. This operation needs to look like a case of Muslims taking care of their own, so Ahmed here can make the case for an Islamic community that isn't hell-bent on death and destruction."

"As for the second reason," Renate said, "while Al-Khalil is working alone so far as he's aware, I think he's getting help. He's being funded by a banking cartel called the Frankfurt Brotherhood. They're worldwide, and they have contacts at the highest levels of any number of governments. They are very sophisticated, and very dangerous. They paid for the ricin attack in Prague, and for Black Christmas, as well."

"The Frankfurt Brotherhood almost certainly

has contacts in the EU security apparatus," Lawton said, interrupting when he saw Renate's anger begin to flash. "In fact, there is no other way that Al-Khalil could get anywhere near the parliament building today. The complex is on security lockdown. The Brotherhood probably also has him under protective surveillance, to make sure he doesn't run afoul of the local cops before he can carry out the operation."

"So we should expect resistance," Niko said. "And not just from Al-Khalil."

"Exactly," Renate replied, nodding. "It may even come from French or EU security people, people in uniform. And that's why you're here. Your men will cover Ahmed's team. If it turns into a firefight, Ahmed's men are to seize Al-Khalil and take cover. We don't want armed Arabs shooting at French policemen, even if those policemen are corrupt. Your men will give covering fire and do whatever else is necessary to make sure Ahmed's team can get Al-Khalil out of the area and into our custody."

"So Europeans shoot Europeans to protect Arabs trying to stop an Arab from killing Europeans?" O'Connor asked. "It's bloody insane."

"It is also your mission," Niko said, his dark eyes flashing. "You follow orders, or we'll get someone else who can."

"Aye-bloody-aye," O'Connor said. "I'll follow

orders, but it's a fucking mess is what it is. If the Frenchies want to shoot Ahmed's men, that's fine by me, so long as they get this Al-Khalil fellow in the cross fire. We didn't start this bloody war, after all."

"Yes, you did," Ahmed said quietly. "You started it when you decided that Muslim lands— my people's lands—were yours for the taking. You had your 'empire on which the sun never sets,' and if that meant enslaving those of us who lived there, well, that was the white man's burden. 'Wave the flag and flog the wog.' Oh yes, you started this, my friend. Have no doubt of that."

O'Connor stepped forward, but Niko held him back.

"Enough!" Renate said in a voice that brooked no disagreement. "If you two want to debate the history of colonialism, do it another time. We have a job to do. O'Connor, you have your orders. If following those orders is going to be a problem for you, tell me now and you're off the team. If any of Ahmed's men gets hurt because you blew an assignment, I'll kill you myself."

Something in her eyes left no doubt as to her resolve. Even O'Connor's face went slack. For a long moment no one spoke. No one moved.

"Yes, well, I am sure that won't be necessary," Margarite said, breaking the silence that hung like a toxic cloud. "We are all a bit tense. Putting an operation together on short notice and such. I'm sure Mr. O'Connor was just letting off steam, right?"

O'Connor paused and finally nodded. "Yeah, sure. I was just letting off steam, like she said. Like I always do, right, Niko?"

"If you say so," Niko said quietly, releasing him.

O'Connor shrugged his jacket back into position, took a breath, then looked at the map. "Right. So where are we going to take down this Al-Khalil?"

_31_

The Indian Ocean

"Black Rock One, Tower Three, Over."

Commander Timothy Wilson keyed his microphone. "Black Rock One, go ahead."

"Black Rock One, cleared for launch. Check your deck crews and happy hunting."

"Black Rock One, roger and out," Wilson said.

He and his weapons officer, Lieutenant Alan Keys, held up their hands to signal the deck crew of the U.S.S. _John F. Kennedy_ that they were clear of any controls, and the deck crew made a final weapons check before backing away to recessed shelters. Only the launch controller remained on the deck, and now he gave them the signal to power up the engines of their FA-18 Super Hornet strike jet.

Wilson eased the throttle forward and felt the

rumble of the twin jet engines as they rose to max power. When he was sure they were ready, he signaled the launch controller with a crisp salute. The launch controller pushed his two lighted batons down toward the end of the flight deck, and the catapult officer triggered the steam catapult that slammed the aircraft into the air.

In less than two seconds, the FA-18 was airborne and climbing to rendezvous altitude to link up with the other eleven jets of VFA-41—the "Black Aces"—who would fly the attack element for today's mission. Already in the air were two E-6 Prowlers, electronic warfare aircraft whose mission was to mask the approach of Wilson's squadron, as well as an AWACS airborne command-and-control aircraft, six tanker aircraft for in-flight refueling and two lumbering rescue aircraft flying along their planned route.

Wilson had flown hundreds of missions in his twelve-year navy career, including combat operations over Iraq, but never before had he been ordered to deliver the payload that hung beneath him today. Its official designation was Tactical Nuclear Bunker-Ground Munition, or TNBGM. With typical military irony, the pilots and weapons officers of the *Kennedy* called it "Tiny Bang'em." But Wilson knew this would be no tiny bang.

As the squadron commander, Wilson had decided that only he and his executive officer would carry the TNGBMs. Only one was required for the mission; the other was a backup in case something went wrong with Wilson's aircraft en route. The remaining ten jets provided escort for Wilson and his XO, armed with radar-seeking, air-to-ground missiles designed to take out any Pakistani SAM sites that might somehow pierce the electronic masking of the E-6s.

"We are formed up and ready, Skipper," Keys said through the aircraft's intercom.

"Roger that," Wilson replied. He keyed the radio. "Big Eye, Black Rock One. Black Rock is standing by."

"Black Rock One, Big Eye," the AWACS controller responded. "Turn to heading zero-one-zero and maintain flight level two-five-five, over."

"Roger, Big Eye. Turning to zero-one-zero at flight level two-five-five. Black Rock is on the way."

It was as simple as that. Wilson turned his aircraft and his entire squadron almost due north on the first leg of a flight like no other in over sixty years. Four hours and ten minutes from now, he would drop a nuclear weapon on foreign soil.

The thought gave him pause. Neither the clear, unambiguous orders sent from the president to the Commander-in-Chief Atlantic Fleet to the *Kennedy* to Wilson's wing commander, nor the sterile and precise instructions that Wilson had delivered in the squadron briefing room, could mask the enormity of what he was about to do.

"Don't think too much, Skipper," Keys said, as if reading his mind.

Wilson and Keys had flown together for three years now, and more than once they had found themselves able to communicate without a word passing between them. That was happening now.

"Hard not to, Lieutenant," Wilson replied. "This is the real thing."

"It's above our pay grade, sir," Keys said. "It's not as if we're going to eradicate a city. You heard Admiral Tanley. It's either this or a regiment of marines trying to batter their way into a cave complex. We're saving a bunch of American lives, Skipper."

"That we are," Wilson said. The thought gave some small measure of comfort. "At least until the Pakis launch their own nukes. Then it's all on the table."

"*If* the Pakis launch," Keys said. "I'm sure POTUS is talking with them. And if not, there are other squadrons standing by to take out their launch sites. You know they won't leave us out in the cold, sir."

"You're right," Wilson said. "Like you said, we're saving American lives."

But that didn't mean he had to like it.

Institutions Européennes, Strasbourg, France

Jules Soult sat in his command center on the Rue de Narcisses, monitoring the security operations. He had insisted that his teams oversee the security for the EU parliament reception, and Frau Schmidt had agreed. The Strasbourg *Gendarmerie* were happy for the help, especially when they learned that they had not been superseded by foreigners but by a Frenchman, a highly decorated *Général d'Armée*.

Of course, Soult had his own reasons for wanting to oversee today's security. Across town, at this very moment, Kasmir Al-Khalil would be making his way from his hotel to the EU parliament complex, carrying a book bag over his shoulder, not unlike the thousands of students and tourists who were out on the streets this fine spring day. Although Al-Khalil did not know it, he was under surveillance by one of Hector Vasquez's most experienced teams. His every movement had been reported to Soult, from the time he left Prague up to the present. He had been provided with inside knowledge that would allow him to place the bomb. After that, as he made his way away from the scene, Vasquez's men would "discover" and capture him. In the scramble that followed, Soult would vault himself into history.

The capture would happen as Al-Khalil boarded a bus heading south on the *Allée de la*

Robertsau. It would be a very public capture, fodder for news broadcasts all across Europe. The alert, timely intervention of Soult's troops—and Soult's personal heroism—would be credited for saving hundreds of lives and preserving the European parliament.

Moreover, Soult's survival would seem nothing short of miraculous. The world would neither know nor need to know of the small ruby pyramid that was tucked into one of the many pouches in his combat vest. They would not know that he had been protected by a secret passed down from Moses through Christ to Mary Magdalene, then entrusted by her to her grandson, who had spirited it across an ocean to the Americas. Only days before, the Hunter had returned to France and personally delivered the Codex to Soult.

This completed a unity that had been broken nearly two thousand years ago: the Codex in the hands of a Merovingian heir, completing prophecies that had been passed in whispers from generation to generation in the Order of the Rose.

Soult had accomplished what countless others could not. He had found the Codex and positioned himself to emerge in his true identity, as the heir to the Merovingian crown. With the power of the Codex, he would crush the bastard Church of Rome and unify Christendom under the true faith, the gospel as proclaimed by the First Apostle.

Only then, with the might of the American military at his disposal, controlled through an owned and subservient president, could he crush the last remaining opposition—Christian, Jewish and Muslim—and restore the Merovingian throne to its proper place.

Jerusalem.

Every act in Soult's adult life had been in preparation for that final glorious triumph. Four millennia of prophecy, misunderstood even by those who spoke it, would come to pass. The royal line of David himself, sanctified by the bloodline of the Christ, seated on the Temple Mount. And the entire world would bow to the Kingdom of God.

All of that lay ahead. But first, he must triumph this day. A day that would engrave his name on the tablet of human history.

Place St. Etienne, Strasbourg, France

"We are looking for a needle in a haystack," Niko said over the walkie-talkie. "One man in a city of a quarter million…it is impossible."

The impatience in Niko's voice was echoed in the minds of every member of the team. Renate was patrolling the Rue des Frères, and in alternating moments every face and no face looked like the photo of Kasmir Al-Khalil. Every nerve in her being screamed for his to be the next face she saw, the next man she encountered at a bus stop. The man who murdered her family was *here,* somewhere, and she could not find him.

For months now, her every waking moment had been dedicated to avenging her parents' murder. The Frankfurt Brotherhood had tried to kill her again, in Rome, and that had only made her rage burn the hotter. She would find Al-Khalil, and she would find out who was pulling his strings. Then she would kill them. It was as simple as that.

Five years ago, the thought would have repulsed her. Five years ago, she had been an agent of the *Bundeskriminalamt,* the Federal Criminal Office, and while she had been trained in the use of firearms, she never anticipated using one in anger. She had been a forensic accountant, investigating fraud, money laundering and other financial crimes. Then she had stumbled across the Frankfurt Brotherhood and fallen into a rabbit hole from which there was no escape.

The Brotherhood had tried to kill her once before and murdered her best friend in the process. That had sent her into the netherworld of Office 119, a nonexistence that demanded she surrender all human ties. She had lived in virtual isolation, walking through the world with a false identity, answering to a dozen aliases on different missions. She had forgone that most basic of human needs—love—in order to devote herself fully to the mammoth task that Office 119 faced.

And still they had murdered her parents.

The rational, clinical part of her knew that such emotions were not helpful and were indeed dangerous. She should have been focused on the larger picture, the plot behind Black Christmas and how to neutralize the growing power of the Brotherhood. They now owned a U.S. President, who for weeks had been threatening to escalate the war on terrorism with the use of nuclear weapons. She had no doubt who was pulling that string.

Thousands of people had died on Black Christmas, including three hundred in the bombing at Baden-Baden. And yet she could see only three.

Her father, a gentle man who had taken delight in teaching her the game of poker, always ready with a smile or an embrace. Her mother, a schoolteacher, a quiet but firm voice of discipline in the home, a woman who had made sure Renate had focused on her studies and attended university. And her niece, a young girl whom she had met only twice, when the girl was an infant. Renate had at first quailed at the notion of changing the baby's diapers, and then had come to enjoy it, because her niece had always giggled when Renate tickled her.

Three lives, exceptional only for their ordinariness. And all of them ended because of her.

That was the worst part of all. Whatever the larger motives that had lain beneath the Black Christmas plot, the bombing in Baden-Baden lay on her head. The Brotherhood was willing to destroy three hundred people in order to ensure the murder of three in particular…three people whose deaths would draw Renate herself into their sights.

Hardly a day had passed since Christmas when Renate had not wondered whether she ought to have obeyed the orders of her *Hauptkomissar* and dropped her investigation of the Brotherhood. Her friend would still be alive. Her parents would still be alive. She would not be living in secret, inhabiting the shadows of a world seemingly gone mad with violence. She would not be seething with rage, waiting for the opportunity to kill in cold blood those who had taken her life away.

Yet she knew such wondering was futile. What was past was past, and she steeled herself to focus on a single thought. By destroying the Brotherhood, she would honor her parents in the only way left to her. She would make sure they would not have died in vain.

For that reason, she studied every face she could see on every bus and streetcar that passed, every face that passed on the sidewalk, looking for Al-Khalil. And yet she knew Niko was right. It was a hopeless task to find one man in a city the size of Strasbourg.

"Margarite?" she said into her walkie-talkie. "Is there any traffic on the police frequencies?"

Margarite was back at their hotel, monitoring the scanner for any hint of trouble, anything that might betray Al-Khalil's whereabouts.

"Non," Margarite said. *"Rien."*

No. Nothing. Renate bit her tongue. She was fluent in French and understood Margarite easily, but it was Office 119 policy to use English. Ordinarily, Margarite did that. But here in France, she had reverted to her native tongue, much to the consternation of Lawton and Niko, neither of whom spoke French at all.

"All right," Renate said. "All teams to Checkpoint Echo. We will have to intercept him at the EU parliament complex."

Renate boarded a bus heading northeast, toward the *Parc de l'Orangerie,* designated as Checkpoint Echo in their operational plans. It lay directly across the Avenue de l'Europe from the EU parliament buildings. Margarite had chosen it because the park was always crowded, and their teams could blend into the crowds without attracting any attention. Still, because of its proximity to the target, Renate knew there would be greater security, and a greater possibility of a chance encounter with Brotherhood agents who might recognize her.

But there was no other way, and she knew it. She leaned her head against the glass, looking out as the sights of the historic city moved past, and whispered a silent prayer.

Please, God, let me find them. And kill them.

The God she knew would not approve of such a prayer. But perhaps he would understand it anyway.

32

Washington, D.C.

"You know there's not a lot we can do if they both deny it," Grant Lawrence said, looking across his desk at Miriam Anson. "And Bentley's going to be there."

"Yes, sir," Miriam said. "And I know what this could cost you, sir. If it goes wrong, well, you won't be high on President Rice's friends list."

Grant smiled and shook his head. "Don't worry about that. Harrison and I were never close. We worked together on legislation because we had some common goals, but we weren't friends. And I don't have to tell you what it was like during the primary campaign. We went at each other tooth and claw."

Miriam nodded. "I appreciate your help on this, sir."

"How could I refuse?" Grant asked. "You saved

my daughters' lives. That's a debt I can never repay."

"How are they doing?" Miriam asked.

"They're doing well. They're both still seeing the counselor, of course. Cathy says she wants to become a cop or an FBI agent. And the look in her eyes when she says it…" He paused a moment and smiled sadly. "Well, she reminds me a lot of Karen in those moments. Her eyes have the same haunted look I see in Karen's eyes when she gets home from work."

Miriam nodded, knowing the look. Terry, who was Karen Lawrence's partner, often wore the same expression. She'd seen the look in her own eyes after the messes in Guatemala, Idaho and Montana. Eyes that had seen death up close, in color, without the swelling chords of a Hollywood soundtrack to leave the impression of glory and triumph.

"It wasn't your fault, sir. You know that."

"Wasn't it?" he asked. "I try to tell myself that, that I wasn't the one who kidnapped my daughters, that I wasn't the one who pulled the trigger in Tampa. But they were after me both times, Miriam, and my girls have suffered for it. Now…well, maybe it's for the best that I'm not the president. I'm back to the relative obscurity of the Senate, and that's better for my family."

"And I'm asking you to step into the lion's den again," Miriam said.

"You're just asking me to do my job, Miriam. I swore an oath to uphold and defend the Constitution. Given what you've told me, that's not what's happening in the White House. So I have a duty here, just like you do."

"Duty," she said. "Interesting word. Not one that's real popular nowadays, but you're right."

"Duty has never been a popular word," he said, with an encouraging smile. "It's not in our nature to subordinate our own interests to something else. Most of us, when we do it at all, do it because we think we have no choice. We go to work. We take care of our kids. But we usually don't like it. Duty is never popular."

Miriam chuckled. "You should have been a priest. You remind me of one I met in Guatemala."

"Idealistic fool?" he asked, laughing.

"Not a fool," Miriam said. "Just another person who'd like the world to be better than it is and is willing to work to make it that way."

"Like I said...an idealistic fool."

Now it was her turn to laugh. "Then God grant us more idealistic fools, Senator."

"Amen to that," he said.

Miriam looked at her watch. "Almost time, sir."

"Yes, it is," he replied. "And, Miriam?"

"Yes, sir?"

"Stop calling me 'sir.'"

She smiled. "Yes, sir."

Parc de l'Orangerie, Strasbourg, France

Renate was the first of the group to reach the small garden in front of the *Pavillon Joséphine,* a conference building and one of the most common gathering points in the park. Its snow-white facade could not have been more at odds with her inner landscape. She found herself studying every face she passed, noting every passerby's movement. In the largest and most beautiful park in Strasbourg, where families gathered to walk, take boat rides or watch the animals in the zoo, she saw nothing but threats.

Perhaps it was the contrast between her own anxiety and the relaxation of those around her, but she came to realize that this moment by moment search for danger had become her constant mode of being. She saw peril in the most innocent of gestures, the most casual of glances. It had made her into someone she didn't especially like. On the other hand, there was that American adage: *It's not paranoia if they really are out to get you.*

She tried to muster a smile as Ahmed walked up, the first of her companions to arrive. From the look on his face, she hadn't succeeded.

"I fear this will not be a good day," he said. "If we cannot stop Al-Khalil…the consequences…"

"All we can do is our best," Renate said, trying to sound reassuring, even though her own thoughts mimicked his. "And we *are* doing that."

"Yes," he said, nodding. "But if you will pardon me, that is easier for you to say. The Americans will not use nuclear weapons here in Europe. They will not decide to eradicate Christianity. The war, if war will come, will be fought in the lands of my people."

"Perhaps," she said. "But your parents were not killed on Black Christmas. Mine were."

If she had kicked him in the stomach, he could not have looked more stricken. "I am sorry, Ms. Bächle. I had no idea."

"We have a story in my country," she said. "In August of 1870, when the Germans went to war with the French, a man said to his neighbor, 'I hope the war will end quickly.' In February of 1871, after Paris had fallen, the man returned and said, 'The war is ended quickly!' His neighbor replied, 'The war will never be ended, because my son was killed.'"

"Yes," Ahmed said, shaking his head. "You are right, Ms. Bächle. I spoke foolishly."

"Forty years later, the Germans and French went to war again, and millions were killed," Renate said. "And twenty years later, war again, and even more millions were killed. That is why we created the European Union, Mr. Ahsami. So we would never again destroy one another. You have seen the statue in front of the parliament building?"

"Yes," Ahmed said. "An embrace."

She nodded. "That is what the European Union

means. That is what Al-Khalil and his masters wish to destroy."

"There is great evil in this world, Ms. Bächle. But there is also great good. We are both trying to be part of that good."

"Then we need to try harder," Renate said.

Lawton and Niko joined them moments later, followed by the remainder of the team.

"We're getting nowhere fast," Lawton said. "Niko and I tried to go to the Parliament building. There are metal detectors at every entrance. There's no way we could get in there. Not armed."

"And the city buses drop people off almost at the entrance," Niko added. "The crowds are heavy, and there are French police and EU security officers all around. If we try to intercept him there, it will be a bloodbath."

Renate paused for a moment, then nodded. With their original plan scuttled, she had to think quickly. "But we must at least know when he arrives. Al-Khalil is not a martyr. He will give himself plenty of time to escape. We take him after he leaves the parliament complex and then alert EU security. Their dogs will find the bomb."

"Sounds good," Lawton said.

"I agree," Ahmed added. "This is all we can do."

The other members of the team concurred. Even O'Connor voiced no objection.

Renate keyed her walkie-talkie. "Margarite?"

"Oui?"

Renate explained the new plan quickly. "Lawton, Ahmed and I will go to the parliament complex to watch for Al-Khalil. Niko and the teams will be standing by. Once we know how Al-Khalil will return to his hotel, I will need the exact route at once. We will plot an intercept point, dispatch Niko's and Ahmed's teams, and rendezvous onsite. You will call in the bomb threat, and we will let EU security take care of that."

"Oui," Margarite said. "That is the best way."

"Merci," Renate said. She lowered the walkie-talkie and turned to the others. "Let's go."

Washington, D.C.

Miriam had been to the White House only once, when she had received her commendation after the Montana incident. Grant Lawrence had been there many times in his career, and he seemed at ease as they were checked through security and escorted to the West Wing. Miriam, however, felt anything but at ease. She was not here to receive a commendation this time. She was here to confront a president and his National Security Advisor, to accuse them of conspiring to take the nation to war using the most horrific weapons that had ever been created.

"Relax," Grant whispered as they strode through the corridors to the waiting area outside the Oval

Office. "This building is designed to intimidate guests, but the people who work here are just that…people. And you know how to work people."

Miriam nodded, hearing the words but not feeling them in her heart. She had to focus on the specific tasks at hand. Kevin Willis had taken the tapes of the Katherine Dixon interrogations, along with the documents she had given them, to a federal judge with a reputation for both courage and discretion. Still, the judge had not felt the evidence was compelling enough to issue a warrant for the arrest of Phillip Bentley on charges of conspiracy and murder. Without a warrant, all Miriam could do was bluff. And while she had never been a poker player, she had more than once bluffed a suspect into a confession. She would simply have to try to do it again.

"Senator," the receptionist said. "The president will see you now."

Grant nodded amiably and rose with only a slight grimace. It was, Miriam thought, an indicator of his true feelings. When he was tense, the knee injury he had sustained in childhood seemed to trouble him more.

Still, he managed to walk without a limp, and she followed him into an office that she had seen countless times in movies, television series and news reports. But for a handful of personal articles that Harrison Rice had brought with him—most notably an old, cracked football that seemed to have been signed by an entire team, resting in a glass case on a side table—the room looked exactly the same as she had expected, albeit somewhat smaller.

Harrison Rice was standing behind his desk as they entered, and he quickly rounded it, approaching Grant with a smile and his hand extended. "Grant Lawrence. It's been far too long, my old friend."

Grant shook his hand, returning the smile. "Thank you, Mr. President. And this is my... keeper...Special Agent Miriam Anson. I'm sure you remember her from the news reports."

"Yes," Rice said, turning to her. "You were quite the hero in Guatemala, and then again in Montana, Special Agent Anson. The Bureau can be proud to have people like you."

"Thank you, Mr. President," Miriam said, shaking his offered hand. "It sounds clichéd, but I was simply doing my job, sir. Our tactical teams did the hard work."

"You're too modest," Rice said. "I read the news coverage. You were no mere desk jockey. You put yourself in the line of fire, more than once, to rally your people and provide leadership. I don't know if I could have done that."

"I'm sure you would have," Grant said, nod-

ding to the football. "You have a knack for stepping up to the task at hand, Mr. President."

The door opened, and Phillip Bentley entered
the room. "Ah, you're here already, Senator."

"They were just shown in, Phillip," Rice said.
He made the introductions and turned to Grant.
"I'm sorry to say I'm on a tight schedule, Grant."

"Yes, of course," Grant said. "As I told Mr.
Bentley, I wanted to thank you personally for the
Medal of Freedom. It meant a lot to my family,
even if I wasn't fully aware of what was happening at the time."

"You're welcome," Rice said. "Though it is the
nation who should thank *you* for your courage
and sacrifice. You have given much to this country, Senator Lawrence. A Medal of Freedom was
the least the country could do in return."

Grant smiled. "Thank you, sir."

"And thank you for coming," Rice said. "After
what happened in the primary fight, it's nice to
know that we're still friends."

"Politics and friendship are separate spheres,"
Grant said. "When we forget that, democracy
suffers."

"Yes," Bentley said. "Well, Senator, if you will
excuse us, the president has a briefing soon."

"He may need to postpone it," Grant said, his
smile fading. "My friend Special Agent Anson
has come to me with some concerns. Evidence

that requires our attention. *Your* attention, Mr. President. And yours, Mr. Bentley."

Institutions Européennes, Strasbourg, France

"I've got him," Lawton's voice said.

Renate whipped her head around, almost dislodging the tiny earpiece through which the alert had come, as she began to scan the crowd. She keyed her mike. "Where?"

"Second bus," Lawton said. "There's a clump of people who just got off. He's toward the back. Jeans, a brown sweater, brown hiking boots, dark green backpack over his right shoulder."

Renate spotted him and felt a predatory surge flow through her. "Yes, I see him. Ahmed?"

"I see him, as well," Ahmed said.

"Lawton, you are the eagle," Renate said, referring to the standard surveillance techniques she and Lawton had both learned in their law enforcement training. "Ahmed and I are the foxes. We will exchange when he comes out."

"Roger," Lawton said.

Lawton, the "eagle," would follow Al-Khalil at a discreet distance, always keeping the target in sight. Renate and Ahmed, the "foxes," would trail Lawton, keeping him in sight while avoiding direct sight lines to the target himself. Thus, should Al-Khalil spot anyone, he would see only Lawton. After he emerged from the EU complex, Renate would become the eagle, and Lawton and Ahmed would be the foxes. Even if Al-Khalil saw her, he would have no reason to associate her with a man he had seen earlier, and no reason to believe he was being followed.

Renate and Ahmed had another task, as well, for the foxes were also responsible for countersurveillance. Even as she watched Lawton, she scanned the crowd, looking for other people who might be following or observing Al-Khalil. Unless she was gravely mistaken, Al-Khalil's masters would have their own team observing him to ensure that he completed his mission. It fell upon the foxes to identify any other surveillance, warn the eagle if they moved on him or the target, and find a way to distract them when the time came for the takedown.

The carefully choreographed dance had begun. When Lawton disappeared behind a crowd, Renate keyed her mike again. "Do you have eyes on eagle, Ahmed?"

"Yes," Ahmed said. "Moving toward west past the tower, toward the river."

"Roger," Renate said, maintaining her pace so as not to attract attention. As she rounded the crowd, she saw Lawton's back once again. "I have eyes on eagle."

"Roger," Ahmed said.

She was not surprised that Al-Khalil was not

using the main entrance. Just as they could not pass through the metal detectors with their weapons, he could not pass with a bomb in his backpack. He would use another entrance, probably one he had scouted in advance, or one that had been scouted for him.

Moments later, her suspicions were confirmed when Lawton spoke. "Target has entered through a fire door. Target is on-site."

"Roger," Renate said. "He will plant the bomb in *la Tour,* so he will probably come out the main entrance. It would be the fastest exit. Ahmed and I will cover there."

Then she would be the eagle, with direct surveillance on the man who murdered her family. And she would fight the urge to swoop in, talons exposed, and kill him.

She hoped she had the strength not to do it.

33

Off the coast of Pakistan

"Black Rock One, Big Eye, over."

The voice in Commander Timothy Wilson's helmet grated on his raw nerves. He knew what the controller in the AWACS plane was going to say, and he didn't want to hear it. Still, his training took over, and he reported in.

"Big Eye, Black Rock One. Go ahead."

"Black Rock One, you are at Papa-November-Romeo."

"Copy, Big Eye. Black Rock at Papa-November-Romeo."

It sounded so sterile, as if this were an ordinary position check on an ordinary flight. It was anything but. *Papa-November-Romeo,* or PNR, stood for *Point of No Return.* His squadron was now circling just outside the airspace of Pakistan. Once they broke north, their ordinance would be armed and they would be committed to the mission—and the rules of engagement. Before that happened, Wilson had a final task to do: contact Command Six, the fleet admiral aboard the *Kennedy,* and secure the release codes for the nuclear weapons he and his XO were carrying.

"Switching to one-one-four-point-nine," Lieutenant Keys said from the seat behind him, announcing that he was changing to the radio frequency for fleet command. "Ready to contact Command Six, sir."

Wilson nodded, though Keys would not see it through the high padded headrest behind Wilson's seat. Once he requested "weapons hot," the fleet admiral would contact the White House. Only the President of the United States could issue release codes for nuclear weapons. Wilson had no doubt that President Rice would issue those codes. The fleet admiral would forward them to Wilson, and he would type them into the keypad of his instrument console. And then, for the first time in sixty years, a U.S. warplane would be carrying a live nuclear bomb with the intent to drop it on foreign soil.

"Sir?" Keys asked. "Command net is active."

"Thank you, Lieutenant," Wilson said.

If he went forward, he would be a hero to some and a monster to others. His name would be inscribed alongside those of the men who piloted the *Enola Gay,* the B-29 that dropped the atomic bomb on Hiroshima. If he refused and turned his squadron back toward the *Kennedy,* those who would otherwise have celebrated him a hero would brand him a traitor and a coward. He would undoubtedly be court-martialed. And those who would otherwise have reviled him as a monster would celebrate his "act of conscience."

And that, he supposed, was what it came down to. Was this an act of conscience or cowardice? Was he morally opposed to deploying the weapon that hung beneath his sleek jet, or was he simply quailing at the thought of doing it himself?

From his plebe year in the Academy, he had been schooled in the *Uniform Code of Military Justice* and the doctrine of lawful orders. Since the horrible events that had come to light at the Nuremberg trials after World War II, every American fighting man was taught that the final responsibility rested on his shoulders. "I was just following orders" was not a legal defense. If the lowliest private believed an order was unlawful, he had not only the right but the duty to refuse that order.

So, Wilson asked himself, was the order to attack the terrorist stronghold in Pakistan with a nuclear weapon a lawful order? Wilson was not carrying an indiscriminate area weapon that would vaporize a city. This bomb would burrow down into a cave complex that intelligence sources had confirmed to be a headquarters for the Al Qaeda terrorist network. The surface release of radiation would be minimal, and those who would be vaporized in that cave had both the intent and the means to murder American citizens. Unlike Wilson, they would not agonize over that decision.

But the consequences of his dropping the bomb might go far beyond simply eradicating an Al Qaeda planning cell. If Pakistan launched its own nuclear weapons in response—perhaps in the form of a missile strike on the *Kennedy* battle group—then India would certainly jump on the opportunity to resolve long-simmering hostilities by launching their weapons at Pakistan. And once someone had broken the unspoken agreement that nuclear weapons were too horrible to be used... That was the prospect that had cold trickles of sweat running down Wilson's back. Because he would have been the man who started that avalanche.

"Skipper, command net is active," Lieutenant Keys said again, concern and impatience clear in his voice. "We have to make the call, sir."

"Yes, Lieutenant," Wilson said. "I know. Thank you."

Ultimately, Wilson concluded, Keys had been right. These decisions were above his pay grade. If this weapon were not used, hundreds of young U.S. Marines would die in the assault on that cave complex. The President did have the lawful authority to issue the release codes that would spare those men's lives. The President also had the diplomatic responsibility to handle the Pakistanis and the Indians and whoever else might want to jump on the nuclear bandwagon, and forestall that escalation.

The order was lawful. It would save hundreds of American lives.

Wilson spoke in clear, crisp tones. "Command Six, Black Rock One. Black Rock is at Papa-November-Romeo and requesting weapons hot. I say again. Black Rock is at Papa-November-Romeo and requesting weapons hot. Over."

"Black Rock One, Command Six. Copy you at Papa-November-Romeo and requesting weapons hot. Stand by for national command clearance."

"Copy, Command Six," Wilson said. "Standing by."

Institutions Européennes, Strasbourg, France

There he was.

Renate spotted Al-Khalil as he emerged from *la Tour* and for the first time looked upon the face of the man who had killed her parents. Even as she reached for the Glock 9 mm pistol in her purse, she knew this was not the time or the place to use it. Instead, she raised her wrist to her face, as if wiping away a stray lock of hair.

"Eagle has eyes on target," she said.

"Roger," Lawton replied.

Ahmed acknowledged a moment later, and the dance of eagle and foxes began again. She followed Al-Khalil south along the *Quay Chanoine Winterer* to a bridge that crossed the canal to the *Boulevard Paul Déroulède* and on to the *Alleé de la Robertsau,* reporting at each location. Lawton and Ahmed acknowledged her reports, letting her know they had her in sight.

"Any sign of other surveillance?" Renate asked.

"I need to confirm that," Lawton replied. "I think so, but you're on a popular pedestrian route. I want to know who's who first."

"Well, find out fast," Renate said. "If they're Brotherhood, they may recognize me."

"Doing my best," he replied.

"Do better," she snapped.

Even as she said the words, she knew she was foolish to have done so. The simple fact was that it was difficult to pick up skilled surveillance operatives when moving with a crowd. Any of the people in that crowd—or none of them—might be following her, waiting for an opportunity to move in for the kill.

But there was no alternative. Margarite was needed to man the police scanners, for only she could follow the rapid-fire French transmissions. Niko was commanding the operations team and had to be there with them. Lawton had already been the eagle, and if he moved in again Al-Khalil might spot him and bolt. Ahmed, patently Arab, would be more likely to attract Al-Khalil's attention.

Renate had to be the eagle, however exposed she might feel. She would simply have to rely on Lawton and Ahmed to alert her if anyone began to move on her. She would have to trust, and that alone was the most disquieting part of the operation.

Al-Khalil boarded a bus outside the *Parc de l'Orangerie,* and Renate boarded behind him. Once the bus was in motion and passenger conversation resumed, she leaned her chin on the heel of her hand, as if resting, and reported the bus number.

"That bus is going to the *Place de Bordeaux,*" Margarite said. "There he will switch to the tram and ride back to his hotel."

"Margarite, have you reported the bomb threat yet?"

"*Oui,*" she replied. "I just did."

"Copy his route," Niko said. "We'll take him at the transfer."

"It is a large plaza," Margarite said. "There may be civilians everywhere."

"We have no choice," Renate whispered insistently. "Once he boards the tram, he will be back at his hotel before we get another chance. And the crowds in *La Petite France* will be even worse. It has to be at the transfer."

"We're on the move," Niko said.

"Copy," Margarite said. "Niko, deploy your snipers atop the Holiday Inn on the east side of the plaza. That will offer the best sight lines in the area."

"Copy," Niko said.

"Foxes, did you see anything?" Renate asked.

"Three men," Lawton said. "Early middle-aged, fit, all wearing jeans, one with a black leather jacket, another with an old army coat and the third with a green sweater. The one in the green sweater looks to be the leader. And he looks like one tough son of a bitch."

Renate quickly identified the three men, who had disbursed throughout the bus. There was no way Al-Khalil could get off the bus without passing one of them. She knew that Niko's team would make it across town before the bus did. But then again, so would whatever backup these three men had. They were after Al-Khalil, she was sure. Or tried to be sure. And very likely these three men had known what route Al-Khalil would take days in advance. They, too, would realize that the *Place de Bordeaux* was their best choice for the take-down.

It was going to get bloody.

Washington, D.C.

"This is preposterous!" Bentley shouted. "These are the ravings of a woman with a grudge."

"Perhaps," Miriam said. She had carefully laid out the case she had built based on the interviews and documents that Katherine Dixon had provided. "But it raises grave concerns about your role in the shooting of Grant Lawrence and the ascendancy of President Rice."

"Absurd!" Bentley said again.

"Mr. President?" Grant asked. "I won't even ask if you had any role in this. I know you better than that."

"I did not," Rice said. "I didn't know about it until after the election."

"Shut up," Bentley said, wheeling on Rice. "Don't say another word."

"Despite what you believe," Rice said, his voice rising as he stood, "I am still your boss, Bentley. You don't give me orders. And your dirty secret is out."

"It's *your* dirty secret, too," Bentley said. "You think you can survive this? I don't tolerate betrayal. Especially not from the likes of you."

"If I go down, so be it," Rice said, pounding a fist on his desk. "At least I can go down fighting."

Just then there was a knock at the door, and a young Marine captain stepped into the room. The captain carried a small black briefcase. "I'm sorry to interrupt, Mr. President, but we have Admiral Rickings aboard the U.S.S. *Kennedy* on the phone. It's time to issue the release codes, sir."

"Release codes?" Grant asked. "My God, you're not going to…"

"He is going to protect the United States from its sworn enemies," Bentley said. "Come in, Captain. Have them patch the call through to here."

The captain nodded, and moments later the red phone on the president's desk began to blink. The captain picked up the receiver. "National command is standing by."

"You can't do this, Harrison," Grant said. "You know what will happen. The Pakistanis will launch on us, and the Indians on them. It will be Armageddon."

"It's a tactical weapon," Bentley said. "We can control the situation, Mr. President. You have to give those pilots the release codes. Think about the hundreds of marines who will die if they have to assault those caves on foot."

"There are other options," Grant said. "Conventional bunker-busting bombs. You're being set up, Harrison. They want you to escalate this war."

"Enough!" Rice shouted. "I can't hear myself think!"

"National command is standing by," the captain repeated into the phone, his voice muted.

After a long moment, Rice shook his head.

"There has to be another way. National command denies release."

"No!" Bentley shouted. "You have to order release!"

"National command denies release," Rice said again, his eyes fixed on the captain.

"You'll be killing marines if you relay that command," Bentley said, now turning his rage on the captain. "Young men just like you will crawl into booby-trapped caves. You will attend their funerals, Captain, and you will know *you* put them in their graves."

"I have the President's orders," the captain said. "National command—"

Before he could finish the sentence, Bentley was charging, hands reaching for the briefcase. Known as "the football," it contained the release codes for the nation's nuclear arsenal. Miriam instinctively reached for her weapon, only then remembering that she had checked it at the White House security desk. She tried to cut Bentley off, but a wingback chair was directly between them. She caught only his sleeve as he passed, but she tightened her fingernails into flesh and muscle, shoving the chair out of the way with her free hand, stepping behind him and trying to twist his arm behind his back.

The captain still carried his sidearm, and the moment that Bentley spent wrenching his arm loose from Miriam's hold gave the captain time to draw and level the pistol. Bentley shoved Miriam to the floor and turned just as the captain fired.

Only her fall saved Miriam. The bullet shattered Bentley's sternum, exploded his heart and burst out through his back to lodge in the wall. His body crumpled atop Miriam's, and within seconds the Oval Office was flooded with Secret Service agents. Amidst the chaos, Rice shouted to the captain.

"Give the order!"

The captain dropped his weapon in the face of six agents whose weapons were trained on him, then reached for the receiver, dangling from the cord where he had dropped it. Never taking his eyes off the Secret Service agents, he groped for a moment before finding the handset and bringing it to his face.

"National command denies release," he said, firmly. "I say again, national command denies release."

Miriam pushed Bentley's body from atop her as she heard the words and looked at Rice. "Thank you, Mr. President. Thank you."

Rice simply shook his head as he helped Grant pull her to her feet. "Please, Special Agent, don't call me that. I'm not worthy of the office."

"Oh yes," Grant said. "Yes, you are."

34

Institutions Européennes, Strasbourg, France

Soult heard the report on the police band. *Bomb spotted in Tour Européenne.* Someone must have seen Al-Khalil plant the bomb. While the report was premature, it changed nothing about Soult's plan.

As he scrambled out of the command van, a French police officer was running to meet him. "I heard," Soult said. "I will lead the search team personally."

"Oui, Général," the police officer said.

The officer had to hurry to catch up as Soult ran past him and across the Rue du Levant. Soult had an advantage over the others who would be searching the magnificent glass tower. He knew where the bombs were to be planted.

Already, members of parliament were streaming out of the building and scattering across the surrounding grass. Soult yelled to the officer to push them farther back. If by some chance either of the bombs detonated before Soult could disarm them, flying glass would cut to ribbons anyone standing within fifty meters of the building.

Soult fought his way upstream through the surge of panicked dignitaries, finally emerging into *la Tour.* Two flak-jacketed policemen were beginning to search the area. More would be arriving in minutes, with search dogs trained to sniff out explosives. Soult could not let that happen. He had to find the bombs himself for today to have any meaning at all. He had to work quickly.

The first bomb was easy to find. It was, as Soult had directed, near the back of *la Tour,* beside the corridor that led to the Louis Weiss Building behind. This would be the bomb that would mark his holy anointing. This was a simple pipe bomb, without any backup detonation circuitry, and Soult quickly but gingerly tucked it into a thigh pocket of his fatigues. But the cesium bomb was not where Soult had instructed Al-Khalil to plant it.

Perhaps Al-Khalil had felt too exposed placing the bomb so near the podium from which the Commission President was to address the members of parliament. Or perhaps he had simply chosen another location on his own, believing that his engineering background had led him to a better solution than the one with which he had been provided. Regardless, Soult had to work quickly. If he did not find the cesium bomb, the entire operation would be a failure.

He tried to project himself into Al-Khalil's mind, estimating where the engineer would have placed the bomb, but found himself drawing a blank. He was a soldier, not an engineer. Desperation grew as he saw the Strasbourg Police bomb squad assembling outside. Acting on impulse, he pulled the ruby pyramid from his pocket and held it in his palm, then slowly turned in a circle, hoping against hope that it might act as a divining rod, guiding him toward his destiny.

The faintest glow within the ruby seemed to call to him as he faced one of the concrete-and-steel pillars on the southern face of the building. The nearer he got to the pillar, the brighter the glow, though never did it seem to leave the stone itself. It was as if the stone were merely illuminating itself, allowing only him to see it. Perhaps it was the power of the stone reacting with the radioactive emissions from the bomb.

Or perhaps it was destiny guiding his footsteps.

As he neared the pillar, the stone began to give off heat. The heat quickly became intolerable, and Soult had to put the stone back in his pocket.

It was then that he saw the bomb.

Al-Khalil had been instructed to booby-trap this device, and Soult studied the bomb without moving, without touching it. It consisted of a black metal cube perhaps twenty centimeters on a side, connected to a sphere only slightly larger. The timing and triggering mechanisms were in the cube; the sphere would be the bomb itself. On the back side, steel conduit led between them. Al-Khalil had been thorough. This would not permit the absurd "red wire or blue wire" scenes so common in American movies. Inside the box, Soult was certain, lay a mercury switch that would trigger the detonation if anyone tried to move the bomb.

"Over here," Soult called out as the bomb squad technicians entered the building. "I have found it."

As they approached, he pointed to the device. "It appears to be very sophisticated. As you can see, the detonating cables are sealed within steel conduit. I would be very surprised if it were not also booby-trapped."

"I have worse news than that," the technician said, sweeping a multiband scanner over the device. He flipped a switch, and Soult could hear the ragged, telltale ticking of a Geiger counter. "It contains radioactive material, General. You should leave now, sir. We will attempt to disarm it."

"No," Soult said firmly. "I am the senior EU security official on-site. An officer cannot lead from the back of the column. I will stay with you."

"Sir, please. I do not wish to be responsible for the death of a *Général d'Armée*."

Soult finally nodded. He took the pipe bomb from his pocket. "I found another device. This one appears to be much cruder. I have disarmed it."

"You are a brave man, General," the bomb technician said, quickly looking at the dummy wires Soult had pulled from the pipe bomb. "We have a disposal mortar beside the river. Give it to the men there."

"I will," Soult said.

"And I will work on this one, General. Trust me. We are good at what we do."

Soult nodded and walked away slowly, holding the pipe bomb as if it were a baby. Everything was perfect. Noting with satisfaction that he had the full attention of the television news cameramen who had swarmed to the scene, he walked toward the river. He slipped a hand into his pocket and gripped the ruby tightly, murmuring a prayer that had been passed down for nearly two thousand years through the Order of the Rose.

Then he pressed the button on the side of the bomb.

He did not hear the explosion. There was only a blinding flash, and then blackness.

Place de Bordeaux, Strasbourg, France

"Snipers in position," Niko said as the bus carrying Al-Khalil and Renate pulled into the vast grass expanse of the plaza.

Renate glanced up and saw that the man in the green sweater was now standing beside her seat, as if he were preparing to get off the bus. Unable to respond verbally, she simply pressed the microphone key...one quick tap, one long tap, one quick tap. It was the letter *R* in International Morse Code, the signal for a message received. She hoped Niko and the rest of the team would understand it.

Al-Khalil rose and headed for the front of the bus. Renate sat for a moment, allowing the three men to close on him, one in front and two behind, with three other passengers behind them. She rose and headed for the rear exit of the bus. As she neared it and leaned against a vertical rail for support, she brought her face to her wrist.

"Target will exit front. Bandit surveillance team is with him, leather jacket in front, army coat and green sweater behind. Have snipers put sights on bandits."

"Copy," Niko said from atop the roof. "Snipers, put sights on bandits and give me shot-or-no."

Renate stepped off the bus and immediately scanned the area for Ahmed's men. They were there, thirty meters away, the four of them casually kicking a soccer ball as if they were students on a break from classes. The three men from the bus ignored them, following their quarry. As she followed Al-Khalil across the grass toward the tram stop, she glanced back over her shoulder at the roofline of the Holiday Inn hotel behind her. Four heads edged above the parapet, almost invisible unless one knew where to look. Niko and his sniper team.

"Shot-or-no?" Renate asked, still walking toward the tram.

"Sniper one has shot," she heard one of the men say.

"Sniper two has shot," another added.

"Sniper three has no shot," O'Connor said.

Renate glanced around. Although the plaza was mostly open, it was dotted with trees. O'Connor's shot might be obstructed by one of them. Or perhaps O'Connor himself was the obstruction.

Seventy meters to the south, a minivan pulled into a parking place alongside the plaza. Renate recognized Lawton behind the wheel. There was no way for him to bring the car closer, and no chance of herding Al-Khalil into the van before the three men could react. She needed all three of them taken out, and at the same instant. That was the task of Niko's snipers, and two were ready to act. But O'Connor was not.

Renate could use her own weapon to take out the third target, but not without drawing attention from the dozens of people who were wandering the plaza on this warm spring evening. Three momentary muzzle flashes and inaudible *spits* from silenced sniper rifles on the roof would likely go unnoticed. Perhaps the strollers would see the three men topple to the ground, perhaps not. Regardless, Niko's men were well trained, and they would leave no trace of themselves or their weapons on that roof. But if she were forced to fire, the report of her 9 mm pistol would not go unnoticed.

"O'Connor, shot-or-no?" she asked impatiently.

"Fifteen more meters," O'Connor said. "Then he will clear the trees."

"And twenty meters after that, he will be at the tram stop," Renate said.

"I can't guarantee a clean hit," O'Connor said. "I can't make the bloody tree move."

"Sniper one and two, shot-or-no?" Niko asked.

"Sniper one has shot."

"Sniper two has shot."

"Sniper three stand down," Renate said. "If we let him get closer to the tram stop, we endanger civilians. I will take green sweater."

"Sniper three standing down," O'Connor said.

Renate could not tell whether she heard relief, disgust, disappointment or anger in O'Connor's voice. They would sort that out later. Right now, she had to act, and act quickly.

"On my mark," she said, drawing the Glock from her purse and squeezing the grip to release the safety.

From the corner of her eye, she saw Ahmed's men abandon the soccer ball, preparing to move. She raised the pistol and centered it on the back of the green sweater.

"Three. Two. Mark."

The two snipers fired a split second too soon. As she was squeezing the trigger, Renate heard the buzz of their rounds passing, the quiet thuds as their bullets struck the targets, and the men's almost silent grunts as they slumped to the ground.

But so did the man in the green sweater.

As Renate's pistol fired, he was already dropping to the ground and rolling. She tried to sight on him, but he was moving quickly, eyes up and alert, seeking the threat, seeking her. He raised his pistol as their eyes met, and Renate knew in an instant that this was not a battle she could win. He was prone, a more stable firing position and a smaller target. She saw the muzzle flash and ducked to the left, hearing the bullet buzz past her right ear. He would not miss again.

But neither would he fire again.

As Renate sighted on him, she saw his face explode in a pink mist.

"Sniper three has him," O'Connor said a moment later.

Al-Khalil was left standing alone, frozen in place as Ahmed's men moved in on him. As they grabbed his arms and began to steer him away toward the van, Renate walked over to the dead man and looked back up at the hotel roofline. Through the thin outer springtime growth of a tree, she saw O'Connor's head for just an instant, before he disappeared beneath the parapet.

"Good shot, sniper three," she said.

"Bloody good for you that he rolled to his right," O'Connor replied. "And thanks, gov."

Renate joined Ahmed's men. They were talking to Al-Khalil in Arabic, but she knew he spoke flawless English. As he tried to twist away, Renate stepped in front of him and jammed her pistol into his belly.

"Give me an excuse," she said.

Al-Khalil looked resigned but defiant. "Allah be praised."

"Allah didn't kill my parents in Baden-Baden," she snapped. "You did, you filthy dog. And my six-year-old niece. And three hundred other people who wanted nothing more than to worship their God on Christmas morning."

From the corner of her eye, she saw Lawton approaching. He had left the van. She stared into Al-Khalil's eyes, searching for any sign of remorse, any hint of humanity. She saw only emptiness, an emptiness that seemed to mirror her own soul. Anger surged within her, and she brought the pistol up beneath his chin. She would end this here and now.

"Renate, no," Lawton said. "Not here. We're too exposed as it is."

"He doesn't deserve to live," Renate said quietly.

"Perhaps not," Lawton said, stepping closer. "But if you do this now, we lose our last lead. He's a puppet, Renate. We want the puppet masters."

"I'll settle for the puppet," she said.

He lifted his hand and placed it over hers.

"You're not him, Renate. You're not."

Something in his voice, in the touch of his hand, found the last shred of the person she had once been. She looked into Al-Khalil's eyes again. He deserved to die. But it was not her place to kill him.

She lowered her pistol.

"Take this shit away," she said quietly. "I never want to see him again."

As Ahmed's men pushed Al-Khalil toward the van, Lawton looked at her. "You're not coming?"

"I'll take the tram," she said.

"But…"

She met his eyes. "Leave it be, Lawton. Please. Just leave it be."

He nodded. As he turned and headed toward the van, Renate put the Glock back in her purse. She walked across the plaza, not looking over at the three dead bodies sprawled on the grass, not looking up at the hotel roofline for any sign of Niko's men departing, not looking back as the van pulled away, not looking at the startled people around her.

Instead, she looked forward, at the new spring growth on the trees.

35

Renate glanced around the café as the news came on a television behind the counter. The bustle of conversations quickly quieted to murmurs.

Once again, the news networks showed the by now familiar footage of General Jules Soult coming out of the EU parliament building, gingerly holding the bomb in his hands, seemingly oblivious to the cameras that had recorded his every move as he walked around the building to the bomb disposal squad waiting on the riverbank. Every time, it almost seemed as if he would make it to the detonation mortar, a thick steel container in which the explosion would have been contained and vented harmlessly. Every time, just as he drew near the mortar, the crowd gasped as the bomb went off. Every time, the cameraman's breathless

"Merde!" was audible before the camera whipped around to show the dignitaries crouched with their hands over their heads or lying facedown on the ground.

Next came the interviews with the bomb disposal men, who had defused the cesium-laced bomb inside the building with only seconds to spare. They could not have neutralized the bomb in time, they assured the cameras, had Soult not entered the building and found the devices. An attack intended to kill hundreds and poison thousands more had instead wounded only one man… Soult himself.

His survival was nothing short of miraculous, the doctors said. Perhaps it was the position in which he had held the bomb, the police speculated. Or his fitness and stout constitution, the doctors wondered. Regardless, except for flash burns on his hands and face, he had been almost unscathed. The shards of twisted metal that should have riddled his body had somehow missed him. Although his uniform was shredded—photos of it had appeared in almost every newspaper in Europe in the days after the attack—he had only a few small cuts.

The clamor for the vote of no confidence against the President of the European Commission had been swift and loud, and with its outcome a foregone conclusion, the president had dissolved the commission and resigned. The search for a successor had been equally swift, for it had centered on the man who lay recovering in a Paris hospital, the hero of Europe, the savior of the European Parliament.

Now the coverage returned to the present and the image of Jules Soult, still bald and without eyebrows, still wearing the gauze gloves that protected the skin grafts on his hands, standing on the podium, ready to be sworn in as the new President of the European Commission. He had been, news anchors reminded the audience, the near-unanimous nominee of the European Council—the committee of elected heads of state from each of the member nations—and overwhelmingly approved by a grateful parliament.

He promised a new Europe, a stronger Europe, more united under the banner of the Union, fully committed to prosecuting the war on terrorism. This would require changes, he said. Sacrifices for the common good. But such was the price of liberty and safety. The parliament roared in approval.

No one, Renate realized, had paid the slightest attention to the apprehension and trial of the man who had planted the bombs. Al-Khalil's trial, conducted in Saudi Arabia, had been broadcast on the Al Jazeera network but had received only passing mention in the Western press. The chief witness for the prosecution, Prince Ahmed Ahsami, had detailed his investigation of Al-Khalil's role in the Black Christmas bombing in Baden-Baden, the ricin attack in Prague and the attempted bombing in Strasbourg. The verdict had been unanimous, and Kasmir Al-Khalil had been executed under Islamic law before jeering crowds chanting "Innocent blood is not justice."

By prior agreement, Ahmed had not mentioned Renate, Lawton or their companions. He could not have identified Office 119 even had he been inclined to do so. After their interrogation of Al-Khalil, so far as Ahmed knew, Lawton and Niko had vanished into the ether.

But that interrogation had yielded fruit. Al-Khalil had identified a Swiss Arab banker as his recruiter, and already Niko and Assif were in Zurich, tapping into yet another bank's communications. The results would, Renate hoped, provide the evidence needed to roll up the Frankfurt Brotherhood once and for all.

That would be a victory, yes. But a hollow one. The Brotherhood had extracted from her a price that could never be repaid. Now she was truly alone in the world.

"You look pensive," Lawton said, leaning over to her.

"Pensive?" she asked. Despite years of training and study, she still sometimes had to ask the meanings of obscure English words.

Lawton nodded. "Sad. Melancholy. You're thinking about unhappy things."

"Yes," she said. "It is difficult not to. They are gone. I cannot even visit their graves."

"No," he said. "You can't. Not yet. But perhaps soon, when Niko and Assif have found more, we can bring their killers to justice. And that's the best tribute you can ever give them."

"Is it?" she asked. "What do we really accomplish, my friend? What can we really accomplish, when the hearts of men can conspire to such evil?"

"Consider this," Lawton said. "Today we are watching the inauguration of a new president. But what might we be watching instead? If you hadn't brought me to Idaho, if we hadn't built the case against Wes Dixon and Jonathan Morgan, if Miriam hadn't intervened with President Rice against Phillip Bentley, what would we be watching right now? We would be watching India and Pakistan in nuclear ashes, Renate."

She nodded. That was true. Few knew how close the world had come to nuclear war three weeks ago. Few knew that the bombers were already in the air, their pilots awaiting only the final release codes.

"We saved a lot of lives, Renate," Lawton said. "Lives in India and Pakistan. Lives in Strasbourg. At the end of the day, that's what we have to focus on. Or else you're right, it's just hopeless. And it's *not* hopeless. Jonathan Morgan has been indicted on conspiracy charges. We know he's one of the Brotherhood's inner circle, and right now he's sitting in an eight-by-ten cell. They're not untouchable. We can win."

"Yes," she said, although she heard the tired sigh in her own voice. He was right, and she knew that in her head, but her heart still grieved. "We can win. But at what price? At what price?"

Epilogue

Steve Lorenzo looked across the café at the striking blond woman whose eyes bespoke so much pain. Beside him, as if reading his thoughts, Miguel nodded.

"_Sí, Padre._ She has seen too much."

"Yes," Steve said.

The woman's eyes reminded him of another woman, on a night that seemed a lifetime ago, after that woman had helped to protect the villagers of Dos Ojos. It was the same haunted look he had seen in Miriam Anson's eyes. Did he have the same look? Was it the look borne by anyone who tried to stand up to the evil around him?

Jules Soult's eyes did not have that look. Instead, Steve realized, Soult had the look of a man who had just won a championship. Proud. Jubilant. Victorious. Not the look of a hero at all.

"He is no hero," Miguel said, nodding toward the TV. "His eyes betray him."

"Ahh, there you are!" Guiseppi Veltroni said, making his way to their table. "I apologize for my tardiness."

Steve rose to shake his hand. "There is no need for apologies, Monsignor."

Veltroni took the hand briefly, then drew Steve into a tight embrace. "I am so happy to see you, my friend. I feared that I had sent you to your death."

"Quite the contrary," Steve said. "You sent me to my life, Monsignor. Please, join us. This is my friend, Miguel, who came with me from Guatemala."

"You have come a long way," Veltroni said, shaking Miguel's hand.

"And we have a long way yet to go," Steve said, leaning close. "There is much that I must tell you. And we will need to act quickly."

Renate watched idly as a monsignor entered and embraced a priest across the room. Now, as the monsignor sat, she noticed for the first time the young man who sat with them. The face was familiar, and for a few moments she struggled to remember it. Then she turned to Lawton.

"To our left, third table from the back. The young man with the two priests."

"I think I recognize the face," Lawton said, scratching his head. "But I can't remember who he is. Was he on one of our watch lists?"

She shrugged and returned her gaze to Lawton. "I'm not sure."

Lawton looked at the young man a moment longer. "We should check him out. But why would he be with two priests?"

Renate's expression suggested that he should stop being so naive.

"It never ends," she said. "It never ends."

The latest historical romance from

NAN RYAN

Kate Quinn arrives in Fortune, California, with little but
a deed to a run-down Victorian mansion and a claim to an
abandoned gold mine. But a beautiful woman on her own
in a town of lonely, lusty miners also brings trouble.

Sheriff Travis McLoud has enough to handle in Fortune,
where fast fists and faster guns keep the peace, without the
stubbornly independent Miss Kate to look after. But when
a dapper, sweet-talking stranger shows a suspicious interest
in Kate, Travis feels it's his duty to protect her. And he's
about to discover that there are no laws when it comes to love.

The Sheriff

*Available the first week of February 2006
wherever paperbacks are sold!*

MIRA®

www.MIRABooks.com

MNR2272